Dennis Brooke read the newspaper headline:

SHAITAN GETS NO. 283

The article claimed that the man-eating leopard had killed in broad daylight.

Impossible, Brooke thought.

Unless this was something else. Unless Shaitan was some strange mutation of his species. Unless he was, as all the Hindus claimed, some kind of devil or evil spirit.

Of course, all this was rubbish.

Or was it?

A slight chill ran up his spine.

ATTENTION: SCHOOLS AND CORPORATIONS

TOR Books are available at quantity discounts with bulk purchases for educational, business or special promotional use. For further details, please write to: SPECIAL SALES MANAGER, Pinnacle Books, Inc., 1430 Broadway, New York, NY 10018.

WRITE FOR OUR FREE CATALOG

If there is a Tor Book you want—and you cannot find it locally—it is available from us simply by sending the title and price plus 75¢ to cover mailing and handling costs to

Pinnacle Books, Inc.
Reader Service Department
1430 Broadway
New York, NY 10018

Please allow 6 weeks for delivery.

_____Check here if you want to receive our catalog regularly.

SHAITAN

MAX EHRLICH

TOR

A TOM DOHERTY ASSOCIATES BOOK

FOR MARGARET

A Tor Book

Published by Tom Doherty Associates, 8-10 W. 36th St., New York City, NY 10018

First printing, June 1983

ISBN: 0-523-48075-X

Printed in the United States of America

Distributed by Pinnacle Books, 1430 Broadway, New York, NY 10018

PROLOGUE

IT IS HARD to imagine a place less important than the village of Chakrata.

In 1927, it was part of the district of Dehra Dun, located in the United Provinces under the rulership of the British Raj. Regionally, it was just another village among hundreds of others in the province of Uttar Pradash, in northern India.

The village of Chakrata has a population of some seven hundred souls, mostly Hindu. From here, the snow-topped ranges of the Himalayas can be clearly seen, and through this area several small streams wind their snaky way to ultimately empty into the mighty Ganges—or the *Ganga Mai*, as every Hindu calls it. It is a village remote from any town of any size, and untouched by any modern techniques of farming or sanitation. There are no tube wells, drainage pipes, compost heaps or pits built to contain runoff. Chakrata has two or three small shrines, a temple, and is located next to a pilgrim road. It has a central drinking trough fed by a tiny stream which flows down from the mountainside and is diverted into the trough by a man-made channel of rough-cut saplings. This might be called its main feature. Otherwise, Chakrata is lined with grass-thatched houses, and the largest house, made of brick, is occupied by the *padhan*, or village headman. It has the usual fixtures of the Indian village, a blacksmith, carpenter, barber, potter, oil-presser, public washerman, sweeper, cobbler; a scavenger, weaver, temple servant and, of course, a money lender. In all respects,

Chakrata is a carbon copy of a thousand other northern Indian villages.

Only the largest and most detailed maps of India acknowledge its existence. The others simply ignore it.

Yet there was a time when the village of Chakrata became famous all over the world, a name and a place known to people everywhere, of whatever language or nation.

It all began with the arrival in Chakrata of a certain pilgrim in the year 1921.

He called himself Ram Gwar. Now this is a name fairly common throughout India, but to the villagers of Chakrata, the man himself was most uncommon. He appeared in the dead night, wearing a huge leopard robe over his simple *dhoti*. He was a *sadhu*, or self-professed holy man. He told the villagers he was a pilgrim on the way to the ancient shrines of Kedernath, there to purify himself in the sacred pools and do *darshan* at the many temples. It was unusual for a lone *sadhu* to make this kind of pilgrimage. For they almost always traveled in groups, for companionship and mutual protection. And although they were holy men and wore different garments than most, usually saffron-colored robes, the villagers had never seen one wearing a leopard skin. At any rate, Ram Gwar had begged shelter for the night. And because he was a *sadhu* the villagers gladly fed him and gave him a place to sleep.

But instead of proceeding on his pilgrimage, the *sadhu* decided to rest for a few days before continuing his arduous journey. The few days became a few weeks, and the few weeks became a few months. Finally, the *sadhu*, professing a liking for Chakrata, built a hut by a ruined temple and became a resident.

No one knew why. Chakrata itself has nothing to offer outside of its small shrines and single active temple. The villagers wondered why he did not proceed on his pilgrimage. Or why, if he wished to settle, he did not choose more important places like Hardwar or Dehra Dun, which were not too far away and had many more temples and shrines, and far more opportunities for alms.

From the very beginning, there were things about this particular *sadhu* that deeply disturbed the people of Chakrata.

First of all, there was the leopard skin.

He wore it every day and was never seen without it, even when the weather was warm. When he slept, he used it as a blanket. The leopard coat itself was ancient and mangy, and the inner skin was filthy and stank of the *sadhu*'s sweat. But he treasured it more than anything else. Once, he had left the leopard skin out in the sun. Some boys had picked it up and started to play with it. He came rushing out from his hut, furious, and beat them with a stick until they ran off.

But there was more than this.

The *sadhu* was a man of enormous girth; the fat rippled along his arms and legs, and his belly bulged over his waist. Yet, he was seen to eat little or nothing; he fasted frequently, or so it seemed, and the people of Chakrata thought this very strange.

Stranger still, unlike any normal man, he slept by day and stayed awake all night. He was rarely seen at his hut after sundown, and it was assumed that he was off somewhere, wandering in the woods, meditating perhaps, or keeping some strange rendezvous. No one knew for sure.

But most disturbing of all, was the appearance of a man-eating leopard in the vicinity, shortly after Ram Gwar had come to Chakrata. For some years now, the village and its environs had been spared the menace of man-eaters, either tiger or leopard, although they were very active in the Punjab.

Yet this leopard—they knew its species by its pads—
had already taken a toll of four or five lives in and
around the village.

It was then that certain tales and rumors about Ram
Gwar came to be heard in Chakrata. These were
brought to the attention of the villagers by pilgrims who
had heard of this particular *sadhu* in places like Hardwar, Shreenagar, and even as far away as Delhi. And
because of these tales, the villagers of Chakrata treated
him like a pariah. None would speak to him, or even go
near him, as though he were an Untouchable.

His name, it seemed, was cursed in other parts of
India, particularly in the north. He had built for himself
a black and monstrous reputation wherever he went. It
was said that in those villages where he had set up
temporary residence, certain disasters came about. The
monsoons mysteriously stopped, and because of the
lack of life-giving rain, the crops withered and died.
Babies were stillborn, and the wells became polluted. It
was said that he preached certain heresies, and secretly
ate the flesh of sacred cows. The *sadhu*s of India are
generally known as holy men of great piety and compassion, doing all manner of good deeds. But it was well
known that Ram Gwar belonged to a certain evil sect,
disciples of Siva, the god of destruction, with a lust for
human flesh and blood. And that they were able, magically, to transfer themselves into animal, and then back
to human form, at will.

But most important of all, their favorite animal, in
terms of this transference, was the leopard.

One evening in August, just before darkness fell, the
sadhu was dozing in the shade of a great banyan tree
immediately in front of his hut.

He was rudely awakened by the sound of angry voices
coming toward him. He threw off the leopard skin

which covered him and sat bolt upright, staring down the wide path leading to his hut. What he saw chilled his blood. It seemed that the entire population of Chakrata was coming to see him. Some carried clubs, others carried flaming torches dipped in pine resin. The furious mob was led by the village headman, Bahalji Singh, and his son, Ranga. And beside them walked a man, one of the residents of the village, who carried a shapeless mass in his arms, wrapped in a white sheet.

The *sadhu* knew why they had come. He rose to his feet and tried to run. But he was fat and slow, and was easily caught by some of the young men. The mob closed in on him, shrieking curses and oaths. They held him by his arms, and the man carrying the bundle now took off the sheet, to let the *sadhu* see what was contained within.

It was the bloody remains of his fourteen-year-old son, all that was left after the leopard had feasted.

They accused Ram Gwar of turning into the leopard and then devouring the boy. The *sadhu* tried to plead his innocence, but no one would listen. They set upon him with clubs, beating him mercilessly, until he became unconscious. Then they burned down his hut and threw the leopard skin into the flames as well.

The mob had brought a bamboo litter with them, and they rolled the body of the *sadhu* onto it; four young men lifted it and began to carry it. The *sadhu* was a heavy burden, but they did not have far to go. In a few minutes, they had reached the edge of a cliff, looking down over a steep gorge, perhaps two hundred feet deep and covered with jagged rocks at the bottom.

Now, this was an extraordinary thing for the people of Chakrata to do. It showed their great hatred for the *sadhu*. The Hindus almost always cremate their dead, usually on the bank of some river or stream, so that the ashes can join the waters that eventually flow into the sacred Ganges. The *sadhu* was obviously a Hindu, and more than that, a holy man. But the villagers would not even accord him the comfort of this rite.

As the *sadhu* lay on the litter, he recovered consciousness for just a moment. He began to scream at them "*Main phir aunga, hum phir malenge,*" which in a threatening sense means "I will come back, we will meet again." But in the blindness of its anger, the mob was unimpressed by this threat.

Ram Gwar continued to scream at them. But then the headman signaled to the bereaved father. The man stepped forward with a heavy club. He beat the *sadhu* over the head again and again, until the *sadhu* was dead. The people did not even allow the corpse of Ram Gwar the small comfort of the traditional live coal in its mouth. The young men simply picked up the litter, dumped the body of the *sadhu* over the cliff, and watched it fall until it smashed onto the rocks far below.

After that the mob, now quiet, walked back to the river, burned the last remains of the half-eaten boy, and gently deposited his ashes into the water.

The next day, a curious thing happened. Those who looked down the gorge expected to see the skeleton of the *sadhu*, since there had been vultures waiting in the trees to devour his flesh.

But there were no bones to be seen. The remains of the *sadhu* had mysteriously disappeared.

Suddenly, the village of Chakrata was no longer threatened by the man-eater. The British authorities in the area concluded that the bloodthirsty cat had decided to seek a new territory, and perhaps gone into Himachal Pradesh or the Punjab, which at that time was infested by man-eaters, both tiger and leopard. But of course, the villagers knew better.

Still, they did not suspect, they could not have foreseen, the consequences of what they had done.

PART ONE

1

THE LEOPARD CROUCHED low, completely hidden in a dense growth of waist-high basonta bushes. His opaque yellow eyes looked down a short slope toward the brook below.

His prey stood drinking from a brook gurgling through a crevasse of rock. It was a spotted chital, a hind. The deer was totally unaware of the hunter's presence since the big cat, while stalking his quarry, had made sure to keep downwind.

The leopard was a huge male, much bigger than the norm of his species. His coat was dark and glossy, as soft and sensuous as velvet. Its rosettes were glowing patches, small glittering jewels shining against the rich dark satin of the skin. His body was coiled, tense, ready to spring. His tail twitched straight up and down, slowly, a sure signal of a leopard charge to come.

The big cat was hungry. His stomach gurgled. Saliva dripped from his whiskers as he thought of the taste of the deer. His mouth was already open, the cruel, sharp teeth already bared, as though he were already crunching through the delicious meat. His body was flattened out now, tense as a steel spring, forefeet tucked under him to give impetus to his charge. He knew the prey would be easy. One bound down the slope, one leap into the air, and he would be upon the startled deer. His huge jaws would clamp onto the hind's neck, the sharp teeth would bite into the flesh, and with one twist he would break his prey's neck. After that would come the feast.

Yet the leopard hesitated.

He did so because he remembered the taste of a sweeter meat than this. A meat he had become accustomed to, a meat he had come back into this area once more to seek out and devour. At the last moment, he decided against the deer. He was willing to wait a little longer for what he wanted. He would wait until the sun went down and night came.

Then he would hunt out his prey. It would be as easy as this deer. Even easier. For the prey he wanted more than even this was easy to stalk. It could not run as fast as the chital, nor could it detect his scent from far away. His mouth slavered at the very thought of tasting that special flesh once again. He had tasted it many, many times, and never sickened of it.

But to the big cat it was more than just that.

He lay there, watching the deer drink its fill, and then moved away.

After that the big cat rose and leisurely glided through the forest. He had been here many times before, and he knew exactly where he was going. This terrain was home to him. Always, no matter how far he wondered, he returned to it, was mystically drawn to it.

The monkeys swung through the branches of the trees, chattering at him, throwing nuts and twigs down at him. Birds flashed out of the trees, red jungle fowl, pea fowl, white capped babblers, warning of his approach. Other species, like bronze-winged doves and upland pipits, had no alarm calls, but nevertheless took flight. Once or twice he heard the distant alarm bark of a langur, but he took no notice. Now and then he looked up through the high branches of the trees, their leaves dappling the sun, knowing he had plenty of time.

2

IN CHAKRATA THE days are somewhat shorter than those in the villages of southern India. This is because Chakrata is almost in the shadow of the Himalayas, and as a result the sun disappears more quickly behind the barrier of the mountains.

On this day the sun was already lowering and tinting the snow-topped peaks with a pink and reddish glow. For the people of the village, it was near the end of another ordinary working day. Men herded buffalo from one grazing ground to another. Fathers and sons worked together, ploughing the fields, urging the bullocks on to pull the primitive ploughs, harder and harder. Other men were returning to Chakrata after buying or selling produce and livestock in nearby villages. The women of Chakrata were on the upland slopes, cutting and bundling grass for thatching or for feeding the cattle. Young boys were returning from school, and the older ones grazed goats or collected dry sticks to use for firewood. A group of pilgrims in saffron robes, each carrying a stave, walked barefoot over the stony scrabble of the pilgrim road.

Suddenly, from the nearby forest, the villagers heard the warning of a kakar, or barking deer. The kakar barked again and again. Almost simultaneously, a huge flock of kalagee pheasants whooshed upward in alarm from the bush, and quickly flew away from the area.

At this, the villagers froze. The men stopped ploughing, the women stopped swinging their scythes, the boys stopped gathering twigs. All of them turned and looked in the direction of the forest, where the covey of pheasants had taken off in such obvious alarm.

Once again, the kakar barked his ominous warning.

Bahalji Singh, the headman, turned to his son, Ranga.

"Shaitan," he said. His face was white. "Shaitan."

"Yes," said his son. "He's come back again."

The bark of the kakar and the flight of the pheasants were a sure warning of a leopard in the vicinity. The people of Chakrata knew this leopard only too well. He was a man-eater, and they knew him as Shaitan, which in Hindustani means devil, or demon, or evil spirit. He had taken a terrible toll of the village for three years. But for the last six months he had not appeared, and the people of Chakrata had been lulled into a false sense of security.

But now he was back again, the devil was back again, and people cried "Shaitan, Shaitan" over and over again, in despair and in terror. Bahalji Singh shouted orders for all to get back to the village at once. But he could have saved his breath.

Everyone was already running for home, knowing that at any moment, if Shaitan so decided, he could come out of the forest, a streak of furry, spotted death, and take any one of them.

Now the village was in shadow as the sun vanished behind the mountain range.

For a time there was frantic activity. The shutters of the bazaar were slammed shut. People ran to the central drinking trough, filled jars with water, drew thornbushes before their doors, and barricaded themselves inside. All doors were barred, and some had additional doors built to supplement the outer ones; Shaitan, with his great strength, had often charged and crashed through ordinary doors in search of his prey. He seemed to know which doors were weak and which were strong, and of course the villagers knew why. Anxious mothers cautioned their children not to go outside in the middle of the night to urinate, but to stay indoors and use certain jars specifically set aside for that purpose. A few chosen men, previously selected by Bahalji Singh, clambered to the roof of his stone house, which had the highest location in Chakrata, and began to beat drums. The beat was done in a certain warning cadence, signaling that their spotted nemesis had returned again. The drums would be heard by a few who lived outside the village, in the forests and jungles, people like charcoal-burners and woodsmen. But more important, it would be heard in the neighborhood villages close by, and passed on in relay to villages like Gangotri, Baijnath, Pauir, and Najibabad, and from these places relayed to other villages in Uttar Pradesh, and even those as far away as Himachal Pradesh and parts of the Punjab. For Shaitan was known to range hundreds of miles in all directions and make his kills in many of these places. But his favorite target was Chakrata and its vicinity. And of course everyone in the village and in all of northern India knew why.

Dusk came, and then the night, and the village was deserted. It was ominously silent, a ghost of a place, a graveyard. Not a soul ventured outside. There was no movement, not even the whisper of a sound. Even the animals in their pens were silent.

Darkness fell, and the people within the houses huddled together by the light of their oil lamps, frozen with terror, whispering to each other, afraid to make any sound loud enough to attract the man-eater. They had done this many times before, for weeks on end, forced to this awful curfew by the man-eater. And now they waited as always.

They waited and wondered where Shaitan would strike next, and whom he would take this time.

The man-eater they called Shaitan lay on his belly at the edge of a forest bordering a terraced clearing. His yellow, unblinking eyes were fixed on the village beyond.

He was hungry now, very hungry. His belly rumbled in its demand, the hot saliva flooded his mouth. He growled and hissed a little, flexed his claws, and waited for darkness.

Finally it came, and he saw a few dim lights go on in the village; in the sky there was a half-moon.

He new it was time now. He rose and began to walk toward the village. He walked in a lordly way, totally unafraid, knowing there was none who could harm him. He passed the tethered buffalos, and they milled about, yanking at their stakes, terrified at the sight and smell of him, trying to get away. The bells around their necks rang and clanked loudly in the night, warning the villagers beyond that Shaitan was coming.

The man-eater ignored the buffalos and continued on toward the town, his great body a symphony of power and rippling grace, his coat glinting and shining in the light of the moon.

He did not know, nor did he care that in this, the year 1928, he had become one of the world's great celebrities, and that his name appeared frequently in the headlines of newspapers everywhere.

The gruesome story broke in the press, not only of India itself, but in Hong Kong, the United Kingdom, Australia, the United States, in places like Kenya and Malaysia, Paris, Rome and Berlin.

The man-eater had appeared during the night in the village of Chakrata. He had paid no attention to the goats in their pens, but began to scratch at the doors of the various houses, as if testing their strength. He had

contemptuously pushed aside, with one great paw, the
thornbushes protecting the entrances. Finally, he had
found the entry he had been looking for.

He had backed off a short distance and then charged
straight at the door. He had smashed through, landing
in the middle of a frightened family, a man and wife,
and four children. He had clawed the husband into a
bloody mess, then selected the wife. He had broken her
neck with one sharp twist of his great jaws and then
carried her off, moving across the terraced fields, dis-
appearing in the forest. All this was witnessed by
horrified neighbors in the next house who saw it all
happen through a tiny grilled window, high up in the
wall of their storage room. The leopard had made
several previous kills by standing on the roof of the goat
pens and then leaping through the windows of the
houses themselves. The people of Chakrata, as well as
those in many other villages, had made their windows
small enough so that the great body of the leopard could
not get through, and for further insurance had barred
these windows.

The eyewitnesses reported that the man-eater had
carried the woman in his jaws across the terraced fields,
and then disappeared in the jungle. The next day her
remains were found several miles from Chakrata by a
charcoal-burner who lived in the forest. The man-eater
had carried her an incredible distance before finally
setting her down and devouring her. She was identified
only by what was left—a string of beads, scraps of a
bloody sari, and her sandals.

The professional hunters of big game testified that the
leopard, either the species found in Africa, or that of
India, was not a particularly difficult animal to track
down and kill. But this Shaitan seemed a different
breed, some kind of strange mutation from his own

species. Any number of men, hunters with expertise, Muslim *shikari*s, big-game sportsmen, and British officers on leave from the Indian army, had tried to track down and trap Shaitan. He had eluded them all with an ease and an intelligence that was astonishing. It seemed that he was indestructible, that he was laughing at all of them. Most of them dropped the hunt and went home, baffled and frustrated. Several never came back. The latest story of this kind had broken a month before. Two young British officers from the Second Lancers had undertaken to hunt down and kill the man-eater. They were found under a *machan*, or waiting platform, they had built in a tree. Or rather, *evidence* of them had been found. All that had been left were their boots, belt buckles, and rifles.

Of late, some of the bigger newspapers around the world had begun to keep a box score of Shaitan's victims. They recorded the names of the various villages where the kills had been made, when they had been made, and how many.

At the top of this list was Chakrata, in Uttar Pradesh. Strangely, it led the others by far. The man-eater had killed and eaten some eighty people who lived in and around that village, during the four years he had ranged the area. Its nearest competitor, the nearby village of Sadhaura, had ten. After that, had come settlements like Gangotri, Surnar, and Barhaj, with four each. Then a long list of other villages two or three victims each.

To those who lived in the West, this discrepancy seemed strange. But to the Hindus of the north, and particularly those in and around Chakrata, it was no mystery whatever. It was all natural and perfectly understandable.

3

TWO WEEKS LATER, a special and urgent *panchayat*, or public meeting, was scheduled to take place in Dehra Dun.

The official residence of Sir John Evans, the deputy commissioner of the district, was a spacious two-storied house of ten rooms ringed by a very large veranda. Some of its furniture had been imported from England, but much of it was built of native woods, beautifully wrought by local craftsmen, under the watchful eye of Memsahib Evans. She had some fifteen servants at her command in one capacity or the other, including, of course, the inevitable *chowkidar*, or watchman. On this, the day of the meeting, the *chowkidar* stood guarding the fence, arms akimbo, glowering at the crowd walking up the dusty road to the assembly hall, which was located only a few hundred yards away.

Sir John Evans was one of the Brahmins of the British Raj. He was a covenanted Indian civil servant, highest in the caste of his social order. As deputy commissioner, he administered a huge district peopled by hundreds of thousands. His staff included a number of assistants, and under his personal authority was the superintendant of police, the public works engineers, the forest officers, the opium inspectors, the subinspectors of posts and telegraphs, and myriad other departments and bureaus. Together with his colleagues men like Evans ruled over the 250 districts of British India, embodying the authority of the Raj over some two thousand castes, religions and sects which made up the general population.

Evans was a tall, thin, sunburned man, once a colonel in the Central Indian Horse, and in every sense an old Indian hand. At the moment he was entertaining a visitor who had just come up from Delhi. Sir John was a busy man, and he considered his visitor somewhat of a nuisance, especially on this, the day of the *panchayat*. Still, he respected his guest. He happened to be Peter Wilkes, the internationally-known correspondent for the *London Times*. Wilkes had landed in Bombay only a few days ago, and had been sent by his newspaper to cover exclusively the ongoing story of the man-eating leopard. He seemed to fascinate the public; the readers couldn't get enough of him. All the newspapers had correspondents in Delhi, but Wilkes was considered someone special.

Now the commissioner and his visitor were in Evans's office, studying a large wall map of the United Provinces. The map was covered by a thicket of colored pins. Each pin marked a killing by Shaitan, noting the place and date.

"Incredible," murmured Wilkes, staring at the map.

"This is an incredible beast," said Evans. "You take an ordinary leopard. He'll roam in a limited range, perhaps twenty-five or fifty miles if he gets enough food. But as you see, this one ranges hundreds of miles in every direction. If one area gets a little hot for him, he simply moves to another where they're not expecting him."

Wilkes studied the pins, then made a note in the notebook he carried.

"What's the latest count?"

"Two hundred and eighty-two official kills."

"The last four at Chakrata?"

"Right. As a matter of fact, over half of his kills have

been in or around Chakrata.''

"Interesting," said Wilkes. "Very. More than that, it's odd." He paused for a moment. "By the way, Sir John, you made a reference to 'official' kills."

"Yes."

"Would that imply there are more?"

"Right. We're sure there are additional kills, not even reported, in tiny and distant villages far out of reach of any modern communication. Shaitan has probably killed and eaten as many as three hundred and fifty human beings." Evans shrugged. "But that's just a guess. And your guess is as good as mine."

"How do you determine when a kill is official?"

"Well, the government follows a certain procedure. If someone is killed by a man-eater, the relatives or friends of the victim report this with the *patwari*." Wilkes looked blank. "Sorry. The *patwari* is an official in charge of a group of villages. When he gets the report, he goes to the spot where the alleged killing is supposed to have taken place. If no body or remains have been found, he recruits a search party and then scours the area, trying to find it. They make a special search of the trees in the vicinity."

Wilkes stared. "The trees?"

"Right. The leopard is a great climber, and he likes to leave what's left of his prey high up, wedged between the branches of the tree and protected by overhanging leaves. This keeps the vultures and other predators away, at least to a certain extent. The leopard likes to take his naps stretched out along the branches of the same tree, so the search party has to be damned careful. Anyway, to get back. If the body is found, the *patwari* conducts his own investigation, right there at the scene. If he decides that the deceased is the true victim of a man-eater, and hasn't been murdered by someone else, or anything of that sort, then the remains are given to the relatives so that they can cremate it. The *patwari* registers the kill in his record book and passes it on to one of my assistants, who then officially notes it in our records as an official kill.''

"Interesting," murmured Wilkes. "And very thorough."

"We think so."

Evans studied Wilkes, a somewhat corpulent man of middle age with a huge walrus mustache and sleepy, heavy-lidded blue eyes. He sensed that Wilkes was only half-listening, preoccupied with something else.

"Sir John, getting back to this village, Chakrata."

"Yes?"

"How do you account for so many of Shaitan's kills taking place there?"

"I don't know."

"There's the story of the holy man these people killed some years ago. The one they thought was a man-eater in human form. He threatened to come back. The Hindus, I gather, believe he's the reincarnation of—what's his name?"

"Ram Gwar."

"Yes. Ram Gwar. As you of course know, and better than I, they think this Shaitan is actually Ram Gwar wearing a leopard skin, with claws and teeth. And that he has come back to revenge himself on these people, particularly those in Chakrata." Wilkes paused. "An intriguing premise. But pure nonsense, of course."

"Of course."

"Still," said Wilkes. "When you think of it, well, it makes the skin crawl. However it *is* odd, don't you think?" He pointed to Chakrata on the map. "Look at the kills registered here. Far more than any other settlement. One has to ask *why?*"

"I'm damned if I know. Maybe the animal just *likes* the place. Maybe he was born near there and sees it as his special territory. India's a strange place, my dear Wilkes. You live here long enough, you begin to half-believe some of these Hindu superstitions. It's insidious, but the country works on you in that way; you have to watch yourself, remember what you are and who you are. Reincarnation is more than just an idea here, it's a religion. Of course, it's absolute rubbish, but the Hindus believe in it totally. And in a way, it's given us a lot of trouble in this particular situation."

"How so?"

"Well, I'm sure it's been reported, but I'll repeat it for you. The trouble is, the Hindus in Chakrata and these other villages won't really defend themselves against Shaitan. If they kill him, they're afraid the demons inside of him will be released, and in their fury, attack and destroy them. By drought, plague, starvation."

"Dead is dead."

"I know that. And *you* know that. But again, let me repeat. This is a different part of the world. The people all through these provinces believe that their only chance to get rid of Shaitan is to have him hunted down and killed by a Christian. But that damned man-eater has been raising bloody hell around here for years, and we haven't been able to do a thing about it."

"And you've tried."

"Oh, yes, we've tried." The commissioner laughed, almost derisively. "God knows, we've tried. But the bugger's been too smart for us. Either he slips away or he turns around and makes a meal out of the poor devil who tries to hunt him." He looked at Wilkes. "Of course, the answer, as we both know, is living in London."

"You mean Dennis Brooke, of course."

"Exactly."

"Interesting that the natives here never refer to him

by his proper name. They simply call him the Sahib."

"That's because they consider him almost a kind of god, a deity. Someone superhuman, so to speak." Then Evans exploded, suddenly. "Damn it, Wilkes, we've got to get him back here."

"He keeps insisting that he's retired."

"He *can't* retire. Not yet. Not till he comes back here and hunts down and kills this damned leopard once and for all. You understand, this is not just a matter of saving a few more lives. This is far more important than what has been happening to these poor beggars up here. There's the humane element, of course. These people have been living in terror for years now. But over and above that, this is a political problem. You follow me?"

"I do," said Wilkes. "I do indeed."

Evans checked his watch. "Time for the *panchayat*. I must add that this is the biggest and most important meeting we've had in years. We've got people in here from villages all over the United Provinces. Some of them have come hundreds of miles by foot and bullock carts just to be here today. I'm to be the *panch*, or chairman." Then with a bitter laugh. "Or more like a master of ceremonies, you might say. Except that I can't think of anything clever to say to them. This is one day I hate my bloody job."

"Who asked for this meeting?"

"The headmen of the villages. In a petition signed and attested by them, and presented formally to me, which I passed on to the governor general. Normally, in times past, His Excellency might have given this petition the back of his hand, unless it came up through channels in a proper fashion. You know, through civil service, the bloody bureaucracy we have to deal with here. I'm a part of it, of course, and I shouldn't stick a needle into it, but sometimes a thing like a native petition takes forever. But in view of the present political situation, His

Excellency expedited this one directly, ordered me to quickly set a date, and here we are.''

The meeting was held in the large administration building, just down the dusty road from the district commissioner's house. In it were contained a post office, a health clinic, the office of courts and justice, the officer of tax registration and district security, and a number of others.

It also contained a large assemby hall where public meetings were held on occasion. It could seat some five hundred people, and besides its function as a place for public meetings, it was also occasionally used as a court-room and sometimes served as a theater for the showing of films sent up from Delhi.

Now the place was jammed, every seat taken, and many had to stand outside, listening to the procedures through the open doors and windows. It was intolerably hot. A great blade fan rotated slowly from the ceiling, but did little to help.

From the platform, the crowd presented a sea of turbans. Beside the headmen of the various villages, there were the local and regional officials, the *patwari*s and *tahsildar*s, not only from the Uttar Pradash, but from Himachal Pradash and a few from as far away as Nepal. Present also was a delegation of Kalakamli Wallahs from Rikikesh, a cult dedicated to protecting pilgrims on their way to the various shrines. These pilgrims had always been one of Shaitan's favorite sources of dinner. Shaitan had picked off many of stray *guru* or *sadhu* walking along some jungle path, lost in meditation or kneeling at some shrine along the way.

On the platform behind a bare table sat Sir John Evans. Next to him sat his first deputy, Henry Lang. They were flanked by two British flags, and just behind him on the rear wall, was a large portrait of King George VII. The crowd was abuzz when Sir John finally

picked up his gavel and rapped for order. A dead silence
fell over the audience. First, there were some small
formalities in which Sir John, in the name of the
governor general of the United Provinces, formally welcomed them to Dehra Dun. He then stated that His
Majesty's government appreciated the fact that many of
them had come a long way, by bullock cart and on foot,
to attend this *panchayat*, and would listen with the
greatest respect to what was suggested or requested
here.

To this, the *tahsildar* of Dehra Dun rose and informed Sir John that the assembly had chosen one man
to speak for them all on the common problem. And that
man was the *padhan* of the village of Chakrata, Bahalji
Singh by name. When the headman rose, a paper in his
hand, the turbaned heads all turned to look at him.
They stared at Bahalji Singh with a certain awe. It was
not just that his village had been hit hardest by the man-
eater. Bahalji Singh was known to be a close and dear
friend of the man they called the Sahib.

Bahalji Singh was now a respected elder of sixty. But
some years ago, as a young man, before he had moved
to Chakrata, he lived in the village of Khurja, in the
Punjab. The town and its area had been tormented by a
man-eater, this one a tiger, and the British army had
given the Sahib leave to come and hunt down this tiger
and thus relieve Khurja and its neighboring villages of
the terrible problem. This the Sahib Dennis did. And
during this time, the Sahib stayed at the simple house of
Bahalji Singh, and ate porridge and that flat *chapatti*s
and drank tea with him, and although a Christian, became as one with the Hindu family. And when the Sahib
became sick with the fever and lay in the house of
Bahalji Singh for many days, near death, it was Singh
and his wife Kasturi who nursed him back to health.
When the Sahib left, they parted as brothers.

Later, Bahalji Singh took his family to live in
Chakrata, where he had relatives. There, after some
years, he rose to be the headman of this village. Meanwhile, the Sahib had become the most famous *shikari*,
the best hunter, in the United Provinces, the Punjab,
and the Northwest Frontier, and his fame had finally
spread through all of India and, indeed, the world itself.
It was he who had built a long list of successes, where
other *shikari*s, many of them experts, had failed. It was
he who had hunted and shot down the Dharkot leopard,
the Bangthal and Dhamak and Sindarwandi tigers,
man-eaters all, with hundreds of kills documented to
their teeth and claws.

Now, Bahalji Singh, who had the petition translated
by one of the forestry officers from Hindustani to
English for the benefit of the deputy district commissioner, began to read haltingly, each word by
rote:

Respected Sir:

We, the subjects of your state and district, and
loyal as always to the Raj, do very humbly and
most respectful, as the favor of your kind consideration, for we are very much in terror, very
troubled, and much needful.

As you are most surely aware, this leopard,
Shaitan, has eaten many of our people, causing
much sadness to widows and children, and families in almost every village. Because of the fear of
people to go out at night, we cannot watch our
wheat crop, and the deer have come down from
the hills and mountains to eat it, so that many of
us now hunger. We are feared to enter the forest
for fodder grass, and many of our cattle and goats
die because of this lack, and so there is no milk.

We know many *shikari* gentlemen have gone to

hunt Shaitan. But all have failed. Including those of your army people. Some themselves have been eaten. There is only one we of the public believe is *shikar* enough to hunt this Shaitan and kill him, and thus relieve us of ruin.

This, of course, is the Sahib. He who is known by your people as Sir Dennis Brooke, but for us is always the Sahib.

We know the Sahib is in England, and has said many times he has retired and will not return to India to do this hunt. We humbly beg that you, through the governor general of the United Provinces, and then through His Excellency, Lord Irwin, the viceroy himself, to beseech the Sahib to return to us once more and do this thing for us. We have faith that he is the only *shikari* in the world who can be our salvation. We pray for him each day at our temples and shrines, that he will come back and save our people from this terrible demon, Shaitan. In this, we see him as our deliverer.

So, to conclude, Respected Sir, we humbly beg that you make some special effort to make known to the Sahib our distress, for we know he has always loved our people, and to me, personally, he is like a brother, and we ask you to beg him to pick up his guns again and come back and save us all. And we will always pray for his long life and his prosperity.

We beg to remain, Sir,

Yours Most Sincerely
BAHALJI SINGH

Dated Dehra Dun,
The twentieth of February, 1928.

Then Bahalji Singh looked up from the petition and

addressing Sir John, said: "This, honorable sir, is signed by seventy *padhan*s of the same number of villages, and it has the thumbprints of many more who are unable to write, and of course, there are the official signatures of all the *patwari*s and *tahsildar*s present here."

He handed the petition up to the district commissioner and sat down.

Sir John studied the document and then handed it to his deputy. He squirmed a little, clearly embarrassed. Then he cleared his throat, and said:

"Gentlemen, we understand your predicament. And you know how hard we have tried to be of help. We have, as you know, sent many of our best *shikari*s, detached them from the army, to hunt Shaitan. As to the Sahib—" unconsciously, Sir John had begun to call him that instead of using his proper name "—we have done our best to persuade him to come back to India and hunt down this man-eater."

"Then why does he not come?" said one of the *tahsildar*s.

"He insists that he is retired. He says he has done what he can, and it is enough. He has other reasons why he cannot come back to India."

"What are these reasons, sir?"

Sir John shook his head. "None of us know. He will not speak of them, other than to say they are private, personal. More than this, he is tired of hunting and wants simply to be left in peace. He says there are other hunters equally qualified . . ."

The crowd dissented. "No," said a *patwari*. "This is not true. Shaitan is not merely an ordinary leopard, Respected Sir. He is Ram Gwar in fur and claws. In him is the spirit of this terrible *sadhu*, this evil holy man. He has sworn revenge on us and especially on those in Chakrata. This he has done, to our ruin. And only the

Sahib has the courage and the skill to deal with Shaitan. All of us here remember the Dharkot leopard. Over a hundred of our people died by his teeth and claws and jaws. It was said that no one could catch this beast, and many tried. Many tried, Respected Sir, and all failed. It was said that the Dharkot man-eater was possessed. That he, too, had a demon within him, that he would continue to kill until he became old and feeble, and could hunt no more. But then came the Sahib. And in two months he hunted down, shot and killed the Dharkot man-eater.''

Another *tahsildar* called for attention. The *tahsildars*, as the chief revenue officers of designated groups of villages, spoke with more authority than most when it came to addressing the authorities.

''Sir John, Excellency, all of us are under the protection of the British Raj. We respect the Raj and obey its laws. In return, it must help us in this matter. Otherwise, our people ask questions. They become restless. They listen to other voices rising in India. The Sahib is part of the Raj, is he not?''

''Of course,'' said Sir John.

''He is only one man, and the Raj is the government. You have a king in London. Cannot he order the Sahib to return?''

''No,'' said Sir John. ''He can request, but not order. The Sahib is a British subject. He is no longer in the army, and he can do as he wishes. However, we shall do what we can. I will see that your petition goes to Delhi immediately. Directly to the viceroy himself.'' Sir John spread his hands, eloquently. ''And this is the best I can do.''

The meeting lasted a little while longer. A few new laws were passed, certain grievances were aired and promised consideration, and finally the men filtered slowly out of the hall, shaking their heads, visibly disappointed. In their view, the *panchayat* had produced little encouragement; they had left their villages and come a long way for nothing.

Later that evening, just before dinner, Sir John Evans and his guest sat in the library over a bottle of Haig and Haig.

"Well," said Sir John. "What did you think of it?"

"Interesting," said Wilkes. "I was fascinated by it. Certainly it gives me a story to cable back to London."

"The trouble with London, or Whitehall or Downing Street," said Sir John acidly, "is they have no bloody idea of how hard we're being pressed up here. Damn it, it's all a matter of getting Dennis Brooke back here. He doesn't have to begin some second career, you know. Just this one animal, and it'll be more than enough."

"We've been trying," said Wilkes. "But you don't know Brooke."

"Oh yes, I do. I know him very well. The best I can say for him is that he's a stubborn bastard. Especially, when it comes to a matter like this."

Wilkes sipped his whiskey a moment. He studied Sir John's face and hesitated. Then, carefully:

"Perhaps I shouldn't bring this up. But do you suppose that incident at Behra has anything to do with his reluctance to come back?"

"Behra?" Evan's voice was bland, but his blue eyes suddenly turned cold. "What makes you think that?"

"Nobody's mentioned it aloud," said Wilkes. "Nobody's dared to. But people are beginning to wonder . . ."

"You know, Wilkes, you're right about one thing."

"Yes?"

"You shouldn't have brought it up." Sir John rose. "Now, suppose we go in to dinner."

A few days later, at the viceregal lodge in Delhi, Lord Irwin looked across the desk at Captain Anthony Lassiter of the Royal Guards.

"Damn this fellow Brooke," said the viceroy, slamming his fist onto the desk. "What the devil's the matter with him? Doesn't he know how badly he's needed here? All of India, and especially the north, is bubbling and stewing, what with Gandhi and his *Satyagraha* movement. What we need there is something spectacular, a showing of the Raj, so to speak. The Indians love a good show, and Brooke can provide it by going out after this man-eater." He paused a moment and then: "I've called you down from Lahore, captain, because I'm told you're one of Brooke's best friends, and you've hunted frequently with him. And of course, everybody knows about the incident at Behra. Perhaps he might listen to you."

"I've written him a number of times, Your Excellency. And the answer's always been no. He seems determined to stay in England."

"But why?"

"I don't know, sir. He simply tells me that he's had it—he's packed it in for good."

"If there was only some way—"

"I've been thinking about it, sir. And there just *might* be a way . . ."

"Yes?"

"I—well, I'm almost afraid to discuss it, sir. I mean, it's so bizarre, you may call it ridiculous. And I wouldn't blame you if you did,"

"Tell me about it, captain."

"Yes, sir. But if you think it has a chance, I'll need a certain amount of cooperation—from yourself, and the government."

"If it has any chance at all," said the viceroy grimly, "you'll get all the help you need."

PART TWO

4

HER NAME WAS Jeanne Cooper, and at the moment she was the reigning star of the London stage. She was presently playing in the new American import *Craig's Wife* at the Theater Royal in Haymarket.

This was the first time Dennis Brooke had taken her to bed. Earlier that evening, he had told his man, Hendricks, to take the night off. He had taken her to dinner a few times before and sent flowers to her dressing room, and on this night he had a feeling that the time had come. In this he had not been wrong. He had picked her up at the theater immediately after the performance. They had had a late champagne supper, and then he had led her to his flat on Eaton Square.

Now it was over and they lay quietly and close together.

"Darling, I must say you've certainly lived up to your notices," the actress purred.

"Oh," he said. "And what notices are you referring to?"

"You know. You may be the greatest in the world when you're prowling around in the jungle, hunting down some horrible animal, and of course, all that's very masculine. Still, the ladies always have a certain amount of curiosity as to how virile this same man is where it really counts. Here, under the sheets. The gossip was that you were just as good as the great white lover as you are as the great white hunter . . ."

"Jeanne." He interrupted her, almost harshly.

"Yes?"

"Don't."

"Don't what?"

"Don't call me the great white hunter again."

She turned her face toward him. "Dennis, why on earth should it bother you?"

"I don't know. I hate the bloody expression. There's a certain malice in it; the magazines like *Punch* are always making some kind of joke about it, and it makes me feel ridiculous. I think that damned young American writer, Hemingway, is responsible."

"Oh?"

"He came from Paris for a fortnight, and I met him at a party. It was for Tallulah Bankhead, I think, the night she opened in *Fallen Angels*. Anyway, he came up and introduced himself, and gave me this little smile, and said he was glad to meet the great white hunter in the flesh, and he had some ideas about writing a story about someone like me. I didn't mind that, it was just the expression he used. Great white hunter. The newspapers and magazines, for some bloody reason, all caught it up."

"Darling, you're too sensitive. I shouldn't think you'd mind. And after all, you're in the newspapers almost every day. You and that awful leopard."

"I still don't like it. It sounds like the title of some third-class film you might see in a cheap cinema. On top of this, this man Hemingway had the gall to ask me to join him on some safari in Africa. I told him thank you very much, but I had never been to Africa, didn't care to go there, wasn't interested in hunting big game any longer, and that I had retired."

Suddenly, he realized he sounded a little pompous, a little too much like a lord of the realm, and warned himself to be careful, not to let it go to his head, all this adulation, all this attention. He had been knighted by the king, and could now be called Sir Dennis Brooke, but he was essentially a simple man, and being addressed in the titled way embarrassed him. He insisted that his friends simply call him Dennis, as always. But in the clubs he now belonged to, the servants and waiters all addressed him as Sir Dennis, and so did the other members. He realized that in these areas he had to go along, there was no way to beat the system any more than you could the caste system in India.

Now, he felt Jeanne's fingers running up his right leg. She was delicately tracing the livid scar running from his knee up through his upper thigh. It ended about an inch away from his testicles.

"So this is where the leopard hurt you. The one you killed at—where was it?"

"Place called Behra, in the Punjab. And I didn't kill the animal. A friend of mine did."

"How did it all happen?"

He felt his whole body tense, and for the moment the new erection she had been caressing went soft.

"I don't want to talk about it."

"But why not?"

"I *told* you, Jeanne," he snapped. "I don't want to discuss it."

She was a little startled by his reaction. "All right, Dennis, all right. It doesn't matter, really." Then her voice turned soft, and she continued to caress him. "That beast came close didn't he, darling? But thank God, he didn't get the best part of you."

After the second time, they lay on their backs and she said it was marvelous, it was divine, simply divine, and every bit as good as the first time. Then she said, suddenly:

"Of course, Dennis, you don't mean it."

"Don't mean what?"

"That you really are retired. I mean, you are going

back to India and kill that horrible man-eater."

"You think so?"

"Of course. You'll simply have to go back."

"Will I?" There was a chill in his voice. "Tell me why."

"Why, because everybody expects you to."

She turned her face toward him on the pillow and looked at him in some surprise. As though he had asked a childish question about something that really was so obvious. He was about to argue the point, then decided to stay silent.

She announced now that she was tired, deliciously tired, and wanted to sleep. He warned her that he had an appointment at eleven in the morning, here in his flat, and gently suggested that it would be discreet if she left before then; his visitor was a very important man, and in a position to really spread gossip if he knew.

She pouted a little at this; in her profession, she never arose before noon, and if she had a lover in her bed, it could be long after that. She informed him that the next time, and of course, there *would* be a next time, they would spend the night at her place. As to the gossip he referred to, it was already all over London. They had been seen together at this party or at that supper club often enough, so that everybody who was anybody in town knew about it, and of course drew their own naughty conclusions. But as far as she was concerned, she found the gossip intriguing and delicious, and there was not a woman in all London who wasn't dying of envy and who wouldn't love to be in her place.

Then she went to sleep.

He tried to follow suit, but it was no use. He tossed and turned and stayed wide awake. He saw himself as a man now haunted, a man in an impossible dilemma, beset by all sides, tormented. A prisoner of his own image.

Everybody expects you to, she had said.

He had heard this said to him a thousand times, in one way or another. And he was weary of it. He reached for a cigarette in the silver case lying on the bedtable, fumbled for a match in the dark. He lit the cigarette, blew a cloud toward the ceiling, dappled with weird light patterns from the moonlight filtering through the blinds, and he thought, damn them, damn them all. Why don't they listen? Why don't they believe me?

I'm not going back.

As the night wore on into early morning, Dennis Brooke reflected on how he had become involved, how he was now in a position he considered impossible, a situation which had kept him awake not only on this night, but on many others.

It had all actually begun when he had been a young lieutenant in the second battalion of the Royal Guards. Like so many other British officers on leave, he had hunted for big game, just for sport. He had developed a particular skill at this, especially in tracking down and killing man-eaters, and his reputation grew throughout the United Provinces. Soon the army was giving him longer leaves, detaching him for special service to hunt down and kill some particular leopard or tiger that was terrifying the villagers, a leopard other hunters were unable to kill. What started out as recreation now became a serious matter, not only to himself, but to the Hindus who were ravaged by the killers, and to the Raj which prided itself on protecting the people over which it ruled.

What began as sport then became a profession. Dennis Brooke had swiftly achieved the rank of major, and by this time he was acknowledged to be one of the best in the world at what he did. By the time he had disposed of the Dharkot leopard, and then the Sindarwandi tiger, he had become a kind of demigod, a legend throughout India. The villagers touched his feet wherever he walked and spread flowers in his path, and in the temples and at shrines they said prayers for him. All the adulation embarrassed him, but there was no way he could stop it. And he, in return, had grown to love these brave and simple people; he had shared their pain and grief when they lost one of their loved ones, a child, or father, or neighbor, to the sharp teeth and ripping jaws of a man-eater.

But at last his luck caught up with him at Behra. He had spent some weeks in the hospital and at a rest billet in a hill station at Rampur. After that, he had done the obligatory thing. With his close friend and fellow officer, Captain Tony Lassiter, he had gone out and killed two tigers. He had emulated a theory made popular by the flyers of the war. If you crashed your plane in training, or were shot down by the Hun, and if you survived, the thing to do was to take the controls of another plane and go right up again. Otherwise, your natural courage would dissipate, and you might never fly again.

After he had sweated through this ordeal, he had resigned his commission in the Royal Guards and had come home to London. That was in 1923, five years ago.

He knew that because of what he had done, he had become some sort of celebrity. But he had no real idea of the magnitude of his fame. The Great War had ended in '18, London had fully recovered from the trauma of that bloody slaughter. The city seemed prosperous, lighthearted, carefree, and although the class lines were still distinct, there was a whole new set of free, postwar mores, the flapper had made her entry, and sex was freely discussed in the drawing room. Above all, there was peace everywhere.

England had duly honored its wartime heroes, and now it was looking for, and needed, a new one. Dennis Brooke had come to London at exactly the right time, and was just the man to fill that need. Especially since he had come from India, where the empire was in deep trouble because of Gandhi's freedom movement.

He had been given a celebrity's welcome wherever he went. He was photographed by Cecil Beaton, the sensational young photographer who had captivated London with his work. Brooke's name was constantly in the newspapers, there was interview after interview. He became an instant social lion. In a matter of months he knew everybody who was anybody in town, from the royal family down. The prince himself had actually become one of Brooke's closest friends.

His father, a colonel in the Royal Guards, now dead, along with Brooke's mother, who had come from a wealthy Sussex family, had left him enough money to live like a gentleman. Two of London's most exclusive clubs, White's and the Travellers', offered him honorary memberships, and each morning his valet brought in a silver tray filled with invitations for dinner, for the opera, for concerts, for charity balls, for everything and anything.

Then, four years ago, this damned man-eater Shaitan began to appear in the news.

As his kills began to mount, Shaitan became, in his own right, a kind of celebrity in fur. When the leopard had passed the hundred mark in terms of humans he had killed and eaten, and had either baffled or devoured every hunter who sought him out, his fame mounted higher and higher. He became more than just a leopard, he became a legend. And with it, impending drama took shape and began to grow. It was a drama with a cast of only two characters, a man and a beast. Both antagonists, both in the headlines, and destined, the press insisted, to clash one day.

Dennis Brooke versus Shaitan.

Meanwhile, Dennis Brooke tried to ignore all this. He moved about London with the greats and the near-greats, he was on speaking terms with people like Winston Churchill, Lord Beaverbrook, Noel Coward, Ellen Terry, Bertrand Russell and Rudyard Kipling. The popular magazines nominated him as Man of the Year, and one of the penny dreadfuls coupled him with D.H. Lawrence as the two most romantic and glamorous British personalities of the decade, after Prince Edward himself, of course. Crowds sought autographs wherever he went in London, and the same was true in Paris, New York, Rome, any major city of the world. His guns, the hunting rifles he had used in India, were now encased in a glass cabinet in the British Museum, with a long list of the man-eaters he had killed posted next to them.

He had given the guns to the museum at its request, and to Dennis Brooke it was a visible sign of his retirement, to the world in general, and a symbol to himself.

But not to the public. Hardly a day passed that his name was not mentioned in the *Times* or the *Daily Express* or the *Telegraph*, especially in conjunction with this damned man-eater. If he was simply a celebrity before this, now he became a super-celebrity. The pressure was on him from all quarters to go back to India, for one last and glorious trophy, the pelt of this leopard, Shaitan. The public, egged on by the newspapers, began to see it like a boxing match, as a one-to-one sporting contest—Dennis Brooke versus Shaitan—and may the best man (or animal) win. The idea was being blown up out of all proportion, Brooke thought bitterly. The confrontation of the decade. As the *Daily Express* put it in a headline:

SUPERMAN VERSUS SUPERBEAST

The headline caught on not only in London, but everywhere else in the world. It seemed to stimulate the viscera of the public; people seemed to drool in anticipation of such a match, and were ready to wager with their bookmakers on the outcome. And the odds, they said, would be no better than even. A lot of hunters of great reputation, it was repeated, had gone after Shaitan. Many of them had never come back alive.

SUPERMAN VERSUS SUPERBEAST

Well, thought Brooke, to hell with them all. He was thirty-seven and now, lying here wide awake in bed, Dennis Brooke knew that his stamina wasn't what it used to be. For four years he had lived the soft life, the life of a gentleman, a London clubman. He no longer relished the idea of walking mile after mile through narrow jungle and forest paths, climbing up rocky slopes, wading through rushing streams of ice-cold water, sitting in *machan*s, platforms built high up in the trees, sometimes drenched with heavy rain, waiting for a quarry that more often than not never came. And although he loved and respected the Hindus who lived in the shadow of the Himalayas, he no longer relished sleeping on mats, in the dirt or on the stone floors of their huts, or living on gruel and rice and tea. There had been the excitement, yes. Waiting for the big cat to cross his path, playing point and counterpoint, matching wits, always alert for the charge that might come from any quarter. He had not fired a gun in some four years, apart from some shooting for grouse in Scotland, and he knew he would be slower in his reflexes now, a little rusty. And that could make the difference.

But there were other reasons too, why he dragged his feet and would continue to do so.

Suddenly he felt a little queasy. He went into the bathroom, washed his face in cold water, and then stared at the reflection of his naked body in the full-length mirror.

He turned his body, swung his head around, and caught a glimpse of the long claw marks along his back. Then he stared at the ugly red scar running straight up his leg, ending just short of his sex. He shuddered a little, and for a moment felt the familiar surge of nausea rising in his throat.

Behra. *Behra.* He lived it still and dreamed it and could not forget it, even now.

It had been close, so damned close.

He looked into the blue of his eyes in the mirror, and he did not like what he saw.

He came back into the bedroom, and gazed down at the sleeping woman. Her long hair was flung across her face; she slept on her stomach, arms flung out on either side, like the wings of a pinioned bird. The posture reminded him suddenly and vividly of Ootacamund, and of Nora.

Nora.

She was still back there in Delhi, living in the house on Prithviraj Road. And he thought of the month they had spent together in Ootacamund. How could he tell them what had happened there, in the hill station high in the Nilgiri Range and Blue Hills of southern India? How could he tell them the truth? That this, far more than Behra, was the real reason he could never go back to India.

5

WHEN BROOKE AWOKE it was eight in the morning, and Jeanne Cooper was gone. All that was left of her was the scent of her lingering perfume in the sheets.

He felt tired and out of sorts. He had had three hours of sleep. When he came in for breakfast, his valet, Hendricks, was waiting to serve him. Hendricks was a tall thin man and, as usual during the morning, he wore no waistcoat, simply a red leather vest over his blue working shirt.

"Morning, sir."

"Morning, Hendricks. What time did the lady leave?"

"I don't know, sir. It must have been very early. She went out before I came in. Left you this note, sir. I found it on your desk."

He sat down to his bacon and eggs and read the note. It was brief. She said he had tossed and turned so that she had awakened and then was unable to go back to sleep. She had risen at dawn, she wrote, like some barbarian, and called a taxi to take her home, where if the Lord was kind, she could catch up on her sleep. She wrote, furthermore, that she expected to see him, as arranged, after the performance tonight. Supper at Romano's, and after that, he would be the beneficiary of her own hospitality at *her* flat. She concluded by saying that she had enjoyed the night no end, that she adored him, and that he was a darling.

"More tea, sir?"

"Thank you, Hendricks. This will be enough."

"Very good, sir. What shall I lay out for today?"

"I'll leave that to you."

"May I suggest one of the gray tweeds, sir? You've worn blue for the last two days."

"Very good, Hendricks. You take very good care of me, and I do appreciate it."

"Thank you, sir."

Hendricks permitted himself the ghost of a smile, and began to gather up the dishes. He had been Brooke's man for over a year now. He had come to Brooke highly recommended by a bachelor and fellow clubman named Standish, who had employed Hendricks, but had had to dismiss him, since Standish was getting married. At first, Brooke had been a little embarrassed by having a valet at all. Not that he wasn't used to servants. In his rank he always had a batman, and a bearer, and of course any number of Indian servants wherever he billeted. But somehow this was different. He was not really born and bred to be a London gentleman, although since his return he had lived in high style. The point about Hendricks was that he was totally reliable and, like any good valet, absolutely discreet. He wasn't the Jeeves that P.G. Wodehouse was lampooning to everyone's delight. Brooke knew that Hendricks would never dream of breathing a word of his master's liaison with Jeanne Cooper or anyone else; it would never be bandied about in gossip at some servant's pub or tavern. Hendricks was close-mouthed, even in his relationship with Brooke. He spoke rarely, and sparingly. He did not intrude.

"Shall I draw your bath now, sir?"

"Please."

Brooke lit a cigarette and leaned back, leisurely. He had known extreme hardship in his life. He was a veteran of the war, he had slept in many an open trench, half-filled with mud, with the rain beating down on him. He had fought with his regiment through Belgium, had been slightly gassed at Ypres, where he had caught a piece of Hun shrapnel in the side. He had marched countless miles with his regiment in India, drenched in sweat, across sun-scorched plains, forded rushing rivers as they cut their way through dense jungles, tormented by flies and mosquitoes, trying to avoid lethal snakes. Later, as he developed his skill at big-game hunting, he had literally walked hundreds of miles through rock-strewn country, up hills and down hills, virtually living almost as a primitive in some of the more remote areas, freezing in some mountain areas and through some of the passes where it was so cold that his fingers stuck to the barrels of his guns.

Now he lived the life of the London gentleman, and found it easy. He had to confess that he liked it, he liked it very much. He liked his big and comfortable duplex flat, with a view of the grassy and tree-lined Eaton Square through the big front windows. He liked to have his bath drawn, his clothes laid out, his meals cooked for him. He liked the feel of good leather, of good worsted, the smell of good cologne. He liked to have Hendricks around to fend off unwanted callers, to remind him of his schedule for the day, and he appreciated the thousand and one suggestions, made discreetly and obliquely by his valet, designed to fit him snugly into the gentleman's mold, and make him more comfortable. He was not a rich man, not really rich as some of his friends at the clubs or elsewhere understood it, but he was well-off, and he knew where tomorrow's dinner was coming from.

He liked the theater and the opera, and the fine restaurants, the beautiful women and important men he had met in London and elsewhere. Being human, and entirely honest with himself, he enjoyed their respect and admiration. And there was something in the fact that in what you did, you were at the very top, the best in the world.

Yet in all this he felt a certain threat. A threat to his own identity. In a sense, he no longer belonged to himself. Not really. He was an exhibit in a glass case. He was a public possession, the darling of the crowds, their man, not his own. They could elevate him or destroy him, depending on the circumstances. As they saw it, they owned him; he was their creature, and they expected him to perform. More than that, they now demanded it. Sometimes they almost frightened him in their intensity. Often, when he was entering some theater or shop, he would be instantly recognized and people would swarm about him, asking for an autograph, or wanting simply to get close to him. Sometimes they clutched his clothing and tore it, and he would have to muscle his way through the crowd roughly. It was true not only in London, but everywhere else he had been, in Paris, New York, Hollywood. Even his face was no longer his own. It was photographed, duplicated endless times in newspapers and magazines, caricatured in publications like *Punch*, and by this time probably known to the tribes of deepest Africa.

Somehow he had to make them understand that he had a mind of his own.

"Your bath is ready, sir."

When he stepped out of the tub, his valet wrapped him in a great warm turkish towel. After that Hendricks shaved him, and reminded him of his schedule for the day. There was an eleven o'clock appointment with Lord Ellsworth here at the flat, a luncheon meeting with Fred and Adele Astaire at one o'clock at the Colony, and a three o'clock meeting with the secretary of state at the India Office. Of all these, he looked forward with pleasure only to the meeting with the Astaires.

Brooke asked his valet to select a sweater, rather than

a jacket, for time being. He still had plenty of time before his meeting with Lord Ellsworth. It was a beautiful spring day and he was in the mood for a brisk walk. He heard Hendricks chuckle a little as he helped Brooke on with the sweater, and Brooke was intrigued. Hendrick's face was usually set in the same serious expression, and this flicker of humor on the valet's part was very rare.

"What seems to amuse you, Hendricks?"

"I was just thinking of Lord Ellsworth, sir."

"Yes?"

"I mean the fact that he's coming *here* to see you."

"What's so strange about that?"

"It's very unusual, sir. You see, I know Lord Ellsworth's man. We happen to be old friends. And he tells me that His Lordship *never* goes anywhere to see *anyone*. One is always received at his office. *Always*. You seem to be the one exception, sir."

There was a note of pride in Hendrick's voice. Almost gloating. Brooke was dimly aware that there was a certain aristocracy among the manservants in London. It was important whom you served. The more celebrated, the higher the status.

"I suppose," said Brooke. "I should feel flattered."

"Yes, sir."

"The fact is, I think I know why Lord Ellsworth insisted on seeing me. Even if it meant coming here." Brooke sighed. "And frankly, I'm not looking forward to it."

He fitted on a cap, pulled the brim down low, and then put on a pair of dark glasses. This was something he had learned in Hollywood, where he had spent a few weeks a year ago. People there wore them to dull the glare of the sun, and in some cases to go about unrecognized. London, considering its climate, was not the place where one wore dark glasses, but in his case they did serve to conceal his identity somewhat. People stared at him and wondered who he was. And if they thought they knew, they didn't have the nerve to stop him and ask him if he were, indeed, Dennis Brooke. They hesitated because it would be a cheeky thing to do, bad manners, and very embarrassing if they were wrong. Especially when the dark glasses meant that the wearer was interested in his own privacy.

It was a sparkling June day, and when he stepped out of his flat the small park in Eaton Square was a patch of rich, lush green. He walked over to Sloane Street, and at Knightsbridge came to a newspaper kiosk. The chalk legend scrawled on the slateboard which advertised the headline of the day was short and succinct. SHAITAN GETS NO. 283.

Dennis Brooke stopped for a moment, staring at the slateboard. A slight chill ran up his spine. He bought a copy of the *Times* and the news vendor, who knew him, said:

"Well, he's got another one, sir."

"So I see, Alfred."

"Seems like there's no one who can stop the murdering bugger."

"Yes," said Brooke. "So it seems."

The news vendor had rheumy blue eyes, and now they stared directly into Brooke's and the message was clear; they said something very specific. The question in them was: *when?* Brooke turned away and walked the short distance into Hyde Park. He walked across meadows, along shaded walks, past flower gardens. Nannies paraded their charges in perambulators, or sat on benches and gossiped. Old gentlemen in golfing knickers swinging their walking sticks, were out for their morning constitutionals. Small boys, some of them wearing white gloves, rolled hoops along the walks or kicked a soccer ball about. Smaller children sailed toy sailboats on the edge of the whale-shaped Serpentine, and there were a few boating enthusiasts testing their craft on the surface of the lake.

Brooke followed the tail of the lake as it curved upward through Kensington Gardens, until he came to a favorite retreat of his. This was a secluded garden done in the Italian style, marble and water. Formal in style, with an imposing assembly of fountains and clear pools, balusters and statues, demigods and conch shells, all elaborately done, very baroque and un-English.

Brooke found a bench, sat down, and ran his eye over the front page of the *Times*. There were several newsworthy items. But the one given the most prominent position and most important headline was the story of Shaitan's latest kill, as written by the *Time*'s crack correspondent, Peter Wilkes. The account had been telegraphed to London via Dehra Dun and Delhi.

Two days ago the Devil came once more to his favorite killing ground—the village of Chakrata, and its vicinity.

This time Shaitan took his victim. The grisly event, as related by Bahalji Singh, headman of the village, and officially documented by British officials in the area, took place in the following manner. A group of Kalakamli Wallahs had come up the pilgrim road which runs just outside Chakrata. Thousands of pilgrims travel this road on their way to various shrines and temples, or to the Ganges itself, and the Kalakamli Wallahs are a religious brotherhood dedicated to the welfare of the pilgrims all along the road. Their name comes from the fact that the founding father of the sect wore a black blanket, and many of his followers still wear this blanket held to the body by a belt of goat's hair. They are what we might call the Hindu version of Good Samaritans. They feed the hungry, build shrines and, most important, pilgrim shelters along the road.

On this occasion, they had come to inspect the pilgrim shelters in the vicinity of Chakrata, knowing of the depredations of the man-eater, and planning to strengthen the shelters against possible attack.

Around noon, one of the Kalakamli Wallahs left the main group to go off into the jungle and relieve himself. He never came back. An inspection by his comrades showed bloodstains, and nothing more.

Later, the remains of the body were found wedged into a banyan tree some five miles from Chakrata.

Bahalji Singh concluded his story with the following remark, and I quote him verbatim. "Where is the Sahib? If the Sahib had been here, this might not have happened."

Dennis Brooke felt the small stab of guilt. And then he began to feel a little sick. He could almost see Bahalji's face, almost hear the reproach and regret in his old friend's voice. He swore at Wilkes for adding this fillip at the end of the article. He knew it was not gratuitous, something the correspondent had just thrown in to elaborate his story. He knew it was deliberate, and that Brooke would be stung by it. It was just another point of pressure on him, of course. The old Chinese water-drop treatment.

His anger rose. Why didn't the bastards just let him

alone? He thought of his coming meeting with Lord
Ellsworth. His Lordship was involved in this dispatch;
in a way, he was responsible for it. He, Dennis Brooke,
might have a word or two to say about this kind of
tactic.

He found a trash receptacle nearby, dropped the
newspaper into it, and began to walk in the direction of
his flat. He had walked perhaps a hundred yards when
he suddenly remembered something. A tiny nerve
quivered and nagged him. Something in that article
didn't make sense.

He walked back to the trash receptacle, reached in,
and fished out the newspaper. He stood there, scanning
the story again, and found what had disturbed him.

According to Wilkes's account, the leopard had killed
his unfortunate victim in broad daylight. But, Dennis
Brooke thought, this was impossible.

The fact was that Wilkes had made a mistake. Man-
eating leopards, to Brooke's knowledge, only hunted
and killed by night, never by day. It is the tiger that kills
by day. In all his experience, he had never heard of a
daytime victim taken by any leopard.

Unless this was some strange mutation of leopard, an
animal completely atypical of his species, the victim had
been killed by a tiger. There were always tigers roaming
the United Provinces, and some of them were man-
eaters.

The article had made no mention of pugmarks, the
animal had left no tracks. But his friend Bahalji Singh
would know the simple fact that leopards killed only by
night.

Unless this leopard was something else. Unless he was
some strange mutation of his species. Unless he was, as
the Hindus claimed, one kind of devil or evil spirit. Of
course, all this was rubbish. Of course. A leopard was a
leopard was a leopard.

He wondered why Bahalji Singh, who knew better, had blamed the leopard Shaitan for the killing? Had Wilkes put him up to it? Or was it Bahalji's own idea? Another small cut, from another scalpel.

He shrugged the thought off, and walked rapidly back to his flat.

6

At eleven o'clock sharp, Lord William Ellsworth, publisher of the *London Times*, rang and was shown in by Hendricks.

"Can I get you something, Sir William? Coffee? A drink?"

"No, thank you. I'm here on business and I'm pressed for time." He looked around the flat, then stared at Brooke. "I've telephoned you twice and asked you to come around to my office. You've refused on both occasions. Why?"

"I meant no disrespect, sir. But I had a pretty good idea what the interview would be all about. In fact, you gave me a broad hint on the phone. I told you on the telephone that I simply wasn't interested. There was no point in wasting your time—or mine."

"So you've made the mountain come to Mahomet."

"Again, sir, I meant no disrespect."

The publisher was silent for a moment. Brooke studied his guest with some curiosity. He had met Lord Ellsworth casually at one or two receptions, but this was the first time he had come face-to-face with a legend. And Lord Ellsworth was exactly that.

Physically, he was a huge bulk of a man and exquisitely tailored. He still wore the traditional heavily-starched high collar, the kind that detached from the shirt itself. He had steel-blue eyes, a ruddy complexion, and wore muttonchop whiskers in the old Victorian style. He seemed to wear a perpetual frown. His manner was authoritative, almost arrogant. This was a man,

thought Brooke, used to being on top of the pyramid,
aware of his power and not afraid to use it, a man used
to giving orders and never taking any, an executive impatient with the slightest evidence of weakness or
mediocrity on the part of his subordinates.

Those who knew or worked with him on Fleet Street,
or were his competitors, like Beaverbrook and the
others, either swore at him or by him. But he had
maintained the traditional high standards of the *Times*
and the excellence of its reportage. Its influence was felt
throughout the dominions and the colonies, and the
leading politicians in both houses of Parliament came to
his office in Fleet Street to see him. It was said of Lord
Ellsworth that he would leave his office and answer
summons from only two places—Buckingham Palace
and 10 Downing Street.

"Suppose I come directly to the point, Brooke?"

"Please do."

Brooke was amused that Lord Ellsworth had called
him simply by his last name, instead of Sir Dennis. Old
aristocracy's contempt for new aristocracy, perhaps. Or
more subtly, Lord Ellsworth was making the point that
although the mountain had indeed come to Mahomet,
there was still a difference in their status; they were not
really equals.

"You know, of course, that Shaitan has made
another kill."

"Yes."

"How many more of these poor Indian beggars does
he have to devour before you take some action?"

"This is an illusion that you and the public seem to
keep alive, Sir William. That I'm ready and available.
But I've said it over and over again. I've retired from
big-game hunting, and I propose to take no action, as
you put it."

"Brooke, I know that Beaverbrook has offered you

fifteen thousand pounds for your exclusive story on the hunting down and killing of Shaitan. I know the *Daily Express* and the *Telegraph* have offered a similar sum. I also know that William Randolph Hearst has offered you a hundred thousand dollars for the exclusive rights to your story for his newspapers back in the United States." Lord Ellsworth paused. "The *Times* is prepared to offer you twenty thousand pounds for the exclusive rights to your story."

"Twenty thousand pounds."

"Precisely. We have a correspondent already in the area, a man you must certainly know of—Peter Wilkes. He is now established at Dehra Dun. As the hunt continues, you can relay reports to him as to how it is progressing . . ."

"Damn it, sir. There's something you and the others just can't seem to understand."

"Yes?"

"I'm not for sale. This isn't a matter of money at all."

Lord Ellsworth studied Brooke for a moment. Then he asked softly:

"Then what is it, Brooke? What keeps you from going? If it isn't money, what is it?"

"I've gone into all that a hundred times, Lord Ellsworth," said Brooke wearily. "Both in public and in private. I'm tired of hunting man-eaters. I feel that I've done my bit in this respect. I'm out of shape—not as fit as I used to be. And my reflexes aren't what they used to be. I found that out in Scotland." Brooke was referring to two trips he had made to Scotland with Prince Edward shooting grouse. He was slow in his reflex action when the grouse sprang from the bush. His bag had not measured up to what it had been four years ago. He had joked about it, and the newspapers had caught it up. "I've simply had enough. I'm convinced that there

are other men capable of hunting down and killing this
animal. My friend Captain Lassiter, for instance.''

''He's tried. Several times. And it's been fruitless.''

''I know. He's written me. But I have great faith in
Tony Lassiter. If he keeps trying . . .''

''We've just had word from Delhi. He's given up. In
fact, he's on his way home at this moment—on extended leave.''

''Is he?'' Brooke was surprised. ''I didn't know
that.''

''That leaves only you,'' said Lord Ellsworth. ''And
so far, the reasons you give, while they may be
legitimate, aren't really enough to convince anyone.''

''I'm sorry about that. As I've publicly stated, I also
have personal reasons for not returning to India.
Private reasons that I'm not at liberty to reveal. They
may not be good enough for yourself, or your newspaper, or the public in general, but they're good enough
for me.''

Lord Ellsworth studied Brooke for a moment. ''What
about your pride?''

''What about it?''

''Surely you must consider your self-respect. You're
letting down the side, so to speak. Everybody expects
you to back and do the job.''

''I can't help what they expect. I'm my own man, and
I've made my decision.''

''You're wrong, Brooke. You aren't your own man.
You're a prisoner of your own reputation. To be
honest, I don't really respect your position, but still, I
understand it. If everyone in the world expects you to go
back and hunt down this beast, I don't know how you
can stand up against it. It's like trying to stand up
against a tidal wave. A tidal wave of public opinion. Of
expectation. All they're asking is that you do the same
job you've always done—just one more time.''

''Damn it, Lord Ellsworth, that's just the point. The

whole thing is obscene. People like yourself, the newspapers, have made a circus out of this affair. They see
this as some kind of sports affair, a one-to-one combat,
like two gladiators, two boxers in the ring. Every time
Shaitan kills another poor devil, it means he's scored
another point. They see it as some simple game played for
high stakes. They want a primitive spectacle, with only one
coming out alive—either this bloody leopard or myself.
My friends tell me there are wagers already being placed
on the result, not *if* I go to India, but *when*. I don't
know what the current odds are, and I don't care. Let
me put it to you plainly. I am not some creature to be
manipulated by you, or the other press lords, or by the
public itself. I am not in servitude, and I am not in the
public employ. I've done enough, and I have nothing to
prove."

"No?" said Lord Ellsworth, softly. "I think you are
mistaken, Brooke. I think you do."

"And what does *that* mean?"

"Well, there's talk."

"What *kind* of talk?"

"You really wouldn't want me to be more specific,
would you?"

"Yes," said Brooke, "I really would."

"Very well, then." Brooke was aware that the
publisher was watching him intently now, that the blue
eyes had become even colder, that the man's lips had
tightened into a thin, curved line. "I am, of course,
referring to the incident at Behra."

"Behra?" said Brooke. "And what are they saying
about Behra?"

"I'll let you draw your own conclusions about that,"
said Lord Ellsworth. "And obviously they won't be
pleasant ones. It's a question of pride, of course, your
self-respect. *And* your courage. Now, if you don't
mind, Brooke, I'll bid you good day." As Brooke
reached for the cord by the window to summon Hen-

dricks, the publisher said coldly, "That won't be
necessary, thank you. I'll show myself out."

Brooke walked to the Strand and had a very pleasant
lunch with Fred and Adele Astaire. They were sailing
for New York in a few days to star in the latest Gersh-
win musical comedy, *Funny Face*. The Astaires were
two of his favorite people.

"The best of luck to both of you," he told them. "I
know you'll charm the Americans right out of their
boots." And then he added fervently, "Damn! I wish I
were going with you."

And he meant it. Anything to get out of London. He
had been to the United States the previous year, and
enjoyed it. He had many invitations to return, and for a
minute or two he was tempted to accept one of them, on
the theory that putting distance between himself and
Sahitan would relieve the pressure. Unlike the British,
he tried to tell himself, the Americans were not really
involved, emotionally or politically. He knew, of
course, that this was wishful thinking, fantasy. They,
too, had been caught up in the sporting aspect of the
situation; the one-to-one confrontation stirred their
imaginations almost as much as the English, and their
newspapers gave much prominence to this prospect.

He took a taxi to the aging mid-Victorian jumble of
buildings known as the government offices, and there he
was led past a rookery of small offices to the anteroom
of the secretary of state, the Earl of Birkenhead. Ten
minutes later he was admitted into the huge and
luxurious office. With the secretary was a man Brooke
already knew—Sir Bruce Wellham, first advisor to His
Excellency, Lord Irwin, Viceroy of India. Brooke shook
Wellham's hand, inquired as to the health of the
viceroy, and then was waved to a seat by the secretary.
The Earl of Birkenhead was a tall man, thin and
austere, with piercing gray eyes and a hawklike nose. He

was elaborately polite, and his voice was soft, but Brooke could sense the shrewdness in him, and the toughness. Brooke had a quick and perhaps ridiculous impression. This is a man he would not care to play cards with. Not for money, at least.

"Sir Dennis," said the earl. "First of all, I'd like to express my pleasure in meeting you personally. You have created quite an impression. I must say. Not only in England but throughout the dominions. And that impression, I must say, has been eminently favorable."

"Thank you, sir."

"Perhaps you wonder why I have asked you to come here."

"Frankly, sir, I *am* curious."

Brooke lied a little. Actually, he did have an idea why the secretary wanted to see him. He knew what the theme of the discussion would be, but not the specifics. It had to be something about Shaitan. Everything was about that bloody leopard these days.

"Sir Dennis, I'll come directly to the point. From the government's point of view, it is imperative that you return to India and dispose of this animal, Shaitan. There is a political aspect to this matter that perhaps you are not fully aware of."

"I don't quite understand."

"Then let me explain. Perhaps I can crystallize the problem in one name. Gandhi." He paused for a moment.

"You have spent much of your life in India, and obviously I do not have to acquaint you with the problems this half-naked fakir has given us in that country." The earl's description of the Mahatma, "half-naked fakir," had been coined by Winston Churchill, now Chancellor of the Exchequer. "Every day his demands for self-rule, or *swaraj*, as he calls it, become more strident. And you know about the policy he is preaching to the people of India, the idea of non-

cooperation—" at this point, the earl frowned and
turned to Wellham. "What the devil does he call it? The
Hindu name, I mean."

"The *Satyagraha* movement."

"Ah, yes. Never could remember how to pronounce
it. It's been embarrassing at times, in certain meetings
when I—but that's another matter. To get back, Sir
Dennis. You've been away from India now, for let's
see—how long?"

"Four years."

"Ah, yes. Well, the situation has deteriorated a good
deal since then. The Indians following Gandhi are
refusing to a man to accept British honors; they are
taking their sons out of our government schools and
refusing to send them to our universities here. They are
boycotting our army by refusing service. They have pro-
claimed that they will not recognize decisions made by
our courts, and have refused to serve on any of the
councils set up by the Raj, municipal, provincial or
central."

"Let me add to that," said Wellham. "There have
been riots in Calcutta. We regard them as seriously as
we do the Amristar massacres some years ago. They've
burned good British cloth in ceremonial fires in Calcutta
and everywhere else, including the United Provinces and
the Punjab, with which you are most familiar. There's
been a bomb outrage, as you know, in the Assembly,
and Lord Irwin is planning to come here for consultations. And there have been some assassinations of
several minor officials serving the Raj. All this, of
course, you have read about. But there is something else
you might not yet be aware of. Gandhi is planning a
march to the sea at Dandi, some time in the near future.
His idea is to pick up a lump of natural salt there, as a
symbol of Indian independence, and thus break our
monopoly."

Brooke was puzzled. He stared at the two men.

"This is very interesting, gentlemen. But what's it got to do with me?"

"We've asked you here because we feel you can be of real service to the empire. By going back to India at once and hunting down that damned man-eater."

Brooke was sure now as to what the secretary had in mind. But perversely, he wanted Lord Birkenhead to spell it out. He said:

"I'm sorry, Your Excellency. But I'm not sure I see the connection."

"Politically speaking, as you are well aware, His Majesty's government in India is slowly being pushed to the wall. We need all the help we can get, all the points we can make, so to speak, in crushing this fellow Gandhi. And especially in the north, where this man-eater is loose. It is a matter of prestige, don't you see? If you can go there and kill this animal, it will help illustrate to the Hindu, in a rather dramatic way, that he still needs the power and the protection of the Raj."

Brooke thought about this a moment. Then: "Your Excellency, isn't this really a small matter? Suppose I did dispose of this leopard? What real difference could it possibly make? How could it be important when you compare it to the magnitude of everything else that is happening in India?"

"I agree that it appears to be a small matter," said Lord Birkenhead. "But anything we can do to give us even a small leg up, to illustrate the British superiority in any way possible, is important. The hunting down of this animal may in itself appear to you to be only a drop in the bucket. But the point is, it is highly dramatic in its effect. An event given enormous publicity. Like it or not, Sir Dennis, you are a hero in all of India. You now have the opportunity to be even a greater one. If you kill this Shaitan, the Hindus in the United Provinces are going to be enormously grateful. And this is a region of great unrest at present."

Broke was silent, and now Sir Bruce Wellham broke in:

"I might point out something else. Already some of the Muslims in the area, without this superstition about Shaitan, are demanding high-powered rifles to defend themselves against this man-eater. This, of course, is against British law. Some day those guns could be turned on our own people. If Shaitan is killed, obviously this demand would be vitiated."

Brooke was silent for awhile. He was conscious that they were waiting, expectantly. Damn them both, he thought. Another drop of water. There had to be a breaking point somewhere. Give the boiler enough pressure, build up enough steam, and it had to burst.

He thought of Behra again, and then of Nora. Nora would know why he could not and would not return to India. She was, in fact, the only person, outside of himself, who *did* know. Perhaps in some way, by a simple and great effort of will, he could overcome the memory of Behra.

But Nora?

Suddenly, he was angry at the two diplomats waiting for him to speak. *Will you stop pushing me around, you bastards! It is still no, no, NO!*

"I'm sorry, gentlemen," he said. "But I've announced publicly that I've retired. I'm finished with big-game hunting. And I mean that, although no one seems to believe me."

"Surely," said the Earl of Birkenhead, "under these circumstances, you might reconsider."

"It's a matter of service to the empire." said Sir Bruce. "To be blunt, I think it is a matter of your patriotic duty. And it's simply a matter of doing something you've always done so well—one more time. Really, Brooke, I don't understand . . ."

"No," said Brooke. "I suppose you don't."

They were silent. And Brooke saw the expression creep into their eyes, the same subtle contempt he was seeing increasingly in the eyes of other people. Sir Bruce had said he didn't understand. But he understood only too well. And so did the earl.

"I'm sorry, gentlemen," Brooke said, rising. "I appreciate your interest in me concerning this matter, and I understand the importance of it. But I insist that at the present time there are other hunters who can do this job equally as well as I. If I did not have personal reasons . . ."

"We think we know the personal reasons," said the secretary acidly. "Thank you for coming, sir. And I bid you good day."

Brooke felt the blood heat his cheeks. The dismissal was brusque and contemptuous. He left the office and walked past the dusty little cubicles lining the long corridor, where the underlings, the drones of the civil service, put in their long hours and their lives. He was conscious that many of them recognized him; they stepped out into the corridor to watch him go, and called to their friends to do the same. He looked neither to the left nor the right.

He still felt the eyes of the two diplomats boring into his back when he left the secretary's office. And he thought savagely, to hell with them, both of them. They had soft jobs. They sat on their bloody asses in their soft chairs and big offices, and ordered their minions about, manipulated people and populations, pulled the strings of the empire. They had never walked hill after craggy hill, with blistered feet, tramping through jungle and underbrush, looking for some murdering devil. They had never sat exposed all night in a driving rain, slept on the ground, or lay on a mat in some villager's hut, burning or shivering with fever. They had never wagered their lives on a small fraction of a second, on a quick reflex, on a steady aim and a sure shot. Brooke resented in particular Sir Bruce Wellham's remark about this being a patriotic duty. Brooke had had enough of that, he had his bellyful.

He remembered the slogan enshrined in the annals of British history: England expects every man to do his duty. Certainly it had a ringing sound, and it had excited Englishmen everywhere for years. But this was 1927, and now many regarded it as a kind of cliché. Because of it, he, Brooke, had seen thousands upon thousands of fine young men, the so-called flower of England, die in the cootie-infested mud of the trenches, or end up as shattered bodies hanging on barbed wire, or hopeless cripples with amputated arms and legs. He himself had been lucky to have escaped alive. He now considered the slogan pure rubbish. Put it down to the munition makers, the politicians like the Earl of Birkenhead and Sir Bruce Wellham, and others of their kind. Brooke had been in the army, and of course he had never mentioned ths cynicism about all this and would not now. In India, you and your companions in the Royal Guards were there to keep order and to keep the peace, and of course, to keep the empire alive. But in order to do this you had to keep the people down, the native people, the Hindus and the Muslims and the other races and religions that checkered the country. Basically you were top dog, they the supplicants and servants.

You were British Soldier Sahib. And to some in the army, especially those in the ranks, the natives were monkey-nut *wallahs*, or beer *wallahs*, or vegetable wallahs, all with their hands out, all petty thieves—Hindus, Muslims, or Parsees alike, it did not matter. And the leader of them all was this skinny bag of bones, this old and shriveled little fanatic, this fakir called Mahatma Gandhi, who had the brass, the unbelievable gall, to challenge the Raj, and the empire itself.

Brooke woke from his reverie to find himself walking along Downing Street. He entered St. James's Park, walked past the flowerbeds, and found a bench facing the lake, and watched the pelicans and the ducks sailing majestically by.

His head ached, he felt feverish. His mind spun around and around. He felt trapped, as though in some nightmarish room with the walls closing in on him, the ceiling slowly lowering on him, so that ultimately it would squeeze him and finally crush him. There was a door out of the room, to be sure. And he was being assaulted on all sides by demons who demanded that he open it and walk through. He knew it was the only exit. But he still did not want to take it.

He wondered how long he could stand the pressure. Maybe, he thought, it would be better if he came right out and told them the truth. Make a clean breast of it. Let them think what they wanted to think.

But of course, that was impossible. He was, after all, Sir Dennis Brooke. The great white hunter to end all great white hunters, a national monument, a legend. They had great expectations. The legend had to live up to itself. They were not about to let him off the hook. Just one more time, o great white hunter. After that you can retire to the country and cultivate your roses, or write your memoirs, or do whatever it is that big-game hunters do when they retire.

Just one more time.

Suddenly he was caught by an impulse. He tried to brush it away, but then it started to torment him, it became a driving demand. It was something he really

did not want to do, but knew it was something he now
had to do. He was consumed by his own curiosity; he
could not resist it.

He walked out of the park, hailed a taxi, and told the
driver to take him to the London Zoo.

7

HE GOT OUT of the taxi on Prince Albert Road and started to walk down Broad Walk, which took him toward the interior of the zoo. He knew exactly where he was going and what he wanted to see. He passed the area housing the flamingoes, the British crows' aviary, the cages of parrots, cockatoos and birds of prey. Finally, at the South Gate, he turned in toward a building where the big cats were caged.

There were two leopard cages. One held the African species, the other the variety inhabiting India. He went directly to the cage holding the Indian leopard. His hands gripped the protective rail and he stared at the animal crouched in the corner.

The brass sign said the animal was the species *Leo pardus*, taken from the Punjab, in northern India. It differed in some respects from the African or North American leopard. Its body measured eighty-four inches in length and its tail was three feet long. Its shoulder height was twenty-eight inches. The sign pointed out that no two members of the species had identical patches or spots—they were as different as fingerprints. The sign also said that the leopard was an agile climber, a good swimmer, and liked to store what remained of its kill in the branches of trees. It listed some of the leopard's favorite prey which, in some cases, included man.

But Dennis Brooke was not interested in this information. He did not even glance at the sign. His eyes were riveted on the great cat on the other side of the bars. His

blood began to quicken, he felt a chill run up his back,
he could feel the hairs rising on the back of the neck.
His adrenalin began to flow as he sniffed the familiar,
fetid odor of the animal, and his mouth was suddenly
dry.

Brooke was alone at the moment. The big cat had
been sleeping but now, aware of a human presence, he
opened his eyes. His fur shone like yellow silk, the
rosettes black and brown, with blurs of gold and
orange. In the half-light of the cage, they seemed to be
iridescent and to move and vibrate as though with a life
of their own.

The opaque yellow eyes looked straight into
Brooke's.

The leopard rose to its feet. His eyes were still fixed
on Brooke. They began to burn with a terrible intensity.
Hate spewed from them, an awful, shivering, murderous hate, along with suppressed rage because he
could not get at Brooke, rend and tear at him, claw him
into bloody strips of flesh.

Brooke knew that the leopard had seen many humans
on the other side of the bars, and had become in-
different to their stares. It may have been that the
leopard had had some kind of bad dream. Yet, at this
moment, he seemed to regard Brooke as some kind of
personal enemy, different from the others.

Brooke watched, fascinated, as the leopard began to
pace counterclockwise around the cage with a kind of
lazy and silken sway, shoulder and torso low. Around
and around the big cat went, his eyes never leaving
Brooke's. The animal was terrifying; he could sense all
that hidden power and swiftness. And at this moment
Dennis Brooke had never seen a more beautiful animal,
although the beauty was frightening and deceptive. On
too many occasions he had seen how ugly and obscene
that beautiful coat could turn when splattered with the

blood of some helpless prey.

Suddenly the leopard changed his walk. Instead of circling, he began to pace the cage from one wall to the other, back and forth, back and forth, his eyes fixed on Brooke's, intense, full of yellow fire, hypnotic, and Brooke found it impossible to turn his head away.

Then the cat stopped in mid-walk, and began to inch across the cage toward Brooke. His head was low, his body scraped the floor of the cage. He began to spit. Brooke could see his teeth now, shining wetly, long, curved and cruelly sharp, the mouth partly open, the tongue dripping saliva. The tip of his tail flopped up and down, nervously, unlike the sideways motion of most cats. The yellow eyes continued to stare into Brooke's.

Brooke stared back at the cat, rooted to the spot. And he thought incredulously, *he's stalking me. The bastard's in a cage, and he knows he's in a cage, and still he's stalking me!*

Now the leopard put his face against the bars of the cage, whiskers drawn back, spitting his hatred; his yellow eyes fixed on Brooke's. They were only a few feet apart now, eyeball to eyeball, separated only by the bars and the protective rail behind which Brooke stood. And now Brooke could smell the hot, stinking, obscene breath of the animal, could look straight into the mouth, see the curved teeth now in closeup, watch the saliva drip from the animal's jaws.

Brooke stood there, paralyzed, transfixed. He shivered and once again remembered the same sudden nausea, the fear bellying within him and choking his throat so that he could not even scream in his terror. Once again, he remembered another time, and another place . . . when he had looked straight into another whiskered face, almost exactly like this one . . .

The place was Behra, in the Punjab. The time was four years ago, and he and Captain Anthony Lassiter had been given leave from the Guards to hunt down the leopard that was then known as the Man-eater of Pindi Gheb. This particular man-eater, so-named because of the place of his first kill, was not the current heavy-weight of his time, but he had a respectable score of some fifty kills, including three professional hunters who had tried to bag him. Brooke and Lassiter knew they would not have an easy time of it.

Basically, Brooke liked to hunt alone. He had a special way of doing things, and he felt another man, well-intentioned as he might be, could sometimes be an encumbrance. This was not true of Tony Lassiter. Lassiter and he, besides being fellow officers in the Guards, were close personal friends. They hunted well together and were occasionally sent out as a team when some man-eater was spreading terror in the provinces. As a hunter, Tony Lassiter had a few faults which Brooke tried to correct in an oblique and diplomatic way. First of all, Lassiter lacked a certain patience; he wanted to close in for a kill a little too soon, to move toward the quarry instead of letting it come to him in good time. They had sat in tree *machans* on many a night, and Lassiter had been fidgety, waiting for the quarry to appear, suggesting that perhaps they should go straight after the bugger, as he put it, and take their chances of finding him. But Brooke had pointed out that this could not only be dangerous, it might warn the leopard off when he sensed he was being tracked. Whenever possible, he told Lassiter, *let him come to you*.

More than this, Tony Lassiter did not read a trail as well as Brooke, and he did not have Brooke's instinct in knowing the animal was nearby, even if there was no clear evidence of it. But that was something you could not acquire; it was born into a man. Aside from this,

Lassiter had very quick reflexes and he was a dead shot, absolutely a dead shot at any reasonable distance. Not only that, he was a man of great courage, if not of caution.

At any rate, they had been trailing this particular cat for a week, in the area around the village of Behra. They had caught the animal's pugmarks on a dirt path after a rain, then lost them in an area of rocky outcrop. The day after this, the animal had made another kill, this one a charcoal-burner living in the forest. They had found the man's grisly remains in a tree, about a mile away from the man's hut. And this tree was on the edge of a meadow.

They had caught the man-eater running across the meadow, and Brooke had had a shot at him with his .275. The leopard was a definite hit. They saw him leap high in the air, turn and head for them, then reverse himself and run into a clump of underbrush, zigzagging through it and leaving a trail of blood. They had seen him go down once, roll, rise, and then continue. Both had fired again, and both had missed.

The man-eater had left a big splash of blood where he had been hit, and Brooke thought he had been caught by a lung shot. The trail of blood leading into the brush was heavy as well. It was, of course, foolhardy to go in after the animal. By the amount of blood, Brooke was sure the animal would simply hemorrhage and bleed to death. Yet, he could never be sure. He and Lassiter knew that it was never safe to assume a leopard was dead until it was skinned.

Then they saw vultures starting to circle overhead just over a point a few yards into the brush. He and Lassiter would simply wait until the vultures told them that the man-eater was dead. That was the simple thing to do. Then they could safely move in, skin the animal, and take the pelt back into the town. And then bring back witnesses to make it official.

They had just started to turn away from the area of undergrowth and walk across the meadow when Tony Lassiter, who was looking back, uttered a piercing yell.

The leopard, his entire body stained with blood and his face flecked with it, had come out of the brush and was charging directly at Brooke.

Brooke was totally unprepared. He turned, but he could not even get his rifle up in time.

The man-eater sprang high in the air at him, jaws open, teeth and claws bared. And Brooke, standing there, immobile, paralyzed, knew this was death. He heard Lassiter fire, heard the bullet thud into the man-eater's head. Then the animal completed its spring and was upon him. The great weight of the man-eater knocked Brooke to the ground; he looked straight into the open mouth of the leopard, saw the teeth, smelled the stink of the animal's breath, and then felt sharp, excrutiating pain as the claws of the leopard ripped at him, one tearing furrows through his back, the other ripping up his left leg.

Suddenly, the clawing stopped abruptly, the jaws ceased grinding at his neck, the animal's mouth remained open. Blood and spittle gushed from it and ran onto Brooke's face. He lay there supine, wondering how it was that he was still alive.

Later, he learned that the clawing he had received from the man-eater was a kind of reflex action. The animal was already dead in the middle of his leap. Tony Lassiter had caught him with one perfect desperation shot, right through the head.

After that, Lassiter bound him up, stanching the flow of blood as well as he could. The man-eater, with one great stroke of his clawed paw, had almost ripped away his penis and testicles. Another inch, and he would have been a eunuch. When Brooke realized this, he vomited and passed out. Lassiter sent to the village for help, and men carried Brooke there in a litter. It was a miracle that he had survived the bleeding at all. Later, he was taken to the hospital at Lahore. And after that, he had resigned from the Guards and come home, knowing that he would never be the same, knowing that he could not go on any longer, that the memory of that awful experience would always lie deep in his brain, and the fear remembered in his belly.

He had looked into the whiskered, fanged face of Death at Behra, and he was looking at the same face now, except that now there were bars in between . . .

Suddenly, he was startled by a flash of blinding light.

He turned to see that a news photographer had just taken a flash photograph of himself and the leopard staring at each other. The man wore a press card in his hatband which read *The Daily Mail*.

When Brooke had first approached the cage, he had been alone. Now a small crowd had gathered. And they knew who he was. Brooke glared at the photographer.

"What the devil do you think you're doing?"

"Just doing my job, Sir Dennis. And thank you very much. My newspaper will like this one."

The man turned and walked rapidly away. He wondered how the photographer had found him here. Then he recalled reading a day or two before that a large American eagle had escaped from its cage. Fortunately it had been trapped and brought back to the zoo, and presumably, the photographer had been here to cover the story, and stumbled on Brooke's presence. For a moment, Brooke had an impulse to run after the man, catch him, and smash his camera. But he knew that would be foolish. He hadn't wanted any picture taken. Not here. He had seen the smirk on the photographer's face, and the malicious smile. Of late the press was

becoming sharp and impatient with him. Fleet Street
had begun to chide him openly for sitting on a story that
would make sensational copy. And one reporter had
dubbed him "The Reluctant Gladiator," with all its
accusing implications.

The crowd pressed around him now, asking him
questions, beseeching autographs. But Brooke, upset,
uncharactertisically ungracious, paid little attention to
anyone, pushed through the crowd, almost roughly, and
went outside. He headed down the Broad Walk and
entered Regent's Park.

He found a bench and sat down, glad to be alone. He
felt shaken, disoriented. He was perspiring heavily. He
took out a cigarette and lit it, his fingers trembling.

He had come down here to test himself. He had
hoped that by facing the leopard, he could somehow
face down his deep and suppressed fear. But he had
failed.

It was still there. Just as deep and virulent as ever.
After Behra, he had never really been the same. He was
a man who had had it. He knew it, but nobody else did.

And that was the trouble.

When he got back to the flat, Hendricks handed him
two messages which had been delivered in his absence.

The first was a cable from Hollywood, California. It
read:

GOOD LUCK ON SHAITAN STOP PREPARING BIG
GAME HUNT PICTURE AT METRO STOP TENTATIVE
TITLE QUOTE TIGER UNQUOTE STOP OFFER YOU
STARRING ROLE ON YOUR RETURN STOP BLANK
CHECK DEAL NAME YOUR OWN PRICE STOP L.B.
SENDS WARM PERSONAL REGARDS

                                        IRVING THALBERG

The other messages had been delivered by an equerry of Edward, Prince of Wales. It was addressed to "Dear Dennis," and it asked if Brooke would do the prince the honor of joining him for a private lunch at York House at one o'clock the following day.

The note was in the prince's own handwriting. And it was signed: "Affectionately, David."

Brooke slept badly that night. The experience at the zoo had upset him. He had hoped that over the last four years the passage of time would have softened the impact of Behra. But the mere sight of the leopard was enough to start his nerves jangling again.

He thought of the telegram Irving Thalberg had sent him. The previous year he had visited the United States, spending most of his month there in New York and Hollywood. Hollywood was a place full of celebrities, but one film star was not very different from another, and Brooke had been welcomed as a special kind, an original.

He had become, to use the cliché, the toast of the town. They saw him as some kind of virile and masculine personality, the real thing, and not some synthetic, carefully built up through studio publicity. His arrival had come at a time when animal and nature films had suddenly become of high interest. The film *Simba* was a big hit, and they were making movies with titles like *Grass* and *Chang* and *Nanook of the North*. And names like Mrs. Martin Johnson, Captain Bob Bartlett, Roy Chapman Andrews and William Beebe took on sudden glitter.

Brooke had also arrived at a time when British films had begun to make an impact, films like *Downhill* and *The Lodger*, created by a young English director, Alfred Hitchcock. Brooke was immediately adopted by everybody who was anybody in Hollywood. He was a guest in the home of Charlie Chaplin, and at Pickfair. He met them all: Greta Garbo, Lillian Gish, William Powell, John Gilbert, King Vidor, Raoul Walsh, and Cecil B. de Mille. There was already a solid colony of British-born actors in Hollywood: Herbert Marshall, Clive Brooke, Ronald Colman, Basil Rathbone, and C. Aubrey Smith. They begged him to stay on. They even arranged a screen test for him. Brooke saw this as some kind of joke, but he agreed to take it. It had been a lark to Brooke, but not to others. The trade press reported that his test was sensational, that he would illuminate the screen. They predicted that he would captivate every woman who saw him, that he would draw them into the movie houses by the millions. They predicted that he would be a star of the first magnitude.

An avalanche of offers poured in, but Brooke politely declined. He did not, and could not, see himself as a film star, and had no desire to act. They persisted and he continued to decline, although the money offered to him was unreal. He knew that if he pursued this kind of career and was successful, any chance of personal privacy would be lost forever. He could not fade away gracefully, as he now wished to do. He would be in the fishbowl to stay, more exposed than he was even now, a super-celebrity for years to come, stared at, dissected, interviewed, judged, adored or envied, praised or reviled, but always a puppet, manipulated to titillate the public, and never enjoying the luxury of being alone.

Yet now he toyed with the idea of going back to Hollywood. At the moment he wanted to escape, some-where, anywhere. He was sick of London, fed up with this bloody man-eater Shaitan because it had brought this terrible pressure on him, and threatened to ruin his life, or at least his permanent peace of mind. He thought of California, the sunny climate, the palm trees and the desert and the swimming pools, and in terms of distance it seemed a planet removed from India. And he thought wryly, well, why not? He was still comparatively young. And after all, what was there to do for a big-game hunter, once he had retired? Do nothing? Live out the rest of his life as a London clubman? He had had four years of that and enjoyed it, but now he was becoming just a little bored with it. He could, of course, write his memoirs. He had already written a certain number of articles, not only for the English press, but also for William Randolph Hearst and his newspapers back in the United States.

Now the cablegram triggered a certain fantasy in Brooke's mind, and nourished it. He had terminated his trip to California last year as a guest of William Randolph Hearst and Marion Davies, and had stayed at an incredible castlelike place called San Simeon. Hearst himself had taken Brooke for a limousine ride some miles orth into an area called Big Sur. He had been fascinated by what he had seen. The great cliffs, the booming surf, the marvelous seascapes, the absolute beauty of the place. And the loneliness. He had seen a house here and there, nestled in the lee of a cliff overlooking the sea, and had thought if there were any place in the world he would prefer to live, it would be here.

But with Nora, of course.

Just the two of them, living and loving out there, away from everything, the crowds, the traffic, the pressures, getting to know each other, just being alone and together. Some day, so went his fantasy, a miracle would happen, or perhaps the inevitable—the door would be open, and she would be free, as well as he. He would cable her to leave Delhi at once and come to England, and they would be married and they could love together and sleep together as husband and wife, without guilt and without torment, and then after that they would go out to Big Sur, and build a house on one of those magnificent cliffs overlooking that incredible sea, and stay forever.

But once again, reality intruded. They knew all about Shaitan in Hollywood, as they did in London. There would be the same pressures to perform, the same questions asked. He could not run nor hide from his dilemma; distance was meaningless. He would be under the same pressure in Timbuktu or Samarkand.

And Thalberg's cablegram was explicit. "Good luck on Shaitan," it had said. They had taken it for granted that he would return to India and take care of what they saw as unfinished business.

Then, *after that*, they would offer him a blank check.

8

THE NEXT MORNING Brooke took his customary walk to Sloane Street. As he approached, he could see chalked on Alfred's slateboard the single number: 284. Alfred had apparently decided it was a waste of chalk to explain the number. Everyone knew what it referred to.

"Hungry bugger," said Alfred. "Never seems to get enough. This time he got himself a little tyke."

He snapped off a copy of the *Times* from the top of the pile and gave it to Brooke. Then, just as Brooke started to turn to walk away, the news vendor said:

"Excuse me, sir. But you may be wanting to see a copy of the *Daily Mail* this morning."

His watery blue eyes stared straight into Brooke's, and now there was something faintly hostile in them, a little contemptuous.

"They've got quite a picture of you. Here. Right on the front page. Thought you wouldn't want to miss it."

Alfred handed him a *Daily Mail*, and the smile on the pimply face was almost malicious.

Brooke took the newspaper and stared at the photo on the front page. It was in juxtaposition to the story of Shaitan's latest killing. The photographer at the zoo had caught him faithfully. Brooke was staring directly at the eyes of the leopard through the bars of the cage, and the leopard's jaws were open, his burning eyes fixed on Brooke. Brooke had his head thrust forward, over the edge of the guardrail, staring hypnotically at the leopard. There was a strange, tense look on his face. The eyes wide, the muscles taut. The look was de-

ceptive, subtle, haunting. You could define it as a look
of respect for the leopard—or a look of fear.

But it was the caption that struck home. It read
simply:

AT LAST
SUPERMAN FACES SUPERBEAST

The caption and the picture were clearly malicious. It
was the first overt criticism of Brooke's shilly-shallying.
It was also the first public implication that Dennis
Brooke was actually afraid, that he had lost his courage
at Behra, and for this reason had refused to go back to
India and face Shaitan.

Brooke looked up from his paper to see that not only
Alfred but three or four others who had stopped to buy
their newspapers were watching him silently, their faces
curious. He glared at them, turned and walked swiftly
away.

When he got back to his flat, Hendricks was out on
one of his morning errands.

Brooke sat down to read the story of Shaitan's latest
kill in the *Times*. Again, it was written under the byline
of Peter Wilkes.

This time the killing had taken place near a small
village called Chandigarh, in Uttar Pradash, and not
too far from Dehra Dun itself. A cobbler, Devaka by
name, his wife and small son lived in one of the small
huts of the village. The cobbler had buttressed his door
with an extra panel and wooden lock bar, had barred his
windows, and felt reasonably safe. He reminded his
wife and son that Shaitan had come back to the area,
had already made a new kill at Chakrata, and could
possibly be somewhere in the vicinity. He had then
ordered that instead of going outside during the night to
relieve themselves in the ordinary way, they were to use

the jars he had provided in the rear of their tiny store-house. When darkness came, they had eaten their meal of *chapattis* and goat's milk, Devaka had smoked his evening hookah, and they had all gone to bed, the boy sleeping between the father and mother.

Sometime during the night, the small boy had been awakened by a call of nature. Drugged with sleep, he had forgotten his father's warning and according to habit and normal routine, had stepped outside to urinate. The parents were awakened by a piercing scream, and rushed out of the open door to see a great pool of blood lying in the yard, and a huge leopard running down the road, carrying the limp body of their son clamped in his jaws. They had roused other villagers to the alarm, and in the early morning a search for the missing boy was begun.

His body, or what remained of it, was found in an open field about three miles away. Whatever the leopard had not taken, the vultures had picked clean. And so, wrote Wilkes, kill number 284 was duly record-ed. And the chances were that the man-eater would go on indefinitely unless he was stopped by a miracle, or by someone professional enough and courageous enough to put a stop to this monstrous predator for all time.

At quarter of one it began to rain. A chauffeured Rolls Royce sent by the prince drew up in front of Brooke's flat. A few minutes later, he was driven through the gates of St. James's Palace and delivered in front of York House, where Edward made his home.

He was led to a small dining room, where a table was set for two. A cheerful fire was burning in the grate. From the window, Dennis could hear the faint sound of traffic, and he could see the chimneys of Westminster and faint curls of smoke patterns eddying against the dark, angry sky. Below, he could hear the clickety-clack of soldier's heels, and an occasional thump of a rifle butt on the cobblestones.

The prince came in immediately. Brooke knew that Edward, Prince of Wales, was now thirty-three, just two years younger than himself. But somehow he still looked boyish, not much more than twenty-five, and this was part of the youthful charm that endeared him to his subjects and to the world. He was dressed casually, in dark checked trousers and a crew-cut sweater of fine Irish wool. Brooke knew that the prince would never dream of dining in this kind of casual dress except with very close friends. He greeted Brooke with a firm handshake and a warm smile.

"Good of you to come, Dennis. Awfully good of you to come. It's been a long time."

"Yes, sir."

The Prince frowned. "Damn this 'sir' business. Have you forgotten my name?"

Brooke grinned. "I'm sorry. David."

"That's better. Much better."

The Prince had been christened Edward Albert Christian George Andrew Patrick David. But only his immediate family and a few intimate friends, a very few intimate friends, called him David.

"Now, my dear fellow, let's get down to serious business. How about a drink?"

Brooke ordered a gin and soda, and the prince, signaling to a manservant, ordered the same. Edward studied Brooke for a moment.

"I must say you look a little peaked—done in."

"Well, I haven't been sleeping well—."

"Never mind telling me why. I know. Tell you something, Dennis. I'm pretty well done in myself at the moment. This last trip took something out of me. Oh, everyone in Canada was marvelous, of course, and I love the place. But that damned schedule they prepared

for me. Kept me running like a fox away from the
hounds. Ontario, to Manitoba, Alberta to British
Columbia, Saskatchewan, Quebec. Making speeches,
laying cornerstones, reviewing troops, you know, the
usual thing. To tell you the truth, Dennis, I'm pretty
well done in myself. Got some rest aboard the *Empress
of Scotland* on the way home, but it wasn't quite
enough. Tell you what, Dennis. Why don't we *both* get
away, for a few days. Just put everything behind us,
have a good time, rest up a bit."

"What do you have in mind?"

"I was thinking of running up to Scotland and doing
a little shooting. Say for a week. Just you and I. Might
be just the ticket. What do you say?"

"I'd like it very much."

"Jolly good. I'll tell the people up at the lodge to get
things ready. We'll leave on Monday."

Over lunch they chatted for awhile. Then the prince
turned the conversation to India.

"You know, Dennis, I found the country fascinating.
I loved the trip there back in '21, and I'd like to go back.
But papa thinks it's too dangerous, what with this
fellow Gandhi and his people giving us all sorts of
trouble. I tried to point out that he gave us some trouble
back in '21, but nothing happened. But papa wouldn't
hear of my going back. Said the situation is a lot worse
now. So they're planning a trip to Africa this time.
Political, of course, but I suppose it should be interesting. Egypt first, then Sudan, Kenya, Uganda. Safari
in Kenya I think. Big-game hunting. God, I wish you
could go along with me on this one. But they need your
expertise elsewhere, of course. Speaking of India,
Dennis, I need not remind you that's where we first met.
Six years ago. Jove, how time flies. I recall, you'd already built your reputation then."

They talked at length about that particular trip, and

Brooke remembered it well. The Prince of Wales was
aboard the H.M.S. *Renown*, due to land at Bombay
sometime in the middle of November. The viceroy, then
Lord Reading, had chosen a selected number of officers
from various military units, all highly experienced India
hands, to travel as escort for the prince. Brooke, then a
lieutenant, had been selected to represent the Royal
Guards. He was the lowest rank present, the others
being colonels and captains from units like the Central
India Horse and the Welsh Fusiliers. The viceroy had
selected Brooke because the prince anticipated doing a
little big-game shooting in the Punjab, and he could
have no better aide than Brooke at this sport.

Brooke remembered that cloudless warm November
morning when the *Renown*, to the shrieking of sirens
and the blast of whistles, steamed into the harbor and
landed at the Apollo Bunder, the famous gateway to
India. It was a sight that Dennis Brooke could never
forget. Lord Reading, standing in front of everyone to
receive the prince, was an elegant symbol of the British
Raj, wearing a formal gray morning coat and a white
sun helmet, the famous Star of India pinned on his
breast. With him were other important British officials,
and drawn up behind them were the ruling princes of
India and their sons, sovereigns of their domains,
dressed in rich shining silks and jewelled *pagaris*, the
fabulous names of the subcontinent, the maharajahs of
Patiala, Jodhpur, Dholpur, Dahr and Rutlaim; and the
nawabs of Bahawalpur and Palanpur. And beyond
them, in one great unending, seething mass, the
ordinary people of India, thousands upon thousands of
them, come to greet and shout welcome to the "Shah-
zada Sahib."

After that came a state drive through the city of
Bombay. The route led to Government House at
Malabar Point. The prince, looking stunned by the

tremendous reception he was receiving, rode in a horse-drawn carriage decorated in gilt, with a servant holding a gold-embroidered umbrella over his head. On either side of the carriage, as escort, rode the governor's mounted Indian bodyguard in full dress uniform, the sunlight glinting on their steel lances. Looking across the table now at Edward, it was hard for Brooke to believe this man, in the casual sweater and trousers was the same man who rode in the carriage that day.

What was especially memorable was that the ordinary people of India had turned out in tremendous numbers to greet the prince, and all along the parade route they cheered and shouted out their delight, and clapped their hands in the traditional sign of approval. They had ignored the pleas of Gandhi and his chief lieutenant, Pandit Jawaharlal Nehru, who had asked the people not to receive the prince, to stay indoors and close their shutters. The British had been concerned, even worried, but their fears were unfounded. The Indians simply could not resist a "good show." And Brooke remembered that the Earl of Birkenhead had used the same phrase. He, Brooke, would be a "good show," to the benefit of the Raj.

Brooke had traveled with the prince all through the length and breadth of India, and Edward seemed to gravitate toward Brooke and request him at his side more and more, and their friendship had ripened. When Brooke had returned to England, four years ago, the prince had made a point of renewing the friendship. And now here they were.

All through the lunch, Brooke noted a certain tension in the prince; he was not as relaxed as usual when they dined together. It was clear that he had something on his mind, something that seemed to disturb him. Finally, Edward came around to it.

"That photograph of you and the leopard," he said,

suddenly. "The one in the *Daily Mail*. They gave you
the dirty end of the stick, Dennis. You must have found
it—" and here the Prince fumbled for a word "—quite
cutting."

"Yes," said Brooke, wearily. "Naturally, I did. But I
suppose a man can get used to hanging—if he hangs
long enough."

"Dennis," said Edward. "I think I know how you
feel. I mean, I know what it is to be humiliated by the
press. Not the British press, thank God. But the
American newspapers. Every time I fell off a horse, they
featured it in their headlines. Made jokes about it, you
know. When papa heard of this, he was furious. He'd
never been to the United States, you know, never understood the American idea of humor. Anyway, he's for-
bidden me to ride horses any more. I mean, where there
is the slightest danger, steeplechase or point-to-point
races. He advised me to take up golf." The prince
snorted. "Golf, by God." He looked at Brooke.
"Sorry, old boy. I'm getting off the track. Let's get
onto it again." He paused. "Dennis, I'm going to
presume on our friendship. Anything you say to me I
will keep in complete confidence, if you so wish. I give
you my word, my royal word, on that. And if you wish
to say nothing, for personal or private reasons, I would
understand that, and never bring up the matter again."

"I think I know what you're going to ask me. What
am I doing in London when I should be in India, hunting this man-eater, Shaitan."

"Yes." Edward hesitated. "I'm amazed that you've
resisted this long, with everyone after you, including the
press. You realize, Dennis, that photograph in the *Daily
Mail* is pretty damaging. You know what it implies."

"Of course. It implies that I'm showing the white
feather."

"I know you too well for that, Dennis. I know it's a lie. But there's talk of it everywhere."

"I know. and it isn't quite a lie."

Edward stared at him. "You mean that attack at Behra?"

"I'll be honest with you, David. It *did* take something out of me. It's made me afraid, in a way. But that isn't the *real* reason. Every man's afraid of something, now and then. I was afraid just before going into battle in the Somme, at Ypres, and any man who says he wasn't is a damned liar. You were at the front, and you understand what I'm saying. But just knowing it was dangerous to go after this particular leopard, just being aware that he could kill me instead of my killing him, isn't the real reason. If it had only been that, in spite of the fact that I might be a little rusty in my professional skills by now, in spite of the fact that I could conceivably face another Behra, that, I repeat, is not the real reason. If it were only that, I'd have been back in India months ago."

"Then what *is* the real reason?"

The prince stared at him, and Dennis realized that he had to tell someone at last, that if he did not he would go insane, he would explode. And so he told Edward about Nora, how he had met her, and what had happened after that, at Ootacamund, how they felt about each other, and why they had parted. The reason he could not go back to India was that he knew he could not possibly stay away from her, nor she him, and the consequences of that would be frightful.

The prince listened quietly, never interrupting until Brooke was through. He nodded now and then, his face filled with compassion. And then he said:

"So it's a woman. And not the animal."

"Yes."

"Now I understand. And believe me, Dennis, I

sympathize. I'm not in your position, but in a sense I could be. If there was a woman I loved, I couldn't have her either. My future wife will have to be chosen for me—approved by the family and tradition, and all of that. It would all be *arranged*—by others. At least you have some freedom of choice, even if you don't wish to exercise it. The fact is, Dennis, we're both in very similar positions. We've both got the same problem."

"I don't understand."

"The problem is simply this. Neither of us is our own man. We belong to others. We're both public property. The only difference is, I was born into it, and you created your situation yourself. But because we are who we are, we have to pay the piper. We're expected to perform in certain ways, do what we're expected to do, and there's no way around it. They expect you to go to India to hunt down this man-eating beast, and sooner or later you will."

"I've just told you, David, why I can't."

"Dennis, listen to me. It's *their* decision, not yours. Your experience in this kind of thing is fairly recent, but it's been impressed on me the day after I was born. Do you think I like all those rules I was born into, all those rituals, all the saluting I've done, all the hands I've had to shake, all the speeches I've had to deliver, all the speeches I've had to listen to, all the cornerstones I've had to lay, all the troops I've had to review, all the standing I've had to endure, watching parades, the monuments I've had to unveil, all the uniforms I've had to wear, all the trips I've had to make, when all I wanted was a chance to sit down and think and rest, and find out who I really was? Do you think I like standing still for all those idiots who want to take snapshots, and all the babies I have to hold and kiss, and all the dinners I've had to attend, and all the toasts I've had to listen to, and the tours I've had to take through this factory or that, this coal mine or that, when I'd rather be quietly reading a book somewhere, or taking a walk through the country, or simply getting drunk. From the day of my birth, it's been listening to papa saying a royal prince can do this, but cannot do that, and mama saying the same thing, and the prime minister and the Church of England all telling me what I must do, and what I must not do. Everybody in the world seems to envy me, as they do you. But being a prince, at least much of it, is a damned bore. And when I become king my life will be even more rigid, more circumscribed. It's all ordained, simply an accident of birth.'' Then he hesitated. ''Between you and me, Dennis, and I don't think I'd say this to anyone else, my brother Bertie would make a much better king than I. But I can't walk away from who I am, and neither can you. If you'll take my advise, old friend, I'd simply go, do what I have to do, and get it over with.''

''I can't go, David.''

''You must. And you will.''

Brooke studied the prince for a moment. Then he said:

''With all due respect, David, may I ask you a—well, a rather delicate question? You can answer or not, as you wish. The last thing I should want to do is embarrass you.''

''Yes?''

''Was this your own idea, this luncheon? Or did someone put you up to it?''

The prince looked straight into Brooke's eyes. He reddened a little. And finally:

''Dennis, you have a perfect right to ask that question. And I want to be as frank and honest with you as you have been with me. The answer is yes. Directly after your interview with the Earl of Birkenhead, the earl asked for an immediate audience with papa. He explained that he was unable to persuade you to return to India, and emphasized the importance of the mission. He knew that you and I were good and close friends, and he persuaded papa to talk to me—'' The prince shrugged. "Well, here we are. The son of a king must do his duty, you see. And I *am* embarrassed, Dennis. I hope it does nothing to affect our friendship in any way. Perhaps I should have told you about it straightaway, at the beginning. But I want you to believe one thing."

"Yes?"

"Whether I had been instructed or not, as dear friends, I would have told you the same thing. You can't wait much longer. Sooner or later, you've got to go back. There's no way out of it. Any more than there's a way out—for me. Even if I wanted it."

9

WHEN HE RETURNED to his flat, he telephoned Jeanne Cooper and told her he could not see her that evening. He had developed a head cold, he was already running a fever, and his entire body ached. He could only hope this was not a prelude to influenza. There was a lot of flu going around in London lately, as she knew. And of course, at the moment, what he had was clearly infectious. He apologized profusely.

She was disappointed, of course. She had looked forward to the evening with great anticipation. But of course, he was right. She made him promise to call her when he felt better.

After his talk with the prince, after he had opened the door for the first time and told someone else about Nora, his head was now full of her. On this evening, he had no desire to bed down with Jeanne Cooper or any other woman. Nora Clymer was thousands of miles away, in Delhi, but she was still alive. Yet she was a ghost, haunting him. To lie close to another woman, to whisper in her ear, to touch her flesh, to enter her, seemed on this night to be a kind of sacrilege. He knew he was being a fool. He knew that perhaps the best way to forget Nora, or at least to dull the edge of his desire for her, was to supplant her entirely.

He dismissed Hendricks, and feeling very tired, went to bed early. But she still whirled around in his mind, the images and memories came back again, and he could not sleep.

Long before he had ever met Nora, he had known her husband, Sir Hugh Clymer.

They had first met as boys at Cheltenham. They were the same age, came into school at the same term, and became warm friends. They wore the traditional top hats, stiff collars, and straw boaters of the old English schools. They played rugger together, studied together, fenced each other, cursed their headmaster and housemaster together. In their last term they became roommates.

After that, they parted for a long time. Brooke had chosen the army, and went off to Sandhurst. Hugh Clymer opted for a diplomatic career, went to Oxford, and began his career in the Foreign Service in London. A year or two after Sandhurst, Brooke went to India to serve in the Royal Guards. For several years they corresponded fitfully. Then, a year after the Great War, Clymer had written Brooke that he had married. Her name was Nora Blythe, and she was the daughter of a prominent Harley Street surgeon. And by now his friend had become Sir Hugh Clymer, while Brooke himself had risen to the rank of captain.

The next year, in 1921, Sir Hugh Clymer was appointed an aide-de-camp to the viceroy, and he and his wife, at the end of that year, had come to Delhi.

Brooke had not seen them immediately. He was off on duty with the Guards near Ahmadabad, where there had been some trouble with one of the Gandhi factions, and some minor violence. His regiment had been posted there for some time.

Then one day he was shocked to read, in the *Times of India*, that his old friend had been felled by a stroke. He was paralyzed from the waist down and confined to a wheelchair for the rest of his life. The doctors had no idea as to the cause, nor of any treatment that might do any good. The news item went on to state that, fortunately, Sir Hugh's affliction was purely physical, and that his brain had in no way been affected. And although he was now handicapped, and would be confined to a desk, he would still continue to serve the viceroy in his capacity as ADC. His release from the hospital was expected in a week.

As soon as the Guards were relieved at Ahmadabad some weeks later and given a short leave, Brooke telegraphed that he was on his way, and took the next train to Delhi. There was a tiger, now called the Man-eater of Gujranwal, terrifying a number of villages north of Lahore, and normally he would have volunteered to go after it, as he had so many others. But this time he declined.

The Clymers had a large bungalow on a quiet lane leading off Prithviraj Road. Behind this, at the far end of the garden, was a spacious guest house. When Brooke arrived, he was admitted by a servant, and Nora Clymer came out to meet him.

This was the first time he had ever seen her, and he simply stood there and stared at her. And to this day he remembered every detail of that meeting, everything he saw, and everything that was spoken.

He remembered exactly what he thought at that moment—very simply, that she was the most beautiful woman he had ever seen. He remembered that he had just stood there, and gawked at her, like some acne-skinned, feckless schoolboy.

She was a tall woman with purple eyes and high cheekbones, the kind that are acquired only through generations of proper breeding. Her face was sculpted in its contours, almost gaunt. Her skin was flawless, tanned by the sun, and her hair, tied in a bun in the back, was a rich, vibrant chestnut. There was a slender elegance about her, and when she walked, or even moved, it would be with the grace of a cat. There was a coolness about her, but no hint of rejection. It was totally natural, totally a part of her, very polite and very much in control. It was the coolness of the well-bred English lady, very composed and still not distant. She was the kind of woman who looked directly at you, without exercising little feminine artifices with eyes and mouth.

He remembered she was not wearing the normal and proper dress of the English lady in India. Instead, she wore the Hindu *salvar*, an ankle-length pantaloon, deep blue in color, and a light blue *cumeez*, which resembled a man's shirt, loose fitting around the waist and reaching down to her knees. The effect was exotic. He knew instinctively she had not deliberately dressed this way to achieve some studied effect. His impression was that these were casual garments she liked to wear in the privacy of her home, simply because they were cool and comfortable.

She smiled at him as he stood there. He remembered the warmth and radiance of that first smile, and the first electric touch of their hands.

"Welcome to our house, Captain Brooke. Of course, I know you by reputation. But it's more than that. I feel that I *really* know you—as an old friend. Hugh's told me so much about you, of course, how close you were. And he can't wait to see you . . ."

At this moment Hugh Clymer entered in his wheelchair. Brooke was shocked at his appearance. Once a handsome, virile-looking man, he now looked twenty years older. His face was pale and drawn, and he had lost at least twenty pounds. He had a blanket around his waist and legs, as though to hide the obscenity of what had happened to that part of his body. But his blue eyes lit up when he saw Brooke. He rolled himself forward, and extended his hand:

"Welcome, Dennis, welcome. God, it's good to see you again."

Brooke mumbled something about being sorry for what had happened. There was nothing he could really say. Under the circumstances, he felt embarrassed about saying anything at all. But Clymer waved him off, with the typical British stiff upper lip.

"It's just bad luck, Dennis. Something, I suppose, that could happen to anybody."

But Brooke immediately thought of what a tragedy this must be, because he knew that Clymer was paralyzed from the waist down, he was crippled sexually, and could no longer perform as a man. With a beautiful woman like his wife, this must be particularly hard to take, both for him and for her. He felt guilty; he did not like himself for letting this thought pop into his mind. Yet he could not help it. He looked at Nora Clymer and caught her eyes. He saw the shadow in them, and in her face. He knew she sensed what he was thinking, and she turned her head away. He was suddenly embarrassed, as though he had unintentionally caught her naked and exposed.

He had arranged quarters at Delhi's military post, but Hugh Clymer would not hear of it.

"You're staying here, old man. There's a perfectly good guest bungalow at the rear of the garden, there'll be servants waiting on you hand and foot, Nora's trained a marvelous cook, and for the week you're here, you can be a pampered gentleman. Besides, we've got so much to talk about, you and I." Then he laughed. "After all, you're now such a damned celebrity, what with hunting down all those man-eating tigers and leopards, everybody who's anybody in Delhi is going to be impressed. Give us a certain prestige, you know. Might even give me a leg up at the Viceregal Palace."

Then he laughed. "Oh. Sorry. No pun intended."

Both Nora and Brooke heard the bitterness under the laugh, and the anger and helplessness, and the question, *Why me? Why did this have to happen to me?*

Most of the two weeks in Delhi was spent with Nora Clymer.

Her husband was at his office every day, transported there by a chauffeured car. She was curious as to what Brooke would be doing in Delhi, and he told her that he had come mainly to rest, and that there was no one special he wanted to see in the city. And so, almost by default and quite naturally, they saw much of each other. He was not, of course, a surrogate husband, but he was a friend and he had legs and Hugh Clymer was delighted that there was someone about to entertain Nora and take her around. And so they walked in Lohdi Park, and bicycled along Babar Road and down wide, tree-lined Barakamba Road to Connaught Circle, and from there to Queensway. They shopped together at the bazaars, and went to the theater twice, and he remembered that at the time there was a traveling Gilbert and Sullivan company imported from England, and they saw *Iolanthe* and *Pirates of Penzance*. Like tourists new to Delhi, they visited the Fort and the great Friday Mosque. There were garden parties and receptions, and the press, both English and Indian, came to Prithviraj Road to interview him. Nora was there, watching all this fuss being made over him, and smiling; he was embarrassed by this, he felt like an idiot.

The days of this particular holiday went by all too quickly, and when the last day had come around he was sure of one thing.

He was in love with Nora Clymer.

There was nothing spoken. But it was there, on her part as well. In the way she spoke his name, in the touch of their hands, in the way he slipped his arm around her waist as they inched their way through the crowded bazaars, and the way her body responded. It was there in the long silences between them when they sat on the ridge overlooking Delhi, and the plains beyond.

On the last day, Nora had the cook pack a picnic lunch, and now Dennis Brooke, lying sleepless in his bed, remembered every detail of it.

She told him she would pick the spot, and he would not know where it was until they got there. On her instructions he drove the car over the bridge spanning Jumna River. He remembered the traffic jam at the bridge, hundreds of bicycles, horse-drawn tonga carts, bullock carts, little carts pulled by men, automobiles, produce trucks, empty ones headed for the Punjab, others inching their way in toward Delhi, filled with produce. There were rickety buses, wandering cattle, flocks of sheep, buffalos, goats, all being goaded on by their sweating shepherds, and then, added to this, thousands of pedestrians.

Once over the Jumna River bridge, Nora instructed him to follow alongside of the river, until they finally reached a quiet spot near a field of sugar cane, growing tall and ripe in the late-morning sun. Here, in the shade of a banyan tree, they had lunch and watched the washermen on the other side as they spread the clean clothes on the grass to dry in the hot sun.

Finally, after lunch, they lay on their backs together on the cool grass, content with this moment and with each other. Then, while they looked up at the leaves of the banyan tree, dappling sunlight and shadow, he reached out his hand and caught hers. She held his hand, and he could feel her tremble, and he began to tremble himself, and then he turned his head toward her and kissed her.

It was a long, sweet, deep kiss, and it told them both

everything. But she pulled away suddenly, and said:

"We can't, Dennis."

"I know."

"And you know why."

"Of course."

"Damn it, darling," she said. "Damn it, damn it!"

Then she began to cry, and he took her in his arms and held her till she stopped. They both agreed that it was lucky he was leaving Delhi.

"I couldn't have stood it much longer, Dennis. I don't think I could have held out, I know I couldn't stop myself. If it had happened, I would have hated myself. And you would have hated *yourself*. And in the end, perhaps we would have hated each other."

He was an officer and a gentleman, of course. And she was another man's wife. Under ordinary circumstances, according to the code under which they both lived, this was nasty, but it was not an insurmountable obstacle. A man could conceivably take another man's wife away, *if* the husband was sound in body and able to defend himself.

But Hugh Clymer was a ghost of a man now, a paralytic in a wheelchair. And to take Nora from him, under these circumstances, was indefensible and dishonorable. In the very British circle in which they lived, he would be violating a very deep code of honor, as would she. Together, they would be snubbed, isolated, treated as pariahs even by their best friends.

He left Delhi, and they both agreed that it would be best if they never saw each other again.

And now, tossing and turning in his bed, he thought *what a damned fool I was.*

If I had only gone to Simla, instead of Ootacamund, I might have been able to forget her.

10

HE HAD HOPED that the shooting week with the prince in Scotland would be a blessed relief after the pressures of London. He had looked forward to tramping the moors and forests and breathing the sharp, cold clean air of the highlands, hoping that this would somehow provide some kind of special magic and rejuvenate his spirits.

This did not prove to be true.

First, the weather was bad. On three of the days, they were confined to the lodge because of heavy rain. When they did get out, walking for miles on the moors, Dennis Brooke realized how far he was from being in shape. At the end of the day he was exhausted, and could not wait to fall into bed. Four years ago, this kind of exercise would be child's play compared with what he had endured in the hills and forests of northern India. But since then he had lived the soft life in London, and it had taken its toll. His reflection in the mirror told him he was still a fine physical specimen. But he had not taken any kind of exercise, and his body had taken on a certain amount of flab.

His shooting had not been bad; he had taken full bags of grouse and pheasant. But he knew that his reflexes were not as good as they once were. He reasoned that he was four years older and a bit rusty because he had not held or fired a gun in such a long time. He rationalized that, of course, the guns used in shooting birds were much lighter than those he had used for big game, and perhaps this had made some difference. But he knew

that he was lying to himself. When the birds suddenly
flared up from some bush, in a noisy rush of flapping
wings, he knew that he was just a little late in getting his
gun around, just a fraction of a second. He knew also as
a professional, that a fraction of a second could be the
margin of life or death when it came to the charge of a
wounded leopard or tiger.

As to the matter of Shaitan, the prince never once
mentioned it. And he had ordered his attendants at the
lodge never to mention it, either. He wanted Brooke to
enjoy a complete escape, if only for a week, from the
dilemma that was tormenting him.

But there was no escape. The London newspapers
were delivered to the lodge each day. Ever since that
photo had appeared in the *Daily Mail*, the press had
changed its stance where he was concerned. Previously,
it had been impatient with his stubborn refusal to return
to India, his insistance that he had retired. Now it had
turned critical and almost hostile. One of the trashy
weekly penny newspapers, which specialized in shock
and cheap sensationalism, boldly printed an article
headed "Let Us Call A Spade A Spade."

The article was blunt. The truth was, it said, that Sir
Dennis Brooke was afraid to go back to India and hunt
the man-eater. The fact was that the incident at Behra
had emasculated him, and that he was not the man he
once was. There was no other reason why he should not
volunteer his skills, why he should not go back to fulfill
such an urgent mission. Innocent people were being
eaten by this voracious man-eater. The animal left
widows and orphans wherever it went. It was still at
large and the world believed, rightly or wrongly, that
only one man was capable of hunting down and killing
Shaitan. It would be better, continued the article, if
Brooke admitted to the world that the incident at Behra
had taken his courage, that he was indeed afraid. If he
came forward to tell the truth, to confess openly and

frankly to this, the public would understand. The public would, in all probability, forgive. What could not be forgiven was Brooke's feeble attempts to ward off the expectations of the public, his pitiful efforts to save face. Let him, it concluded, come forward, and simply admit that he was afraid to face Shaitan. This could be called in itself a certain act of courage. The question was asked. Did Sir Dennis Brooke actually have enough courage left to step forward and simply tell the truth?

The newspapers, of course, knew nothing of Nora, or Ootacamund.

In the week Brooke had been in Scotland, Shaitan had taken two more victims.

A priest was caught one night on the pilgrim path outside of Bisalpur. He had been bound with a group of fellows for the shrines in Hardwar when he had fallen behind. The others had found a stout pilgrim shelter on the road, and then discovered their companion, one Pattu Lal, missing. They had been deep in meditation as they walked, and did not notice that he had lagged behind. Fearful of going back in the night to find him, because they knew Shaitan was in the vicinity, they waited till morning. All they found of Pattu Lal was a few torn and bloody remnants of his robe, and his walking staff.

The villagers of Bisalpur were called, and they began a hunt for the remains. They found them in an open field a mile away. All that remained was a skull and a few broken bones, and a scared amulet that Pattu Lal always wore.

Three days later, a well-known Sikh big-game hunter from Amristar, Nanak by name, was caught and eaten by Shaitan outside of a village named Ramnagas, not far from Bisalpur. The Sikhs, like the Muslims, gave no credence to the Hindu belief that Shaitan was a reincarnation of the *sadhu*, Ram Gwar. The Sikhs were people of great courage, and a number of them had become accomplished hunters of man-eaters, though not in a class with the British army officers. The government had licensed the necessary weapons to a few who were qualified to hunt down and kill man-eaters. The body of Nanak, so named after the founding father of the Sikh faith, Guru Nanak, was never found. All that was found, under a tree, was his belt buckle, his rifle, and scraps of his boots, all lying in a pool of blood. This in itself was enough to document the killing.

The Sikh hunter actually had volunteered to hunt down Shaitan for altruistic reasons. It was interesting to note that all the victims so far taken by Shaitan were Hindus. Not a single Moslem or Sikh in the area had been attacked.

The newspapers reported, with some irritation, that Dennis Brooke was in Scotland shooting birds while all this was going on. The newspapers also reported that as of now, Shaitan had taken victim number 286.

When Brooke returned to London he immediately sensed a change in attitude toward him.

None of it was overt and much of it was subtle. But the elements were there, suppressed yet controlled. His own man, Hendricks, seemed to look at Brooke in a different way. He seemed to become more starched, more formal, more distant. He did his work quietly, unobtrusively; he seemed glad to quickly disappear from the room when not needed. When Brooke tried to draw him into some kind of conversation, any kind, Hendricks simply replied in monosyllables. It was "Yes, sir" and "No, sir" and that was about it.

Brooke came to the painful conclusion that Hendricks was ashamed of him, that he had lost some face and prestige among his own peers. Up to recently, it had been an honor to serve a man like Sir Dennis Brooke,

second only to the Prince of Wales in the public eye.
Hendricks was still loyal, but Brooke sensed that now he
was sorely tried.

The newspapers continued to become hostile. The
humorous publication, *Punch*, ran some wicked and
biting illustrations concerning him. One really hit home.
The artist had drawn Brooke as a shrunken figure, bent
nearly to the ground, trying to carry an enormous
smiling leopard sitting on his back, the great paws
wound around Brooke's neck. The illustration had no
caption, and clearly needed none.

On the street, the faces of the people who recognized
him somehow seemed different. There was a certain
curiosity reflected in their expressions, a certain
wariness, a disappointment, almost reproach. They had
built a hero—more than that, a superhero—and he had
let them down. They expected him to perform, and he
did not, and they began to resent him for it. What they
had thought was a giant was now turning into a pygmy.
They were polite, of course, almost too polite, but they
kept a certain distance. There were some people who
still asked for his autograph, but fewer than before. The
invitations for dinner, for the theater, for the opera,
stopped coming.

He called Jeanne Cooper. "Darling," she said. "I'd
love to see you, I'd simply *love* to, but I've been so
busy. We're having some changes in the cast of the play,
and you know how unsettling *that* can be. Besides, I'm
booked for every night for the next two weeks and
besides—" she hesitated, and then "—well, there's this
man, darling. I've become rather attached to him. He's
a producer, and he's promised me the leading role in his
next play, and well—what can I say? It's all been lovely,
darling, you're really such a dear. But why don't you go
back to India and kill that wretched animal, and stop all
that awful talk?"

He began to waver. Maybe Jeanne was right. Go to India and get it over with. Damn the consequences. Either you will get Shaitan or he will get you. That wasn't important now. It's Nora. You managed to say goodbye to her in Delhi once. But you couldn't do it again. And you know damned well you couldn't. Not after what happened at Ootacamund.

And she could not leave you. He remembered her exact words, there in his bungalow that night. "*If you ever come back to India, Dennis*," she had said, "*I'll never let you go.*"

It was all too much, he thought. Go or not go. My plate is too full, he thought; it's more than I can handle.

He had been in London for a week, and was at breakfast when the phone rang. Hendricks answered it on the kitchen extension. A few moments later he came in and said:

"There's a gentleman on the telephone, sir."

"Who is it?"

"He wouldn't give his name, sir. Just asid it was a friend."

Brooke hesitated. During the week he had had three or four anonymous phone calls. All had been abusive. Two of the callers had called him an out-and-out coward. Hendricks waited.

"Shall I put him off, Sir Dennis? Tell him you don't speak to people you don't know?"

"Yes, I think so, Hendricks. Do that."

Hendricks picked up the phone on the end table and said stiffy:

"I'm sorry, sir. But Sir Dennis is not interested in speaking to anyone who does not identify himself." Brooke heard the man's voice coming out of the receiver pressed against Hendricks's ear, but could not make out what he was saying. Hendricks listened for a moment, then put his hand over the mouthpiece and turned to Brooke, his face puzzled.

"He said he knows you very well. In fact, he says, you owe him a drink or two for all those bottles he bought you from every beer *wallah* in Madras after you got the Dharbanga tiger—."

Brooke grabbed the phone from Hendricks's hand.

"Tony! Tony Lassiter. By God, I don't believe it!"

"Hello, Dennis."

"When did you get in?"

"Late last night. Came on the *Eastern Star*. Long, long trip. Seems forever since I left Bombay."

"What are you doing here?"

"On special assignment. Directive straight from Lord Irwin himself."

"Sounds formidable."

"It is." Brooke could imagine Lassiter grinning over the telephone. "Dennis, I've missed you. Missed having you around, especially on the hunt. Just doesn't seem the same these last four years. Can't imagine why you're still here. I know everybody thinks of this as home, but India's *your* home, it's where you belong."

"Never mind all that," said Brooke, impatiently. "Are you free? When can we meet?"

"Free as a bird, sir. And at your service, major."

"How about lunch?"

"Today?"

"Why not?"

"Where?"

"At my club . . ."

"Tell you what, Dennis. Why not make it *my* club. The Explorers'. You know where it is. Just off St. James's Street. Haven't seen the inside for years, but my father is still a member, and by virtue of that, so am I. Be much more convenient for me. Have to meet a few people there after we finish. Matter of fact, my father and a couple of my uncles, county people, are all coming down to London to present the family greetings to their prodigal boy. I'll arrange for a private dining room."

"Look, Tony, I'm the one who owes *you* the drinks . . ."

"Don't worry," said Lassiter, "I'll collect later. The Explorers' then. Right?"

"All right," said Brooke. "What time?"

"One o'clock?"

"Done." Then: "Damn it, Tony, I still can't believe you're here. We've got a lot to talk about."

"We have indeed," said Lassiter.

The Explorers' Club was recessed somewhat from the street itself, and was fronted by a Victorian-style porter's lodge, presided over by an ancient concierge of indeterminate age.

Brooke entered through two swinging doors and introduced himself.

"I'm a guest of Captain Lassiter's. Has he arrived?"

The concierge recognized him instantly.

"Yes, sir. He's waiting for you in one of the upstairs dining rooms. Please go in. I'll see that you're taken to him at once."

The concierge pressed a buzzer and a young page in livery came forward quickly to meet him.

"This way, sir."

The page led Brooke along the white marble floor of the entry hall, then to the main room of the club. Men in easy chairs, reading or engaged in low conversation, turned and watched him go. His face was almost as familiar now as the prince's, and he was recognized immediately. A few of the members watched him curiously. He was aware that one or two of them looked at him with ill-concealed contempt, and then turned

abruptly back to their newspapers. He had had the same
reaction at his own clubs, at White's and the Travellers'.
Everyone was scrupulously polite, but he was conscious
that now he was subtly being snubbed. Some of the
members who had once greeted him warmly did not
even respond to his "good morning." Others simply
turned their heads away when he walked by. Even the
servants seemed infected. They no longer smiled at him,
they were overly polite, stiff. Now, he rarely went to his
clubs.

The page boy led him up a carpeted stairway and
opened the door to admit Brooke. Tony Lassiter was
seated at a table already set for lunch. He was wearing
his Guards uniform, and it seemed to Brooke that time
had forgotten about Lassiter, he hadn't changed a bit
since Brooke had said goodbye to him four years ago.
Still the warm smile, the lean, ruddy, windblown face,
the laughing gray eyes, the great, curly military
mustache.

They spoke each other's name and then embraced, in
a most un-English way. Brooke said:

"You look fit, Tony. Damned fit. God, I'm glad to
see you!"

"And I you, Dennis. Or should I say, Sir Dennis."

"You do, and I'll punch that bloody grin right off
your face."

They each ordered a gin, and Brooke asked:

"How long will you be in London?"

"That all depends."

"On what?"

"On you."

Brooke's face clouded.

"I see."

They were silent for a moment. Suddenly, there was a
small distance between them. Lassiter said:

"Look, Dennis. I know how you feel. I know you're

getting it from all sides. Your letters have explained that. I'm sorry I'm adding my weight. But I simply have to. The fact is, the viceroy's sent me here on a special mission, as I told you. You can guess what it is."

"I thought I made my position clear, Tony."

"You have. But it seems nobody will take no for an answer." He hesitated, then looked Brooke straight in the eye. "What is it, Dennis?" Brooke was silent, and Lassiter said: "Never mind. I know. It's Behra. Damned close call you had. And of course, you keep on doing things like running down man-eaters, your luck can run out, sooner or later. Personally, I don't blame you for balking. Enough to shake any man. If that claw had caught you just one inch higher—well, you'd be better off dead, as far as the rest of life was concerned. Still—here's this beastie they call Shaitan—and here's the man they call the Sahib. It's very simple. One and one make two. And you're still the best in the world, Dennis."

"I was."

"No. You are. Even if you walked with a limp and one hand tied behind your back. Everybody is beginning to think you've lost your nerve. I don't. I know you too well. Listen, old man. We'll hunt Shaitan together. You'll get back into it soon enough. You'll find this beastie a real challenge. Now you see him, now you don't. He doesn't do all the usual leopard tricks. He's crafty, Dennis. You think you have him, you think you've cornered him, and he isn't there any more. Another thing. This animal is big. I mean, really big. Almost half again as big as the ordinary species. The Hindus think he's some kind of devil, some special mutation. Those that have seen him claim he's two or three times ordinary size. But of course, that's hysteria. They see his shadow in the dark, catch just a glimpse of him, and of course they exaggerate. Scared to death, of course.''

"Tony," interrupted Dennis, sharply.

"Oh. Yes.''

"It isn't Behra alone. That *did* shake me up, to be frank. But if it were just that, I'd be on my way now, I think. It's something else. It's a private reason. Something personal.''

There was a long pause. Then Lassiter said:

"I see. Anything you might want to talk about?''

"No. I can't.''

Lassiter was silent. Brooke studied his friend. He had an idea that Tony Lassiter *knew*. Or if he did not know, he at least suspected. Lassiter knew that he, Brooke, had taken that holiday at Ootacamund, when he had almost always gone to Simla. He knew that Nora Clymer had been in Ootacamund at the same time. The tales of who was with whom at the British hill stations, and who did what, was common gossip in the regiments. Lassiter was not stupid. It was conceivable that he might put two and two together. But at best it would be an educated guess, and knowing Tony, he would never mention it.

"Oh, Tony. Something I forgot to ask you.''

"Yes?''

"How long will you be in England?''

"That depends. On you.''

"I see. Well, you already have your answer. Sorry.''

"That's all right. Didn't expect I could move the mountain all by myself." He paused. "By the way, before we have lunch, I'd like you to meet a friend of mine—and yours.''

Brooke looked at Lassiter, puzzled. Lassiter grinned, rose from the table, and opened a door to an adjoining room.

"*Ia*," he said.

Brooke rose in shock, unbelieving, stunned by the sight of the man in the doorway. It was his old friend, Bahalji Singh, headman of the village of Chakrata.

"Bahalji." For a moment or two Brooke was unable to continue. Then: "What the devil are you doing here?"

"Took him along with me," said Lassiter, blandly. "Thought you two might want to say *ram ram* again, after all these years." Then, grinning at Brooke: "He's been through a lot getting here, Dennis. Hadn't been more than thirty miles outside of his village for years. Seasick almost all the way from Bombay to Southampton."

Brooke had always seen Bahalji Singh in his simple cotton *dhoti*. But now, the effect was startling. Bahalji Singh still wore his turban, but otherwise he was dressed in an ill-fitting English suit a size or two too big for him, and shoes, which Brooke knew the Hindu must find extremely uncomfortable. The headman carried a suitcase, which he set on the floor for a moment. Then, he gestured with his hands and gravely spoke the greeting used throughout northern India.

"*Ramasti*, Sahib."

Brooke returned the gesture. "*Ramasti*, Bahalji Singh."

To anyone else, the Hindu might have looked small in this room, pathetic in his ridiculous clothes, totally out of place in this mahogany-paneled English dining room. He knew he was in this sanctuary of British sahibs only by sufferance and special arrangement. Yet there was a certain dignity about him, he did not cringe or seem embarrassed, he was not obsequious. He was, after all, the *padhan* of his village.

Brooke saw that there were tears in the Indian's eyes. Then the headman said, in Hindustani:

"Sahib, I have come on a long journey to this place. And it is good to see you again. Long ago, we spent many days together, and my son, Ranga and my wife, Kasturi, still think of you as one of our family, and our house is always your house."

Brooke felt his own eyes water. He wanted to embrace Bahalji Singh, to hold him close, so deep was his love and respect for this man, but he knew he could not do it, not here at the Explorers' Club. And so he gripped Bahalji's hand tightly in his and said, rather stupidly:

"It's good to see you again, Bahalji. It's so damned good."

Brooke, still bewildered at finding Bahalji here in London, glanced at Tony Lassiter, knowing there had to be a reason, and already suspecting what it was.

"The reason he's here, Dennis," said Lassiter, "is because he wants a few words with you. Personally. On behalf of the people in his village, especially. But also on behalf of all the people in the other villages of his district."

Then Behalji Singh said:

"Sahib, we of our district are in great distress. It is not those in my village alone, in Chakrata, which has felt the teeth and jaws of Shaitan many more times than any other place. He roams like an evil demon, and he has eaten many in Rampur, Pauri, Bijnor, Chandpur and many other villages nearby. Great sahib *shikari*s have sought to kill him. They themselves have been eaten. He is a fiend, Sahib Brooke, bigger and fiercer and faster than any other man-eater or tiger ever known in Uttar Pradash, or even the Punjab and Nepal. But it is the people of my village he favors for reasons we all know.

"Our people love you, Sahib. Many tmes you have saved them from terrible death. They remember well the tiger of Ramnagas and the leopard of Baijnath and

how you came into our country and killed them.
But you came not only into our country, but into
our hearts. You were our deliverer, and in every
temple and at every shrine our people prayed for
your long life and eternal joy afterward. They are
praying again, Sahib, for your return, to save us
from this calamity. For if you do not return, we shall
be ruined. Because of Shaitan, we dare not go out at
night, we cannot watch our wheat crop, so that the deer
have eaten it, we cannot graze our goats after darkness
falls, we cannot enter the forest for wood or fodder for
fear of this demon. At night we sit in our houses,
frightened that he may come through our windows and
doors, and this he has done many times. Sahib, we love
you as one of our own, we love you as a brother, we
pray for your return, to deliver us from the devil. There
is no other *shikari* but you who can do this.''

He picked up the suitcase he was carrying and placed
it on the table.

''Sahib, the people of the district ask you to accept
this.'' He opened the suitcase, and Brooke stood there,
staring at its contents. It was packed to the brim with
Indian money in small denominations, crumpled rupees
and annas and coins of all kinds. ''We, the *padhan*s of
each village, have collected this money from our people.
The poorest of the poor have given something. They
asked me to bring it to you as a token of their love and
esteem. They ask you for the sake of their wives, their
mothers, their little children, to come back and kill
Shaitan. For only you can do it, Sahib. This we know.
And we shall pray for your joy in some other world, for
all our lives, and our children shall do the same.''

There were tears in Bahalji Singh's eyes. Dennis
Brooke felt tears springing to his own eyes as well. He
stood there, shaken. He did not move as Bahalji Singh
knelt and touched Brooke's feet with his hands, his tur-

baned head bowed in supplication. Then he rose, turned, and abruptly left the room.

Brooke looked at Lassiter. "You bastard."

Lassiter shrugged and grinned. "Sticks and stones . . ."

"I suppose this was your idea."

"Well, I *did* discuss it with the viceroy."

"Bringing Bahalji here. That was *really* ingenious, Tony."

"I thought a direct appeal from him to you would do it. I know how you feel about him, Dennis. And about his people. But of course, the whole thing wasn't easy. The club here was a little sticky about allowing Bahalji Singh to even enter its premises. The committee shouted sacrilege, but they were shouted down by the right people . . ."

"The money," said Brooke, sarcastically. "I suppose that was your idea, too."

"Yes. But now I'll admit, old man, it did seem a little overdone. Gilding the lily, you might say. Sorry about that."

"And your father and uncle. They're all waiting to meet you here later, of course."

Lassiter fidgeted a little, then grinned. "Well, actually, no. To tell you the truth old man, that was a bit of a white lie. What I mean to say is they're waiting to meet me, to be sure. But it seems that they just couldn't make it to London so soon. In other words, they're still in Worcestershire."

Suddenly Brooke started to laugh. He simply couldn't help it. He laughed and laughed until his sides hurt, knowing that it was over, and there was no way he could stand up to it any more.

The newspapers bannered the announcement:

SUPERMAN VERSUS SUPERBEAST

SIR DENNIS BROOKE TAKES UP CHALLENGE
LEAVES FOR INDIA AT END OF WEEK

The next evening, Brooke entered the Bristish
Museum after hours, accompanied by Hendricks and
Tony Lassiter. They went immediately to the Indian
Room of the King Edward VII Gallery. They walked by
the various exhibits, the erotic stone carvings, the
Gandhara sculptures dating from the first to the sixth
century, the Buddhist sculptures from Amaravati, and
the Jain and Hindu sculptures from Orissa.

Finally they came to the huge glass case holding the
exhibit of Brooke's guns. A crowd of photographers
and newsmen were there to record the event. The
curator solemnly opened the glass case, and Brooke
took out the guns one by one, holding them, examining
them, getting the feel of them. Then the curator, by
previous arrangement, instructed two of his assistants to
box the guns and take them immediately to Brooke's
flat.

The following day Brooke left for Worcestershire as a
guest of Tony Lassiter. There, in the country, he could
enjoy the privacy he needed. In the morning he ran
through the woods and fields with Tony Lassiter, mile
after mile, trying to run off some of his flab, and to get
his wind back. In the afternoon he practiced firing his
various weapons, the Mannlicher, the .275, the
.450/500, testing his aim and his reflexes. He found
himself somewhat rusty, he knew that he was not quite
as fast and sharp as he once was, and he worried about
it. But Lassiter assured him that he would come around
in time.

During his stay in Worcestershire, the press reported
that Shaitan had killed and eaten two more victims, one

in Kotdwara and another near the man-eater's favorite haunt, the village of Chakrata.

By official count, Shaitan had now taken his 288th victim.

On Monday, a week later, Dennis Brooke, along with Lassiter and Bahalji Singh, boarded the *Dover Castle*, bound for Bombay. In a press interview on the dock, Brooke announced that if he were indeed successful, and managed to kill the man-eater, he would accept the reward offered by the *Times*, as well as any from other sources, and distribute it among the bereaved families of Shaitan's victims.

On his first night at sea, Dennis Brooke found it impossible to sleep.

He put on his trousers, a heavy sweater, and a short-coat, and went up to the deck. He lay back on a deck chair and stared out at the sea, its greasy swells undulating in the half-light of the moon. A sharp, nipping night wind was blowing in from the northwest. A heard the steady throb-throb of the engines far below sending their faint vibrations through the hull, and by turning his head and looking aft, he could see the wake of the ship boiling its way toward England.

He remembered, suddenly, another deck on another ship at another time. On this occasion, the bow was pointing toward England, and the wake was headed the other way.

It was five years ago, aboard the Peninsular and Orient liner, *Sussex Downs*, the ship which had brought him to England. On the morning the ship finally left the Suez Canal and entered the Mediterranean, there was the usual ritual observed by all the British passengers, who had left India and were going home. On this morning, the male passengers, all wearing their topees, paraded

once around the main deck, while the ship's band
played a lively Scottish tune. Then, at a command from
the captain, the men stopped and stood solemnly at the
rail, standing at attention and still wearing their topees.
The band then played "God Save The King." Then,
after the last notes had died away, the captain gave
another command, and with a great cheer the men all
took their topees from their heads and flung them into
the sea. The pith and cork helmets quickly bobbed and
floated on the current, were caught in the wake and then
disappeared. Again the men cheered, while the women
applauded. The topees symbolized India, and the
Orient, of course. And leaving them behind meant that
they had finally left the subcontinent—for many, forever—and were going home.

Dennis Brooke had watched his topee float along with
the rest of them, and to him, the symbolism was
particularly poignant, because he knew he could never,
and would never, go back to India again.

Yet, strangely, unbelievably, here he was, five years
later, on the deck of another ship, going back to India,
something he had never in his wildest imagination ever
expected to do.

He leaned back and shut his eyes, and his head
whirled with a hundred confused pictures of the strange
land he would see once again, the land of hill stations
and *gymkhana*s, of topees and spine pads, of monsoons
and the hot season, of bullock and tonga carts and rick-
shaws, of chota pegs and burra pegs and Brahmins, of
*sadhu*s and Untouchables, of water wallahs and
sweepers and *punkah* coolies, of *guru*s and *khitmagar*s
and bejeweled maharajahs, and nizams and rajas, and
mehtars and ranas, each with their allotted gun salutes;
of langurs and kakar deer and black crows and vultures,
jackals and leopard and tiger and wild boar and
Himalayan bear, of mango trees and bamboo forests

and temples and shrines and pilgrims by the thousands;
of sedan chairs and gilded elephants and palanquins—
the land of Vishnu and Siva and *purdah* and *dastur* and
royal durbars, of curry and *chapatti*s, of cholera belts
and *shikar*s and pig-sticking contests, of Bengali *babua*s
and *dacoit*s and the murderous sun, baking the land and
frying the brains of all who lived there.

Finally he fell asleep, and when he opened his eyes
again, the red glow of sunset was tinting the sea, and he
felt still and cold, very cold.

PART THREE

11

Nora Clymer would never forget that particular Thursday in early October. It began like any other day in the life of a memsahib of her class.

The monsoon rains had ended, and now the climate in Delhi was delightful, cool and dry. After Hugh had left for his office, she had called for her *syce*, or groom, and asked him to bring out the black mare. Then, after a short ride, she had had breakfast served to her by her *khitmagar*, the man who waited on table, and then gone over the household accounts. As befitted her station as wife of an ADC to the viceroy, there were some twenty servants in her household, at a cost of some five hundred rupees per month. The key servants were the cook and the *khansamah*, or butler. Then there was Hugh's valet and bearer, Badri Prasad, the watchman, the scullery man, the sweeps, and under housemaids, the *bhisti*, or water carrier, Nora's personal maid, the washerman, the groom, the grasscutters, and the gardener. And of course there was the indispensable *derzi*, or household tailor, as well as a number of part-time servants.

In India, the British memsahib left everything to her servants. Nora knew that she could get along very well with one third of her staff, but as the wife of an ADC she had to abide by *dastur*, or custom. *Dastur* was the key word. You observed it to a T or you ran into trouble. The day before, for example, she had run into a vexing problem. Her small terrier, Perk, had made a mess under her bed. She had asked the *khansamah* to see that it was cleaned up. But the butler had been shocked at her request. "Memsahib, I cannot do as you say. This is a task for a lowly person," he had said. She had then asked the scullery man to clean it up and he, too, had demurred, almost indignantly: "Memsahib, this is not my task. It is beneath me. It is against custom. It is not *dastur*." In desperation, she had talked to the *dhobi*, the washerman. He too, was shocked at her request. His job, he insisted politely, was to wash the family clothes, and that was all. Finally, she had been forced to send to the marketplace for a *dome*, an Untouchable sweeper. The collection of offal was in his domain, and he consented to come to the bungalow and for a few annas do what was necessary.

At any rate, there was the morning consultation with the cook, the routine chores of seeing that the ashtrays were cleaned, the decanters and cigarette boxes filled. Then there were the consultations with the gardeners, and a discussion with the *derzi*, sitting on his little carpet on the veranda before his little sewing machine, on what sewing and mending was to be done on this day.

By eleven o'clock, Nora occasionally had people over for bridge and coffee. There was the usual scandal and gossip. Normally her husband, like the other men, would come home for lunch. But because of his handicap, he had lunch at the Viceregal Lodge. After lunch she took a siesta, and after that she usually played tennis at the club. There was time for a drink with the other ladies in the set, and after that it was home for dinner.

Nora Clymer found the life stifling and boring. Because of Hugh's condition, it was difficult for them to get around, and the Clymers seldom went out at night. She hated the deadly sameness, day after day. She became a volunteer worker at the Children's Clinic three times a week. She waited eagerly for the *dak* wallah, the postman, to bring her periodicals and occasional letters from her parents and a few friends in England. Sometimes there were small events to brighten the day. The Chinese trader who came to the bungalow and made marvelous shoes to measure, or the merchant from Kashmir who sold sensuous underthings of pure silk and bright shawls and rugs. She read the *Statesman*, which some called the *Manchester Guardian* of the East, and the *Times of India*, and she avidly consumed some of the more popular magazines posted from England, *Blackwood's* and *The Tatler* and of course *Punch*.

At five o'clock Nora saw the big Rolls Royce come up the road. It was a Phantom One Hooper Tourer with an open-bodied canvas top, and its hood and accessories of polished aluminum shone in the sun. It was one of the viceroy's fleet of cars; Lord Irwin had lent it to Hugh Clymer, so that he could enjoy easy transportation from home to the palace and return.

Badri Prasad, Clymer's huge Hindu bearer, was waiting on the veranda, standing next to his master's wheelchair. When the chauffeur stopped the car, the bearer went down, opened the rear door, gently gathered Clymer in his arms, and carried him like a child up to his wheelchair, and deposited him carefully into it. After that, Badri Prasad whipped out a cloth, kneeled down, and polished the dust from Clymer's shoes. Then he wheeled him inside the house. The *khansamah*, who stood attention at the sideboard, then mixed Nora and her husband a gin and soda.

She kissed her husband on the cheek and sat down wearily. She asked him as a matter of routine, in the way wives ask their husbands, whether anything important had happened at the office.

"No," he said. "But there's a bit of news just come in by telegraph. From England, and it may interest you."

"Yes?"

"Dennis Brooke is coming back to India."

"Oh?"

She caught her breath. She sat perfectly still, trying to digest this news. She had had her glass halfway to her lips, and now she held it there, suspended. She was conscious that her husband's eyes were on her, and that they were smiling. There was a long silence. Then Hugh Clymer said:

"Bit of a shock, isn't it?"

"Oh. Yes, yes."

"Well, the newspapers will be full of it tomorrow, of course. Naturally, he *had* to come back sooner or later, under the circumstances. No matter what his personal inclinations. Everyone's delighted, of course, from the viceroy down. We need a Dennis Brooke here right now, if only to earn a few points."

"When is he expected to arrive?"

"He's sailing on the *Dover Castle*. Means he'll be here in four weeks, more or less. Unfortunately, I don't think we'll get a chance to see him this time. Not until after he kills that damned man-eater, at least."

"But I don't understand . . ."

"I know. He's our dear friend, and all that. But this trip will be all business. Time is of the essence, my dear, to use the cliché. He'll probably stay in Delhi overnight, when he gets here from Bombay, and no longer, and of course he'll stay at the lodge. They'll want him to go north as soon as possible. He has a job to do, you see."

"Yes. Of course."

"According to what we hear, however, he'll make one stop before he goes out into the Dehra Dun district and the villages. He's to be a guest of the Maharajah of Patiala for two days. It's a matter of politics. Putting it simply, the maharajah has been a very good friend of the Raj, insists on entertaining Brooke, and of course it would enhance his prestige. There are other reasons, of course, but they're much too complicated.''

"Then," she said. "That's that. We won't be seeing Dennis at all. At least, not in the near future."

Hugh Clymer sipped his drink, and smiled at his wife. "I wouldn't quite put it that way, my dear."

"What do you mean?"

"I mean, I may not see him. But *you* will."

She stared at him. Then, stupidly:

"I?"

"You see, my dear, Lord Irwin is sending up a small delegation to the maharajah's entertainment. By invitation, of course. The usual thing, the usual courtesy. The viceroy himself can't go, pressure of work and all that, but he's already selected four or five couples. We were among them."

"Then we're *both* going . . ."

"No," he said. "I begged off. Too arduous a trip for me, what with being a prisoner in this damned wheelchair, and all. But I suggested to Lord Irwin that you might go. This on the basis of the fact that we were very close friends of Dennis, and he would miss seeing at least one of us. The viceroy agreed. So there you are, Nora. It's off to Patiala for you when the time comes."

"Hugh," she said. "This is ridiculous. I won't go unless you go."

"Don't be an idiot," he said. "It'll give you a chance to see Dennis again, and give him both our regards. Besides, I hear the maharajah is going all out for this one. It should be something to see."

Later she watched as Badri Prasad gently lifted her husband from the wheelchair and gently deposited him on his bed. She leaned over and kissed her husband on the mouth, and for a moment he held her hand. Then he said, softly:

"Thank you, darling."

"For what?"

"Just for being here. Just for being—my wife."

She wanted to cry. She turned and went into her own room. They had separate bedrooms. This was at his insistence, not hers. He was a restless sleeper, he said. He would require help if he had to get up in the middle of the night to go to the bathroom. He did not want to have to wake her. Badri Prasad slept on a cot in the hallway, just outside of his bedroom. The servant was a light sleeper, and he awoke immediately at his master's call whenever necessary.

But Nora Clymer knew there were other reasons. His legs, twisted with the paralysis, were ugly when exposed, and she knew her husband was very sensitive to this. Moreover, if they slept in the same bedroom, somehow both she and he, by their very physical proximity, would be constantly reminded, and painfully aware, of his impotence.

Back in her own room, she undressed slowly. Somehow she had known that Dennis Brooke would come back some day. The last five years had been hell for her. Not a night had passed that she hadn't thought of him, thought of what it was like to be in his arms, to feel his body against hers, the way it had been the month they had spent together at the hill station.

Now, she studied her naked body in the full-length mirror. Her reflection sent an erotic thrill through her. She studied herself critically, and was pleased at what she saw. She imagined Dennis Brooke in the room with her, watching her. She trembled a little at the mere thought of it. She felt deliciously wanton. She caressed her breasts, her hands following the smooth curves and contours, sensitive to their ripe fullness. She brought her hands down to her hips. lightly tracing their sensuous curves, and finally held the full cheeks of her buttocks in her hands. She stared at the lush black triangle between her legs and thought, Oh God, he's coming back, Dennis is coming back.

She began to wonder about her husband's decision to send her to the gathering at the palace of the Maharajah of Patiala. Had Hugh deliberately arranged to throw Dennis and herself together? There had been gossip, of course. There was always gossip about what went on in the hill stations in India. Did Hugh suspect, did he *know*, what had happened at Ootacamund? He knew she was a healthy woman in her prime, a sexual woman. He knew that she was being denied through no fault of her own. Was this his discreet way of providing her with the outlet she needed, with a man he admired and considered his best friend, a man whom he could trust to be entirely discreet? Was this a rare act of thoughtfulness and generosity on the part of her husband? To provide a surrogate lover, to arrange a discreet affair, knowing that under the mores of the rigid society in which they lived, she could not divorce a man simply because he had suddenly been struck down, she could not just walk away and desert him. You took what you had and lived with it, in good times and bad. And always kept a stiff upper lip.

But of course, thought Nora, the whole idea was absurd. Her husband was not a saint, and he had his pride. He was still a man, in spite of his infirmity. And yet—yet, he *did* seem to be throwing them together.

She lay on her bed, and slept fitfully that night. Shortly after dawn, she awoke to hear the familiar sounds on the street outside her window. The creak and squealing of the bullock carts, the jabbering and laughing of small children, the shouts, the tinkling bells of the *tonga* carts, the cries of jackals in the nearby park, the wail of a snake charmer's flute, the bells and whistles of the passing cyclists.

It was a morning like any other morning, she tried to tell herself. But she knew, of course, that it was not, that it was something special.

All she could think of now was Patiala.

On the second night out, aboard the *Dover Castle*, Dennis Brooke was vividly reminded, too, of Ootacamund.

He was seated at the captain's table, and among his tablemates were Sir Alan Bradbury and his wife, Lady Diana. He had served for years in India, reaching the rank of colonel in the Fifteenth Hussars, but had long retired. They were both well along in years, a very proper English gentleman and his lady, and when the captain began to make introductions Sir Alan beamed.

"No need to introduce Sir Dennis Brooke to us, captain. We know him personally. Met at Ooty a few years ago. I'm sure Sir Dennis remembers."

"Oh," said Brooke, blankly. "Yes."

Brooke tried to remember where in Ooty he had met the Bradburys. They looked so much like a hundred other couples he had met at the same place.

Lady Bradbury must have noted the puzzlement on his face.

"Actually," she said, "it was at a garden party given by Colonel Wheeler, at that lovely house of his, Grassmere Lodge. You know, just off Cheltenham Road. It was during one of those weeks they always have in Ooty. Was it Race Week, Hunt Week, or Planter's Week? I simply can't recall, but . . ."

"It was Hunt Week," said her husband. "I distinctly remember—it was during Hunt Week."

"Yes. But there was still another time, Sir Dennis. You remember that marvelous dinner at the Maharajah of Jodhpur's summer residence. On Rajah Square. I remember you were with that beautiful lady, Mrs. Clymer, I think her name was. Or is it Lady Clymer?

Anyway, she was absolutely stunning. I must say, you two made a fine pair."

"Thank you," said Brooke. He hastily changed the subject. He asked politely:

"Are you going back to India just for a visit, Sir Alan?"

"No, This is much more than what you might call a sentimental journey. We're going back permanently. To live in Ooty."

"We've already bought a cottage there," said his wife. "Marigold Cottage, it's called. It's quite convenient, very close to Charing Cross."

"Funny thing," said Sir Alan. "When I retired from the service, Diana and I couldn't wait to come home. But I don't know. After a few years in Surrey, we began to yearn for India again. I mean, it seemed that we couldn't get the place out of our blood, kept talking about going back all the time. To put it simply it seemed, at least to us, to be home, not England. And so we arranged, through an agent, to buy a cottage in Ooty. No better place in the world to live, in our opinion. It's a bit of England right in the heart of India, so one gets the feeling of both places."

"We do hope, Sir Dennis, that after you get rid of this dreadful man-eater, you'll come up to Ooty and see us."

"Always room at the inn," said Sir Alan. "And we mean it."

"Thank you," said Brooke.

They began to talk of Ooty again, and every word sharpened Brooke's memory of what had happened there. After brady and cigars, he excused himself and went out on the deck.

For the second night in a row, he sat in a deck chair, huddled in a greatcoat against the cold. The sky was blazing with stars, dappling the waves of the ocean with iridescent glints of silver. But Dennis Brooke saw none of this.

His mind was somewhere else, in a different place than this, and at a different time.

It had all happened because he could not say no.

It was the April after Delhi, when he and Nora had said goodbye. He was on manuevers with the Guards on the blazing hot plains of Madras, and he remembered it as being stinking hot, with many of the officers as well as the ranks suffering from sunstroke and dysentery. He had returned to his regiment in Madras, after hunting down and killing the Chapra tiger, and he was exhausted.

It was during that time that Brooke received a letter from Hugh Clymer. Clymer told him that Nora would be spending the month of July in Ootacamund. He himself could not make the trip to the hill station, which was situated high up in the mountains, and reached by a rough and winding road. The trip would be too arduous, but more than that, there was pressure of business at the Viceregal Lodge, especially since the pro-Gandhi demonstrations and small riots throughout India seemed to be springing up like mushrooms. Clymer understood that he, Brooke, had a month's leave coming, and nothing would please him more than if Brooke chose to go to Ooty and "look after" Nora. Clymer made the point that it was always awkward for a married woman to be at a hill station alone, without an escort, and if Brooke, who was known by everyone to be a very close friend of the Clymers, were there to escort Nora, everyone would understand, there would be no gossip.

"I know you always go to Simla, Brooke," concluded Clymer in his letter. "I know you like that particular hill station, and you have friends there. I wouldn't dream of asking you to change, of course, just on my behalf. But give it some thought, old friend. And if you *do* decide on Ooty, I would really appreciate it. I would appreciate it no end. Nora's looking pretty wan lately. Seems nervous, on edge, and she needs that cool mountain air and a good rest. She's very fond of you, you know, and you could make her stay very pleasant. But again, dear boy, and I sincerely mean it, if you say no, I would most certainly understand. The truth is, I am embarrassed to write this at all. I presume on our friendship too much. It just occurred to me that I am not being very thoughtful. You may, for example, have a lady in Simla. If so, I beg of you—tear up this letter, and we'll say no more about it. With warm regards and sincerely, Hugh." Then Clymer added a postscript: "I have told Nora nothing about this letter. I don't want to disappoint her if you decide to go to Simla. If she doesn't know you're coming, and you appear, it will be a very pleasant surprise for her."

Brooke had agonized over that letter for days. He was scheduled for a month's leave in August, and as usual, he had planned to go to Simla. His head told him it would be wise, very wise, to stick to his original plan.

But he spent too many sleepless nights, thinking of Nora.

Finally, he went to his commandant, Colonel Sir Gilbert Cashmore, and asked if he could have his leave switched from August to July. He told the colonel that the hunt for the Chapra tiger had taken something out of him, he was exhausted and sleeping badly, and he would appreciate it if his leave was moved forward a month. His commandant readily gave Brooke the necessary permission. He was fond of Brooke personally. But more than that, Brooke had brought both honor and prestige to the Royal Guards, and because of Brooke, the regiment itself was now a household name, not only in India and Britain but throughout the empire as well.

Brooke had never been to Ootacamund before.

When he finally finished the trip up the steep, tortuous road, and approached the town, he was startled at its appearance.

It was as though some giant hand had lifted some Victorian town in England, complete to the last cottage, gable and rose garden, and gently deposited it, intact, high into the hills of southern India, over seven thousand feet in altitude.

The air was crystal clear, with an invigorating snap, and the pungent scent of the eucalyptus trees was everywhere. Brooke found it enormously refreshing after the brutal heat of the Madras plain. Everything about it reminded Brooke of some town in Herefordshire or Devonshire, right down to the names of the houses and public buildings. There was Woodcock Hall and Squire's Hall, Castle Hall and Shire Hall, representing the larger establishments; those with romantic names of literary fame, Kenilworth, Bleak House, and Harrow-on-the-Hill. The more modest cottages carried names like Ethel Cottage, Hopeful Cottage and Cheerful Cottage, and other whimsical names like the Castlet and Idyll Hallo Ween. Each had a garden of some kind, filled not with indigenous species but such imported English blooms as geraniums, roses, heliotrope, mignonette and violets. There was the collector's office, and the law court and the post office and, of course, the inevitable club, all done in quaint Victorian style.

Brooke had written Clymer that he would be happy to go to Ootacamund. And his friend, delighted and almost effusively grateful, wrote that Nora had taken a lease on a place called Apple Cottage for the month.

After he had checked in at the hotel, Brooke inquired as to the whereabouts of Apple Cottage. The desk clerk told him it was easy to find. Just off Charing Cross, he said, on Hartford Lane. When he found it, Brooke saw that it was isolated, set back from the lane itself in a small forest of eucalyptus trees.

He would never forget the look on Nora Clymer's face when she opened the door to his ring. Her great violet eyes stared at him as though he were some ghost, her face went pale, her mouth began to tremble.

He remembered smiling at her, and his first inane words:

"May I come in?"

She opened the door, still wordless, and when he entered, she spoke his name once, only once, and then they were in each other's arms, and lost themselves in one deep kiss after another. Finally they separated, breathless, and she gasped:

"Dennis, what on earth, how on earth . . .?"

He simply grinned, and showed her Hugh Clymer's letter, and when she finished she looked at him soberly.

"You shouldn't have come. You know that."

"Yes."

"If I had known what Hugh had been up to, I'd have cancelled my plans. You know that, too."

"I'm sorry," he said. "I couldn't stay away. Just didn't have the will power. Just too damned weak."

"I'm glad, darling," she said, softly. "I'm glad you were so weak. I know what we said in Delhi. I knew we were lying to each other. And to ourselves. I've read every newspaper, trying to keep track of where the Guards were. Simply because I wanted to know where you were. Somehow, I knew we would meet again. It was something that *had* to be . . ."

"But there's still Hugh . . ."

"I don't want to think of Hugh now," she said,

firmly. "For this month, I simply do not want to think of my husband. I hate myself for this, and I know I'll feel awful about this later, but I want to put it way back in my mind, and reserve the guilt and the suffering for later. I love you, darling. I know I'll pay a price for it, and I don't know whether it will be worth it in the end, but I can't weigh the consequences now, I simply don't have the will or the power. All I know is that you've come from the sky, like some ancient Greek god, and descended on Ooty, and you're here, you're actually here, *we're* here and together."

He took her in his arms and tasted the salt of her tears, and the soft, hungry yielding of her lips. Suddenly, she broke away from him and locked the door, and pulled down the bamboo blinds and then turned to him and began to unbutton her blouse. He did not know what to say, he could only stammer her name, as felt the sudden hardening in his groin.

"Nora."

"I don't want to waste any time, Dennis. I want it to begin *now*, darling. There's nothing we can do to stop it. So why wait?"

And so they went to bed, on his very first afternoon in Ooty, and they stayed in bed all day and through the night, without even arising for dinner. And now, sitting here on the deck of the *Dover Castle*, staring out at the ocean and the night, he was drunk in memory, drunk with the scent of her, of her warm feminine flesh and perfume, the exquisite feel of her soft, curvaceous body; he remembered how perfectly her rounded firm breasts felt in his hands, how he fondled and caressed them and held them like two precious jewels, and he remembered the heat of her passion when they kissed, and her cries when he entered her, her animal cries of delicious agony and exquisite delight, and crying, as she twisted and turned, the same words over and over: "Oh, darling,

darling, darling, Dennis, Dennis, darling . . . ."

He remembered everything that happened in that month, the places they had gone, the gin and limes they had drunk at the club, watching the rugger games, the garden parties, and receptions by the rajahs, and attending all the various events of the Ooty high season. They went through Race Week, Hunt Week, Planter's Week, they saw the Dog Show and the Flower Show, they went to the bazaar, and bought fresh strawberries from the strawberry-wallahs, squatting beside their woven fruit baskets in front of Spencer's or Higginbotham's. They mingled with the innumerable gentry in commerce or civil service for the Raj, and with the Brahmins, and with the young officers stationed at Coonoor, some twelve miles of corkscrew twists down the valley.

They were a distinguished-looking couple and very correct in public, very English and very formal, and they were besieged by more invitations than they could possibly accept. During the day they were together and seen everywhere, and if there was gossip at all, they were not aware of it.

But every night he left the hotel, and walked the short distance to Hartford Lane, and from there into the cottage hidden in the small forest of eucalyptus, the place called Apple Cottage.

Finally, the end of the month came and it was time to say goodbye, and in that last dawn, when he held her naked in his arms, he kissed her and said:

"Well, darling, it's over."

"Is it?"

"You know that. It has to be."

"We'll see," she said. "We'll see." Then: "What if I ask Hugh for a divorce? In order to marry you?"

"You can't. You know that. Everything's against it. He needs you. They'd crucify you, if you ever did that.

Not just you. Us.''

"Suppose I did," she insisted. "What would you do?''

"Damn it, Nora. What do you expect? He's my friend. And I've betrayed him. I've got all I can stand on my plate now. I just couldn't do it.''

"Then we'd better say goodbye, Dennis. I mean this time, for *good*. I couldn't stand seeing you again. Not because I hate you for the way you feel. It's because I love you. The thing is, I've got to live through the same guilt you do. Maybe I will in time. But if that time ever comes, I just couldn't go through all this again. I couldn't. Do you understand?''

"Yes," he said, miserably. "I do.''

And so they had said goodbye to Ooty. He had gone back to his unit, and then had been detached from duty to hunt that damned leopard who had done him in at Behra.

And then, he had resigned his commission and come home, and in this way defended himself from Nora.

And again he thought, it's impossible. Yet here I am, bound for Bombay, and Nora is still in Delhi and waiting, and God only knows what will come of it.

By the time the *Dover Castle* had come down through Suez and set course for the Indian Ocean, the ship's wireless reported that Shaitan had killed and eaten four more victims. Two of them were Hindus, and both had been taken in the vicinity of Chakrata. The third victim was a lieutenant in the Highland Light Infantry, and the fourth a captain in the Royal Irish Rifles, both of whom had attempted to hunt down the man-eater. In each case, nothing was found of the man except his rifle, scraps of his leather boots, and his belt buckle.

The kills officially recorded to Shaitan now numbered 292.

12

EVEN BEFORE THE *Dover Castle* actually tied up at the Apollo Bunder, while it was still outside the harbor of Bombay itself, Dennis Brooke knew, with his eyes closed, that he was in India.

It was the land breeze wafting off from the mainland that carried the unforgettable scent of India, the sharp tangy mixture of cow dung, of burning charcoal, of dust and ashes and the faint perfume of flowers.

His arrival had been well publicized, and when he came down the gangplank, accompanied by Lassiter and Bahalji Singh, there was a tremendous crowd waiting to greet him. Immediately behind, Indian stevedores, naked to the waist, carried the boxes holding his weapons. The crowd, held back by police, broke into a roar of applause, and began to rhythmically clap hands in their delight. In their many languages, they cried welcome back to the Sahib, welcome, *Burra Sahib*.

Brooke was met by Sir Thomas Allison, chief secretary to the government of the United Provinces. The viceroy had ordered a military guard, a detachment of the Black Watch, to augment the Bombay police, fearing that the crowd could break through and in its show of affection literally do Brooke bodily harm. He was escorted through a lane formed by the men of the Watch and the police combined, and it was all they could do to hold the surging crowd. A few of the spectators broke through, and were able to lean down and touch Brooke's feet, when they were savagely thrown back by the Guards.

Finally, Brooke was ushered by Allison into a waiting
Rolls Royce, and Lassiter and Bahalji Singh rode in a
second Rolls behind them. As they began to move, the
howling mob broke through, pounding at the windows,
smiling at Brooke, calling his name. Police beat them
off with clubs, and they started slowly to move in the
direction of Malabar Point, dodging bullock carts,
bicyclists, trucks laden with produce, stray cows and
swarms of pedestrians waiting for his approach. Rhythmically they clapped their hands, shouting in delight,
and women held up their babies so that the Sahib might
glimpse them as he passed by.

"Damn," said Allison. He was a tall, distinguished
looking man in a gray felt topee and gray morning coat.
"This is the biggest demonstration I've seen since the
prince came here, back in '21. Of course, there's no real
comparison in the size or importance of the event, there
never could be. Still, it's very impressive. You're an old
India hand, Sir Dennis, you know how much the
Indians love a good public show. But it's more than
that. You've caught their imagination, in a different
way from the prince. You've really come to help them,
and they know it. There was a certain hostility to the
prince among some sections of the people, especially the
fanatics following Gandhi. But the people in general are
happy to see you here, and of course *we're* delighted.
His Excellency is very pleased. There'll be a dinner in
your honor, of course, when we get to Delhi. You'll stay
at the lodge overnight. Then it's on to Patiala."

Brooke stared at Allison. "Patiala?"

"The old maharajah wants you as his guest. At the
palace, of course. For three or four days at least. Big
party in your honor, that sort of thing."

Brooke frowned. "Can't we beg off, Sir Thomas? I'd
rather get on with it. Get it over with."

"Sorry, old man." Sir Thomas shrugged and spread

his hands. "Politics. A royal summons, practically, and no way to get around it. The Maharajah of Patiala happens to be one of His Majesty's most loyal supporters, and he sees it as a feather in his cap to entertain you. Better to please him than to offend him. Not ours to ask why, ours only to—well, you know the rest. And later, you have invitations from the Maharajah of Jodhpur and the Nizam of Hyderabad, to name a few. That is, of course, after you've caught this bloody man-eater."

"You may have to send them my regrets, Sir Thomas."

"I don't understand."

"Suppose," said Brooke, sardonically, "the leopard catches *me*. Sir Thomas looked at Brooke, startled. "Surely you don't think—"

"I think of it all the time."

"I know you had a close call at Behra, Sir Dennis. But still—you're the best in the world at what you do."

"Perhaps. But so is this animal Shaitan—at what *he* does."

They rode for a moment or two in silence. Sir Thomas, Brooke noted, seemed a little tight-lipped. He seemed almost ready to rebuke Brooke, disappointed in him for flatly admitting that he was vulnerable. This was rather not the thing to do for the man who represented the finest the Raj could produce. Definitely not the thing to do. Brooke found this rather amusing.

He stared out of the window, and then:

"By the way, where are we going?"

"Government House at Malabar Point. You're scheduled for a press interview there."

"Isn't there some way we can avoid that?"

"No. It's mandatory, old man—an absolute must. The Indian press will be there, of course, but there'll be several correspondents from the international press as

well. You're the biggest news in India at the moment.
You must know that, of course. And the people of the
villages—I'm talking about those in the Dehra Dun
district and beyond—well, they know you've come
back. The word's spread by drum, by runner, by every
pilgrim on the way to every shrine in the United
Provinces and the Punjab. Knowing the feelings of the
villagers, even the most fanatic of Gandhi's followers
haven't dared to call you some puppet or tool of the
Raj, or even hint that the real reason for your visit is
political. Even the Indian newspapers who have
supported Gandhi strongly, like the *Madras Mail* and
the *Amrit Bazar Patrika*, have publicly welcomed your
coming, as well as people like Motilal Nehru and the
Mahatma himself. You've created an unbelievable kind
of excitement by coming here, Sir Dennis. Something
about it, the whole drama of the thing, matching up
with Shaitan, and so on. People have been praying for
you to come at the temples and shrines, and I'm talking
about all sects . . ."

"Damn it, Sir Thomas, I find that frightening."

"In what way?"

"This isn't the coming of the Messiah. I'm not a
bloody god. I'm just a man."

"True. But they see you as something more than just
that. At any rate, you've put this self-rule thing, *swaraj*,
and even the Mahatma himself, on the back pages for
just a little while."

Brooke leaned back in his seat. For the rest of the ride
he said nothing. A deep depression enveloped him like a
shroud. *Great expectations*, he   thought,   *great
expectations*. Why can't they ever understand? All I can
do is the best I can. And it may not be good enough.

He stared out of the window. It was hard to believe
that he had actually come back to India, but there was
the proof, right through the window. The bullock carts,

the two-wheeled, horse-drawn *tonga* carts, the swarms of people wearing their cotton *dhoti*s or saris, choking the streets, the sidewalk merchants sitting cross-legged, hawking their wares, the hundreds of sweepers at work, undernourished and ragged figures pathetically swinging their twig brooms, stirring up the dust of the street, the stray cows, the hemp-eating *bhangi*s, the priests in saffron colored robes, the beggars and the Untouchables, the starved pi-dogs, with the bones showing through their skins.

From here he would take the train to Delhi, and then go on dutifully to be entertained by the Maharajah of Patiala. Then he would go to Dehra Dun and, finally, Chakrata, and do what he had to do, or what everybody expected him to do. He wanted to see Nora, he ached to see her, but he decided against it. He knew how upsetting that would be emotionally. It would be wise for him to concentrate on Shaitan, and only Shaitan, attend to his work with all the professionalism he had, and not be distracted. More and more he realized that this man-eater was a really formidable animal, far more clever and dangerous than any leopard he had ever hunted, and he had better have his guts and his wits about him. As to Nora—he knew he could not avoid seeing her, he knew that he *must* see her again. But he would wait until afterward.

He turned to Sir Thomas and asked:

"About Shaitan."

"Yes?"

"What's his latest count?"

"Well, don't know if you heard while at sea. But in the last week he's got two more. Caught a boy in the yard of his house one night, while the child was relieving himself. That kill was at Rampur. Caught another in Chakrata. A bullock driver, this time."

"Chakrata . . ."

"Yes. The bastard always seems to come back to that particular village. In any event, the official number of kills is now 294. And only God knows how many kills he's made, unproved or unreported."

At Government House, Dennis Brooke was led into a large hall which served as an interview room. He was given a seat on a raised platform; behind him were the usual huge photographs of King George and Queen Mary, and flanking them the usual Union Jacks.

The room was filled to overflowing with sweating reporters from many of the great newspapers of the world. India itself was represented by the *Calcutta Bengali*, the *Times of India*, the *Indian Patriot*, the *Madras Mail*, and the *Bazar Patrika*, as well as the local Bombay press. The place was stuffy, the heat and humidity almost unbearable, and stinking of human perspiration. The ceiling fans revolved lethargically, their blades listlessly seeming to stir the thick blue tobacco smoke, rather than the air itself. Brooke's shirt, like those of the others in the room, was soaked in sweat and he wished heartily that the occasion was over even before it had begun.

Sir Thomas Allison introduced Brooke, stating the obvious—that, of course, no introduction was necessary, and that the British authority, as well as the people of India, were happy to have Brooke back. He asked that the questions be brief, and that the correspondents state their names and the names of the newspapers which they represented. Then he said that questions would now be allowed.

A forest of hands shot up. The first correspondent identified himself as a Steven Lawrence, from the *New York Herald*.

"Is it true that you have accepted twenty thousand pounds from the *London Times* for exclusive British feature rights, and one hundred thousand dollars for the Hearst syndicate for similar American rights . . . ?''

Brooke was tired, and it irritated him that the interview should lead off with this particular question. He interrupted:

"Do you mind if I comment on this in my own way, Mr. Lawrence?"

"No, sir."

"There is one thing I'd like to settle in the minds of everyone here, gentlemen. I have not come to India for the money. I will not accept a shilling or a dollar of it personally. It will all go into a special fund and will be distributed in proportionate share to the families of the victims of this man-eater. I'm not here for glory, or for sport. I'm here to dispatch, if I can, an animal that is killing people, people I know and have grown to love, who cannot defend themselves." He paused a moment, and then sardonically: "Of course, If I don't come back, and therefore have nothing to report, your query becomes academic. Next question, please."

This one came from a correspondent named Van Klee, from the *Cape Times* of South Africa.

"Sir Dennis, will you hunt this animal alone?"

"Normally, I prefer to hunt alone. I learned that lesson while hunting a man-eating tiger near Mandi. I had a Hindu *shikari* who was somewhat less than a total expert, and had a near accident. The man was extremely nervous, and I had been walking just behind him, when he tripped on a tree root and fell. He had been carrying a rebuilt .275, and he had the safety catch off. When he tried to recover his balance, the gun swung around in the general direction of my head, and went off. The blast almost resulted in my obituary. It's bad enough to have to protect someone with you who isn't armed. But when your companion has a gun, and is an amateur, you're always in a certain amount of danger for one reason or another, and not necessarily from the animal you are hunting.'' Brooke paused. ''But I am afraid I'm getting a little off the field, away from your question. The answer is that I will not be alone when I hunt Shaitan, but with another man. This will be Captain Anthony Lassiter, a close friend of mine, and expert hunter and complete professional.''

''This is the Captain Lassiter who saved your life at Behra?''

''That is correct.''

The next question came from a Lee Hang Yung, a correspondent for the *Hong Kong Sun*.

''What weapons will you take with you, sir?''

''A variety. Depending on the circumstances of the hunt at the time. I expect to bring along a Mannlicher with a hair trigger, a Martini Henry rifle, an .800 modified cordite rifle, and probably guns of .275 and .450 calibers.'' Brooke paused again. ''There's a special point I'd like to make here. I may succeed in getting a shot at this animal, and I hope I do. But this is not a game, or a sporting contest. This is a serious business. We are dealing with a man-eater here, and I'll try to get him any way I can. By using a pit trap, by poisoning bait . . . I emphasize again, by any way I can.''

Next came a question from the correspondent of the *Montreal Daily Star*.

''When it comes to man-eaters, sir, which do you consider the more dangerous—the tiger or the leopard?''

''The leopard, by far. First of all, he can be a wanton killer. Kill just for the pleasure of it. Generally, the man-eating tiger will kill only because he needs food. The leopard is much faster than the tiger on a charge, much smarter, much shrewder. He can wheel and turn faster. And when he is cornered or wounded, he will show unbelievable courage. If you think you've hit a leopard, and start to track him, you have to be damned careful, because he'll turn on you, even if you've shot most of the life out of him. A tiger will do the same, but not with the same desperation. And leopards die hard. You think they are dead, and they can spring up and claw you to death. I respect the man-eating tiger; believe me, he can be a real bastard in his own way. In some ways, he's much harder to track than a leopard. But if you're looking for the worst kind of trouble—I give you the leopard."

Now, a correspondent from the *Calcutta Bengalee*, V.N. Mehto by name, was selected by Sir Thomas to ask the next question.

"Sir Dennis, the people in Uttar Pradash and the Punjab believe that Shaitan is the incarnation of an evil *sadhu* named Ram Gwar. And that this man-eater may have a furry body and sharp teeth and claws, like any other leopard—but that he also has a human mind. Inherited from the *sadhu* himself. You have heard this story?"

"Yes."

"But you put no credence in it?"

"I know the Hindus believe this," said Brooke carefully. "And I respect their religious belief in reincarnation. But as a Christian, my beliefs are quite different. I have tracked and destroyed a very large number of predators in my lifetime, Mr. Mehto, large and small. And in my view, an animal is an animal. From one to another, they vary very little in the habits of their species. I don't expect this Shaitan to be any different, fundamentally. However, I do make the point that when a leopard develops a taste for human flesh, you've got a different kind of cat. This is to say, he is much smarter, more treacherous."

"Then, Sir Dennis, may I ask another question?"

"Yes."

"There are a number of Muslims and a few Sikhs living in the area in which Shaitan operates. Yet all of his victims have been Hindus. *All* of them, sir. And many have come from in and around the village of Chakrata. The same place where Ram Gwar met his death. Does this not seem strange to you, Sir Dennis? How do you account for this, what is the word one would use—oh, yes, phenomenon?"

Brooke thought for a moment. "I don't know. It *is* strange, of course. But then, it may simply be coincidental. The great majority of the people around Chakrata are Hindus, after all. As for this Shaitan striking so often around this particular village—it could be where the man-eater has staked out as his personal territory. Usually tigers and leopards do cut out a piece of territory they consider theirs—and will fight interlopers to maintain it. And in the case of man-eaters, they usually roam the territory in which they made their first human kill. It becomes home to them, so to speak. They know that in this area there's more where the first one came from." Brooke paused. "Still, it is puzzling. I can't give you any definite answer, of course. I don't suppose anyone can. It's all conjecture."

There was a question from the man from the *Auckland Star* and another from the *Times of India*, and finally Sir Thomas announced:

"Gentlemen, this press interview is now over. Sir Dennis is tired, and we have a train to catch to Delhi. Thank you very much for coming here."

13

THE DINNER IN Brooke's honor was held in a private
dining room of the Viceregal Lodge, and it was for men
only.

The aide-de-camp to the viceroy on duty for that day
had spread the word that Lord Irwin wanted no talk of
politics at this dinner. He had had a hard day, what with
the Northwest Frontier boiling with small insurrections
and riots. He had received a number of confusing
directives from Whitehall in London. On this day, he
had received His Exalted Highness, the Maharajah of
Gwalior, and had had tea with Their Highnesses, the
Nawab and Begum Sahiba of Rampur, to discuss the
problems of the Princes of India in view of Gandhi's
new demands for self-rule. Lord Irwin did not, on this
night, even want to hear the words *Satyagraha* or *swaraj*
mentioned in his presence. Moreover, he had had tiring
interviews with General Sir Kenneth Wyndham and
Lieutenant-General Sir Peter Briggs, concerning the
military situation and disposition of troops, and the
loyalty of the Indian troops in case of a general
uprising. And much to the viceroy's disgust, he had to
leave immediately after the dinner to attend an affair
sponsored by his wife, a charity affair in aid of the
Diocesan Women's Hostel of Delhi.

It was, therefore, to be an early dinner, and Brooke
was just as glad. The train trip up from Bombay had
been tiring, and he was ready for a good night's sleep.

In certain ways, the pecking order of the Raj was
similar to the caste system of the Hindus. Only the top

echelon of the British bureaucracy had been invited, and
were now enjoying their chotapegs of gin or whiskey
before going in for dinner. The Indians considered these
men "heaven born" in the same sense they regarded their
own Brahmins. These were the senior members of the
Indian civil service, the Indian police, forest and
medical services, and top officers of the provincial
government services who happened to be in Delhi at the
moment. And sprinkled among them were four or five
generals or lieutenant generals of the British army in
India.

They all regarded Brooke with a certain respect, and
even awe, and wished him luck, old man, the best of
luck. As the guest of honor, he was to sit on Lord
Irwin's right. The viceroy was particularly warm in his
welcome.

"I'm delighted you've come back, Sir Dennis. But I
must say, it took some doing. I suppose you know by
now that Captain Lassiter's responsible."

"Yes sir, I do. He made a complete confession."

"I know this was . . . oh . . . inconvenient for you,
but we really needed you here. Especially since you'll be
hunting this man-eater up in the United Provinces.
We've been having a bit of trouble in that area, far more
than in the Central Provinces, and killing this
animal—well, I don't have to explain how that will help.
But I mustn't discuss politics. At least not tonight.
Violating my own order, you see."

He smiled warmly at Brooke, gripped his hand again,
and moved on. Brooke watched him curiously. Lord
Irwin, later to become Viscount Halifax, was a tall and
imposing-looking man. His power was enormous. He
ruled ten provinces and two hundred and fifty districts
of British India, and was the symbol and the embodi-
ment of Pax Britannica and western enlightenment to
more than two thousand castes, religions and sects that

made up the Indian population. He traveled only in motor cars or palanquins, and had several thousand servants, of one kind or another. When he went to Simla during the hot season, he brought with him a retinue of some five hundred underlings, dedicated to the task of making him comfortable. Brooke remembered a remark that Prince Edward had once made to him: "I tell you, Dennis, I never knew how true royalty lived until I went to India."

The viceroys had little or no contact with the ordinary people of India. They were insulated, kept in a silk-lined cocoon by virtue of their eminent station. They dealt with their own establishment and the royal Indian princes, and that was all. It was said that one of the viceroys had never actually had in his hand a rupee, or anna, and did not even know what the money looked like.

The talk among the guests naturally was of hunting, keyed to Brooke's presence. Many of the men present were excellent *shikaris* themselves. Some of them had shot the mandatory tiger as guests of one prince or the other, but most went shooting "for the pot," which meant such game as quail, partridge or other jungle fowl, and occasionally even a black buck. They spoke wistfully of big game and trophy hunting, of traveling to the high Karakoram and stalking the rare mountain sheep called *Ovis poli*, so named because Marco Polo had been the first Westerner ever to see one. Or perhaps having a go at the rhinoceros whose home territory was the *terai* country, along the borders of Nepal of Assam. And some of the older men reminisced about hunting alligators on the Ganges, just down river from Allahabad.

They deluged Brooke with questions about how he would go after Shaitan, and he answered mechanically. His mind was on Nora, and now he thought that since it was to be such an early evening, perhaps he would run

over to the bungalow off Prithviraj Road and say hello
to the Clymers and there, at least, have a glimpse of
Nora, the real Nora, not the one he had kept as an
artifact in the museum of his memory for such a long
time. He had half-expected Hugh Clymer to be present
at this dinner, since the viceroy knew Clymer was his
best friend. He was puzzled that Clymer had not been
invited.

But a moment later he saw Sir Hugh wheeled into the
room, and he rushed forward to greet him.

Clymer looked ghastly. He was pale and seemed to
have shriveled in his wheelchair. Five years ago, Hugh
Clymer had seemed as robust as any man could be who
was confined to a wheelchair. But now it was clear,
terribly clear, that his old friend had gone downhill.

After they had greeted each other, Clymer said:

"Sorry I'm late, Dennis. Didn't know whether I
could make it at all. Been feeling a little out of sorts
lately."

"I'm glad you came, Hugh," said Brooke, simply.
He almost wanted to weep at what he saw. "I'm so
damned glad you could make it. I was planning to come
and see you." Then: "How's Nora?"

"She's very well. But she's not in Delhi at present."

"Oh?"

Clymer saw the disappointment on Brooke's face.

"My dear Dennis, I guess you haven't heard."

"Heard what?"

"Nora is up at Patiala."

"Patiala?"

Brooke was startled. The word burst from his mouth.
Clymer laughed.

"A bit of a surprise, eh?"

"I just don't understand . . ."

"Why, it's very simple, old man. The maharajah's
invited a delegation from the Viceregal Lodge to attend

the celebration. Nora and I were invited, and I must admit I was surprised. I mean, I didn't think we were high enough on the Brahmin list to rate such an invitation. It's very prestigious, you know. Well, mysterious or not, there it was—an invitation to Patiala. Obviously I couldn't make the trip. Impossible in this wheel chair. I have to be close to my doctor now, and besides, the viceroy wants me here; the work load these days is monumental. So I sent Nora up alone. In the escort of a number of respectable ladies of course, in the official party. They left for Patiala yesterday by special train." He looked at Brooke. "As matters stand, she's still a lady without an escort. I'd appreciate it, Dennis, if you'd sort of—well, rather look after her. The way you did at Ooty. She's very fond of you, you know. Sometimes these maharajahs run some pretty wild celebrations, and if you'd simply keep an eye on her, see that she enjoys herself . . ."

"Of course," said Brooke. "Of course I will."

"Damn it, old man," said Clymer. His eyes were shining. "I can't tell you how grateful I am."

After that they adjourned to the great banquet hall, toasted Their Majesties first, then Brooke, and finally sat down to a sumptuous dinner on viceregal silver.

The newspapers the next morning announced that Shaitan had caught and eaten his two hundred and ninety-fifth victim. This one was a young girl from the village of Ramnagas, who had left a friend's house just a little too late to return home. All that was found left of her was a section of her arm, from the elbow down, a bracelet still dangling on the wrist.

Brooke shared his compartment in the private car with Tony Lassiter. Lassiter had not been invited to Patiala, and was leaving the train at an earlier station to rejoin his unit briefly before going to Dehra Dun.

Bahalji Singh had left the day before for his village.

In a minute or two the train was scheduled to leave the Delhi railroad station, and Brooke stared moodily out the window. Again the sight before him reminded him that this was not a dream after all, he was truly back in India, back in the India he had always known. And nothing had changed.

The station was deluged in a manswarm of activity, the place was a bedlam of noise.

There were the water-bearers, both Hindu and Muslim, the sweetmeat-wallahs hawking their sticky wares, servants with tea and toast which they served up to their masters and mistresses through the windows of the first-class compartments, cigarette boys and newsboys, vendors selling rice and lentil cakes shouting their wares along the sides of the trains. There were children running about and howling, the clanging of gongs, engine bells, steam hissing, men waving copies of the *News of the World* and *True Story Magazine* to the sahibs in the first-class cars. There were starving yellow pi-dogs, one or two minus a leg, limping along the platforms, hoping to find scraps of food. Several people were lined up before a water tap, and one of them was using his wet finger to wash his teeth. The din was frenzied, incessant. Coolie-porters carried great loads on their heads or shoulders, boxes and heavy trunks, searching the windows for empty seats, or even a place where a man could stand. Families trailed after them, shrieking. Beggars and cripples, the blind, even the legless solicited alms. Men who carried their own huge water jars, brass *lota*s, washed by pouring water over themselves, then skillfully changing to clean *dhoti*s. A water-*wallah* passed along the windows of the trains filling the brass and clay jugs of his clients with drinking water. There were the vendors who sold oranges, crying "*Narangi, narangi*" and the vendors of hot milk "*garm*

dudh,'' as well as potato stick-*wallahs* and tea-*wallahs*.
One vendor sold a variety of western medicines,
shouting that he had in stock the most necessary,
entirely indispenable Beacham's Famous Pills.

It was a sight that Dennis Brooke had seen many
times before, and it was always the same, whether the
station was Delhi, Bombay, Calcutta, or some smaller
place like Wardha or Shahdara. But he became particularly interested in something he saw on an opposite platform, where a train had just recently pulled in and
discharged its passengers.

A space had been cleared on the platform for a
sahib's hunting party. It consisted of three Englishmen
and their wives, hunters all, bedecked in safari clothes,
pith helmets, puttees, bush jackets and boots, the ladies
dressed appropriately for the hunt, sporting wide hats
and veils. The men carried the newest in high-powered
rifles, and were perched in front of a pile of trophies,
the spoils of what seemed to be a highly successful war
against the wildlife of India. The prizes consisted of
animal heads of many kinds, the pelts of two tigers, and
other game. The leader of the group, a portly gentleman
looking for all the world like a *Punch* caricature, stood
at the front center of the group, a stout, florid and
pompous-looking man with a huge walrus mustache.
They were posing for a photograph, a memento of the
trip. An Indian photographer begged and pleaded with
them to stand a little closer together. Then he put the
hood over his head, pointed his camera, and set off the
flash gun he held high in his hand.

Brooke, for some reason, felt a little sick. He turned
to Lassiter, who was also watching through the wide
window.

"What do you think of that, Tony?"

Lassiter turned and looked at him, puzzled. "What
do I think of it? Don't know what you mean, old man."

"I think it's disgusting."

Lassiter stared at him. "Disgusting? What the devil are you talking about, Dennis? All they've done is gone out and done a little shooting. The old boys will hand the trophies to one of the clubs they belong to, if they can find room. The photograph they've just taken will be pasted in some album—so when they become really old boys they can back up their stories of big game hunting to their grandchildren." He stared at Brooke. "What the devil's wrong with that?"

"I don't know. All that killing."

"It's just sport. You and I have done a lot of shooting in our time, Dennis. Long before we started going after man-eaters."

"I know. But somehow it bothers me now. I keep thinking of what it might be like fifty years from now. The way we've been killing off all that game. The tiger, for instance, and the leopard. If we keep on with all this shooting, maybe there'll be only a few left by that time. Maybe the species will even become extinct."

"I can't imagine that, Dennis. There'll always be plenty of game in India. More than enough to go around. And shooting for sport will always be going on. There's no way anyone's going to stop it."

Lassiter stared at Brooke curiously, started to ask another question, and decided to remain silent instead. The train began to pull out of the station, bells jangling, whistles blowing, with a great rush of steam spouting onto the platform.

Finally, as it began to roll, Brooke leaned his head back and closed his eyes, mesmerized by the clickety-clack, clickety-clack of the wheels.

He wondered why and how Sir Hugh Clymer and his wife, Nora, had suddenly received an invitation to be the guests of the Maharajah of Patiala. While Hugh Clymer was high in the caste system and the rigid social

order of the Raj, he was not quite high enough, as
Clymer himself had put it, to rate this invitation. The
princes of India were very particular and rigid themselves, when it came to inviting representatives of the
government to their great *durbar*s.

Then how had it happened?

Suddenly, he had the answer.

It must have been arranged, he reasoned by the Prince
of Wales. By David himself, back in London.

The prince and the Maharajah of Patiala had got
along famously when Edward had visited there, back in
'21. And the prince was the only man to whom he,
Brooke, had talked about Nora. Now, he could see
David's fine hand in this. A message to the maharajah,
a small personal request. He would very much
appreciate it if the Maharajah could see his way clear to
invite a favorite couple, Sir Hugh Clymer and his
memsahib to the celebration for Sir Dennis Brooke. He
could not reveal the reason for this, except that it was
highly personal.

Coming from the heir to the throne of England, the
maharajah, of course, would be delighted to oblige.
And David, through his own sources, knew that Sir
Hugh could not possibly make the trip, and that Nora
would go alone.

Brooke smiled mirthlessly. He had no idea that
David, with his fresh, ever-young, innocent face, could
be so devious.

But there it was. He would meet Nora at Patiala,
whether he wanted to or not.

And he knew he wanted to. Now, as the train gathered speed, it could not get him there fast enough.

14

WHEN BROOKE FINALLY stepped off the train at Patiala, the maharajah was waiting on the platform to greet him.

His Highness, Sir Bhunpinder Singh, was a giant of a man, over six feet tall and weighing some two hundred and eighty pounds. Very little of this was fat; he was mostly hard muscle and bone. His mustache was well-waxed, curled stiffly upward, his thick black beard was rolled neatly in the Sikh manner and he wore a daffodil-yellow turban. His black patent leather boots were hip-high, over a tunic of bright red, lined with four rows of solid gold buttons. At the throat was an enormous emerald, and around his waist he wore a belt of precious rubies. He stood in military stance, legs parted, his back ramrod-straight, and extended his hand to Brooke.

"Welcome to Patiala, Sir Dennis. It is good to meet you once again."

"I am delighted to be here, Your Highness."

They shook hands in the English way. This was not the first time Brooke had met this Indian potentate. They had met once before, when the prince had been a guest of the maharajah's during his trip to India, and Brooke had been one of Edward's aides. Brooke noted that over the years the maharajah had changed very little. He had the same oval face, the same intense, arrogant black eyes, the same patrician nose, the sensuous lips. If anything, he looked handsomer, more powerful, and virile than ever. Sir Bhunpinder was noted as a ladies man all through India, and with very good reason. His appetite for women was insatiable. It was known that at the Pink Palace he had more than three hundred women for his exclusive pleasure behind the walls of his harem.

"I bring you greetings from the viceroy, Highness," said Brooke. "His Excellency regrets that he could not come. These are busy times, and he has orders from London to stay in Delhi for a time."

"Ah, yes," said Sir Bhunpinder. "These are busy times, indeed. Everywhere in India. And especially for the Raj." He smiled. "But this is not the time to talk of politics. Come."

The maharajah turned and began to stride toward the entourage which had accompanied him to the railroad station. A troop of Patiala lancers stood stiffly at attention, the famous and magnificent Sikh fighters, regarded as the best and the fiercest in India. Behind them were the officers and high dignitaries of the maharajah's court. The maharajah was known to own twenty Rolls Royces, and a fleet of ninety-three other cars from America and elsewhere, and had seven English mechanics imported to look after their maintenance. But Brooke did not see a car in sight.

Instead, two huge elephants waited, their legs painted in gold, their tusks ringed with straps of gold, their tough, wrinkled flanks covered with red silk and decorated with gold tassels, their faces painted with vermillion designs, and their foreheads sprinkled with gold dust. The *howdah*s, or palanquins, perched on their enormous backs were encrusted with plates of gold, which glittered brightly in the morning sun.

Brooke remembered that the Prince of Wales had been transported to the palace by elephant, and now he was being given the same treatment, welcomed in the royal way, although on a much smaller scale. Trumpets were sounded, as the *mahouts* waited silently beside their charges. Then Brooke and the maharajah were hoisted up to their *howdah*s. They proceeded toward the palace, followed by the others, some on foot, some riding other elephants, those which were considered inferior, and decorated only in silver.

All this was very impressive. But Brooke was looking for one face and did not find it. He assumed that the guests would all be waiting at the palace. The maharajah rode on the front elephant, as befitted his station, and Brooke, staring at the broad back of his host, reflected that this man, one of the great princes of India, was truly a legend, and much larger than life.

The maharajah's palace was tremendous in size and estimated to be a quarter of a mile long. He had some thirty-five hundred servants, all dedicated to making him personally comfortable, some five hundred horses in his stables, and any number of top flight gun dogs in his kennels. On the grounds of the Pink Palace were a polo field, a cricket field, several tennis courts, and carefully manicured gardens. Brilliant-hued peacocks strolled around the immense and lush acreage surrounding the palace. Roaming the area were Afghan stag-hounds, and he had a small zoo, with chained tigers pacing angrily beyond the pools of lotus.

The extravagance of his private quarters was legendary. During the blazing heat of summer, Sir Bhunpinder Singh kept coolly comfortable by occupying a great room in which a pool of water was constantly supplied with huge blocks of ice, dropping the temperature by fifty degrees. Surrounding this cooling area were rooms for the current favorites of his harem, who were constantly present to serve their master with food, gin, whiskey, aperitifs or provide more intimate services. The prince's harem itself was equipped with beauty salons and staffed with hair-dressers, experts in the use of exotic perfumes and skin makeup, and masseurs. Occasionally, Sir Bhunpinder Singh called in various doctors from other nations, skilled in the arts of plastic breast surgery, and the mysteries of gynecology. And since, because of the sheer numbers in his harem, the maharajah clearly needed all the help he could get, he was in constant consultation with Indian doctors regarding the latest discoveries in aphrodisiacs.

The Maharajah Bhunpinder Singh was one of the most powerful leaders of the Sikh nation. He was also one of the last princes to exercise absolute power in his state, yet he was loyal to the Raj and the establishment in Delhi, and London did not dare offend him. All the princes of India were extravagant, but none more than the Maharajah of Patiala. He owned a fabulous pearl necklace worth at least five million dollars, as well as the famous Sancy diamond. It was estimated that he spent over fifty percent of the entire income of his state on his personal needs.

Brooke remembered a visit the maharajah had made to England two years ago. He arrived with more than two hundred trunks and a vast entourage. In London, the Hotel Savoy virtually surrendered to him. It reserved all of its thirty-five suites on its fifth floor, and each of them was perfumed with fresh roses every day. He required a special kitchen and a private elevator decorated in his colors of gold and scarlet. A special chef, employed by the Savoy, spent the entire day carving out a huge replica of a Patiala elephant, made of pure rice and sherbet, to grace the maharajah's tables. Bodyguards stood before the doors of each of his suites, and twenty chauffeurs waited in the driveway and garage beside his fleet of limousines. He brought along several trunks, loaded with hiw own saddlery and cricket gear, as well as half a dozen of his favorite polo ponies. The visit was a sensation, and the London newspapers played it to the hilt.

Brooke thought he understood why Hugh Clymer was
so pleased that his good friend would look out for Nora
at Patiala. As part of his reputation, the maharajah had
an eye for non-Indian women. He was not only
attractive and very rich, he was also a determined man
when it came to getting what he wanted. And it was
rumored that more than one of Britain's high-born
ladies had shared his bed.

Sir Bhunpinder Singh was a shrewd man, and when
the Prince of Wales had asked him to invite the Clymers
as a personal favor, so to speak, he had probably
figured out why. He would know that Clymer himself
was too ill to make the trip, and had insisted that Nora
come along anyway.

Bobbing around in his golden *howdah* on top of the
decorated mountain he was riding, Brooke felt a strange
mixture of guilt and exhilaration. He had spent every
day for five years dreaming of Nora Clymer. Now they
were coming through the gates of the Pink Palace itself,
and in a very short time the dream would come true. He
knew how he felt about her; nothing had changed.

But five years is a long time, and he wondered
whether she still felt the same way about him, and
whether Patiala would turn out to be a more exotic
Ootacamund.

Brooke was taken to his room by a bearer designated
to serve him personally while he was a guest at Patiala.
The room was vast and, to Brooke's astonishment,
completely equipped with furniture imported from
England. Even the wallpaper and paintings had been
imported to give the bedroom this flavor. Close the
drapes, thought Brooke, and you could be in a bedroom
anywhere in Belgravia or Eaton Square.

The bearer, a tall bearded Sikh, Akbar by name,
helped Brooke undress, drew his bath, and informed

him there would be a two-hour siesta before meeting in the great *durbar* hall, where the maharajah held court. After that, dinner would follow in the great banquet hall. Then the servant nodded toward a connecting door leading to another room.

"The Sahib is no doubt tired from his journey," said Akbar. "And no doubt will wish to rest. There is a guest in the next room, but I am sure she will be very quiet, and not disturb you."

"She?"

"A memsahib from Delhi, Sahib."

Brooke stared at the tall Sikh.

"*What* memsahib, Akbar?"

"The Memsahib Clymer, Sahib. She is the wife of a *burrah-sahib* in the service of the viceroy. Unfortunately, I am told, her husband was ill and could not come."

"I see."

Brooke sat back and relaxed in the hot, steaming bath. The maharajah apparently had seen to everything. The whole thing was incredible. Here he was, in the next room to Nora, in a great pink palace straight out of an Indian version of the Arabian nights. He was sure that she knew he was here, her female counterpart of Akbar had probably made sure that Nora was informed as to the identity of her next-door neighbor.

She was in there now, he was sure, waiting for him.

His body tingled all over, the excitement rose in him. Lying here, in the steaming hot water, and just thinking of her, thinking of her as being so near, was enormously sensual. He felt himself harden quickly, his penis floated upward and straight out of the water, he was filled with aching desire, ecstasy that was almost painful. He got out of the tub, expecting his bearer to come in and wrap him in one of the great towels hanging on the rack. But Akbar did not appear. When Brooke left the bathroom and came into the bedroom, Akbar was nowhere to be seen. His boots had been polished, his clothes laid out, including a luxurious silk robe, which the maharajahs of India usually provided their guests as a routine part of their hospitality. His bearer, thought Brooke, had done something unprecedented. He had left the room without having first requested permission from his master. This was a pure violation of custom. And Brooke knew the servant would have never dared to do this unless he had been instructed to do so by His Highness himself.

He put on the robe. The feel of the silk against his warm and tingling skin was sensuous. He thought of this moment, and how he had savored it in fantasy, convinced that it would never happen, that Ootacamund was a memoir, a precious artifact to be preserved in the museum of his memory, never believing, never even dreaming he would ever see this woman again.

And yet there she was, and waiting, beyond that wall, a few steps away.

He knew how he felt about her. But he did not know how she felt about him. Five years could be forever. Perhaps she had met someone else. Someone with whom she was having an affair. Or perhaps she was now in love with someone. She was a full blown, passionate and totally feminine woman, elegant and even fragile in her delicate beauty, but with a marvelous appetite and lusty joy when it came to bed, when it came to pleasing a man as well as herself.

But Brooke knew it wasn't just sex that drew him to Nora Clymer. It was a hundred other things, a gentleness and a sweetness, a deep strength and dignity. This was a lady who would nourish, help, support, sustain and make a man strong and confident. It was Nora Clymer's *womanliness* that had attracted and held him.

He was in love with her, had known it at Delhi and

Ooty, and during all the years he had exiled himself in London, and he knew it now, here in the Pink Palace of Patiala. But again came the nagging fear.

Perhaps she had changed.

He walked to the connecting door and knocked gently on it. and he heard the voice say "Come in."

She was standing there, waiting for him, dressed in a sari of turquoise silk. Behind her was a huge canopied bed with the silken cover rolled back.

They looked at each other for a long time, and then she smiled and removed the sari. She stood there, naked, straight and unashamed, her skin glowing, her mouth parted, her eyes on his.

"Hello, darling. I've been waiting for you a long, long time."

Afterward, sated and sleepy, they lay in each other's arms, and she said:

"I still don't believe this."

"Neither do I."

"You know, when the maharajah's invitation came, I didn't want to come. I knew you would be there. I knew what would happen. I told Hugh that I wanted to stay with him in Delhi."

"But you didn't."

"No. I wanted to come so badly—well, I just couldn't stand it. I looked at Hugh, and I knew how much he needed me, and I wanted to cry. But then I said—damn my guilt. I just had to see you. Still, up to the last minute I was on the fence. I knew if we ever started again, we could not stop. Then, when the maharajah insisted that I come alone, Hugh made a point of it. I guess you could almost call it a political point. It would be some kind of insult, a breach of protocol, not to accept. And so I came."

"Any regrets?"

"Not now, darling. I'm in heaven right now. Perhaps later—when I get a chance to really thing about . . ."

"About Hugh."

"Yes."

"I feel the same. No regrets at the moment. But I'll hate myself later. The thing is, Nora, we've got to face up to it. There *is* Hugh."

"I know."

"Do you think he knows about us? I mean, Ooty . . ."

"I really don't know, darling. Sometimes I think he does—sometimes I think he doesn't. You know the old cliché—the husband is the last to know. But there's always gossip about what goes on in all the hill stations. Ooty's no different. There are the Indians, of course. The *chowkidars*, the watchmen, see everything, know everything. They pass on gossip, to other watchmen, other servants, about all the sahibs, and memsahibs, and what they've been up to. It's impossible to keep a secret from them, you know. But it isn't only the Indians. It's the British, especially the ladies. Gossip is the stuff of life for them, darling. They saw us together so much at Ooty, of course. Some just say 'How nice of Sir Dennis to watch out for his best friend's wife, to escort her about.' But the others—well, you know what they'll gossip about." She paused and leaned over and kissed him. "Darling, I still don't believe you're here. In my bed, beside me. But there's a third party here."

"Hugh."

"Yes. I can't tell you, Dennis, how it's been since you were away. I was so split down the middle. I wrote you a hundred letters, begging you to come back—and tore them all up. It wasn't just that I was worried about what people would say if we came together and abandoned him. The whole establishment, from the ICS down through the military to the most junior clerk would cut us. We'd be pariahs everywhere, including England, where at the moment you're some kind of celebrity. I think I could live with that, darling. It's just that Hugh—well, he needs me."

"So do I."

"It isn't that he needs me—physically. He can't do anything that way. He knows I'm a—a passionate woman. He knows that I need a man in that certain way. I have to cry every time I think of the humiliation I know he feels. I almost believe he wanted to have us get together—just so that I could have what I needed, what I had a *right* to have, as a woman. I almost believe he would have tolerated this, just to see me happy, to see me—satisfied. I know this kind of talk is terrible, darling. I feel awful discussing it. But it's something I must talk about. The point is, I still love Hugh—in a certain way. He doesn't need me in the ordinary sense—I don't have to provide any wifely services—heaven knows, we're up to our necks in servants we don't really need. Bearers, cooks, gardeners, chauffeurs, watchmen, sweepers, scullions, everything. In that sense, I'm as useless as any British woman in India in my position. Everything is done for us, whether we really want it or not. We literally don't have to lift a finger, and that can make life terribly boring. But I'm getting off the track. Hugh needs me simply to be *there*—to be near—to come home to. And he loves me still, Dennis."

"All right, then. What are we going to do?"

"I don't know."

"One thing, Nora. I'll never let you go again."

"Then we'll have to tell him."

"Yes," she said. "I suppose we will."

"When?"

"I don't know."

"If you ask me, the sooner the better. Let's get it over with, Nora."

"No. No, not yet. I can't think of it—yet."

"Then *when?*" he insisted.

"Later. After you kill that man-eater, that Shaitan."

"Suppose he kills me?"

"Oh God, darling," she said. "Never, never say things like that again. I know how dangerous it is. I know they're saying you may never go back. But please—don't ever say it again. Don't even think of it. I couldn't bear it."

"Look," he said. "All that's some other time, some other place. The only thing I'm going to think about it now."

"I love you, darling. Please don't let anything ever happen to you. Please be careful . . ."

She buried her face in his shoulder and began to cry.

The maharajah had invited some five hundred guests to the festivities honoring Brooke, and now they were gathered in what was acknowledged to be the largest and most elaborate *durbar* hall in India.

It was here that Sir Bhunpinder Singh normally held court, listening to petitions from his subjects, dispensing alms and instant justice, making political decisions and receiving emissaries, not only from the other princes but from the Raj. The hall had a carpet which was reputed to be the second largest in the world—the first was owned by the Maharajah of Gwalior. The hall itself was walled in glass, with gleaming crystal everywhere, mirrors reflecting images in other mirrors, the great crystal chandeliers glinting and gleaming in the light of the many candelabra. From crystal fountains sprays of cool, clear water shot upward.

Among Sir Bhunpinder's royal guests, apart from the

lesser princes, were the Maharajah of Kapurthala, also a
Sikh from the Punjab; the Maharajah of Cooch Behar,
whose domain was in Bengal, and the Nizam of Hyderabad, who, it was rumored, had stored some eight
million dollars in bank notes somewhere in his palace,
only to later find that the money had been eaten by rats.
This was eminent company even for the Maharajah of
Patiala to entertain, but they had come out of curiosity
to see and meet Brooke. Their survival depended on the
survival of the Raj, and they saw in Brooke a man to
their own liking and a political asset, even though his
contribution would be small when matched against the
great sweep of events now taking place in India.

But perhaps the guest who aroused the greatest
curiosity, outside of Brooke, was His Highness the
Maharajah Jagatjit Singh of Kapurthala. At the age of
nineteen, he found it impossible to copulate with the
willowy ladies of his palace. The problem was not that
he was impotent. The problem was that he had weighed
some two hundred and seventy-five pounds, and much
of this weight was in his great, protruding belly. Thus,
the nubile young ladies who were dedicated to
teaching the fat young prince the arts of love were
completely frustrated by what might be called a problem
in logistics. Professional dancers of great beauty, and
experts at the complicated sexual arts and positions
known to the Hindus for centuries, were brought from
Lucknow to deal with the situation. They too failed
miserably. Naturally, the court of Kapurthala was
deeply upset. It was important that His Highness have
an heir some day. Finally, someone had suggested that
if the main barrier to both heavenly bliss and an heir
was the royal belly, the master of the royal elephants
should be consulted. He reported that on occasion,
when male elephants were too heavy to reproduce, they
had built a ramp on which the female could lie on her

back and thus be able to carry the great weight of the
male. The idea kindled hope in the court, and the chief
engineer of the palace was summoned. He was ordered
to build such a structure. For the bedroom of course,
and not for the woods. He thereupon designed a kind of
ramp bed, which could be inclined or declined at various
angles, and equipped with a spring mattress. Happily,
this proved to be the ideal solution, and the maharajah
was able to marry. He took the bed with him on his
honeymoon, and handsomely rewarded the engineer so
that the man could retire for life. Later, the maharajah
went on a determined diet to lose weight and now, here
at Patiala, he had thinned enough so that he would no
longer need the contraption.

The British contingent consisted of the cream of the
establishment and their ladies. Those invited and sent
up, not only from the Viceregal Lodge in Delhi, but also
from government houses in Bombay, Calcutta and
Lahore, were the pukka Brahmins of the Indian Civil
Service, senior members of ten years standing and
"Majors." Included among these were members of the
elite viceroy's diplomatic corps. Just a notch below
these were the lesser, but still ordained, Brahmins of the
many special services, and the provincial service. There
were the ambassadors, of course, and then the military,
generals and brigadiers. There was not a single British
businessman present. No matter how wealthy or powerful, especially in the large cities, they were considered a
cut below the ICS and the military.

Brooke entered the *durbar* hall first. He was
immediately surrounded by an army of admirers and
well-wishers. Sir Bhunpinder Singh was now dressed in
a garment of pure canary-yellow silk, which rippled and
glistened in the lights of the candelabra. His turban was
black and orange, the colors of his famous polo team,
known throughtout India as the Tigers. At his throat he

wore, on a short chain, a tremendous diamond, called the Star of Africa, said to be one hundred and twenty-five carats in weight. This particular occasion was informal. His Highness moved easily among his guests, laughing and chatting as they drank whiskey, gin and champagne.

Brooke saw Nora enter, and excused himself to move toward her. Just as he reached her, he heard a voice behind him:

"I assume you two know each other."

Brooke and Nora both turned to see the maharajah smiling broadly at them. There was a twinkle in his eye. Almost a wink. "And I hope you both enjoy your stay here."

Nora made a brief curtsy. "Thank you, Your Highness."

"I'm honored to be here again, sir," said Brooke. "It brings back old times."

"I remember. When you were escort to the prince. You had already achieved some reputation in your dangerous but fascinating vocation. A fine man, your prince. Very engaging. Most charming. And despite rumors to the contrary, a fine horseman. I recall his heat had a bag of five pigs when he was here. His Highness himself, if I remember, was personally responsible for two of them. I had none that morning, myself. To use your western phrase—I take off my turban to him. I understand you have seen him lately."

"Yes."

"I trust he is in good health."

"He is, sir."

During all this, the maharajah spoke almost absently. His eyes were on Nora. They were glittering, intense. She flushed under his direct stare and flashing smile, and turned her head away in embarrassment.

"And Lady Clymer," said His Highness. "I am sorry

as to the state of your husband's health. And I regret
that Sir Hugh could not make the journey." He flashed
another of his smiles, and nodded toward Brooke. "But
I gather you are in good hands."

"Thank you, Your Highness. I think I am."

"Lucky man, Sir Dennis. To squire a beautiful lady
like this. There is no gift I could give you in my palace
that is more exquisite—or exciting. Frankly, I envy
you." He made a mock bow. "But nothing is too good
for my guest of honor."

The maharajah left them and mounted a platform to
a raised throne. He announced that in the morning there
would be a polo game. In the early afternoon, a tiger
hunt. And in the late afternoon, weather permitting,
something for the ladies. A tea and garden party. "Personally, their amusement has always been my very large
concern." He smiled. "And as you know, I have always
found them most enchanting."

There was a round of applause from the women, and
a ripple of laughter. Then the maharajah clapped his
hands, and servants opened the huge doors to the
banquet room, where dinner waited.

From the balcony in the enormous banquet room a
string orchestra, led by the maharajah's personal
bandmaster, an Italian imported from Milan, softly
played, in honor of the British guests, such standards as
"Blue Bonnets Over the Border" and "Bonnie
Dundee." These selections were better rendered by a
band of Scotch bagpipers, but nobody seemed to mind.

Behind each diner at the vast table was a servant, turbaned and barefooted, who stood immobile against the
wall, waiting for signals from the head *khitmagar*. The
service was gold-encrusted and fashioned by craftsmen
in Bond Street; the table linen had been especially
woven in Ireland. On the table also was a kind of toy

train, operated by a miniature electric locomotive pulling tiny freight cars. Later this train, its cars filled with such after-dinner delicacies as candy, cigars, cigarettes and liquor, would ride completely around the table, stopping for five or ten seconds before each guest, so that he or she could make a choice.

Brooke, as the guest of honor, sat on the maharajah's right, and Nora sat next to Brooke. This was actually a violation of protocol on Sir Bhunpinder's part, since the wife of the district commissioner of Patiala, the most important representative of the Raj in the maharajah's kingdom, would normally sit next to the guest of honor. The lady pouted and tried hard to hide her irritation. She was, after all, the wife of the DC, Sir Eustace Wiggam, GCMG, KCB, KCIE, CSI, and precedence was precedence. But the maharajah was important enough and secure enough to ignore any warrant of precedence. The food was prepared by the maharajah's French chef. It was delicious and of infinite variety. Brooke ate hungrily, reflecting that in a few days he would be in the remote village areas and would be living on a diet of *chapatti*s, rice, porridge made of wheat ground on stones, tea and goat's milk, with occasional vegetables and fruit.

The conversation was generally shallow. Brooke wished he had these hours alone to spend with Nora. He was conscious that several of the British, especially the women, eyed them both curiously. The eyes formed a consensus. Two and two equal four.

The talk turned to Shaitan. Brooke politely answered a number of questions. About tigers, leopards, man-eaters in general. He had given the same answers to the same questions a hundred times, but the public curiosity was insatiable. He understood that. It was only natural. He sensed that the others regarded him with some awe. Not because he was such a public figure. But because in view of Shaitan's reputation, he was soon to be engaged in the most desperate gamble a man could make, putting his life on the line. Even the maharajah was somewhat awed:

"Four of my best *shikaris* went out to kill this devil," he said. "My men are Sikhs, and they have no regard for the superstition that this animal is an evil spirit. They are men of great courage and exquisite skill. Yet, three of them never came back. The fourth did—but he was broken in spirit. He saw Shaitan snatch one of his comrades, break his neck with one twist of his jaws, and simply trot off, ignoring this man. My *shikari* fired at Shaitan. Now, I know this man; he is very cool and an excellent shot. The man-eater was only fifty yards away. My *shikari* was using a .275 rifle, and he swears that the bullet simply bounced off Shaitan. He also swears that the leopard was huge, abnormally so, the size of a small elephant. Put it all down to hysteria, but still, one must be impressed. Perhaps, as the Hindus believe, this animal is indeed the incarnation of Ram Gwar." He smiled at Brooke. "I am terribly sorry, old man. I didn't mean to worry you with this grisly account. But of course you know what you're in for. As an Indian, of course, I believe in reincarnation myself." He looked at the district commissioner. "I suppose as a Christian, Sir Eustace, you must find this absurd."

"With all due respect, Your Highness," said Sir Eustace, carefully. "We cannot accept that idea, precisely. We are taught that when the body is dead, the soul goes to heaven. It belongs to God, Christ, so to speak, it is in His hands. But to appear again in somebody else's body, human or animal, well—" Sir Eustace Wiggam shrugged—"I must say, we find that rather hard to take."

"Interesting," said the maharajah. "This whole subject of religions. We have so many of them here in

India, as you know. Most of them believe in re-incarnation as a central thesis. And when you think of it, it's the most comforting of all the religions in the world. Much more than yours in the west. The point is, you get another chance. A beggar dying on the streets of Calcutta, or Lahore or Bombay or anywhere, who has lived on one handful of rice per day, can expect in his dying moments another chance at life, dictated by his *karma*, where his lot will be improved, providing he has lived a worthy life.''

"You mean," said Sir Eustace, "he might hope to improve himself sometime in the future—to the tune of *two* handfuls of rice."

"Perhaps." The maharajah shrugged. "But again, the most important point. It is easier to die peacefully, if you know you will live again, some time, some place, as something. And if you believe it, really believe it, it's true."

"Your Highness," said Brooke. He simply could not resist the question. "What or who would *you* like to be in your next incarnation?"

Sir Bhunpinder Singh laughed. "A good question, Sir Dennis. But it really doesn't take much thought. The answer is quite obvious. In my next life, I'd like to be—myself."

Everyone laughed and applauded. Then the conversation turned to the weather. The overwhelming subject was the scorching heat of India. Not only the blast-furnace heat of the plains, but the murderous, debilitating heat of the cities and villages during the hot season. People by the thousands each year wilted and died because of it. The maharajah had a theory about the heat of the subcontinent. He maintained that it was the greatest ally and benefactor the Raj could possibly have. This aroused some curiosity and raised eyebrows.

"Your Highness," said Sir Eustace. "I cannot, for

the life of me, see the connection.''

''Why, it is quite simple,'' said the maharajah. ''The key to who holds India is the climate. And that, gentlemen, is the heat. You British took this land because the races that conquered it before, the Moguls and the others, could not hold on because they were exhausted by the heat. The Raj continues to rule here because you British are able to refresh yourself and renew your vitality by returning frequently to your native land.''

He had just finished when a servant came in, bowed to the maharajah, and presented him with a message on a golden tray. Sir Bhunpinder read it, hesitated a moment, as if debating as to whether to communicate it to the rest of the diners. Then he made his decision.

''Ladies and gentlemen, I have just received some news. I trust it will not in any way interfere with your pleasure on this occasion. I debated for a moment whether to read it to you. But since our guest of honor is Sir Dennis Brooke, it seems apropos that he, as well as you, be informed of it.'' Sir Bhunpinder paused a moment. ''Yesterday, near the village of Chakrata, the man-eater Shaitan caught a Muslim *shikari* named Shakur just as he was climbing down from his tree platform. The time was shortly before dawn. The remains of the body were found in an open field three miles away. What flesh remained was devoured by vultures, but the hunter was identified by a necklace and other jewelry left on the ground. This man Shakur came from Peshawar, and had a considerable reputation as a killer of man-eaters, with twenty to his credit. He had hoped to collect the reward offered by the governor of the United Provinces. The number of official kills credited to Shaitan now is 296.''

There was a dead silence. The three hundred guests at the maharajah's table turned as one to stare at Brooke. He did not move a muscle. With a great effort of will he

kept his face impassive. The fear was there, it rose like
bile in his throat. It was a cold fist in his stomach. The
maharajah could have waited till later, he could have
told Brooke privately. But Brooke knew Sir Bhunpinder
was testing him, finding a cruel amusement in it. He
knew the potentate expected Brooke to show some
reaction, perhaps some twitch of concern, some expression of bravado. The hush in the great hall was eerie,
almost a peculiar sound in itself. Brooke saw the sea of
faces, the expectant eyes. They all expected him to say
something, waited for him to do so. The maharajah
looked at Brooke, waiting like the others, a sardonic
glint in his black eyes. And Brooke thought, the hell
with him. I won't give the bastard the satisfaction. Or
any of the others, for that matter.

There was a carafe of beaujolais on the table, directly
in front of Brooke. He picked it up and turned to Nora.

"More wine, Lady Clymer?"

There was a long sigh from the others. It seemed to
ripple up and down the table. The guests who were
British sat back, relaxed, and smiled at Brooke. Some of
them could not help raising their glasses to him in silent
tribute. Their faces reflected their pleasure. He had
shown the Indians present, and especially the
maharajah, how a true Englishman acted. He had not,
as they would put, "let down the side."

Early the next morning there was a polo match
between the black-and-orange-shirted Patiala Tigers,
and a pickup team chosen from the British guests.
Brooke himself played two *chukkers*. He had some
trouble handling his pony, and he realized that he had
grown rusty. Every sahib, in India who was anybody,
including his memsahib, rode a horse.

After that came the tiger hunt. Or so it was called.

It was all done very systematically. A few days before

the event, the maharajah's *shikari*s would locate two or
three tigers in some nearby valley located in the vast
park of the palace. They would keep a constant watch
on the animals, and make sure they did not wander
from the premises by providing them with food—in
tethered goats or even a water buffalo, chained to a tree.
Then, on the day of the event, an army of beaters,
banging drums, shouting, and shooting off ancient guns
into the air, would drive the tigers out of cover and into
plain view of a tower the maharajah had built, bordering the rock-strewn and jungle-covered valley. In this
tower stood His Highness and Brooke alone. A number
of the other English guests, also participating in the
shoot, rode on elephants, guns at the ready. But the
placement of the driven tigers was such that His
Highness and Brooke had the first shots. If they missed,
then the men on elephants could take their turn.

Suddenly, as Brooke and the maharajah waited, two
huge tigers came streaking out of the jungle, straight
toward the tower. Brooke saw that the pair was a male
and a female, and they came on fast. At a range of
about a hundred yards, Sir Bhunpinder Singh fired and
killed the male. He had given Brooke, as a gift, a
beautiful .400 express double-barrel rifle, with a stock
inlaid in gold, made by J. Purdey and Sons of London.
Brooke drew a bead on the female, had his sights
directly on her left shoulder as she began to swerve.
Suddenly he raised his sights a little and fired over the
head of the fleeing tigress. The men behind, on the
elephants, finished the animal off, wounding her first,
then closing in to pump round after round into the
dying beast.

The maharajah looked at Brooke curiously.

"I was certain you would get him, Sir Dennis. At that
range."

"So was I," said Brooke.

"Perhaps it was the gun. Of course, you're not used to it."

"No," said Brooke. "Let's call it what it really was. Bad shooting, I'm afraid. If there's any excuse at all, I'm a bit rusty. I've been away a long time."

"Of course," said Sir Bhunpinder. "I'm sure that's it. A bit rusty, as you said." But Brooke could see that the maharajah did not believe it. Not really. He was still watching Brooke. "I hope when and if you face Shaitan, you'll do—well, somewhat better."

"If I don't," said Brooke. "Then you can damned well hang me—or what's left of me—in your trophy room."

The maharajah laughed. Then he ordered that the pelts be taken care of by an expert called the Naturalist to the Shoots. He cautioned the man and his squad of skinners to be very careful with the pelts. Sir Bhunpinder also instructed that the skull be boiled, and the lucky bones set aside so that they could be made into scarf pins for the ladies.

Later, the garden party was held on a great grassy lawn, next to a lake peopled by graceful white swans. There were tennis courts and ball boys, decked in the colors of Patiala, scampering about. The guests were transported to the garden in ornate carriages decorated in gold filigree, attended by footmen in glittering uniforms, and pulled by bullocks of pure white. The garden party itself might have taken place anywhere in England. The women wore wispy chiffon and great brimmed hats topped with flowers; the men wore uniforms, or blazers, white ducks and their old school ties. Everywhere there were tables under the shade trees, loaded with every variety of drink, from champagne to tea to iced lemonade, and every variety of pastry and other delicacies, cakes and scones and bijou sandwiches.

Sir Bhunpinder Singh moved easily among his guests,

confining himself mostly to the ladies. Nearby, a sedan chair waited, with six servants dressed in orange tunics and black *salvar*s, the pantaloon-like pajamas. Their duty was to carry the maharajah from one section of the garden party to the other, in the event he became weary of walking.

The talk among the gentlemen was all about tigers. Brooke was standing with a group from the ICS, some of the men he had met at the viceroy's dinner, back in Delhi. One of them, a Brigadier Ridgeby Savory, an OBE and MC, with seven bars to his Frontier Medal, was a connoisseur of tigers, and was known to rarely talk of anything else. He claimed that Lord Reading, the viceroy preceding Lord Irwin had, as a guest of the Maharajah of Gwalior, shot one of the largest tigers ever recorded. It was a giant, measuring some ten and a half feet from head to tail, and some five hundred and ninety pounds in weight. The kill had taken place in the valley of Ker Kho. The maharajah, Sir Madhav Rao, who himself had presided over the killing of over a thousand tigers, vouched for these measurements. But of course, there were rumors that His Excellency, the viceroy, might have stretched the statistics just a little. The fact that Lord Reading had been born Rufus Daniel Isaacs, was the first Jew to ever reach this exalted position, and had started his career as a ship's boy on a full-rigged merchantman, might have had something to do with the skepticism.

Brooke was only half-listening. His eyes were searching out Nora. She was strolling about, holding her parasol high against the hot smash of the sun, talking to a group of other ladies. He had been careful not to monopolize her, not to spend too much time in her company. He did not want to enlarge the gossip he knew already existed.

"Well, chaps," the brigadier was saying, "Learned

one thing early on. You never ride after a tiger on a horse. Went after one once with a friend, in the Maharajah of Jodhpur's park. Nicked this bugger with a shot, a big male it was, and went after him in full gallop. He turned on me all of a sudden, and jumped me with his big mouth wide open, and his claws spread. Just missed my leg by a fraction, landed on the back of my horse, dug his claws in deep, then slipped off. Had a devil of a time holding my horse—the beast screamed and ran wild. Damned near threw me before I gained control. Luckily my friend, Major John Chesteron, who was riding behind me, put a bullet into the tiger at close range, while he was getting to his feet.'' He turned to Brooke. ''I don't suppose you've ever tried it, Sir Dennis.''

''No,'' said Brooke. ''And I don't intend to.''

''I know. Of course, I was a young man at the time. Foolhardy. Ready to try anything. What did you think of the hunt today?''

''Hunt? I wouldn't call it that.''

Savory stared at him. ''No? What would you call it, then?''

''Murder.''

''I don't understand.''

''Those tigers never had a chance. It was like shooting fish in a barrel. No sport to it, brigadier. The sport is in stalking and finding your quarry. Not in killing. I mean wanton killing, the kind we saw this afternoon. Killing for food—well, that's different. Or if an animal is dangerous to human life. But this—'' Brooke shrugged. ''This was just a show. A bloody show, I must add.''

He was aware that the group was silent. Their eyes were wary, curious. He knew he was expressing an unpopular opinion. But somehow at this point he did not care.

''I must say that's a strange point of view, Sir

Dennis,'' said one of the ICS men. ''Considering that you've shot several hundred leopards and tigers yourself.''

''True. I have. Especially when I came here as a young man. You know what the game was. You had to make your mark by shooting your first tiger. It was expected of you. Gave you proper status, so to speak. Well, tiger pelts became so common people no longer hung them in their bungalows. Later on, I became sick of the whole business. If I went hunting at all, it was for man-eaters. That's why I'm here now. The tiger and the leopard are beautiful animals, gentlemen. They are two of nature's most magnificent works of art. They fulfill a function in the natural order of things. And they are not normally man-eaters. Some because so because they are too old and feeble to hunt other game. Some develop a taste for human flesh, when there's a plague in some part of the country, and the bodies are just too numerous to burn. In that case, the Hindus may throw the corpses with hot coals in their mouths over the cliffs. Leopards, who will eat carrion, naturally find these bodies before the vultures do, and develop a taste for human flesh. But to get back on the track. I think we're guilty of overkill, in these maharajah or viceregal shoots. Some of these princes, as you know, have shot over a thousand tigers. Not to mention the bags our own British *shikari*s have taken, just for sport. Some day, if we're not careful, the leopard and tiger will become scarce. An endangered species, you might say. I'm not saying in the near future, but in fifty years . . .''

Again, silence. Then Brigadier Savory spoke up.

''Really, Sir Dennis, that's absurd. You might as well suggest that we hunt these beasts with—well, a camera.''

''Why not? An excellent idea. The killing is nothing. If you're siting in some *machan* in some tree, and a tiger is just below you, all you have to do is aim the gun barrel straight, and pull the trigger. Where's the sport in that?''

"Tell me the truth, Sir Dennis," said Savory.

"Yes?"

"You deliberately missed that tiger, didn't you? Raised your sights just a little."

"Confidentially, yes. But I wouldn't want His Highness to know that, gentlemen. He might think I had abused his hospitality."

"I hope you don't have the same compassion for these big cats when you go hunting for Shaitan."

"I'd be a fool if I did, brigadier. Shaitan, as we all know, is dangerous. If I don't get him—he'll very likely get me. It's very simple, you see. It's he—or I. He's become a damned inconvenience to me, and of course I resent him for that. Still, he's doing what comes naturally—for him. Unfortunately, he has chosen the wrong kind of prey, and must be disposed of. As a professional, I intend to hunt down and kill this animal, if I can. It's simply a matter of business, you see. But too many people view it as some kind of sporting event. Two gladiators in some arena, fighting it out to the death for the amusement of the crowd. And there's the rub, gentlemen."

After that, Brooke turned on his heel and walked away.

Brooke and Nora lay in each other's arms all night, knowing they would not see each other for a long time, and perhaps never again. Nora wept a little.

"Damn this beast," she cried passionately. "Damn him, damn him, *damn him!*" Then: "Why you, why you, why *you?*"

They both knew why, and he was silent. And finally:

"Nora, this may sound as though I've gone around the bend. But we really owe him something."

"Shaitan?"

"If it weren't for him, I'd have never come back. We'd never have come together again."

"You *are* dotty, darling. Absolutely and completely dotty. If you hadn't come back, you know I would have come to you some day. Simply appeared in London and said: 'Here I am, you fool.' "

He laughed, and she put her fingers to his lips and closed them shut.

"Darling, be careful, please be careful, don't take any chances."

"With this particular man-eater? Do you think I'm mad?"

"Maybe," she said, hopefully, "you won't be able to find him, to track him down, no matter how you try."

"Anything's possible."

"In that case, you'd have to come home, wouldn't you? I mean, you'd simply have to tell everybody—you couldn't find him."

"I don't think it'll happen that way, Nora," he said gently. "I expect to find Shaitan."

"Or *he* might find *you*."

"Nora, don't think that way—"

"Oh, God, how can I help it, darling? Think of what happened to all those other hunters . . ."

He was silent to that, because he had no answer, and finally she asked:

"You'll write to me?"

"Of course. When I can."

"I'd better write you first. Give you a box number at the post office in Delhi." She stumbled a little. "I—well, you see, I wouldn't want Hugh—I mean, there wouldn't be any point . . ."

"I understand."

"Darling, tell me something."

"Yes?"

"I'll want the truth."

"You'll get it."

"Do you still feel guilty—about my husband?"

He took a little while to answer.

"No. This is the way it ought to be."

"Was meant to be. Yes, I feel the same way."

"Maybe I'll feel guilty later."

"No. You won't, darling. You won't have time to even think about it. You'll be too busy hunting down that creature. But I—I'll be with him—while you . . ." She choked a little. "I know I'll feel hateful. Hugh's such a good man, Dennis. He's been through so much. And I know he loves me—needs me. But I can't—I can't just go on any more . . ."

"Nora, Nora, there's no point in avoiding it any longer. When I get back, we're going to have to tell him."

"*If* you get back."

"I will. I *have* to."

Then she started to cry, and he held her close and began to caress her, and her crying stopped, and he felt her flesh grow hot against his and the nipples of her breasts harden, and he too began to harden, and at last they came together, once again, shortly before dawn. She fell asleep, but he stayed awake, and then he rose and dressed and left her sleeping there, because he did not want to say goodbye to her in a polite and stilted and formal way, before all the others.

Sir Bhunpinder Singh offered Brooke two of his best *shikari*s and any number of bearers for his personal needs. But Brooke declined. He thanked His Highness, and told him he had been promised all the help he needed by the district commissioner in Dehra Dun.

The maharajah wished him luck at the train station. Beginning there, and everywhere else he went on the

journey to Dehra Dun, the Hindus threw flowers in his
path, leaned down to touch his feet, tried to touch his
clothes, prostrated themselves, cried his name, *The
Sahib*. Drums sounded from village to village, pilgrims
spread the word, people prayed for him in the shrines
and temples. Their rescurer had come back. He had
come back to rid them, once and for all, of Shaitan, the
spotted devil.

Brooke was stirred by this demonstration, deeply
touched. But at the same time he felt the weight of his
responsibility. He was the deliverer—and the pressure
was on him now to do just that. Great expectations, he
thought, great expectations. He wished he could feel
confident, but he knew he wasn't. Especially when he
thought of Behra. What had happened there had taken
something off the top, made him something less than he
once had been. He had to face that, in all honesty. And
all this adoration disturbed him. I am not a god, he
thought. I am only a man, for Christ's sake. He wished
he could make them all understand. He was only
human. He would try to live up to his reputation. He
would do his best, and no one could ask more.

At Dehra Dun, the district commissioner, John
Evans, had picked him up at the station in an old Rolls
Royce. On the approach to Government House itself, at
a narrow point in the road, Brooke saw a group of
lepers, some dressed only in filthy loincloths, others
wearing dirty, ragged *dhoti*s. They were gathered at a
shrine, and when they saw him, they crowded toward
the car, crying his name. They held their diseased
stumps toward him begging for alms, the stumps that
had once been their palms. If he denied them, they
would bring down curses upon him, no matter who he
was. He reached into his pockets, threw them all the
coins he had, plus the few rupees he carried. He watched
them scramble and fight in the dust for the money, some

of them picking up the coins with their teeth, since they had no fingers. He knew that it was best not to bring down the curses of the lepers on his head, even though his pragmatic Western mind told him they could not possibly affect his future, one way or the other. Still, he reasoned, why take a chance, when a few coins might buy him a blessing.

And God knows, he thought, *I'll need all the luck I can get.*

He had dinner at the commissioner's house. Evans had another guest, Peter Wilkes, correspondent of the *London Times*. He had been stationed in Dehra Dun to report exclusively on the predatory activities of Shaitan. Brooke knew the correspondent; he had been interviewed by him before in London. He remembered the morning he had sat in Hyde Park, just before his appointment with Lord Ellsworth. He remembered reading a dispatch by Wilkes on that morning, stating that Shaitan had taken a victim in broad daylight. Twelve o'clock noon, if Brooke remembered correctly. He had an impulse to chide Wilkes for his mistake. The man must have meant twelve o'clock midnight. But he decided against it. The dispatch, of course, could have been garbled in transmission.

Evans briefed Brooke on the man-eater's latest activities. Shaitan had been quiet after he had caught the Muslim *shikari* from Peshawar. "This hunter had a big reputation. What was his name? Oh, yes. Shakur. The devil caught him just coming down from his *machan.* Just before dawn. But I suppose you already know . . ."

"Yes. I heard about it at Patiala. As I recall, it was near Chakrata."

"The bugger seems to love that particular village," said Wilkes. "Regards the place as a kind of home, you might say."

"That's not unusual," said Brooke. "Leopards stake out their own territory, like most other animals."

"The Hindus don't see it that way," said Evans. As you know, Chakrata's the place where they did in this Ram Gwar. And he's come back to take his pound of flesh, so to speak."

"Of course," said Wilkes, "it's absolute rot."

"Still," said the commissioner. "It's interesting. We know this man-eater has a very wide range. He kills here, and he kills there. But he always comes back to Chakrata."

"If I worked for one of the penny dreadfuls," said Wilkes, "I could make capital of something like this, write a really big story. You could see it now, let's say, in the London *Illustrated News*. A big picture of a leopard. And the caption: 'Is He Really Human? Or Isn't He?' Be a sensation. But of course, the *Times* won't go in for this sort of thing. They just mentioned the superstition, once, and let it go at that."

"That's why it's such a great newspaper," said Evans. "It tries to report the facts."

"Ah, yes," sighed Wilkes. "The facts. And nothing but the facts. That, gentlemen, is the essence of the good, gray and hoary *London Times*. I enjoy my work, of course. But sometimes if you have to stick too closely to the facts, it can become a bloody bore. Now, if they'd let me do a feature on this Hindu fantasy, this Ram Gwar thing . . ."

"We sound as though we've all gone around the bend, talking about this thing," said Evans. "I could understand it during the hot season, when everyone gets light-headed and slightly insane. If we were sitting here in the month of June, I might really believe this nonsense. What I suggest now, gentlemen, is that we all have a drink and change the subject."

Evans told Brooke a forester's bungalow had been

fixed up especially to accommodate himself and
Lassiter. It was located only a mile outside of Chakrata,
and it would be staffed by a cook, a *chowkidar*, a bearer
for each man, a *khitmagar* to wait on table, and other
necessary servants. Tony Lassiter, who had briefly
visited his regiment at Lahore, was already on his way to
Chakrata.

Wilkes expressed a desire to stay at the bungalow,
since he would have closer access to whatever happened,
but Brooke politely and firmly turned down this
proposal. He told Wilkes that he had contracted with
Lord Ellsworth to give the *Times* the full story of his
hunt for Shaitan, *after* it was finished. Unless, of
course, there was some sort of unfortunate accident,
and it went the other way.

At dawn the next morning, Brooke left for Chakrata.

PART FOUR

15

THE ASSISTANT INSPECTOR general of forests for the district had done himself proud in setting up what had been a simple *dak* bungalow into a reasonably comfortable establishment. The people of Chakrata nearby agreed that a residence like this was only proper for a great, or *burra* sahib. The bungalow had been enlarged to four rooms, and quarters for the servants had been built in the rear. There was fresh mosquito netting and new rattan shades which could be lowered during the day. There were new pull-*punkah* fiber fans suspended from the ceiling which, during hot weather, could be set into motion by a rope pulled from outside the house by a *punkah wallah*. The veranda was spacious and supplied with Indian cane chairs sometimes called "planters' long sleeves," because they had leather or cloth pockets sewn on the arms which would hold drinks.

The arrival of Brooke was a *burra din*, a great day, for the people of Chakrata. They swarmed around the bungalow, waiting for a glimpse of him, as though he were Gandhi himself. They bent down and touched his shoes, and threw flowers in his path, and they did the same for Lassiter. Bahalji Singh insisted on a *burra khana*, or big celebration, to mark Brooke's arrival. There would be a feast, a stick dance, and other entertainment. Brooke protested that this was not necessary, he was embarrassed and touched by what Bahalji Singh said:

"Sahib, you are not a god. You are of human flesh.

195

This we know. Yet to the people of my village, and others nearby, you are a kind of holy man. For years, now, because of Shaitan, my people have not had a *burra din*. They have lived in fear, and been saddened so many times by the jaws of this man-eater. If they have gathered together at all, it has been to burn what is left of their loved ones, and then bring the ashes to the river. But your coming is a matter of joy, of celebration. Now their spirts are high, they feel protected, safe. They know you will kill Shaitan. Then we can burn his body, and thus rid ourselves of the demon of the evil *sadhu*, of Ram Gwar.''

After the headman had left, Lassiter grinned and said to Brooke:

''How does it feel to be looked up to like some kind of saint?''

''Damn it, Tony,'' snapped Brooke. ''I don't consider that amusing.''

''Sorry.'' The grin remained on Lassiter's face. ''No use being touchy about it. And of course there's nothing you can do about the way they feel. Might as well accept it and enjoy it.''

''I wish they weren't so bloody sure,'' said Brooke. ''About our doing in Shaitan, I mean. They've seen all these other hunters fail . . .''

''Look, old chap,'' said Lassiter. ''There are *shikaris* and *shikaris*. But number one is number one. Sooner or later, you—or we—will have the bugger in our pocket.''

''Even *you're* sure.''

Lassiter shrugged. ''Have to look at the bright side of things. Now—it's getting dark. How about asking our demon *khitmagar* to bring us a couple of whiskeys? Doubles this time, of course.''

They sat on the veranda and had their *burra pegs* and watched the dusk fade into sudden, almost instant darkness. Brooke moodily watched the *chowkidar* as he slammed the gate shut, and stood at guard.

"Tony, I hope we can get on with it. Get it over quickly."

"That depends on Shaitan. He's got to make the first move."

That was the trouble, thought Brooke. Usually, you had to wait for him to kill first before you could track him. It reminded him of a foray the Royal Guards had made against the Pathan tribesmen years ago. This was deep in the Northwest Frontier. The tribesmen were hidden in tall grass, so that you couldn't see them. As you advanced, you had to wait till one of their hidden snipers fired. Usually, it meant a casualty. But only then were you able to locate the man who had fired the shot. You had to wait for *him* to kill someone before you could flush him out and kill him yourself.

"You know," said Brooke, "Evans told us Shaitan's been quiet for a few days now. Maybe he'll try again tomorrow."

"Maybe. Let's hope so. Meanwhile, all we can do now is sit here and wait."

In the next three weeks something strange happened. Shaitan did not make a kill anywhere. There were no reports that he had even been seen. He had never before taken this long to make his presence known.

Brooke found this somewhat nervewracking. Somehow, he had imagined that he would come into almost immediate confrontation with the man-eater. He had looked forward to settling the issue one way or the other, quickly. Now it was almost as though Shaitan were taunting him by his very inactivity. Almost as though the animal were deliberately playing out a war of nerves, putting Brooke on edge. Brooke realized, of course, that this was ridiculous. He knew that it was simply coincidence that the animal had stopped his activity practically on the day Brooke arrived.

But the villagers of Chakrata did not think it was any coincidence. As Bahalji Singh explained: "Shaitan knows you are here, Sahib. He is afraid of you and has gone away. Perhaps to the Punjab, perhaps even as far as Nepal. Our people are beginning to feel safe now."

The villagers of Chakrata had begun to violate the curfew, going out at dusk, staying a little later. A man wanted to visit his friends and have a smoke at the end of a hard day. The women wanted to visit and chat with each other. The bazaar keeper wanted to do a little extra business, or the farmer wanted to work later with his crops.

Brooke worried about this. He tried to get the headmen of the villages to persuade their people to observe the curfew. The threat was still not over. But Bahalji Singh spread his hands: "It is no use. They will not listen. They will simply say, what is there to worry about now? The Sahib is here."

Brooke found himself spending many hours on the veranda, idle, drinking too much and fidgeting.

"Where is that bloody leopard, anyway?" he said. "Damn it, Tony, what's happened to him?"

"Maybe the villagers are right, Dennis. Maybe he's roaming elsewhere. Taken a little run over to the Punjab, or maybe into Nepal. True, he's got away with everything, but he must have noted that they expect him around here, it's getting a little hotter for him, and food is harder to find when people are alerted. It could be that he can get dinner easier in some other restaurant, so to speak."

"No," said Brooke. "I don't believe it, Tony. I don't believe it for a minute. I think the bugger's up to a clever little piece of strategy."

"Strategy?" Lassiter stared at Brooke. "What the devil would an animal know about strategy?"

"Ordinarily nothing. But this one seems to be something special. He's outwitted or eaten every *shikari* who's trailed him, so he must be pretty damned intelligent in his own way. Look, Tony, suppose this Shaitan hasn't gone *anywhere*. Suppose he's just playing dead in the forest just outside of Chakrata. Suppose he's practically on our doorstep right now, and we don't even suspect it."

"What are you driving at?"

"Well, we know Shaitan's been quiet for a long time, an abnormally long time. Now that may mean something, or it may mean absolutely nothing. But suppose he's smart enough to know that if he lies low for awhile, people get restless staying in at night, they get careless, they start to go out in the evening. It's what's happening right now. I can't say I blame them, they've been living in fear, huddled up in their houses every night for weeks and months, till they're all ready to go around the bend, to go a little crazy. You can see how they can get lulled into a false sense of security, because they've given me magic powers I don't possess. Three weeks, and no Shaitan. Proof enough for a Hindu, but not for me, Tony. It's possible that Shaitan is just out there a little way, licking his chops and waiting, killing a deer or a wild pig once in awhile to keep his belly full, while he sets up an easy kill. It's easier for him to take somebody outside and unawares than it is someone who's bolted inside and aware."

They waited another week. Brooke paced the floor and drank still more. He wrote letters to Nora and went out occasionally to shoot quail or pheasant for the *bobajee*'s big kitchen pot in the cookhouse. Lassiter, on the other hand, was enjoying the situation. One evening they sat on the veranda in the gathering dusk. Lassiter stretched his long body languorously in one of the big planter's chairs, sipping a gin and soda, and watched his

companion with amusement. Brooke complained, for
the hundredth time, that the man-eater had failed to
appear.

"Be patient, old man," said Lassiter. "If he's around
somewhere, he'll show his teeth sooner or later."

"I'm beginning to feel like Bahalji Singh. Maybe he's
gone somewhere else. If so, there's no point in our
staying around here much longer."

"Ready to move when you are, Dennis," said
Lassiter. "But frankly, don't make it too soon. As far
as I'm concerned, it's more comfortable here than with
the Guards up in Lahore. I'm supposed to report back
for duty in a few weeks, and can't say I look forward to
it. All that damned marching on the parade ground in
that blasted heat, day after day. Just to show the flag,
and the power and glory of the Raj. Even the Indians
are bored with it. And a lot of them are staying away
because of Gandhi and all that. All it means to me now
is blisters on my feet. And then, sitting in mess every
evening, listening to the brigadier and the senior officers
tell the same old stories. What they did against the
Pathans, up on the Northwest Frontier, and what they
did in the big war against the Boche. Colossal bores, all
of them. Well, I don't have to tell you, Dennis, you've
been through this with the regiment yourself. But really,
this is easy duty." He waved his glass and grinned. "All
we need is a couple of supple dancing girls, and a little
music . . ."

"Tony," interrupted Brooke. "Will you please shut
up?"

"Oh. Sorry."

"Look, forgive me," said Brooke contritely. "I'm a
bit on edge . . . nerves."

"That's all right," said Lassiter. "If I were you, I'd
feel the same way. They've given you a full plate—too
full a plate."

"I just want to get it over with," said Brooke. "One way or the other. And get back home."

"Of course." Then Lassiter took a long look at Brooke. "Dennis, there's something I wanted to ask you."

"Yes?"

"It's something I've wanted to ask you straight on. Does Behra still bother you?"

Brooke met Lassiter's blue eyes. "Sometimes it does, Tony. Sometimes I dream of it, and wake up sweating." Then, a long pause. "Why?"

"Nothing. I was just wondering. If it'd happened to me, I'd have nightmares, too."

"I could never thank you enough for what you did."

"Rot. I had an easy shot. Just lucky to be there. You'd have done the same for me."

"Of course." Brooke studied Lassiter. "Why Behra, Tony? Why did you bring it up *now*?"

"Oh, nothing. Just making conversation. But you *do* seem tight about *something*, Dennis." He paused. "Anything you'd like to talk about?"

"No."

Lassiter grinned. "Then let's have another drink."

Brooke studied his companion for a moment. Lassiter's face was impassive, but Brooke was disturbed. Why had Tony brought up Behra all of a sudden? Was he afraid that he, Brooke, had lost a little of his nerve? Was he worried that in a tight spot, where Lassiter might be in danger, Brooke might not be quick enough to back him up, might not have the reflexes to fire instantly and straight? It was unlikely, it always was unlikely, of course, but sometimes it happened the way it did at Behra. A big cat, especially when crazed with a wound, might charge one man and totally ignore the other. If your backup man wasn't sharp with his gun, it could cost you your life. Lassiter, thought Brooke, was perhaps thinking of the week they had spent at Worcestershire, and the shooting they had practiced there. He had, admittedly, been a little rusty. But that was only natural. Still, he supposed that Lassiter had a right to be a little concerned. After all, he, Brooke, had been out of the game for years.

"One of these days," said Lassiter. "The bugger will show up. Perhaps sooner than we think. He seems to like it a lot around here."

In this, Tony Lassiter proved to be somewhat of a prophet.

They had just sat down to dinner when they heard a distant shout:

"Shaitan! Shaitan!"

They left the table and hurried out onto the veranda. On the path leading to the village, they saw a man running, carrying a torch, and shouting again, at the top of his lungs:

"Shaitan! Shaitan!"

The runner was Ranga Singh, son of Bahalji. Panting, he told them that Shaitan had just struck again. This time the victim was a young man named Mothu, son of the village cobbler. Brooke and Lassiter did not wait to hear the rest of the story. They took their lanterns and headed straight toward the village.

When they arrived, they saw a crowd in back of the cobbler's house, carrying torches. They were standing around a bloody patch on the ground. The cobbler and his wife were inside the house, weeping. In the center of the chattering crowd stood a small boy. His eyes were wide, he looked pale, he was still trembling in shock. His name, he said, was Sastri. He was the son of one of the shopkeepers in the bazaar, and he had been with Mothu when it had happened.

They had been visiting friends in the nearby village of

Rapti and had started home a little late. By the time they
had left the pilgrim path and crossed the fields of rice
stubble just outside the Chakrata it had grown dark.
Formerly, they would have made a run for their homes
when it was dark, but this time they were not particularly worried, since Shaitan had not been seen or heard
from in a very long time.

They had just gone into Mothu's yard, explained the
boy, when it had happened, so suddenly that neither he
nor Mothu had time to move. In the rear of the house
there was a goat pen, sheltered by a slanting roof.
Shaitan had sneaked in just after dusk and waited,
crouched on the roof. Mothu had been walking just
ahead of Sastri. When he had just passed under the
roof, the man-eater had leaped straight down onto him.
He had knocked Mothu down, caught him in his jaws,
fixed his teeth in Mothu's neck and twisted savagely,
breaking it. He had taken a huge bite out of Mothu's
chest as well. Sastri simply stood there screaming. He
could not run; his limbs were paralyzed by the horror of
what he was witnessing. The leopard paid no attention
to Sastri. Apparently, he was satisfied with the prey he
already had in his mouth. When questioned by Brooke,
he said:

"He was big, Sahib. Oh, he was so big."

"How big, Sastri?" Brooke wanted to know.

"So big, Sahib. As big as a baby elephant. Bigger
than the largest buffalo or bullock." He picked up a
stick and drew a rough picture of Shaitan's size. "This
big."

Lassiter and Brooke exchanged glances. They knew
the boy was exaggerating out of his hysteria. But the
man-eater had left his pugmarks in the soft dirt of the
yard. And when they leaned over to examine the
pugmarks, Brooke saw that he was at least one third
larger than the largest leopard he had ever seen or heard

of. Later, by closely examining the pugmarks, he would
be able to figure out the approximate measurements of
the man-eater. Now he turned to the shivering boy.

"Which way did he go, Sastri?"

The boy wordlessly pointed across the stubbled rice
fields to the pilgrim path beyond.

With the villagers lighting the way with their torches,
Brooke and Lassiter caught the leopard's pugmarks on
the wide pilgrim path. They proceeded for only a few
hundred yards, and then suddenly veered off into a
rocky area, beyond which were thick woods.

Brooke turned to Lassiter. "What do you make of
this, Tony?"

Lassiter shook his head. "Damned if I know. Doesn't
make sense. No sense at all, Dennis."

Both of them knew that the big cats, the tiger as well
as the leopard, liked to put some distance between themselves and the point where they had snatched their prey.
In their animal minds, this made sense. The nearer they
were to the killing, the easier they could be found and
hunted. It was logical that the man-eater would follow
this path for at least a mile or two before veering off.
The pads of leopards were tender, and they liked to use
forest paths or softer ground. But this particular man-
eater did not seem typical. He seemed to have an idea of
his own. He knew it would be much harder, if not impossible, to track him over these rough stones. Moreover, it was possible that he might meet some hunter
coming down the pilgrim path from the opposite
direction. With his jaws full, and already carrying his
dinner, he would be in no mood to drop his prey in
order to move fast, if it became necessary.

Brooke knew it was pointless to try and track a
leopard over this kind of terrain at night. Pointless, and
dangerous as well. Half the village had followed
Lassiter and himself up the path. A straggler could still

be vulnerable to attack, especially if the leopard thought his meal was threatened.

Brooke issued instructions to Bahalji Singh. They were all to return to the village now. In the morning they would spread out and hunt for whatever was left of Mothu. Meanwhile, the curfew was to go immediately into effect. No one, absolutely no one, was to be abroad after dark.

The next day, if and when Mothu's remains were found, he and Lassiter would go on from there.

In the morning, while the entire village of Chakrata went out in search of Mothu's remains, Brooke and Lassister knelt in the soft dirt of the cobbler's yard and calculated the size and weight of the man-eater. The pugmarks were clear in the soft loam, and by their length of stride and penetration in the ground, it was possible for an expert with the careful use of a tape measure to approximate the size of the animal.

They agreed on the measurements and were astonished by the results.

"Big beggar, isn't he?" said Brooke.

"Christ. I can't believe it. This is no leopard. This is some kind of monster."

"It's a leopard, all right. But some kind of weird mutation."

"Damn it, Dennis. You know, that boy Sastri wasn't far wrong."

They estimated that Shaitan ran about three hundred pounds in weight, almost ten feet in body length, plus about four feet more in tail length, and perhaps three feet in shoulder height. They knew that the average male of this species averaged a hundred to two hundred pounds, was about seven feet in length, plus three feet more in the tail, and over two feet in shoulder height.

"You know, Dennis," said Lassiter, "with all that

bone and muscle, and the speed he must have, he could come down on you like an express train. Might be hard to knock him down with one shot.''

"If we get a shot at him at all."

They noted, by the pugmark in the soft dirt, that Shaitan had a nick in the right front paw. It was from a small wound, long healed. They speculated that some hunter in the past might have nicked the paw with a bullet. Or perhaps Shaitan had a porcupine needle embedded in it, and the man-eater had wounded his own paw by gouging out the needle with his teeth.

Early in the afternoon a runner came to the bungalow, and told them the body of Mothu had been found. Or what was left of him. It had been located about a mile from where the man-eater had veered off the pilgrim road.

Brooke and Lassiter hurried to the scene. They saw the villagers standing in an open field just outside a wooded area. They were gathered around something lying under a white shroud. The cobbler was on his knees, weeping.

"Mothu, Sahib," said Bahalji Singh.

He pulled down the white shroud. All that was left of the cobbler's son was a bloody head. The rest of his body had been almost wholly eaten, but there were strips of flesh still adhering to the splintered fragments of bone. Vultures wheeled about, circling, frustrated. Brooke was immediately interested in their presence. He turned to the headman:

"Bahalji, this is very important. When you found Mothu, were the vultures already here?"

"Yes, Sahib."

"But they were not feeding on the body."

"No. They started to come down, but we chased them away."

Brooke looked at Lassiter. The same thought

occurred to both of them. The man-eater had eaten his fill and had left it in the open field, in plain sight of the vultures. If he had wanted to feed on the body further, he would have concealed it under some rocks, or in the fork of a tree. But the important point was that the vultures had not yet attacked and stripped the body when Bahalji and his people had arrived. That would mean that they did not dare to, for a very good reason. The leopard had still been feeding on the body when the villagers had approached, and as a result had ducked into the forest and left his prey. The vultures were further frustrated by the arrival of new claimants for the feast.

All this had happened in the space of an hour. It was a good bet that Shaitan was lurking around somewhere in the vicinity. He might even be stretched out high on some tree branch, dozing away the day, digesting his meal. Or he could even be watching them from somewhere on the edge of the forest.

What was left of Mothu was wrapped tenderly in the white cloth and placed on a bamboo litter. It would be burned in the traditional Hindu ceremony, and then the ashes thrown in the river, hopefully one day to float down the tributary and enter the bosom of the great Mother Ganges herself.

Brooke and Lassiter watched them go. Then Brooke said:

"Well, let's go find him."

"Shouldn't be too hard to track."

"Nothing to it," said Lassiter, lightly. "Chances are he'll be sitting on his backside, paws up like some friendly bear, just waiting for us to do him in."

The grass in the meadow was sparse, the pugmarks were clear in the soft ground, and they were able to follow the leopard to the point where he had entered the forest.

The forest was a miscellany of eucalyptus and wild cinchona trees, the bark of which was used to extract quinine, mixed with high bamboo, and tall and stately wild rhododendron trees. The turf beneath was damp and springy. Langur monkeys swarmed among the trees, swinging from branch to branch, chattering at intruders. The birds set up their own kind of babbling and whistling clamor. Brooke's practiced eye picked out old friends—blue-necked bee eaters, deccan scimitar babblers, bulbuls which reminded him of the English thrush, crested turban hoopoes, talkative tree babblers and chickadees. They and the monkeys were his friends, for they had often warned him of the approach of a man-eater in the jungle. Most species in the forest had an aversion to the presence of a leopard or a tiger.

Now, standing here in this forest, listening to its sounds, smelling it odors, aware of the life rustling and hidden all about him, holding a gun in his hand, and once again searching out some dangerous quarry, Dennis Brooke felt a sudden and profound change. He was once again the man they called the Sahib. In a sense he had come home again. His sight suddenly seemed to be sharper, his hearing more acute, the adrenalin was flowing, excitement was mixed with caution. And, as always, with some fear. He forgot about London and Delhi, he even forgot about Behra and Nora. There was only one thing on his mind now.

Shaitan.

He and Lassiter began to move, slowly. They found a forest path, made not by men but by the animals themselves. The grass was beaten down and here and there, in areas of the rank soil, they saw the fresh pugmarks of the man-eater. One set had led to the open field, where the remains of Mothu had been found. The other went in the opposite, or forward direction. Distantly, they heard the sound of running water.

They came over a short rise, through a patch of dwarf bamboo, guns ready. Looking down at the stream, which was narrow and shallow, they saw a magnificent sight. A great red Kashmir stag was standing at the edge of the stream, alert, acting as a sentinel. With the stag were two yearlings, two hinds and another stag, heads down, drinking daintily. The two men stood still, hardly drawing a breath. The breeze was directly in their faces, so that the sentinel stag had not yet caught their scent. The deer were a rare sight, and seeing them grouped like this was something neither Brooke nor Lassiter had ever witnessed before.

Lassiter started to raise his gun. The gesture was almost automatic, a reflex. Brooke pushed the barrel down. The sentinel stag, alerted by the movement, or perhaps by the flash of sun on the gun barrel, started to paw at the ground with his two front hooves. In an instant, the entire herd vanished, crashing through the forest.

"Christ," said Lassiter. "There was enough meat there to fill our *bobajee*'s cooking pot for weeks. And we've both got government permits for shooting Kashmirs . . ."

"I know," said Brooke. "But that leopard may be somewhere nearby. We don't want to alert him . . ."

"No," said Lassiter. "I'm sorry. Of course, you're right."

They moved down to the open space, along the stream, where the animals stood to drink. They recognized Shaitan's pugmarks in the oozing mud. But they pointed only one way—toward the stream itself. In other words, the leopard had not walked away from the stream. Clearly, he had walked across to the other side. The water, at its deepest, was waist-high. They expected to find the man-eater's pugmarks where he had emerged from the stream. But they could find none.

Lassiter scratched his head and stared at Brooke.

"I don't understand, Dennis. We saw only the marks of his two hind feet at the edge of this stream, and pointed toward it. Means his front paws were already in the water. We can't find his pugmarks where he came up out of the water on this side. He couldn't hide them on this muddy shore. Yet, no sign of them. I'm sure he didn't drown. Then where the devil did he go?"

"Only one possibility."

"Yes?"

"He walked either upstream of downstream a ways—just to throw us off. You know, Tony. The way a fugitive or escaped prisoner might do to throw the dogs off his scent—wade up a stream a distance."

"How can *any* leopard be clever enough to do that?"

"Apparently this one is."

"But why? How did he know he was being tracked?"

"I don't know. But I've got a feeling that he was watching us all the way. That he saw us walk into the forest from the field."

"Jesus," said Lassiter. He was sweating a little. "That's a nasty thought, Dennis. You know what I could do with right now?"

"What?"

"A drink. Not a little *chota*. But a big glass—filled three fingers high."

They moved a few hundred yards in each direction along the stream. But the going was hard, the underbrush thick. They found no further trace of the leopard. And there were no warning sounds to indicate that Shaitan was anywhere near. No cries of the cheetah or sambhur or kakar deer. No sudden rush of partridge or pheasant. There were the usual sounds of the forest, the humming and singing of birds, the chattering of monkeys, the rustling and crawling and slithering sounds.

Apparently Shaitan was holed up somewhere, lying low. But they both knew he was very near.

Brooke arranged a small *panchayat* of the headmen of the various villages. The meeting was held in Chakrata. Shaitan had returned, as they all knew. And as they could see, Brooke's presence in the area did not automatically intimidate the leopard. It was necessary to enforce a strict curfew again. No one was to leave his house after dark. The district forester would tour the area, show the villagers how to reinforce the doors of their houses in the best way they could. Very few of the doors to the houses, as they stood now, could resist the charge and weight of Shaitan. Thornbush would be cut in greater quantities, and placed high in front of the doors. The big cats did not like thornbush, and avoided it whenever they could. It had been used before, but it had not seemed to intimidate Shaitan. He had brushed it aside with his paws. Apparently, he knew where to grasp it where it would not hurt, between the thorns themselves. Still, Brooke said, it might be some small deterrent. It would take Shaitan a little time to clear a path to the door. During this time, Brooke and Lassiter might be summoned by the beat of drums, and get to the village in time. Also, he and Lassiter would take turns staying at one of the houses in the village every night in case the man-eater was sighted entering the village, or trying to break in. This procedure could take place only in Chakrata, for the time being. This, because Bahalji Singh's village seemed to be the main source of Shaitan's attention. Or, as the Hindus insisted, his revenge.

Meanwhile, Brooke and Lassiter would do everything in their power to rid the people of this demon.

It was Brooke's idea that Shaitan would again use the

water path through the forest. This was deduced on the
theory that the pads of the leopard were tender and,
unlike the tiger, he would be inclined to use the easier
ground. Moreover, the leopard could in this way detect
any porcupines lying before him and thus avoid being
struck by their quills.

Sooner or later, Brooke was sure that Shaitan would
come down that path again, and he set up a gun trap.

He instructed the villagers to drive two long and
sturdy bamboo poles into the ground. He tied both a
.245 rifle and a shotgun securely to them. Then, carefully, he wound fishing line around the trigger guards of
both weapons. He had his helpers drive two stakes into
the ground, one on each side of and a short distance
from the path itself. Then he looped the fishing lines
around the stakes and tied them securely. After that he
released the safety catches. The rifle was pointed one
way, the shotgun another, and the fishing lines were
stretched at a height of somewhat over two feet, roughly
about the height of where the leopard's head, or part of
his body would be. If they were lucky, there was a
chance that the man-eater could walk straight into the
trap, exert pressure on the lines, and shoot himself.

Then the villagers built *machan*s in the branches of
two rhododendron trees flanking the path. Lassiter
would sit and wait in one of them all night, Brooke on
the other. If Shaitan did come down and run into the
trap, the shot could very possibly miss. If it did, the
man-eater would shy away, and start to run. It might
then be possible, in this event, for either Brooke or
Lassiter to get a shot at him.

For two nights they sat in their *machan*s and waited.

On the third night, the shotgun went off with a blast.
There was an anguished grunt, the thud of a heavy
body, and then the sound of whimpering and whining.

Lassiter lit the kerosene lamp beside him on the *machan*, while Brooke had his .450 ready.

It was not what they had eagerly hoped for. What they saw was the body of a huge wild boar writhing on the ground in a pool of his own blood.

Brooke put a shot into the boar to end his agony. Then the next morning they entered the village and told the people what had happened. The villagers went out to bring in the boar.

When they got there, they found the boar half-eaten. And leading away from the remains were the pugmarks of Shaitan.

Once again Brooke had the weird feeling that the man-eater again had been close by, watching as they had set up the gun trap. It seemed absurd to credit Shaitan with such intelligence. But it was apparent that he had simply waited, somewhere close, as Lassiter and Brooke sat in their *machan*s, until the trap produced something worthy of his appetite.

Lassiter was angry and frustrated.

"You know what that bastard did, Dennis? He just thumbed his nose at us. Made us look like a couple of bloody fools."

"True," said Brooke. "And maybe we are."

16

TWO DAYS LATER Shaitan took a victim in the village of Kiuri.

The kill took place in the house of a devout Hindu, Mukandi Lal by name. Lal had built his house with a chimney so that his family could have a small fire inside when the weather became cold. They had a small wood fire going in the hearth in the middle of the room that night, and the entire family had been gathered around it. Mukandi's father, a venerable old man, had been chanting Sanskrit prayers, which he had memorized from the holy book of the Hindus, the Vedanta. At certain times during this ritual of recitation, the others would throw small chunks of pure butter, water, and spices into the fire, symbolically purifying the three necessities of life—air, water and food.

It was during this ritual that Shaitan, who had been lurking outside, with one great charge smashed down the door, leaped over other members of the family, picked up the ten-year-old son of Mukandi Lal, twisted and broke the child's neck with a single jerk of his great jaws, and then walked leisurely through the door and up the main street, his young prey hanging limply, clamped between the sharp teeth.

Kiuri was about twenty miles from Chakrata. It was a difficult journey by foot, along a rocky path part way up a mountain. When they arrived at Kiuri, they began to track Shaitan, but lost his trail in a rocky outcrop. Three hours after they arrived at Kiuri, they heard the sound of distant drums. Men stood on their rooftops and beat their drums, so that the sound could carry on to the next village, which would then take up the drum-beat, relaying the same grisly news.

While Lassiter and Brooke were vainly to track Shaitan at Kiuri, the drums announced that he had taken another victim, this time near the village of Jhirmoli.

Jhirmoli was ten miles west of Kiuri.

Again, the two hunters made the weary journey on foot, followed by their packman and gun bearers. Again, Brooke and Lassiter found that Shaitan could not be trailed with ease because, unlike the ordinary leopard, he did not stick to footpaths or animal trails in order to favor his pads.

In this part of the United Provinces, most of the villages, like Chakrata, were almost a hundred percent Hindu. But now and then a village could be found that was almost entirely Muslim. Jhirmoli was such a village. It had its own small mosque, and at sunrise and sunset the men of the village hurried to answer the bells of their house of worship. Most of the houses had crumbling courtyards, in the Muslim style, and the women of the village observed strict *purdah*, never going outside their homes without wearing the shapeless garment called the *burkha*, which not only covered their entire bodies but veiled their faces from the stares of men other than those of their families.

The victim was the water *wallah*, who carried water taken from a distant well from house to house in a great goatskin bag in his bullock cart, and filled the clay jars of the householders for a few annas.

He had been caught at the well just before dusk, while filling his goatskin container for the next day's rounds.

The interesting point of this killing was the fact that out of a town of three hundred people, the water sales-man, Mohinder Ram by name, was one of only four Hindus living in Jhirmoli.

Brooke brought this to the attention of Tony Lassiter.
But Lassiter was unimpressed.

"Well? What of it?"

"Doesn't it strike you as peculiar, Tony? I mean,
when you figure the odds . . ."

Lassiter stared at Brooke.

"Dennis, what are you trying to say?"

"You'll think I've gone around the bend."

"Say it anyway."

"Maybe the Hindus know something we don't
know."

"You mean about this Ram Gwar nonsense? Swear-
ing to get back at the Hindus for doing him in?"

"Yes."

"You know what that is," said Lassiter. "A lot of
heathen rubbish."

"Still," said Brooke. "It's pretty damned odd, if you
ask me. Out of some three hundred victims, he hasn't
attacked a Muslim yet."

"That's just a coincidence. If you want to talk about
odds, consider this. The Hindus outnumber the
Muslims in this part of the country by perhaps ten to
one." He gave Brooke a long look. "Dennis, look. I
know this bugger's been shrewd. I know he's clever and
he knows more tricks than any big cat *I've* ever come
across. But he's still a bloody animal. No more and no
less. Still a bloody animal."

"I suppose you're right."

"Of course I'm right," Lassiter exploded. Then he
paused and stared again at Brooke.

"You know what, Dennis?"

"What?"

"You're beginning to worry me."

They were unable to track Shaitan very far out of

Jhirmoli. His pugmarks were clear enough at the well, then led a few hundred yards away to a field of stubbled wheat. They were able to follow the direction of a line of bloodstains for a short distance, which indicated that Shaitan had descended with his prey into a gorge just ahead. When they reached the edge of the gorge, they saw that it was filled with great rocks, stone fissures and cave openings. At this point, there was no point in trying to track the man-eater further. It could be not only foolhardy but dangerous. Shaitan could easily be lying somewhere in those rocks, hidden in one of the caves, and he might very well leap from hiding upon his tormentors before they had a chance to raise their guns.

They returned to the village, exhausted by their long trek by foot from Kiuri to Jhirmoli. They spent the night at the headman's house, and decided it was useless to spend any more time in the village. Shaitan might continue to look for another kill somewhere nearby, but Brooke decided to return to Chakrata. They had no way of knowing where he would strike back, but Chakrata was his primary territory, and sooner or later, Brooke decided, he would come back there.

In this, he was proved right. Two days later, as they came up the pilgrim path toward Chakrata, they heard the distant drums of the village. The message was clear. Shaitan had come home again.

This time they were met by a runner from the village, a young man named Jai Gopal, who was a nephew of Bahalji Singh. They were told that the victim this time was the village *banya*, or moneylender, Hanuman Prasad by name. The *banya* had walked up a forest path to collect on a loan he had made to a charcoal-burner living on the outskirts, when Shaitan had leaped out of a thicket, seized the *banya* in his jaws, broken the man's neck, and trotted off up the pilgrim path with him. All this had happened practically at the door of the charcoal-burner's hut, and in front of the man's horrified eyes.

"I thought I told everyone to stay in their houses at night," said Brooke sharply. "Your uncle, Bahalji Singh, told the people this . . ."

"Yes, Sahib," said Jai Gopal. "Yes. We have stayed in our houses at night, as we have been told. But this did not happen at night."

"No?" Brooke glared at the runner. "What time *did* this happen?"

"In the afternoon. When the sun was still high over the mountain."

"Shaitan attacked by *day?*" said Brooke.

"Yes, Sahib. It is so."

Brooke looked at his companion. Lassiter looked bewildered.

"You ever hear of a man-eater, a leopard, attacking by day, Tony?"

"No. A tiger, yes. A leopard—no. But I suppose there are exceptions. I'm not sure it's a hard and fast rule."

"At this point, I'm not sure of anything."

Lassiter was a little shaken. "Nothing ordinary about this bugger, Dennis. We've agreed, he's bloody clever. This time, he's given us something a little extra to worry about."

"If he starts to kill by day, we'll have to find him fast, Tony. Otherwise, people won't be able to work in their fields, harvest their crops, tend their livestock. They can't be on curfew all day and all night, too."

"You're right," said Lassiter. "But it isn't going to be easy. We're dealing with a bloody ghost. Now he's here—now he's not. Now you see him—now you don't."

"And I thought Wilkes had made a mistake."

"Wilkes? The correspondent from the *Times?*"

"He'd reported a killing by Shaitan during the day. I thought he had buggered up the whole thing." He told Lassiter of the day he had read Wilkes report back in London. Then: "You know, Tony, we can't shoot what we can't find or see. Right?"

"Right."

"All right. Then we have to try something else."

"For instance, what?"

"Maybe we can find some way to let him come to *us*. Then we can blow the bastard's head off."

When they returned to Chakrata, Brooke conferred with Bahalji Singh and then wrote a note. It was to be taken by runner to Dehra Dun immediately. It was a request made directly to the district commissioner, John Evans.

The note from Brooke respectfully requested John Evans to requisition half a dozen grenades from the military post at Dehra Dun, and have them sent forthwith to Chakrata. He specified that they should have a highly sensitive trigger setup, so that they would explode at the slightest touch or impact.

It took some time before the grenades arrived. Dehra Dun had none in its small arsenal, and so they had to be brought down from Lahore and then redesigned by an explosives expert to meet Brooke's specifications.

Meanwhile, Brooke and Lassiter traveled many weary miles, trying to track the man-eater. In each case, and after every killing, Shaitan seemed to vanish, disappear from the face of the death. He seemed to know what the hunters would do, and where they were looking for him, and was never there when they thought they had him. Lassiter and Brooke built machans in mango and rhododendron trees, huddled for long hours on the platforms, endured the bites of mosquitoes and swarms of other insects, waiting all night over a path or gully where they were sure that Shaitan would appear. But he never did. On some nights, they waited in driving rain, soaked to the skin, hoping to trap him. Once, during a storm, they saw the man-eater for just an instant, in a flash of lightning. Lassiter fired, but he was a moment too late. The man-eater leaped behind a rock and ran off.

When they descended from their tree platforms, they had to be very careful. Shaitan was known to sometimes attack hunters climbing down from their *machan*s. He had caught John Boyle of Brooke's own regiment in this way. A Captain Peter Myles and Lieutenant Alan Hunt of the Central India Horse had suffered the same kind of fate. Their effects had been found at the base of the tree where they had built their *machan*s. And the same had happened to a Captain Percy Lyons and Alastair Dougall from the Fifteenth Hussars. It was difficult climbing down a tree with your gun at the ready. Brooke and Lassiter made sure to climb down one at a time. One man descended, the other sat on the *machan*, gun at shoulder, waiting for a possible charge. The man on the ground, in his turn, kept his gun to the shoulder as his companion descended. The man-eater, who was a great climber, had been known to attack his prey with a downward leap from one of the upper branches.

Brooke had failed to get a single shot at Shaitan, and he became frustrated, angry. In all his career, he had never had this trouble with an animal. Shaitan was a wraith, a murderous ghost. He was making a fool out of himself and Lassiter. He outwitted them in ways that seemed incredible. Shaitan seemed to have more than just plain instinct. He seemed to *think* and *act* as though he actually had a human brain. And a clever one, at that. Brooke knew this was ridiculous, impossible. Yet, some deep nerve continued to nag him. A tiger acted

like a tiger, a leopard like a leopard. With minor
exceptions, the habits of the big cats were known and
could be predicted. And because you knew about those
habits, as a hunter, you were ahead of the game. You
tracked him this way or that, you could trap him or
maneuver him into a situation where you could get a
shot at him, you could sometimes figure out the path he
was taking, with help from the birds and monkeys and
kakar deer who gave you warning ahead of time. Normally, Brooke thought, he would have bagged this man-
eater in two or three weeks, a month at the most. But he
and Lassiter had been tracking this animal for two
months now—and nothing.

The point was that although Shaitan was a leopard,
he did not *act* like a leopard. He was never where he was
supposed to be, he kept out of sight, he did not follow
the prescribed paths, he would strike in one area and
then another. Physically, he was much larger than any
recorded animal of his kind. And clearly more dangerous. Brooke saw him as some kind of weird exag-
geration of his species, almost a mutation. Now and
then, the thought rose in his mind: *Are the Hindus
right, after all?* Is there a human brain in that big furry
head, with its great jaws and sharp teeth? Is Shaitan
indeed inhabited with the spirit and intelligence of a
human being—Ram Gwar, if you will—with a spotted
fur pelt, claws, a tail, jaws and teeth?

Brooke, of course, was a westerner and a Christian.
He knew most of the people in Asia, and particularly in
India, believed in metepsychosis, the transmigration of
the soul at death from one body to another. They
believed that if that person was evil, or his thoughts
were not pure, or that he gave no love to his fellow man
during his lifetime, then his *karma* would take its
natural course, and his soul could transmigrate into an
animal's body. As a former British officer, he had never

mixed much with the Indians, nor had he thought much
of their religions, but he had a smattering of knowledge
concerning them. He knew about the *Pratitya Samut-
pada*, or the Wheel of Life, and of *Samsara*, the world
of transmigration and its six stages. He was aware of the
Hindu belief that Buddha himself was the incarnation
of Vishnu, the ninth god in the line, and who was once,
in terms of transmigration, reincarnated as the King of
the Monkeys.

But now Brooke learned more. He learned why
Shaitan was particularly hated and feared by the Hindus
of the villages, for a reason he had never known.

"You see, Sahib," said Bahalji Singh. "When
Shaitan kills, it is quick and sudden. A man does not
have time to die on his deathbed."

Brooke was puzzled at that. "But if a man has to die,
Bahalji, perhaps it is better that way. He suffers an
instant of pain, and then it is over. He may suffer for
hours or days if he lingers on his deathbed."

"Ah, yes," said Bahalji. "This is what you in the
west may think. But in our belief, Shaitan is robbing us
of new homes for our souls. For the soul must travel
from death to rebirth, and this takes time. Those who
are suddenly killed and eaten by Shaitan do not have
time to see the Clear Light."

"The Clear Light?" Brooke was puzzled. "And what
is that?"

The headman hesitated for a moment.

"Sahib, I am a simple man, and it is better that a
sadhu or a *munshi* or some other learned man explain
this to you. But since you speak our language, I will try
to explain as best I can."

From what Bahalji told him, the path of the soul
from death to rebirth was extremely important on the
deathbed. In other words, a man who died a natural
death, in the presence of his family and friends, had the

best chance to make this transition gracefully. When the dying man was about to stop breathing, he was turned over on his right side, and a relative or friend then pressed his arteries so that his consciousness would not be able to lower itself from his brain, but would leave his body at its highest and most valuable point, called the *sahasrara padma*. When breathing stopped, the vital force then went directly to the heart, and rested there for a few moments. And during these moments, the Clear Light of Reality would flash in the mind of the man on the deathbed.

"But how can this be, Bahalji?" asked Brooke. "The man now is dead."

"No, Sahib. This vision will remain with him. He will see it and be blinded by it. It is, we believe, to be a glimpse of heaven itself. Those who have lived peacefully and in goodness, those who have known the tranquil state of meditation will see the Clear Light for longer than those who have lived impure lives, and have pursued greed or spread evil.

"So, Sahib, when Shaitan has eaten some beloved member of a family, the widow or widower or fatherless children do not only weep because he has gone. They weep also for the victim's soul. For the man taken by Shaitan has no time to see the Clear Light. Ram Gwar knows this. And this is part of his terrible revenge on all of us, and my village of Chakrata in particular. And that is why, Sahib, you and Sahib Lassiter must find some way to shoot or kill him, so that we can burn him, so that the demon within him will die forever. And then, when the moment comes, we shall each of us have time to see the Clear Light, and our souls can properly leave our body and find a new resting place."

Brooke did not believe in all this mysticism. Dead was dead. They ploughed you under or put your burned ashes in some urn or, as the Hindus did, floated them on some stream, and that was it. The end. Period. The long, long sleep of eternity.

Still, thinking of Shaitan he was shaken. Could it really be that death was simply a long sleep and that life would be renewed some day? Then, feeling slightly ashamed, he resolutely put down the thought. He called himself a fool for even considering it.

Still, this hunt was beginning to get on his nerves, and Tony Lassiter's. It was entirely unnatural, it was against all odds. But the fact existed and they had to face it. They hadn't been able to catch one glimpse of Shaitan, let alone get a shot at him. This might happen to amateurs, but he and Tony were supposed to be top-flight professionals.

When you thought of how the bugger had consistently outwitted and outmaneuvered Tony Lassiter and himself—playing cat and mouse with them—it was not only frustrating.

It was frightening.

When the grenades arrived from Dehra Dun, Brooke went to see Bahalji Singh.

"I want you, Bahalji, to tell the people of your village and every village nearby, to stay in their houses for a week. Day and night."

"Day *and* night? But Sahib, the people cannot do this. They must tend their herds, take care of their crops."

"I know, Bahalji," said Brooke. "It will be hard to do. But it's part of a plan I have."

"And what is this plan, Sahib?"

"In this way, we can deny food to Shaitan—human food. If he is denied this, and he becomes hungry, he will eat what he can find in the forest. And then we shall try to satisfy his appetite for all time."

He explained what he planned to Bahalji. To use the

Western phrase, he explained that there were more ways than one to skin a cat. They had failed to track down the man-eater. Their guns, both his and Lassiter's, had been silent, useless. Now, they would try to lure the big cat into committing suicide.

For seven days, not a soul in Chakrata or the surrounding villages were seen on the streets or roads or fields. It was as though they all had simultaneously been wiped out by the plague, and had died inside their homes. Sturdy barricades and heaps of thornbush were placed around the livestock pens. The only time anyone was seen was when men furtively came out to milk the cows and goats in the pens behind the houses. Relatives watched them through grilled windows. If the leopard was sighted, they would warn the men to rush back into the houses. Chakrata and all the surrounding villages, in effect, were ghost towns.

On the sixth day, Brooke arranged to have a bullock calf killed. They placed the calf under a mango tree on the edge of the field, in an area he and Lassiter were sure Shaitan was patrolling. They had, in fact, found his pugmarks in the area that same morning. While Lassiter stood on guard, Brooke made a careful incision in the neck of the dead calf, and inserted a hand grenade into the neck. It was triggered to go off at the slightest touch. Then he carefully covered the grenade, replacing the folds of flesh over it.

It was a gamble—that the man-eater would be hungry enough to be attracted to the calf. Leopards were notorious scavengers—like the vultures, they would eat any carrion they found, if they were hungry. Brooke knew, as did Lassiter, that leopards always began their feeding at the neck. His hope was that the man-eater would dig his teeth into the neck of the dead bullock, touch off the delicate firing pin, and blow his own head off.

After he had finished, Lassiter said:

"This won't sound like much in the press. They want a little excitement. They expect you to shoot him down on a charge."

"To hell with what the newspapers expect. This is a man-eater. And I'm not proud, Tony. I intend to finish him off any way I can."

"Amen to that," said Lassiter. "I'm tired of wearing out my boots and getting blisters on my feet trying to find the bastard. I'm with you, old man. Let's get it over with, pack it in and go home, any way we can."

They hid the calf under a canopy of low-lying tree branches, so that it would be out of view of the vultures. Then they went back to the village, and waited.

Just after dusk, they heard the bark of a kakar and the agitated chatter of monkeys, and they knew that Shaitan was approaching.

They waited, holding their breath.

Suddenly, they heard the distant explosion.

They ran across the field, until they reached the dead calf. There was an animal lying dead across the calf, with its head and part of its body blown off. But it was not the leopard. It was a jackal.

Yet, there was clear evidence that some big animal had also been feeding on the calf. His pugmarks were evident; they belonged to Shaitan. He, too, had dined on the bullock. But he had fed only on the hindquarters, and then walked away to let the jackal feast on the remnants.

Shaitan had somehow sensed that there was death in the neck of the calf. Or even more mystifying—he *knew*.

For weeks, Brooke and Lassiter continued the hunt. Once or twice, they got a fleeting shot at the leopard, or what they *thought* was the leopard. But the man-eater seemed to lead a charmed life.

Lured by its tracks in various parts of the forest, they waited in their tree platforms, night after night, hoping Shaitan would appear.

Each time they gave up and left a particular *machan*, the leopard seemed to appear in the vicinity the following night, after taking still another victim from whatever village they were near.

It was as though Shaitan was laughing at them, mocking their efforts to find him. Lassiter became short-tempered, and Dennis Brooke, always the cool professional, was shaken himself. Shaitan was making them both look and feel like amateurs.

Brooke no longer regarded the man-eater as simply an animal. He saw him now as a personality. An evil, almost human personality. He began to see this as a kind of manhunt, except that this particular quarry had four legs, fur, huge jaws and a tail. He was convinced that somehow their quarry had turned the tables on them. He was watching *them* all the time they were searching for him. Shaitan, he felt, would not attack as long as he and Lassiter were hunting together. The leopard could seize one of them on a sudden charge, but he ran the risk of being shot by the other. But Brooke was convinced that the leopard was always somewhere near, stalking them. And, like the devil, toying with them. Enjoying his perverse game. Enjoying being the quarry. Knowing that he could outwit them, sensing their frustration.

The leopard had turned the tables on them, had become the hunter, and if they were ever separated Shaitan would not hesitate to attack.

Tony Lassiter pooh-poohed this idea. A leopard was a leopard, he insisted, man-eater or otherwise. He did not play games. When he killed, he usually killed for food. And he knew danger when he saw it. He knew the deadly fire that came out of rifles, he had seen it before. His guess was that the nick in Shaitan's toe had been caused by a bullet from some hunter's gun.

But Lassiter's skepticism was soon shaken.

One day, just after dusk, outside of Chakrata, they descended from a *machan*. Suddenly, they heard the bark of a kakar, warning them that leopard was near. The bark halted abruptly, in rather a strange way. Looking down at the path to the village, they saw the tracks of deer, ghooral, wild pig and serow. But these were old tracks. What mesmerized them was that almost directly over their own footsteps were the pugmarks of the man-eater, moving in the same direction as they. And Shaitan's tracks were very fresh.

For the first time they were aware that Shaitan had followed *them*, and was now somewhere around.

Dusk fell rapidly into night and the moon scudded in and out of black clouds. Lassiter was carrying a lantern, and now the hair rose on the backs of their necks. They knew they were vulnerable. Lassiter's gun was useless; he could not possibly bring it to bear in case the leopard charged, since he was carrying the lantern. If the leopard charged, it would be up to Brooke, and he would have only one shot to do it.

A few feet along the path toward Chakrata, they found the kakar dead, his throat viciously slashed.

Shaitan hadn't bothered to eat the small deer. He had merely shut off any further warning of his approach.

The path ended on the outskirts of the town, in a muddy series of bullock wallows. At the same time, the fuel in Lassiter's lamp was exhausted, and the lamp went out.

"Oh, Christ," said Lassiter. "We could be in for it now. Can't see a damned thing."

If the man-eater had been following them now and was reasonably close, this would be the time for his attack. His quarry could not see in the dark. He could seize one of them in his jaws and quickly carry him off while the other would fire blindly in the dark.

But just at this moment, the moon came out, flooding the area with light. Brooke turned to see the huge shadowy shape racing for the woods at the end of the field. He brought the .245 to his shoulder, but before he could fire the apparition had vanished.

"Damn!" In his frustration, Brooke slammed the butt of his rifle on the ground. "Damn the bastard." Then he looked at Lassiter, a little abashed. "Sorry, Tony. Didn't mean to go off the deep end."

"Nothing to be sorry about. The bugger's getting to me, too. I mean, the idea of his tracking *us*—putting his pugmarks right over our own footsteps—that has to shake hell out of anybody. Brings up an interesting point, Dennis."

"Yes?"

"Right now, I'm a bit confused. I mean—who is hunting whom?"

17

ANOTHER MONTH PASSED, a month in which the man-eater made ten more kills. Six of them were in or around Chakrata. Two were at Chandpur, and one each at Surnar and Khurja. Again, the best Brooke could do was to warn the headmen in the villages to take extraordinary precautions. Keep people together in the open by day. Lock in everyone at night. Continue to strengthen the stockades holding their livestock.

They tracked the man-eater again and again, for many weary miles. He always struck just ahead of them. And then his pugmarks vanished into nothing.

They tried injecting cyanide into dead buffalo or deer used as bait. Shaitan feasted on the animals, but he delicately avoided the areas where the deadly poison had been injected. They staked out huge traps, and the great steel jaws snapped shut to trap other quarry, but not Shaitan.

The newspapers, which occasionally were sent up to the bungalow from Dehra Dun, were becoming testy, even critical. They focused on Brooke and gave little space to Lassiter. They took the view that Brooke was number one, and treated Lassiter as though he were some kind of assistant. It had been months now since Brooke had arrived in India, and the man-eater was still running around wild and untouched. They hinted that Shaitan was making a fool of Brooke. The public was disappointed that nothing had really happened, and Brooke's image was gradually beginning to tarnish. One newspaper observed sardonically that one of the

contestants had changed—now it was Man versus
Superbeast. A consensus was building that Brooke's
presence was futile, that he would never catch the man-
eater. The plain fact that neither he nor Lassiter had
ever been able to even get a good shot at Shaitan. He
might have been a ghost flitting through the countryside. But the fact that he left pugmarks and the horribly
mutilated remains of his victims was proof that he was
real.

Lassiter was angry at the reaction. He sat on the
veranda of the bungalow one Sunday, and rattled the
pages of a copy of the *London Evening News*, now
some weeks old.

"The bastards," he said. "Sitting on their asses in
Fleet Street and writing this muck. They ought to come
up here for a week and see what it's like."

"Maybe they're right, Tony," said Brooke, wearily.

"About what?"

"Maybe Shaitan's just too much for us. Maybe we
ought to pack it in. Admit we can't carry it off. Go
home."

"You couldn't do that, Dennis."

"Why not?"

"Because I know you. You've taken on a job, and
you'll bloody well do it no matter how long it takes."

"Why me? What you really mean is, we."

"I'm afraid not, old man."

"What do you mean?"

"I won't be in on it unless it happens in the next two
weeks. Just got an order from the colonel. I'm to report
to the regiment in Lahore by the twentieth. There's been
some trouble on the Northwest Frontier, burnings and
massacres. The Gandhi people, of course, and the
Guards have been alerted to stand by and move out if it
gets much worse."

In the next week, Shaitan made two more kills. One was a girl who had been picking mangoes near a field where men had been working. Later, he had boldly crept up to a roadside shrine in broad daylight and snatched a worshipper praying before a small image of Lord Vishnu himself.

Again, Brooke and Lassiter walked mile after mile, pursuing the wraith, coming close, but never closing with him. Both men, now exhausted, fell into a state of depression. Again, they were aware that just as they were the hunters, so too were they being hunted. On two more occasions they had found the pugmarks of Shaitan following them.

The Hindus in the area lost heart. They had expected the Sahib to solve their problem, and he had not. They knew how hard he was trying, and they treated him with respect. But their early enthusiasm at his arrival had vanished. They had regarded him almost as a god, and he had proved that he, too, was human. But more and more, they believed in the legend of the man-eater's invincibility. The demon had not been exorcised, Ram Gwar was still running wild, taking his revenge on any Hindu he could find, and everyone knew that demons like this were immortal, they could go on forever, they never grew old or tired. Homes were being abandoned, people had stopped working in the fields and in the forests, food production had virtually stopped.

The pursuit of Shaitan was a small sideshow compared to the main event at the Raj trying to stave off the native discontent in India. Yet, somehow, the hunt for the leopard continued to achieve headlines in the press, given prominence beyond its actual worth. Most of the Indian villagers had no sophisticated conception of the intricate political situation, the formation of the various commissions formed to study the problem, the point-counterpoint moves between the

Mahatma and the Raj. But they did understand the simple situation of Dennis Brooke versus Shaitan; it was one-on-one, a grim show between two gladiators, with death for the defeated. In itself, it seemed to symbolize the whole issue in the main arena: The Raj versus Gandhi and his *Satyagraha* movement. The followers of the Mahatma were jubilant at Brooke's failure. So were a number of the more militant Indian newspapers, which gave Brooke's fruitless hunt an inordinate amount of space. The Raj, as they saw it, was being humiliated. The British sahib, it had once been assumed, could do almost anything he set his mind to do. Now, Brooke was being used as symbol and whipping boy; the sahib could be as helpless as anyone else.

As the days passed, the anger built in Brooke himself. He was tired and discouraged. He had never wanted this damned assignment. He had been forced into it, very much against his will, a puppet of the public and politics. He felt humiliated and frustrated. It wasn't so much what the newspapers said, or what the public thought. It was the fact that he was being kept from going back to Delhi and seeing Nora. He would ask Nora to divorce Clymer, and bring her back to London with him as his wife, and blast what everybody thought.

But he could not go back to Delhi till he had bagged Shaitan. Assuming, of course, he thought wryly, that it did not turn out the other way. Shaitan was the villain in this drama, and although he had never thought of any man-eater, tiger or leopard, in any emotional way, he began to hate Shaitan in a personal way, almost as though the leopard were a human antagonist, and not simply an animal. The bastard, reflected Brooke, was clever, so damned clever and shrewd, that he *thought* almost like a human being. Brooke found himself totally baffled. He began to develop his own super-

stition about the beast. He almost, not quite but almost,
in his angrier or more frustrating moments, believed
what Bahalji Singh and all the other Hindus believed.
That Shaitan was indeed the reincarnation of this
sadhu, Ram Gwar, and that this holy man actually had
perversely decided to wrap himself in a leopard skin,
equip himself with claws, jaws, teeth and a tail, and
therefore had complicated Dennis Brooke's life beyond
all endurance.

He had heard it said that if you lived in India long
enough you could believe anything, even the existence
of Siva or Vishnu, and you would swear that you
actually saw the famous rope trick. But of course, this
was nonsense. Shaitan was a leopard. An animal is an
animal is an animal, and always will be. Brooke yearned
for just one good look at him, for just one shot at him.

But he was still Shaitan's prisoner, and it looked as
though he would continue to be for a long, long time.
Damn it, he thought. If we could only get it over with.
One way or the other.

It was almost as though someone had heard his prayer
and suddenly taken heed.

He and Lassiter had already gone to bed the following
night when they were awakened by their *chowkidar*. The
watchman informed them that half the village seemed to
be coming toward the bungalow. They were carrying
torches and shouting exultantly, something about
Shaitan. But they were too far away for the watchman
to hear what they were actually saying.

Brooke and Lassiter dressed hastily and stepped out
onto the veranda. The crowd was standing behind the
gate, talking and gesticulating, and laughing in great
excitement. The watchman allowed Bahalji Singh within
the bungalow gate, and he came up the veranda. He
could hardly get out the words.

"We have caught him, Sahib. We have caught him."

Brooke stared at the headman in disbelief.

"Shaitan?"

"Yes. We have caught the devil, and he is now at our mercy."

"How?"

"You remember the pit you told us to dig on the path leading to the grove of the mango trees near the shrine?"

"Yes."

"He has fallen into the pit and onto the sharp stakes. He is there now, Sahib. We ask you to come and kill him now with your gun."

A few days ago, Brooke had instructed the villagers to dig deep pit traps along certain of the known routes of the man-eater. These were cleverly concealed by dirt twigs and grass, so that they looked entirely natural. The natives were warned of the location of the pit traps, so as not to get caught themselves. They were designed to cave in easily at the lightest touch, and certainly under the weight of a heavy animal. The reactions of a leopard or tiger were quick in almost any crisis. Yet, in this kind of situation, for some reason they were known to act slowly. They felt their two front paws sink, and because of the weight of their heads and the forward part of their bodies, they were unable to pull back and out in time.

Brooke really had little faith in this kind of trap when it came to tracking an animal like Shaitan. The man-eater, he reasoned, was too clever, too alert to be caught in such a simple way. But Brooke, in his frustration and desperation, had been ready to try anything once.

He picked up his Mannlicher and, with Lassiter, followed the laughing, dancing crowd. The villagers were wild in their relief. They assured Brooke that the leopard in the pit was indeed Shaitan; he was huge, bigger than any they had ever seen, and more than that,

Shaitan had been the only known leopard in the area, although a number of tigers had been seen lately.

Finally, they came to the pit. The villagers crowded around the huge, deep hole, watching in awe. At the bottom of the pit, the leopard, his body bloodied by the sharp stakes on which he had fallen, his paws crusted with dirt as he tried to pull himself out of the pit, stared up at them. His yellow eyes looked straight into Brooke's. He growled and hissed and spat at his tormentors. He tried to leap out of the hole, but it was too deep. His claws caught the edge of the pit and then he fell back. He landed on the bloody stakes again. Then he tried another leap upward. This time he almost made it, and the crowd, suddenly frightened, shrank back. It was then that Brooke put a bullet through the animal's head with the Mannlicher. The leopard's eyes bored into Brooke's for a moment, two orbs of yellow hate. Suddenly they dulled. Then he slid back onto the bloody stakes at the bottom, and lay still.

It took time before the crowd would believe the leopard was actually dead. They gave it the supernatural powers of the demon. They knew, as the saying went, that it was never safe to assume a leopard was dead until it was skinned. Especially this one. Timidly, they came to the edge of the pit, and as was their custom to make sure a leopard or tiger was really dead, they threw stones at the animal to see whether he twitched. The leopard remained still.

Brooke asked Bahalji Singh to instruct his people to haul the leopard out of the pit. This was not an easy task. The man-eater was of tremendous weight, and they would have to contrive a rough pulley arrangement to get him out. No one yet dared to go down into the pit and tie sisal ropes around the body. They still believed that he would spring up from the dead and claw his way out. He was, after all, a demon, the devil, Shaitan.

To make them feel more secure, Brooke put another bullet into the leopard, this time through the heart. The leopard did not move, did not quiver or twitch. Then to illustrate that the demon was really dead, Brooke clambered down into the pit and sat up on the body of the dead animal.

At this, the villagers were convinced, and prepared to haul their nemesis back to the village for the necessary rituals.

Back in Chakrata, Brooke and Lassiter watched with the crowd as the main event was to begin—the burning of Shaitan.

Had this been some other leopard, or tiger, for that matter, the procedure would have been entirely different. The men of Chakrata would have first turned the animal on its back, in a spread-eagle position, then rope each leg to a tree. After that, they would have split open the pads, scraped out the insides until only the fur remained, and finally, made a series of very careful cuts around the mouth and eyes. After that, they would boil the skull and extract the clavicles, small and shaped like sickles, and about three inches long. These they would use as jewelry or charms.

The British who hunted these predators were mainly interested in the pelt and head alone, to be hung in some club, officers' mess or private home. But to the people of Chakrata, aside from the pelt, there were other parts of the leopard that had immense value. The claws and teeth were precious as lucky talismans, and when worn, were said to frighten witches away. To the arthritic and rheumatic, the fat of the animal was a precious salve to take away pain and stiffness. More than this, the gall-stones were fine medicine for watering eyes, the whiskers could tickle a maiden into sudden desire, like some exotic aphrodisiac, and a small portion of fat from the kidneys, when rubbed on the penis, would magically stir it into action. This, of course, was highly prized by the older men. In addition, the leopard provided still more valuable byproducts. Its brain, mixed with a certain oil, was a specific for pimples, and half a pound of the animal's flesh, cooked and eaten, would make any man invulnerable to snake bite.

But this leopard was different. This was Shaitan, the incarnation of Ram Gwar. This was a devil-demon, and the only way to keep his evil soul from returning and haunting the villagers again was to burn the body that carried that soul, pelt and all.

The pyre had already been built, and Bahalji Singh, as headman of the village, had the honor of lighting it. The crowd watched in dead silence as their leader applied the torch, and the brush and wood, mixed with pitch, ignited suddenly, the flames springing high. Four strong men then lifted the leopard up where it still lay on the bamboo litter used to transport it in the village. They upturned the litter, and the leopard fell into the fire. Its flesh sizzled, the stink of it burning was overpowering, and finally, when it vanished entirely in flames and became ash, the crowd broke its silence with a tremendous cry of joy.

Shaitan was now gone forever. The demon was dead for all time, and their travail was over.

Brooke and Lassiter watched the celebration for awhile. It was now almost dawn. Lassiter was in a light-hearted mood, almost giddy with relief.

"Well, old cock, we finally got the bugger. All that walking, all that sitting in trees all night, waiting for a ghost, getting soaked by the rain or freezing our balls off—it's all over." He slapped Brooke on the back. "Damn it, man. Don't you understand? We've done it, and it's over. Let's go back to the bungalow and have a drink. If ever there was a time to celebrate . . ."

"Let's hold off that drink awhile, Tony."

Lassiter stared at him. He saw that Brooke was sober, thoughtful, preoccupied. Not in a holiday mood at all.

"What's the matter, Dennis? You look like you've come from a funeral. But damn, this is a happy one. Look at those people. Monkey off our backs. Devil off their backs. The bastard's gone, we've done him in for good."

"Have we?"

Lassiter looked at Brooke, uneasily.

"What do you mean, 'have we'? Of course we have."

"What makes you so sure?"

"Only leopard in the vicinity. And you saw how big he was. Couldn't be anyone else but Shaitan."

"It could have been some other leopard wandering into this territory."

"Damn it," said Lassiter. He was irritated now. "You're reaching pretty far out, Dennis. I know how you feel. The same way I did. That we'd never get Shaitan. You saw him burn just now, and you still can't believe we've got the bloody job done. I know. It's hard for me to believe, but there it is. So let's get back and have that bloody drink . . ."

"Let's do something else first."

"What?"

"Go back to that pit trap."

"For Christ's sake, why?"

"Look, Tony, forget it. You go back and have that drink. I'll go alone." He was angry at Lassiter, angry at himself. On edge, ready to explode. He did not believe this was Shaitan, he could not believe it. Shaitan was too smart, too clever to fall into a pit trap. He had proved that in many ways. Yet, was he? He could have made a mistake. The pit was well covered, perfectly concealed under a layer of leaves. They had left it alone for days. It was designed so that lighter animals could cross

it without the kit collapsing, but a heavy animal like
Shaitan would fall through. The path was one that
Shaitan took often. The ordinary leopard did not have a
good sense of smell. But Shaitan seemed to be an
exception. He always seemed to sense when he and
Lassiter were nearby. Brooke, after the pit had been
built, had warned the villagers to stay clear of the path
and the area around it so that their odor would not
linger and warn off the man-eater.

Reason told him the animal, now ashes in the
smoldering fire, *had* to be Shaitan. Lassiter was right.
In the weeks and months they had been tracking the
man-eater, they had found the spoor of no other
leopard. Tigers, yes, a few, but no leopard. If another
leopard had wandered into Shaitan's territory, he would
probably be met head-on by Shaitan and driven off.
Leopards, like other predators, usually cut off a piece of
territory, marked it as theirs and drove off any invaders.

Now Brooke began to doubt his own doubt. He told
himself that he had steeped himself too deeply in the
belief of Shaitan's infallibility. He and Tony Lassiter
had walked their feet off for too many weary miles,
climbed too many hills, sat in too many *machan*s, to
find nothing. They had never actually really *seen*
Shaitan. He told himself he was thinking like a Hindu
now. That this devil was immortal, or had been, up to
now. It was almost as though he didn't *want* to believe
the animal in the fire was Shaitan. Almost masochistic.
As though he, Brooke, in some perverse way, wanted
the hunt to go on and on.

"Jolly good, Dennis," he heard Lassiter saying. "If
that's what you want to do, then I'll go along."

They went back to the pit. Starting from there, they
each walked away from the path in the opposite
direction, since they did not know the direction from

which the leopard had come when he had been caught in the trap.

About a quarter mile away from the pit, the path was shaded from the sun by a heavy growth of mangoes, and the soil became damp. There Brooke found a set of pugmarks. They were fresh, and faced away from the direction of the pit trap.

For a long time he stared down at the pugmarks. Then he raised his gun and fired a shot. After a while, Lassiter came running in. He looked at the pugmarks and his face fell. He needed no explanation from Brooke.

"Christ," said Lassiter, fervently. "Oh, Christ." His face sagged in depression. He licked his lips. "I suppose we'd better go back and tell them," he said finally.

"No," said Brooke.

"But this isn't . . ."

"I know it, Tony. And you know it. But let's not tell them yet. Let them enjoy themselves for awhile. This is the first chance they've had to feel free for years. To celebrate anything. To laugh and smile and dance. We can give them the bad news later. What's the difference?"

"You're right," said Lassiter. "But I can't look at their faces after we give them this bloody news."

As it turned out, there was no necessity to tell the villagers that the animal they had burned was not Shaitan. Shaitan gave them the news himself.

A group of merrygoers were on their way home to the nearby village of Bisalpur when Shaitan charged into the group and snatched a woman carrying a child. She screamed once and dropped the baby before Shaitan broke her neck with one twist of his jaws and carried her off.

18

Two weeks later, Bahalji Singh came to the bungalow and told Brooke and Lassiter that he and the other headmen of the area had held a *panchayat* at Kotdwara, a village in the uplands some ten miles from Chakrata. And there they had come to a momentuous decision.

"We have found a way to trap Shaitan." said Bahalji. "We believe it will surely be successful. But it will involve a sacrifice. A very serious sacrifice."

"What kind of sacrifice?" Brooke asked, puzzled.

"A living man," said Bahalji. "We have decided to offer a human person to the jaws of Shaitan, in order that countless others may be saved later."

Brooke and Lassiter stared at each other. Then Brooke said:

"Bahalji, what the devil are you talking about?"

"Come with me to Kotdwara," said the headman. "You will see for yourself, Sahib. It is useless for me to try to explain here. You must see to understand."

At Kotdwara, a group of men stood around a small, stout hut that had only recently been built. They seemed to regard the hut with some reverence, as though it were some shrine. Bahalji led Brooke and Lassiter into the tiny hut.

In the semigloom they saw a naked man sitting cross-legged on a tiger skin. He was absolutely still. Not an eye blinked, not a muscle twitched. For a moment, both Englishmen thought for a moment he was some sort of idol, the life-size statue of some obscure Hindu deity.

Clearly, he was in some kind of total trance. There was
a strong, pungent smell in the hut, and they realized that
the man's skin had been covered with creosote to
protect him against the ants. A small slit in the roof of
the tiny hut provided the only ventilation.

"The name of this man," said Bahalji, "is Munshi
Mahadeo Prasad. He is, in fact, a *sadhu*, a holy man,
and a practioner of yoga. A few days ago he came off
the pilgrim path, entered the village here, and declared
that he wished to become a *samadh swami*. That is to
say, sahibs, that he wished to end his life by going into
perpetual *samadhi*."

Brooke and Lassiter stared at Bahalji, puzzled. It was
clear that they had no idea what the word meant.

"I will explain," continued Bahalji. "It is what you
people call—what is it? Ah, yes. Meditation. *Samadhi* is
a kind of meditation, very, very deep. At the moment,
you see, this holy man is in the last stage of what we call
the Mystic Path. This is the ecstasy, the great joy, the
total release from the cares of the world beyond which
the *yogi* must make a great decision. He must decide
whether to pass into the worlds beyond this one, or
continue to stay on this earth in order to help his fellow
man. This man has made his decision. To pass
beyond."

They stared at the *sadhu*, a kind of still life in bronze.

"He's decided to commit suicide, then?"

"You in the West would call it that, Sahib. But it is
not really so. He is doing this with joy, not regret."

"Isn't there any way to stop him?"

"No. He has chosen this out of his own free will.
First, he expressed this desire to the Black Blanket
Father in Rikikesh. But the Black Blanket Father tried
to persuade him that he was too young to pass on. Still
he insisted on perpetual *samadhi*. And so he began his
initiation by observing the old practices taught by the

Vedas that many holy men of this day still carry out.
For a long time he ate nothing but fruit, milk, and rice.
Then he fasted for four days, drank the holy water of
the Ganges to purify himself within, and practiced many
*kumbakha*s.''

''*Kumbakha*s?''

''Ah, sahibs, naturally you might not know this
word. It means certain breathing exercises, in the yoga
way. This means that finally, in the state of ecstatic
trance and pure meditation, he was able to suspend
breathing for more than five minutes.''

Both Brooke and Lassiter turned and looked at the
holy man again. Still, they saw no sign of life, not even a
faint rising and falling of the chest. Brooke said to the
headman:

''Bahalji, are you sure he's alive?''

''Oh, I am sure, Sahib.''

''How long has he been in this trance?''

''Twenty days. Without food or water.''

''But he doesn't seem to be breathing.''

''Ah, but he is, Sahib. Except not in the ordinary
way.''

''How did he come here to Kotdwara?''

''He was told by the Black Blanket Father to take a
little time. To think and meditate on his decision. To
take the pilgrim path and pray at the shrines, and reflect
well on what he intended to do. Somewhere along the
path, said the Black Blanket Father, Munshi Mahadeo
Prasad would make his final decision. Or rather, the
decision would be made for him, by some power greater
than he. It was here, at Kotdwara, that he decided to
become a *samadh swami*. The people here built this
small hut to protect him from Shaitan, or a tiger, or any
other threat. As soon as the last stone in this hut was set,
this *sadhu* you see, Munshi Mahadeo Prasad, was
seated on the tiger skin, and passed into *samadhi*. He is

now, as you can observe, in a state of deep and final meditation. He has achieved the temporary separation of his soul from his body by means of a trance state in which all the natural functions of the body are quiet, have ceased their work.'' Bahalji moved closer to the *sadhu*. "As you see, his nails have not grown. Neither has his hair. He has passed no excrement and no water from his body. These two jars of water you see beside him are placed there as a matter of ritual in the event he comes out of the trance. But that is simply a formality.''

"Twenty days without food or water?'' Brooke shook his head. "Bahalji, I can't believe it.''

"Neither can I,'' said Lassiter, staring at the silent cross-legged figure on the tiger skin as though he were some kind of apparition. "If you ask me, he's dead.''

"Ah, no, Sahib. He is alive. And will remain so for many days to come.''

They were standing close to the *samadh swami* now. Brooke shared Lassiter's conviction. The man was dead.

"Is it permitted to touch him, Bahalji?''

The headman nodded to Brooke. "It is permitted.''

Brooke reached out his hand and touched the sitting figure's arm. He shivered a little, and withdrew his hand.

"The body's cold. Cold as a corpse. He *is* a corpse.''

"No, Sahib. It must seem so to you, but it is not so. The body is cold, yes. But there is a warm patch at the crown of the skull, as you will see, if you wish to touch the top of his head. This is the *yogi*'s only link with our world, the world we all live in, but in which he does not.''

They watched the holy man silently for a few moments. Dennis Brooke reflected, you live in India for a long time and you see many strange phenomena, things you would believe impossible, people like this *sadhu*, for instance. The surprises in this country never end; there is always a new one every day, the kind that defies logic and cannot penetrate the western mind. Like this *samadhi*, the last stage, which Bahalji called the Mystic Path. Tell your friends in London about this *samadh swami*, he thought, and they would think you mad, or else an accomplished liar.

The still, sitting figure had a hypnotic effect on Brooke and he, as well as Lassiter, could not help staring at the *sadhu*. Finally, he heard Bahalji say:

"Sahibs, I have brought you here and explained all this to you so that you will understand what we decided at the *panchayat*. But it is very close in here, and hard to breathe. Suppose we go outside, and I will explain what we plan to do."

They left the tiny stone hut, which in reality was a simple structure large enough only to shelter the *yogi*. The light blinded them as they came out of the door. The sun hit them like a hammer, and they blinked as a sudden gust of wind stirred up the dust. The crowd of Hindus standing outside the shelter had swelled when it was discovered that Brooke and Lassiter had come there. Now they waited, curious and expectant, silently accepting the headman of Chakrata as their spokesman.

"The plan we have decided upon is this, sahibs. We will remove the *samadh swami* from the hut, and place him in the open, here, in front of the door. He will know nothing feel nothing. Thus he will sit here in plain sight, night and day, and continue his meditation. Sooner or later, thus exposed, he will be discovered by Shaitan."

"And then?"

"What Shaitan will see is a full dinner, easily taken. What he will not know, is that the moment his jaws pull on the *yogi*, it will mean his sudden death."

Brooke was puzzled. "Bahalji, I don't follow."

"It is very simple," said the headman. "You have these explosive charges, these things of war you call grenades. Suppose you attach one to the *samadh swami*'s foot with a thin cord. Then bury it in the ground, so that the grenade cannot be seen by Shaitan. It can be so arranged that the grenade will explode once there is a pull on the cord. Is it not so?"

Brooke and Lassiter were silent for a moment or two. It took them a little while to let all of this sink in. Then Brooke said:

"Yes, Behalji, it can be arranged. The grenade can be set to explode the moment Shaitan pulls at the body. But there is one problem."

"Yes, Sahib? And what is that?"

"You told us the man inside is still alive. And will be for days."

"That is so."

Brooke felt a little ill. He glanced at Lassiter. He could see that he felt the same way.

"This is an interesting idea, Bahalji, my friend. And it might work. But we cannot be party to this. We are Christians, you see. We do not believe in human sacrifice."

"We are Hindus, Sahib, and neither do we. But I do not think you quite understand. This *yogi* has told everyone beforehand that he *wants* to pass into the next world, he wants to die. In this way he will get his wish, and in his trance he will not care, it will make no difference. He feels nothing, as I said, he now knows nothing of this world. Even if Shaitan sinks his teeth into the *yogi*'s flesh a moment before both he and the animal explode, he will feel no pain. In this way, Shaitan will be blown to bits, and many innocent lives will be saved for the future."

"It's still human sacrifice, Bahalji," said Brooke. "I appreciate what you are saying. But I don't think that we can go along."

"Sahib," pleaded Bahalji, "you still do not understand. Not fully. The *samadh swami* inside this hut now would *want* it that way. He would want to die in a cause like this. In order to achieve his status, he has sworn an oath before Vishnu to dedicate his life to others, to help his fellow men on earth. This is his purpose and his desire. And in what better way could he achieve his purpose than this?"

Brooke was shaken. He looked at Lassiter. He knew Lassiter was thinking exactly the way he was. As far as they were concerned, for all practical purposes, this *samadh swami* was dead. If not, technically speaking, he was as good as dead. In a sense, he was now bait meat, in the same way the dead buffalo had been, the one they had laced with cyanide. Except, of course, this was human meat. That was a hard fact you couldn't get around.

To finally end this ordeal, to finally see Shaitan dead, was something Brooke desperately wanted. He could see his mission accomplished. It could end all the weary weeks and months of tramping about the countryside, tracking a ghost, being frustrated time after time. It could free these people at last. It could release him from this prison up here, and he could get back to Delhi and Nora. Of course, the blowing up of the man-eater by using human bait such as this was not a very romantic way to end this mission. He and Tony Lassiter had discussed this once before. The newspapers and the public still wanted something more glamorous, the great white hunter bringing down Shaitan in a dramatic charge, standing firm in the face of onrushing danger, and firing the shot that would finish off the animal. That was what they expected. But as he and Lassiter had agreed, to hell with them, the public and the press, and what they expected. The idea was the same, as always.

To get this man-eater any way they could.

Brooke looked at the headman.

"Bahalji, a question."

"Yes, Sahib."

"You think Shaitan will really attack this *samadh swami?*"

"It is a chance, Sahib."

"Then, in that case, why not use as bait one of your people who has already died. Someone who has just died of the fever, or some other reason. Use him as the bait . . ."

Bahalji Singh shook his head. "No, Sahib. That would not do, Shaitan, as we have said, is a demon. If he takes a bite of a man's body, even before the explosion comes, then the descendants of that man will be visited by his evil spirit forever. More than that, a Hindu cannot go to the other world, to his heavenly peace, his soul cannot find another house someday, unless his body is properly burned and his ashes floated on the river which leads into the holy Ganges."

"But this *samadh swami* is also a Hindu."

"True, Sahib. But he is now beyond all harm of any evil, even the demon of Shaitan. He is, as I have told you, on the Mystic Path. He is in a state of bliss and emancipation, free of all fear, of the consequences of the real world. He is immune from all harm, even the spirit of Shaitan. No devil can enter his body, or touch his soul, or attack his ancestors. He does not have to be properly burned in the usual way, as long as he holds to his vow to help his fellow men. And Sahib, although you cannot speak to him, nor he to you, be assured that he would be ready and willing to do this."

There was a long silence. Then Brooke turned to Lassiter.

"Well, Tony, what do you think?"

"As far as I'm concerned, the man's dead already."

"I agree."

"In that case, why don't we go along with Bahalji here? And get on with it."

Late that afternoon, they tied the grenade to the *swami*'s foot, buried it in a small hole next to the foot, gently triggered it to go off at a slight pull and then filled the hole.

Lassiter suggested they build *machan*s in the trees in the vicinity of where the *swami* sat, but Brooke demurred. In the first place, he pointed out, there was a large open area around the spot where the holy man was meditating. The trees available for this were too far away. If they saw Shaitan coming up on the *swami*, it would take a long and lucky shot to bring him down. In the second place, this wouldn't be necessary, since if Shaitan took the bait he would be blown to hell anyway.

But even more important, Shaitan seemed to have an uncanny power to know when men were in his vicinity. He had painfully illustrated that to both of them, time and time again. They had never, in all these weeks, been able to get a good *look* at the man-eater, let alone get a shot at him. Brooke was baffled by this. The ordinary leopard did not have a good sense of smell. But this wasn't an ordinary leopard. This was Shaitan. A mysterious mutation of his own species. And if it was not his nose that detected humans in the vicinity, then it must have been some instinct, some sixth sense, that one might apply to humans but not to animals, especially the big cats.

The villagers were warned not to go anywhere near the *samadh swami*, either by day or by night. They were told to give Shaitan a clear field of entry. Shaitan was in the vicinity of Kotdwara. They knew this because only yesterday he had taken a small boy who had wandered from his mother, entered a wood, and started to climb a

tree after some birds' eggs. The boy had crawled halfway up the tree when the man-eater had leaped up,
clawed the trunk in his climb, and pulled down the unfortunate youngster. The grisly remains had been found
in an open field of wild arum lilies about three miles
outside of Kotdwara, and the rags of flesh had already
been eaten by the vultures. But a string of beads found
among the bones had identified the boy, and he would
be recorded as an official kill.

For the next three days, the samadh swami continued
on his Mystic Path undisturbed.

On the evening of the fourth night, it rained slightly.
In the morning, Brooke and Lassiter detected the
pugmarks of the man-eater. Also, the heavy impression
of Shaitan's body and the change in the depth of the
pugmarks meant, to the experienced eye, that Shaitan
had crawled up close to the *samadh swami*, so close that
he was only a few feet away.

But he had not touched the man.

After that, the pugmarks showed a normal path as the
man-eater had walked away. And finally, they became
lost in a nearby forest of cinchona trees.

Something had warned off Shaitan. Could he reason,
almost in a human way? Had he become suspicious,
decided that something was wrong here, unnatural?
How could he possibly know that this was a trap? The
samadh swami had lost considerable weight, but even
after these days of fasting still had some flesh on him. It
was an easy meal for Shaitan. All he had to do was
reach forward and take it.

Yet, he did not.

Brooke had one theory. He could not substantiate it,
but he expressed it anyway to Lassiter and Bahalji.

"Maybe he stayed away because his prey, this *swami*,
showed no fear. Every human being Shaitan has faced
has shown fear or terror. The *swami* just sat there. This

must have warned Shaitan off, made him suspicious.
Made him suspect some kind of trap.''

"That could be so, Sahib," said Bahalji. "But there
may be another reason as well.''

"Yes.''

"Remember, Ram Gwar was a *sadhu* before his spirit
entered the skin of Shaitan. Good or evil, he was still a
holy man. It is possible that he recognized that the
swami was also a *sadhu*. And that to attack him, when
he was on the Mystic Path, would bring evil consequences to Shaitan himself. Therefore, he did not touch
the *swami*.''

After a silence Tony Lassiter said, in disgust:

"Hell, Dennis. Who knows? Maybe Bahalji's right.
As far as I'm concerned, maybe his explanation is just
as good as any other. Right now, I'm ready to believe
anything, *anything* about this bloody bastard.''

19

THE FOLLOWING DAY the newspapers and mail were delivered by the *dak wallah* for the Chakrata area. They were sent, once a week, from district headquarters in Dehra Dun, carried a certain distance by a *chaprassi*, an office servant of Sir John Evans and then delivered to the regional postman.

Brooke had expected a letter from Nora Clymer, but was disappointed. He had not heard from her for three weeks. Their correspondence up to now had been fairly regular, but the content of the letters themselves were strangely restrained, almost formal, as though trying not to reveal the heat and passion lurking underneath. But there was always the shadow of Hugh Clymer between them. There was always the implied guilt in the almost stilted lines. She wrote that she hoped he was well, that he would finish off this terrible animal, and come back to Delhi, where he would once again be very welcome. She dreaded the coming of the hot season, which was almost upon them. They would all suffer terribly as usual. Meanwhile, she begged him to be careful, to take care of himself; she understood his frustration in being unable to, as yet, bag this monstrous man-eater.

He in turn wrote her that he was well, although tired and admittedly frustrated, and gave her some details as to the actual hunt itself, and hoped that soon it would be ended and he could get back to Delhi and see both her and his good friend, Hugh, again.

The letters said nothing—and everything. Both of

them ended with "Affectionately."

In the same batch of mail, Lassiter received word from Lahore. He was to prepare himself to abandon the mission at any time, and report to the regiment.

This meant that Brooke would soon have to hunt Shaitan alone. He did not relish the job. He had always been outraged at the way the press had ignored Tony Lassiter. Brooke was the star, the super-hunter; he was the drama on front stage, and they saw Lassiter only as a supporting actor. Tony had never complained about it, had never even mentioned it. But Brooke was infuriated. He loved and respected Tony Lassiter as much as one man could love and respect another. Tony was bloody good at hunting big game, and he was a crack shot. Brooke remembered Behra and what had happened there.

Moreover, Shaitan was five or ten times more dangerous than any big cat, tiger or leopard that he had ever tracked before. With two on one, Lassiter and himself, they would always have a better chance. In a charge, one of them could possibly get it. But in the process, the other man might bag the man-eater, the way it had happened at Behra.

Now, unless they got Shaitan in the next two weeks, it would be one-on-one. Just he and the leopard. Brooke thought of himself as having as much courage as any man. But the thought of this confrontation in view of all the frustrating weeks he had experienced raised the hairs on the back of his neck, and made the adrenalin flow.

Now, sitting on the veranda on this, a quiet Sunday afternoon, and having no mail, Brooke idly scanned the two-week-old newspapers.

He began with the *Times of India*.

The front page ran a series of brief news items. The influenza epidemic which had swept through the United States had now reached England and Europe. It was

announced from Buckingham Palace that Prince
George, the King's youngest son, had retired from the
navy to begin duties at the Foreign Office. The German
dirigible, the *Graf Zeppelin*, had just flown over Egypt
and Jerusalem, dropped mailbags over the Holy City,
and continued onward toward Syria. Fire had damaged
the German-Lloyd forty-six-thousand-ton liner, the
Europa, in Bremen. Daylight Saving Time would com-
mence in Britain at 2 A.M. on April 21. A British
monoplane had left Cranwell Airdrome in England and
landed at Karachi after covering more than four
thousand miles.

The lead story, of course, concerned that perpetual
thorn in the side of the Raj, Mohandas Karamchand
Gandhi.

After months of traveling throughout India, and
preaching his doctrine of *Satyagraha*, he had returned
to Sabarmarti for a long rest. He had celebrated the
marriage of his third son, Ramdas, and was now spending time in his *ashram*, hand-spinning and reading
verses from the *Bhagavad Gita*. His grandson, Rasik,
had died in February. Gandhi had stated to the press
that he had loved Rasik, but felt no grief. "Grief," he
was quoted as saying, "is only an infatuation. All men
die; then why should they fear death? A man is reborn
after death, or else he enters into eternal light, and there
are only these two happy possibilities. Then why should
I weep for my grandson?"

Gandhi was resting, but he had stirred the political
pot to a burning pitch. It was rumored, according to the
article, that he was plotting a symbolic ploy that would
ultimately mean the end of the Raj. The British administration had passed a law which provided that all salt
should be taxed. Gandi proposed to break this law. He
was planning, so it was said, to conduct a long march in
the direction of Dandi and ending on the sea coast near

Jalalpur, where the salt flats were located. There he would pick up a handful of salt and defy the British to tax him for it.

Meanwhile, the Simon Commission, sent out from England to negotiate the situation, was rebuffed. Its arrival was greeted with black flags and a widespread boycott. The viceroy was making heroic efforts to bring the antagonists to the conference table, but in vain. The leaders of the congress insisted that what they wanted, and would accept no less, was complete independence, *purna swaraj*. In counterpoint, the attitude of the Raj began to harden. It sent more troops to sensitive areas. It put more agitators in jail. The Hindus and the Muslims, besides their hostility to the Raj, were beginning to joust at each other as well. Meanwhile the government must face the hard facts, said the *Times*. The new Indian congress was feeling its oats, goaded on by young leaders like Jawaharlal Nehru and Subhas Chandra Bose.

In a box in the lower left-hand corner of the page was a number in boldface type, the number 316.

And beneath that, the brief announcement that Shaitan had taken another victim outside the village of Kornaprayaj, and this was now recorded as his three hundred sixteenth kill.

All of the newspapers in India, and those in England as well, continued to keep a daily box score on Shaitan. It was a regular feature, like the weather or the changing of the tides. And each time a new kill was recorded, it was another unspoken reproach to Dennis Brooke. Since Brooke had come to India, some four months ago, the *Times* had recently and pointedly printed the fact that the man-eater had made some twenty-six official kills, and probably many more that were not even reported.

Brooke's pursuit of Shaitan was still news. It was still

only a sideshow to the main event, especially now, in view of recent events. As far as Brooke was concerned it had little political impact, if any. The Raj was in trouble, and the killing of ten Shaitans could not change that. Still, it was an ongoing drama. Politics could be complicated, especially to people in the remote villages of India. But they understood the idea of the remote villages of India. But they understood the idea of a simple confrontation, man against beast. It had color and excitement and suspense. It was not simple news to the public at large; it was entertainment. At least, to those not directly affected.

But to those closely involved, Brooke and Tony Lassiter and Bahalji Singh and his people, it was far from entertainment. It was grim and it was grisly, and a struggle for survival, since Shaitan had frightened many from cultivating their crops. To the villagers, it was walking death, padding softly along on four paws, it was a ghost that could not be found, and therefore could not be killed. It was immune and it was immortal, a devil-demon who took his revenge with sharp teeth and lethal jaws and ripping claws. And nobody, not a single man, woman or child was safe, not even the Sahib himself.

Brooke turned to the second page.

The first thing to hit his eye was a photograph of Hugh Clymer. It had been taken some years ago, and he looked much younger. And underneath, the caption: ADC TO THE VICEROY SUCCUMBS. And underneath that, a subhead: *Sir Hugh Clymer Dead at 39*.

Stunned, Brooke glanced at the rest of the obituary.

Sir Hugh had prepared to leave in the morning for his office at the Viceregal Palace. He had been struck with a sudden fever. His bearer had immediately undressed him and put him to bed, and his wife, Lady Nora Clymer, had called the viceroy's personal physician, Dr.

C.T. Graham. Just before Dr. Graham arrived, Sir
Hugh was stricken by violent convulsions and died a few
minutes later. Physicians were unable to make a
diagnosis of the sudden fever. Sir Hugh was buried the
same evening in St. Martin's Cemetery. He leaves his
wife, Nora, and a brother and a sister in Hampshire,
England . . .

Brooke threw the paper down, walked into the
bungalow and poured himself a very large whiskey. He
drank it down and poured himself another. And still
another.

All that night he was unable to sleep.

Strange, the way it had happened. If one had made an
educated guess, it would be that if Sir Hugh died of anything, it would be of another stroke.

But if you lived in India, you had to prepare for
surprises. Especially during the hot season. Already it
had come to Chakrata. It stole in almost overnight, like
a thief. There was little or no spring in this part of India.
Brooke and Lassiter awoke to the hammering of the sun
slanting through the windows in the morning. It had a
special glare to it, like some newly-lit heavenly torch, it
had an *impact*, it hit you straight in the eyes, then thrust
through to the back of your skull and down your spine.
The wind died to a whisper, the heat bounced from the
ground, and went through and under your shorts,
scorching the skin, the humidity was like a wet and
stifling shroud. The harbingers of the hot season, the
koels and the brain-fever birds began their weird calls.
The tin-pot birds began their hammering sounds.
Jackals howled against the heat, and in the villages the
pariahs never stopped barking. Dogs went mad, spitting
rabies in their saliva, and most of the strays were killed.

The bungalow itself became a sweat box. Stifling heat
oozed and belched from every door and window.

Punkah wallahs pulled the ceiling fans back and forth, with little effect. Servants stuffed bundles of straw against the windows and doors. These were called *khas-khas* tatties, and water was flung upon them, in an effort to provide some cooling effect in the rooms. The result was very little relief and the terrible stink of mildew. Brooke and Lassiter slept on army cots on the lawn outside, protected themselves with mosquito nets and wrapped themselves in wet sheets so that the evaporation would insulate them a little against the heat. They always left their shoes on a chair; if you left them on the ground you might very well wake up to find a snake or a scorpion nestled in one of them. The *chow-kidar* stayed awake all night, standing guard on the veranda. There was always the threat of Shaitan, and Brooke and Lassiter kept their guns on a table next to their cots.

Brooke stared up at the stars through his mosquito net. He knew that if the heat was bad here, it would be worse, much worse in Delhi. To put it mildly, sheer hell. In the hot season in Delhi, the thermometer could reach one hundred and thirty degrees, even under the shade of a banyan tree. You never went without your topee, or some other kind of sun helmet, not for an instant, and you wore a special spine pad to protect the vertebrae from the relentless smash of the sun. It was a time, in the large cities as well as the villages, when the specter of disease and death was always with you. There were the minor ailments, the skin infections, eczema, impetigo, prickly heat, boils, and *dhobi* itch. But the hot weather also brought on malaria, dysentery, and the haunting threat of such plagues as cholera, typhoid, smallpox and rabies. In addition, the British in India were particularly vulnerable to other and mysterious fevers and infections not yet analyzed or isolated by Western doctors, and to which there were no known antidotes. Death often came suddenly in India, from maladies such as these, and this had happened to Hugh Clymer. Brooke noted he had been buried on the same evening. And he thought, grimly, this was the way it had to be in India. In the hot season, and with no refrigeration, a corpse would stink and start to rot away in a few hours.

Englishmen wilted in the hot season, those who could not get to the hill stations. They cursed it and endured it. It drained them of energy; they worked in darkened offices and darkened homes. It was hard to even stay awake, and some minds could not take it—and cracked. They waited for the first monsoon as though it were the coming of the Messiah. When the rain came on suddenly, perfectly respectable Englishmen and their wives had been known to run out in their gardens, stark naked and shouting their joy. Later, they would curse the rains, because they brought out snakes, cockroaches, mosquitoes, and an infinite number of insects, especially the large, ugly greenfly that seemed to settle over everything. When the greenfly left, you got a black beetle which everybody called the stinkbug, which insisted in getting into your food and your teacup; and after that came a small white species of moth, which in its sheer numbers made life miserable. The rains, as well as the hot season, made India a land of sudden death.

But Hugh Clymer had gone in the hot season, and was a case in point of the old India hands who knew that you could have breakfast with a friend in the morning and bury him at night.

It was hard for Dennis Brooke to really believe even now that the man who had been his best friend for so many years was now dead. And that he and Nora were now free.

He had heard nothing from her as yet. He knew that Nora was mourning her husband. She had loved Hugh Clymer for a long time; she had taken the shock of his

affliction and lived with him, and seen him through to
the end. In time, she would write to him. He could be
patient now. He could wait.

Two days later, her letter came.

My darling,

By this time, of course, you have heard that Hugh
is dead.

His death was so quick, so horrible. He was in
agony. He seemed to be burning alive in his bed
with the fever. He cried for water, and then could
not swallow it. And when he went into convulsions—oh, darling, darling, I do not want to write
about it any more, I do not want to think of it any
more. I know you loved Hugh as a friend, and he
loved you. And I—I loved one, and now another.

So—one part of my life is ended. And another
begins.

With you, my darling. The moment you come
back, the moment you kill this horrible man-eater,
and come back to me in Delhi. Please, Dennis,
please, please be careful. This animal, this Shaitan
is an inhuman beast—although the Hindus believe
he is human. Of course, that is nonsense. But we
all know he is dangerous, terribly dangerous. He
has, I am told, killed more than ten experienced
hunters before you. For months, darling, I have
met each morning with the prayer that you will not
be the eleventh. And I have ended each day in
dread, wondering whether you were still alive.

Darling, is it too much to ask for you to give up
this uselss hunt and come home? Lord knows, you
have tried, you've done your best. There is
nothing disgraceful about an honorable failure. If

anyone dared to criticize you for this, I would personally scratch out his eyes. I know how hard it would be for you to accept this suggestion. I know how proud you are, and I love you for it. But darling, please, think about it, consider it. There is no longer just one life involved here. There are two.

I love you, Dennis Brooke. I miss you. Am I being a hussy, with my husband dead for such a short time? Is this blasphemy for a woman only recently in widow's weeds? Then so be it. Let it be blasphemy. Let the poor sticks here who call themselves responsible women natter and gossip and raise their eyebrows. I don't care, I don't give a damn. I want to see you smile, and hear your voice, and feel your touch and the strength of your arms around me, and the feel of your mouth on mine. I want you in bed with me, as close as a man and woman can get in this world. Am I being immodest, darling? I don't care. I feel what I feel, I want what I want, and if I'm being terribly naughty, so be it.

Each day now is forever while you are away. Sometimes I see you caught by surprise by that animal, and dangling in his jaws, and hear his teeth grinding into your beloved flesh, and I want to scream out loud. The dreams I've had! Nightmares.

Oh God, Dennis, do be careful. One way or another, come back to me. After you do, I want to leave Delhi, I want to leave India behind me forever. I have had enough of it, I hate it, I hate it. We'll go home. Or if it isn't England, then anywhere else in the world you wish to go. Only come back soon.

I love you, I love you, I love you.
NORA

Brooke read the letter three times.

God, he thought, *I'd love to be in Delhi.* Every bone, every muscle in his body ached to be in Delhi. He gritted his teeth, his anger boiled up inside of him, and during the night he swore softly at the stars he saw through his mosquito netting. Damn it, he could be in Delhi with Nora now if it weren't for this damned mission, if it weren't for that spotted furry jailer who kept him here, who held him in thrall.

Shaitan.

All he wanted was to find the bloody bastard. All he wanted was to hopefully close with him, settle the issue once and for all. One way, or the other.

Only then could he be free, in the total sense of the word.

He did not know, he could not possibly know, that he would get his wish. And much sooner than he thought.

20

IT HAPPENED JUST two days later. Shaitan had caught
a pilgrim in broad daylight, just outside of Chakrata.
The report had come in quickly, and the man-eater's
trail would be warm. Tony Lassiter, despite the large
doses of quinine they both took, had come down with
malaria. He had taken to his bed with a raging fever,
and Brooke had gone after the leopard alone.

He had tracked Shaitan along the pilgrim road for
awhile. Then the pugmarks veered off into a ravine,
beyond which was a small valley. He caught a trail of
blood drippings through the undergrowth, and he was
sure that the man-eater had come through the ravine
and entered the valley itself. The valley was unwooded,
and Brooke calculated that if he could now sight
Shaitan on the clear ground ahead, he might have his
first good shot at him. He shivered a little as his excitement mounted. He could feel his blood quickening,
the adrenalin flowing. The undergrowth disappeared,
the bed of the ravine became sandy and Brooke could
clearly make out the tracks of the man-eater. On each
side of the ravine were banks of stone, and gradually
these banks became higher. They were too much for any
man to climb, since the rains long ago had worn the
stone smooth.

Suddenly, the pugmarks vanished, abruptly.

Brooke stopped, stunned. Where had Shaitan gone?
It occurred to him that the man-eater must have climbed
to the top of the ravine, a feat within his power, given
the clutch of his claws. The question was, why? Why

take this difficult route when the path in the ravine led so easily into the valley?

He knew what had happened now. Shaitan somehow had known that Brooke had been following him. He had climbed to the top of the ravine and was somewhere up there now, looking down at Brooke, in a beautiful position for a surprise leap directly down on his pursuer.

Suddenly, Brooke heard a low cough. The cough came from somewhere just above and behind him. And very close. He tensed, sure that the leopard had led him into a trap and was now crouched, ready to spring at any moment.

Brooke turned his head, looked up, and for the first time from the corner of his eye, got a decent look at his nemesis.

Shaitan was standing there, watching him. His recent prey, already half-eaten, was still in his jaws. He dropped the grisly remains, and his yellow eyes looked directly into Brooke's.

What Brooke saw was a cat of all cats, and he had seen many in his lifetime. He was a magnificent animal, huge in size. More than that—gigantic. He was sudden death, but there was an awful beauty about him. His fur glistened and rippled in the high sun, his rosettes were many-colored, gold, orange, black and ocher, an incandescent coat covering the silky, smooth muscles. There was something special about this cat, an aura, something that set him aside from the rest of his species. Brooke, even in his vulnerable position, even in his heart-stopping fear, was aware of this. It did not seem possible that such a beautiful thing, a perfect creation of nature, beyond the brush of any artist to reproduce in its breathtaking beauty, could be such an engine of evil destruction.

His tail beat gently, up and down, like that of a playful kitten. There was no angry growl, no hostile hiss. Strangely, Shaitan was purring. He was not crouched in a springing position, and he watched his pursuer in what seemed to be a familiar way, as though he had seen Brooke many times before.

At the moment, Brooke was carrying his .275 rifle. Shaitan was above, but a few feet behind him, and Brooke knew that in order to get a shot at the man-eater, he would have to swing the gun barrel around slowly, very slowly, to reach the right position so as to get off a full shot. But all this would take time. And at any moment, before Brooke could get the gun around, Shaitan could leap upon him.

Brooke knew he had very little chance, and he knew that the leopard knew it. In fact, he had the idea that Shaitan not only knew Brooke's predicament, he relished it.

Suddenly, he saw Shaitan *smile*.

Brooke stood there, paralyzed, astounded. He knew that animals could not smile. Dogs could not, cats could not. But this was a real smile he saw on Shaitan's face, a *human* smile. The mouth parted, the lips turned upward, the opaque yellow eyes, normally in fixed position, suddenly became animated, they became alive, they *moved*. And Brooke was sure he heard a hoarse chuckle come from the leopard's throat.

It seemed to Brooke that Shaitan was teasing him, laughing at him, was enjoying this game they had played, the game of cat-and-mouse, and wanted it to go on. Otherwise, he could have had Brooke between his jaws with one leap, could have caught him entirely by surprise. The smile seemed to tell Brooke that his time would come. But not now. Not quite yet.

The smile seemed to be friendly, almost affectionate. It seemed to say, let the game go on, we shall see each other again. But it also said, in a condescending way, you do not have a chance, my friend. You will never have a chance, so why try so hard?

Brooke felt faint. He kept his head turned at the same awkward angle so that he could see the leopard over and just behind him, and his neck ached. His eyes began to blur, he felt dizzy. He did not, could not, believe what he was seeing. But there it was. Dimly, he wondered whether Shaitan proposed to simply stand there, and wait for him to make the first move.

Almost automatically, his hand tightened around his gun. He knew that since Shaitan was behind him, he could not get a shot at the man-eater unless he swung his body and rifle around at the same time. He did not want to alert the leopard by trying a quick move with his gun. The man-eater was lightning-fast; he would react to this hostile move before Brooke could get the gun around and up and take aim. He knew that if he got a shot off at all, it would have to be by stealth.

Almost imperceptibly, Brooke began to turn his body and swing the muzzle of his rifle around in a low arc. Luckily, he had the safety catch off. His hope was that he would somehow, in this way, catch Shaitan by surprise. *Slowly*, he thought, *slowly*. He felt the stock of the gun catch him in the side as he turned, then felt it slide by. He continued to swing closely. The leopard merely stood there, smiling down at him. A feeling of exaltation rose in Brooke. His blood quickened, his skin tingled. The leopard seemed unaware of what he was up to. He was only a few yards away. It would be a high shot, thought Brooke, but very close and almost impossible to miss.

The leopard still stood there, watching him.

Another inch or two, Brooke thought feverishly, and I'll be in line, I'll have a chance to wipe that bloody, insane smile off the bugger's face forever. He began to feel the full weight of the rifle in his hands.

With a quick jerk, he spun and fired.

But an instant before that, the man-eater had vanished. Brooke heard the shot echo and reverberate through the valley. A frightened covey of pheasants roared up from a nearby patch of brush. He heard the alarmed chattering of langurs, distant in the mango trees down the valley.

Brooke stared at the spot where Shaitan had stood. At first he imagined he had experienced some kind of fantasy, that he was seeing things, that he had conjured up this beast, as a man can conjure up the mirage of an oasis in the desert.

I never saw him, he thought. *He wasn't real, he did not exist.*

But he had been real, all right. The evidence lay in the grisly remains of Shaitan's recent prey. He had left it on the ground—a headless and half-eaten torso.

Brooke felt weak, drained. His legs trembled; they could not support him. He sat down heavily on the ground, the rifle resting in the crook of his arm. He looked up into the hot blue sky. The vultures had already begun to arrive. They had noted the pitiful remains of the corpse. Brooke thought, perhaps they were somewhat disappointed.

Perhaps they had had greater expectations.

When he got back to the bungalow, he found Lassiter up and around, somewhat weakened but feeling much better. In Lassiter's case, his malaria was unpredictable. Sometimes it came on suddenly. But often the high fever would last for a few hours and then terminate, just as suddenly.

When Brooke came into the main room, he was drenched in sweat. The heat in the bungalow was almost intolerable; the slow-moving pull-*punkah*s in the ceiling did little more than stir the sluggish air. Now, in late afternoon, it was even hotter on the veranda, and they would move outside only when darkness came.

Brooke felt strange, a little dizzy, his mind wandering in some limbo. He stripped naked and stretched out on his *charpoy*. He lay there supine, staring up at the ceiling, watching intently the slow progress of a small green lizard as it made its erratic way across the bamboo surface.

Lassiter looked at Brooke.

"Anything wrong, old man?"

"No."

"You haven't said a bloody word since you came in."

"Sorry."

"You look done in. Pale as my topee. As though you've seen a ghost."

"I have."

"What?" Lassiter's eyes widened. Then he almost yelled: "Shaitan? You saw Shaitan?"

"More than that. I got a shot at him."

"And?"

"He was too quick. I missed."

"Christ, what a bloody shame. Well, at least someone's got a good look at him. I mean, you have. For a while, I was beginning to believe the bugger wasn't really—well, real." Lassiter yelled for the *khitmagar*. "Raju, bring Sahib Brooke and myself two *burra-pegs*, double whiskeys, you understand, big ones." Then he turned to Brooke. "All right, old man. Tell us about it."

For a moment, Brooke was tempted to tell Lassiter about the smile. He felt he had to tell somebody or burst. But he held back. He knew the reaction he would get. Lassiter would think he had gone mad. Heat-crazy. It happened often in the hot season. What was the old cliché? "Only mad dogs and Englishmen walk in the noonday sun." Maybe the heat *had* got to him. Maybe

there wasn't this smile at all, maybe it was all in his
bloody imagination, maybe his eyes and brain had
pasted that smile on the man-eater's face because the
animal had frustrated him for so long and was enjoying
his success.

He was aware of the glass of whiskey thrust into his
hand and he heard Lassiter say again:

"Come on, Dennis. Let's hear about it."

He told Lassiter what had happened, omitting any
mention of the smile. Lassiter thought about it a
moment, then said, puzzled:

"He had you dead on and didn't jump you?"

"That's right."

"Now, he knows about us. He knows we're hunting
him."

"He's known that for a long time."

"Right. Then why didn't he jump you, when it was
such an easy chance?"

"I don't know."

"There's only one possible reason, old man."

"Yes? What's that?"

"He'd just had his dinner. Wasn't hungry. Probably
figured he'd save you for a little later. Make a meal out
of you then." Lassiter shook his head. "Still, it's
damned funny. You're *sure* he had you dead?"

"Absolutely."

They drank their whiskeys and ordered others. They
lay on their *charpoy*s listlessly, the sweat dripping from
their naked bodies. Lassiter lit a cigarette and watched
the sluggish *punkah* fans swirl the smoke into odd
patterns against the ceiling.

"This bloody heat," said Lassiter. "Thank God, I'll
be out of it soon. Should be cooler up on the Northwest
Frontier. And maybe I'll see a little action for a change.
This mission's got on my nerves, I must admit."

Brooke sat up, straight.

"What are you talking about?"

"Oh. Forgot to tell you, old man. Orders just came in from Lahore. Straight from his eminence, Colonel Sir Gilbert Cashmore, KBE, CIE. Definite. I'm to join the regiment in ten days. Leave here in a week, three days travel. The Guards are moving to the Frontier." He paused, and cleared his throat. "Sorry, old man. From now on you'll have to go it alone."

Brooke was silent for a moment. Then:

"I'll miss you, Tony."

"Thanks. The same to you, Dennis. Half of me wants to stay and still have a go at it." He shrugged. "But still . . ."

"I know. I wish I was out of it."

"The bastards," said Lassiter, softly. "I mean, these newspaper people. All that snide complaining we've been reading about. Five months or so up here, and nothing done. They don't know how big or heavy this monkey is. The one you're carrying on your back. Sitting on their fat asses, back there on Fleet Street, counting the kills Shaitan is making, and wondering what you've been doing, *we've* been doing. When I get back to Lahore, I'll have something to say to the bloody press, Dennis. I'm going to blister their dirty ears."

Lying under his mosquito net, staring up at the moon, Dennis Brooke felt feverish. His brain whirled, his mind's eye saw only one thing.

That smile.

Again he questioned his sanity. Did I see it? Did I really see it? Or did I just *imagine* I saw it, through some strange vaporing of my brain. If I was right, that was a human smile, and Shaitan is indeed the incarnation of the *sadhu*, Ram Gwar. Or the reincarnation. He was never sure which word to use.

If you believe the theory of reincarnation, a man

never really dies. His flesh dies but his soul goes on. In time, it finds a new resting place in another body. And he lives again.

But this cannot be. This has to be nonsense, he told himself.

Yet, *was* it?

Brooke was shaken. He tossed and turned. It seemed especially hot tonight, especially humid. The sweat rolled from him in droplets. There was a water jar on a small table next to the cot. He reached under the mosquito net, took the jar, removed the cover, and took a long draught. The water was tepid and stank of chlorine. He forced it down.

Reincarnation.

I saw that smile, I *saw* it.

Damn it, Brooke, what's the matter with you? You saw nothing. You're sick. Your brain is addled. You're thinking like a bloody Hindu.

Now, he told himself, maybe I am.

He knew there were millions upon millions in the world who believed in reincarnation. In India it was a simple fact. People were born, they died, and they were renewed and recreated. In the West there were some who believed in it. But to the majority, they were a bit around the bend, eccentrics, freaks. The British establishment in India made fun of it, privately. He remembered that years ago, he had attended what was called a Reincarnation Party at the Turf Club in Calcutta. The invitation had said: 'Come As You Were.' People showed up in the damnest costumes. The men came dressed as Napoleon, Caesar, King Arthur or Genghis Khan. the women came as Joan of Arc, Mary, Queen of Scots, Cleopatra or Portia. It was characteristic that they had all conceived of themselves, even in fun, as once being personalities of great fame. It was typical of their class, a collective ego. None came as a bricklayer, or a common soldier, or a slave who once helped build the pyramids.

The Hindu was different. In his next life, in the process of *karma*, he did not aspire or expect anything greater than some small improvement. The man dying on the streets of Calcutta, who lived on one handful of rice and owned one dirty *dhoti*, hoped in his next life to have two or three handfuls of rice and one or two clean *dhoti*s. The humble *bhisti*, or water carrier, might hope in his next life to be a *derze*, or tailor, and the lowly Untouchable would pray that in his next round, he would come up a rung in his caste and be a Touchable, *any* Touchable.

The simple Indian peasant or villager lived in two simple dimensions. One was the ordinary world of the sun and the weather, or crops, sex, work and gossip. The other was a dim world, half-lit and mysterious, the world of temple rites and meditation, of contemplation of the gods and the hereafter, and of concern as to what his new life would be. He would think Vishnu or Brahma or Buddha for such small favors as a modest improvement in his status the next time around, and place flowers before the effigy of his deity to remind him of this prayerful wish.

From the beginning, Dennis Brooke had been interested in the legend that Shaitan was truly the evil *sadhu*, Ram Gwar, in leopard's clothes. Bahalji Singh had told him that the Hindus fervently believed that some men, especially those who professed to be holy men, could choose the form of life they wished to live the next time around. Brooke had been in India a long time, and he knew something of its mythology. He knew that the Hindus worshipped a divine trinity of three main gods, Brahma the Creator, Vishnu the Preserver, and Siva the Destroyer.

A few weeks ago, a swami named Jagadish Shandra

had come along the pilgrim path headed for the shrines of Lahore. He had stopped at Chakrata to rest, and he had been a guest in the house of Bahalji Singh. The headman had invited both Brooke and Lassiter to meet the great man. Jagadish Shandra proved to be a highly educated scholar. He spoke English as well as many of the languages and dialects of India. He knew intimately, and could recite by memory, the readings from the Vedanta and the *Gita*, the holiest of Indian scriptures, and he was a scholar in Sanskrit.

Upon questioning by Brooke, Jagadish Shandra had explained how reincarnation really came about. Brooke had previously had an explanation from Bahalji Singh, but Jagadish Shandra went much further into the subject, in detail. And he had explained:

"What we call the Clear Light, Sahib, and what you call the soul leaves the body and begins to wander in the cosmos, in the twilight of the everlasting space. After two weeks or perhaps a little more, the past life of this astral spirit becomes dim. At that time, floating around in the void, it begins to develop a longing to be manifest again, to be something or somebody. If its past life in its past house of flesh has been good, the things of beauty it encountered on earth, the people it loved on this earth, come back to it in memory, and the enchantments of life are illuminated. It remembers what was beautiful and rejects all that is base. It hears the sound of the waves, and the rush of tides, and the happy cries of children and the singing of birds. It recalls again the love of wife or husband and the warmth of friends, and senses those spiritual joys it could never reach in the flesh. There may or may not be any desire for action, or the mind may prefer to rest forever in the smooth, sweet stream of Nirvana. But if there is a desire for action, then sooner or later the soul must return for another cycle of birth and death."

"Then the soul decides whether to reincarnate or not?"

"Precisely, Sahib. So it is written in the *Bardo Thodol*, the Book of the Dead. Most often it decides to return. From the cold regions of the void, of outer space occupied only by gods and demons, it looks down upon the warm and friendly world and remembers the way life was. A spell comes over it. It feels an irresistible urge to be housed in flesh and blood again. It sees the endless union of man and woman on earth, and now has the powerful urge to enter a womb. In its last moments in space, it chooses its carrier, and at the very last moment, it faints into unconsciousness. So, Sahib, the past is forgotten by the soul, and the future assumed."

"You said the soul can *choose* the body it wishes to enter?"

"Within certain degrees, yes."

"Then the soul can choose *any* body—man or beast?"

"If permitted by the gods, yes. It may choose the vehicle or the carrier for his reincarnation, depending on his character and the actions of his previous life. Good tends to choose good, and evil, evil. Sometimes, there are other motives. The soul, or Clear Light, floats into limbo or the void, restlessly. It can be obsessed by some hurt or insult in its previous life. It may lust to return to earth only to seek revenge. And if so, it will find the vehicle to attain this revenge."

"Then in the case of Ram Gwar, he chose—Shaitan."

"Exactly, Sahib. As a man-eating leopard, which they had accused him of being in his previous life, he could thus satisfy his lust for revenge, and wreak destruction upon the people who had wronged him. And this, as you well know, Sahib, he has done."

When Brooke and Lassiter said goodnight, Lassiter was amused.

"These *gurus*. They tell the damndest stories. For a minute or two, he had me half-believing all that rot about your soul floating around in space, looking for a place to settle down." Lassiter laughed. "God, I wish he was right. If he was, and my soul *was* looking around for a new place to park, you know what I'd choose?"

"What?"

"I thought at first I'd like to be reincarnated as the colonel of the Regiment. But then, that seemed rather a modest choice. I think I'd like to crawl into the womb of the queen, and one day be King of England."

Brooke smiled at that, but lying here now, Lassiter's remark somehow did not seem so amusing. There was no way for Jagadish Shandra to prove all this. But in the same sense, no one could prove the existence of the pearly gates, or heaven or hell. On balance, the *swami*'s story seemed almost believable, considering the existence and the strange behavior of Shaitan.

Suddenly he remembered a fragment of a poem he had read. It all seemed a hundred years now, but he had read it at Cheltenham, where he and Hugh Clymer had been schoolmates, and all these years it had been stuck, long forgotten, in some tiny compartment in his mind. There was a class in which they had been studying the great poets of England, and he remembered now, it was something by Wordsworth. He did not remember the name of the poem itself, nor the rest of its contents, but now he clearly recalled the one fragment:

> The soul that rises with us, our life's star,
> Hath had elsewhere its setting,
> And cometh from afar.

He slept fitfully, and awoke just before dawn. He still felt feverish; his brain was still reeling, torn by his own doubts, still thinking that it must have been his imagination, that damn it, no animal can really smile, despite the claims of a few fanatical and overly fond pet owners who swore they had seen their cat or dog smile when they had entered the house after some long absence.

Yet, he told himself, *I saw it*, I swear I saw it.

Whether he did or not, the point was that he had come out here to destroy Shaitan. This had been his mission, whether Shaitan was just another leopard, or the incarnation of this bloody *sadhu*. Now that he and Shaitan had met, eyeball-to-eyeball, so to speak, Brooke had a feeling that somehow this was a symbol, the beginning of an end at last, the first smell of a final confrontation. And Brooke could not wait. The sooner the better. Every day up here was a century, knowing that Nora was waiting for him in Delhi.

In the back of his mind, for the past week, an idea had been growing. A way to trap Shaitan, a way they hadn't tried before. It seemed so simple, so obvious, that Brooke wondered why he hadn't thought about it sooner. It was a plan that *might* work, and it required Shaitan's unknowing cooperation. If he walked into the trap, Brooke knew that finally they would bag him.

If.

21

SOME FIVE MILES north of Chakrata there was a narrow stream of rushing water called by the natives Babu Ganges, or Little Ganges. It was fed by the ice-cold waters that came down from the Himalayas. And at this time of the year, in the late spring, it was running high, at the peak of its power.

This stream separated such villages as Chakrata, Tehri, Ramnagas and Rampur on the south side of the stream, from other villages, notably Chandpur, Bijnor, Gangotri and Pauri on the north side.

At breakfast Brooke said to Lassiter.

"Tony, the leopard operates on both sides of the Little Ganges. Right?"

"Right."

"Doesn't seem to make any difference where he makes his kills. On the north side or the south side. Does that mean anything to you?"

"Not particularly."

"All right, Tony. Follow me on this. If he operates easily on both sides, how does he cross the river?"

"I imagine he swims across."

"My guess is that he doesn't. I agree, a leopard can swim, but he doesn't like it, and he won't if he can avoid it. Not only that. I doubt whether he could get across even if he wanted to. That current is pretty damned strong."

"Well, he'd *have* to swim across, Dennis. There's no other way for him to make it."

"You're wrong, Tony. Suppose he was getting across

on that swing bridge, between Ramnagas and Chandpur?"

Lassiter put down his coffee cup.

"Impossible, old man. Definitely impossible."

"Is it? Why? Men cross it every day."

"Men. Yes. But you're talking about an animal. And I don't think a dog would even try it. And remember, this Shaitan is heavy—I don't know how many pounds he carries, we know he's big. And he's no fool. That bridge is weak and dangerous. Every time I cross it, I get the bloody shivers for fear it'll snap. What makes you think he'd take a chance like that?"

"Because I don't see any other way he can get from one side to the other."

"Maybe he goes way downstream, where the river's quieter."

"No. I doubt that. He'd have to travel miles. And we know from tracking him that he can make a kill on one side of the river, and then the other, all in the space of three hours. I'll wager that he doesn't swim that torrent. Which leaves that bridge."

"If you want to call it that. I call it Suicide Walk." Lassiter stared at Brooke. "All right. Suppose you're right. What then?"

"Don't you see it, Tony? We build two *machan*s, one on the north side of the river, the other on the south. Close to the bridge. Then we sit and wait. If I'm right, sooner or later, Shaitan will cross that bridge. It'll be sometime at night. He knows he'd be too conspicuous during the daytime. Once he starts across that bridge and gets well onto it, we've got him. He can't move very fast in one direction or the other. One of us, maybe both, are sure to get a good shot at him."

Lassiter nodded at Brooke.

"Like a fish in a barrel."

"Exactly."

Lassiter jumped·up from the table, caught by the idea. He walked around the room, exhilarated, his eyes shining.

"Jolly good, Dennis. It *could* work. We'd bag the bugger for good. If he shows up."

"If," said Brooke, hopefully. "If, if, *if*."

The swing bridge, if it could be dignified by that name, was called a *jhula* by the Hindus of the region. It was the only way to cross the stream at that point. Otherwise, the villagers would have to walk some ten miles downstream, where the water was calmer, in order to cross by poled raft.

The *jhula* spanned only some fifty yards from one wall or rock to another, and a few feet below it the water foamed and thundered and shot mist and spray upward onto the walk of the structure, making it dangerously slippery. There were no handrails. The bridge consisted of two cables, made of strips of bamboo connected to each other by knotted strips of sisal rope. This rope had been rotted by time, and weakened even more by the erosive effect of the spray shooting up from the river. The footway itself consisted of sticks and slats separated from each other by a foot or two in an irregular pattern, and hooked to the cables with the same moldy sisal rope. To cross it an any time took a fine sense of balance, and in a good wind this bamboo-and-wood spider web would sway back and forth so much so that no one would even dare try to cross it. The villagers were surefooted, and they used the *jhula* regularly, but now and then someone lost his balance and plunged down into the rushing water. Some were dashed against the rocks by the strong current and died. Others, somehow, managed to evade the rocks and finally emerged, half-drowned, in one of the quiet lagoons which lay off the river downstream.

Since the *jhula* was some distance from the bungalow,
Brooke and Lassiter arranged to have two porters, who
were both gun bearers and packmen, come along and set
up camp not far from the bridge in an open field, where
Shaitan would find it difficult to attack, without
warning. In this way, the hunters could sleep by day, after
staying up all night on their tree platforms, guns ready,
waiting and hoping that the man-eater might appear.

It seemed that if they waited long enough, the leopard
would inevitably show up to cross the bridge. When he
made a kill on one side, at Brooke's urging, people
stayed in their houses during both night and day, for a
few days at a time. This made food scarce, and after a
short period Brooke guessed that the man-eater would
inevitably try the other side.

Brooke occupied a tree platform just beyond the
bridge on the north side, and Lassiter took up his vigil in
a *machan* on the south side. Their positions were close
to the bridge, and such that if Shaitan crossed the frail
structure, they would both have an easy shot at
him—perhaps two.

Night after night they sat in their tree platforms and
waited. And night after night—nothing. They waited
for five nights, sitting through two of them in a drench-
ing downpour.

On the sixth day, they received a report that Shaitan
had waited outside a house in the village of Bijnor.
There he had caught a boy who had simply opened the
door to let out a dog. They knew then that for the time
being Shaitan was roaming on the south side. And if he
crossed the *jhula* at all, he would make his entry on the
south, or Lassiter's side.

They waited during two more fruitless nights. It came
time for Lassiter to get back to the bungalow, pack his
gear and leave for his regiment. On the seventh day

Brooke said:

"If Shaitan doesn't show up tonight, Tony, it's the end. We'll pack it all in tomorrow morning and leave. Can't have you late getting to Lahore."

"Right," said Lassiter. "Maybe tonight will be the night."

"Maybe," said Brooke.

But he didn't believe it. Like it or not, he had to credit Shaitan with a human brain. And Shaitan may have come near the bridge, became aware of their presence somehow and avoided the crossing. Brooke was sure that they would never see Shaitan anywhere near the *jhula*.

In this, he was wrong.

The night, like the others, passed without incident.

Just after dawn Brooke climbed down from his *machan*. He signalled Lassiter to come down from his tree platform and cross the bridge to the north side. The packman, who had been ordered by daylight to come to the bridge area and pickup the guns and any remaining gear, appeared and joined Brooke.

Brooke had his back to the bridge when he heard a sudden yell from Lassiter.

He turned to see Lassiter backing slowly toward the bridge. The sight froze Brooke's blood. Facing Lassiter was Shaitan. He had suddenly emerged from the forest on the other side. He was hissing and growling, his yellow eyes fixed on his prey. After that single yell, Lassiter seemed paralyzed, hypnotized. And he was unarmed. When he had come down from the tree, he had leaned his gun against the tree to exercise and stretch his muscles after a long night of sitting in one position. It was then that Shaitan had surprised him.

Brooke watched in horror as the man-eater took a step or two toward Lassiter, then crouched, ready to

spring. He had Lassiter trapped, his back to the fragile
bridge, now swinging and swaying in the wind.

At the moment Brooke's Mannlicher was in the hands
of one of the packmen. Brooke ran over and snatched it
from him. At the same moment, Lassiter turned and ran
onto the bridge. Brooke watched in horror as his friend
slipped and stumbled on the treacherous, slippery-wet
floorwalk. A sudden gust of wind caught the bridge and
swung it in a wider arc. Lassiter lost his balance,
screamed, and fell over the side into the raging torrent
below.

The man-eater stood still for a moment, watching
Lassiter fall from the bridge. Brooke snapped loose the
safety catch on the Mannlicher and took aim at the
leopard. It was an easy shot, perhaps seventy-five or a
hundred yards. But as he set his aim, he saw the smile
again. The same smile, breaking out on the whiskered
face. Brooke's eyes blurred. His hands trembled. The
minute he fired, he knew that he had missed, the shot
had gone high. Shaitan whirled and darted back into the
forest. Brooke fired again, but his shot was wild. It was
too late.

He heard the packmen shouting. They were running
along the top of the north bank of the stream, trying to
follow Lassiter, who was being borne along helplessly
like a cork in the raging current, buffeted from one side
to another, trying to keep his head above water. The
water in the center of the stream was deep, and each
bank was lined with sharp and treacherous rocks. At
any moment, the rush of water could slam Lassiter
against the rocks with enough force to mash in his head
or crush his body.

Brooke raced after the packmen along the rocky ledge
overlooking the stream, and caught up with them. He
shouted at Lassiter to hang on. He knew it was useless,
that his friend was totally at the whim of the raging

current. Miraculously, it seemed, the river decided to spare Lassiter. When it finally smashed Lassiter to one side, there were no rocks facing him. Instead, he was propelled into a quiet pool of water, a small lagoon formed by a kind of natural basin which caught the overflow of the rushing stream.

Lassiter lay floating on his back for a moment, resting. As Brooke and the packmen caught up to him and stood on the shore watching him, he smiled at them. Brooke said anxiously:

"Are you all right, Tony?"

"I'm alive," said Lassiter. "At the moment, I'll settle for that." He coughed and gagged. Then he gasped: "Took in a little water, I'm afraid . . ."

He stopped floating and treaded water a moment. The water was deep in the pool, but Lassiter was only a few feet away from shore. After a stroke or two, he finally found footing on the muddy bottom. Now, shoulder deep, he was just starting to come out of the pool when it happened.

A thick green and white coil leaped out of the water, topped by an obscene black reptilian head. The jaws of the head snapped open and seized Lassiter's neck in its teeth. It hung on, and a moment later Lassiter was encircled by two more coils of the huge snake's body.

Brooke and the packmen stood rooted in horror. Lassiter's body bulged.

"Oh, my God, Dennis!" he screamed. "Oh, my God!"

He tried to fight the pulling, squeezing pressure of the coils. But he was helpless. He was in the grip of a water python, the anaconda boa, the largest snake in India, sometimes stretching thirty feet in length and weighing over five hundred pounds. The coils of the great snake glistened wetly in the sun as they started to constrict Lassiter's body, squeezing the breath out of him. The sharp, backward pointing teeth of the snake continued to stay fixed in Lassiter's neck.

Lassiter's face was pale, a mask of horror. He looked up pathetically at Brooke, only a few feet away.

"Please, Dennis," he croaked. "Please. Please . . ."

Brooke knew what Lassiter was begging for. The agony on his face, his eyes said it all. He wanted Brooke to end the horror now. The nausea rose in Brooke's throat, he was sobbing uncontrollably, as he raised the Mannlicher and aimed it directly at the ugly head of the python. He fired.

The heavy slug tore through the head of the python, and continued through Tony Lassiter's neck, killing him instantly. The coils of the python began pulling Lassiter back into deep water. His body was inert now, a wet lump, still. Brooke fired again, and then again, ripping the coils of the great snake. But they would not let Lassiter go. Slowly they pulled him beneath the surface of the water, leaving a bubbling, bloody froth on the surface of the pool.

After that, Brooke threw down his gun. Then he vomited. Again, and again.

He sank to his knees, put his hands over his face, and wept until he was exhausted.

He was still in shock when he finally returned to the bungalow. But he knew then that he could no longer go on. He was through. Finished. Tired and beaten. In his body and soul.

The winner and still champion—Shaitan.

And to hell with everybody, and everything.

The following morning Dennis Brooke, still in shock, closed the bungalow and prepared to leave for Dehra Dun.

There he would deliver an official report of the tragedy to the deputy commissioner, and announce that he was abandoning the mission. Then Delhi. But before that, he planned to make an ovenight stop at Lahore, for a special and personal reason.

Now he had to face the agony of going to Chakrata and saying goodbye to Bahalji Singh and his people. He had already arranged for a bullock cart there to take him to the railroad station at Bisalpur, where he would make train connections for Dehra Dun.

He entered Chakrata and walked down the dusty main street, followed by his bearers carrying his guns and other equipment. He saw that everyone in the village had gathered in front of the bazaar. At the central well, Bahalji Singh and his son, Ranga, stood in front of the others. He noted that the bazaar was closed, a sign of public mourning, as though some prominent person had died.

The villagers watched him approach in dead silence. These were the same people who welcomed him almost as a god some months ago, throwing flowers in his path, bending over to touch his shoes, his clothes. Now their faces seemed to accuse him, reproach him for deserting them. Some, as he came nearer, turned their heads away, avoiding his eyes, and a few of the women covered their faces with the folds of their saris.

Dennis Brooke wanted to shout at them, he almost wanted to scream at them, don't you understand? I can't do it anymore. My nerves are shot, I'm sick in my body and my soul, I'm empty and I'm drained, I'm finished. But he was still British, whatever happened, he was still a sahib and under the Raj, and to blurt out your emotions in this manner simply wasn't done. You could not, he was reminded bitterly "let down the side."

And so he said, simply and in Hindi, to Bahalji Singh:

"I am sorry, Bahalji. I have failed you and your people. There is nothing more I can do here. You know how I have tried."

"Yes, Sahib. We know."

"This Shaitan. I now believes as you do. I believe that he bears the demon soul of Ram Gwar. I have reason for this which I shall not discuss now. But he has proved my master. And this I fully confess. As you know, I have always loved you and your people. I am sick to my soul, Bahalji. If I could but tell you . . ."

"You do not have to explain, Sahib. Because of Shaitan you have lost a great and good friend, the Sahib Lassiter. We all know what a shock this is to you. But we are afraid now, Sahib. More afraid than ever before. If you leave us, we will be alone. Shaitan will kill even more than he does now."

"I know, Bahalji. And I am sorry. But still—I can go on no longer. I must go."

"Perhaps you will take a rest, Sahib, and then return. Perhaps you will go to Simla, where the air is clear and cool. You have walked too many miles, waited and watched too many hours in sun and rain. Perhaps, after you have refreshed yourself, you will be ready to come back. And some day find Shaitan and kill him."

"No, Bahalji. I am sorry, but there is nothing more I can do. I am finished here, and I will be gone for good. I am going back to England."

There was silence and Bahalji looked long and hard at Brooke, and knew he meant what he had said. Finally, he bowed his head.

"Go in peace, Sahib. *Shantih, shantih.*"

With that, the others crowded around him, crying *shantih, shantih*, peace, peace, and Brooke got into the bullock cart and turned his head so that they would not see the tears springing to his eyes. The wheels of the bullock cart groaned and squealed as the vehicle started to move, and Brooke wanted to turn back and take one last look, but he couldn't. He couldn't because he was afraid he would break down and in a very un-British way, show tears.

For hours the bullock cart creaked its way toward
Bisalpur. The road, like most Indian roads of its kind,
was made of *kunkur*, a kind of hard lime. During the
rainy season it fell apart, leaving great potholes. But in
the hot season the wheels of even the lightest traffic
kicked up great clouds of dust. In a very few minutes
Brooke's face was caked with it, he gagged and choked
with it, and he took frequent draughts from his water
canteen.

It was not just the dust that stifled him now. It was
guilt, smothering him like a shroud, eating away at his
vitals. He felt as though he were some kind of zombie, a
skin filled with sawdust. He remembered the faces of
those poor damned villagers when he had finally said
goodbye, and he remembered the face of Tony Lassiter
as he begged Brooke to kill him and end the horror, and
most of all he remembered that strange, bewhiskered
bloody smile on the face of Shaitan.

He told himself, in his own defense, that he had tried.
God, how he had tried. But a man knows his own limits,
he knows when he's had his innings, and if he's failed,
so be it. He tried to comfort himself by reflecting that he
hadn't been the first. He thought of all the other
hunters, good men who had gone after Shaitan, and
how many of them had never come back at all, and how
those that did come back admitted failure and nobody
thought the worst of them.

But he was different.

He was Dennis Brooke. Dennis Brooke, he thought
bitterly, the great white hunter, Superman in rubber
shoes and bush jacket and khaki shorts, wearing a
regulation Cawnpore Tent Club pith topee with quilted
khaki cover, and carrying a Mannlicher, or a .250 or
.450 rifle, or some other magic wand calculated to
subdue the devouring man-eating tiger or leopard. They

had made him into a kind of icon; they had created an image, and they expected him to live up to it. Great expectations. Others could fail. But Sir Dennis Brooke? It was unthinkable.

He had never wanted this mission. He had done everything, short of running away or killing himself, to avoid it. But they had forced him into it, pressed him into it, kept at him until he had given in, because they loved theater and they saw the drama of himself versus Shaitan. He knew what the newspapers would do to him in his defeat. And at this point he didn't give a damn, one way or another.

He had no illusions about his future. The public and the press would see him as the boxer who quits in the ring, quits cold after being battered by his opponent. He could look forward to contempt, rejection, perhaps even ridicule.

They would all have a field day, and he would become the pariah of all time.

But at this point he didn't care any more; he was tired and hunted out and ready to admit that he had no stomach for the game anymore, that Shaitan had beaten him. There was no use in telling them what he really knew about the man-eater, or at least believed. They would laugh at him, and say that not only was he a quitter, but that he was insane as well.

Suddenly, he began to worry. Not about himself. But Nora.

Would she see him differently now? She had begged him to give up the hunt and come back to Delhi. But did she really mean it? Would she see him now as some other kind of man—the kind of man who had failed to stick it out?

The consequences of his act would fall upon her as well. It would not be easy to be the wife of a pariah. To take in her own way the slurs, the innuendos, the social ostracism he was sure to inherit. It would be a heavy burden for her to carry, and no woman in her right mind would want to assume it.

He had to prepare himself for whatever happened now. He had already lost a great part of himself. If Nora walked away from him now, he would have lost the rest. And there would be no point in going on any further.

PART FIVE

22

IN DEHRA DUN, Dennis Brooke got his first taste of what was to come.

He sat in the office of Deputy Commissioner Sir John Evans and delivered a full report of the events leading up to and including the grisly death of Captain Anthony Lassiter, late of His Majesty's Royal Guards. This, of course, was required by law. Present also was Peter Wilkes, the correspondent of the *London Times*, especially assigned to the story of Brooke's hunt. Brooke delivered his report tonelessly, leaving out no detail, except, of course, the leopard's smile.

News travelled fast in this part of the United Provinces, and Brooke knew that both Evans and Wilkes had already heard a version of what had happened from the Hindu grapevine. When he finished, he saw both Evans and Wilkes staring at him. The deputy commissioner asked:

"You said you had a shot at this man-eater? A clear shot."

"Right."

"And the range was no more than seventy-five yards."

"Seventy-five to a hundred, I should say."

"And you *missed?*"

"Damn it, John," flared Brooke. "I've already told you that."

The faces of the two men were incredulous. Dennis Brooke turned his head away and stared at the scene outside the window.

Wilkes said, "Do I understand that if you had hit the beast, you might have saved Captain Lassiter?"

"No," said Brooke. He had disliked Wilkes the first time he had seen him, and he disliked the correspondent even more now. "I thought I made that clear, Mr. Wilkes. I had the shot *after* Tony had run onto the bridge and slipped off."

"It's just hard to believe, Dennis," said Evans. "That you could miss at that range. Another man, perhaps, an amateur. But not you."

"I know."

"Any explanation?"

"You mean, any excuse."

"Look here. Dennis, I didn't . . ."

"The answer," said Brooke, evenly, "is no. I have no excuse whatever. I should have hit him, and I didn't. If I had, maybe Tony Lassiter wouldn't have died for nothing. But I missed him completely. As you say—like a bloody amateur. I hate myself for it. I despise myself for it. But there it is. I've given you a full report, and I just don't want to discuss it any more."

"I'm sorry, Dennis," said Evans, heavily. "Didn't mean to push you on it. But surely one piece of news we've heard is wrong. I mean, it doesn't come from what you might call a reliable source . . ."

"What news is that?"

"That you've quit the hunt for good. That you're leaving India and going back to England."

"What you've heard is true."

There was a long silence. The two men watched Brooke, stonyfaced.

"I don't believe it," Sir John Evans said.

"Believe what you like."

"What I'd like to believe, Dennis, is that you'll take a rest, go to Simla or somewhere, take a few weeks holiday, then go back to take on Shaitan again." The deputy commissioner paused a moment. "I do hope you'll reconsider . . ."

"No. My mind's made up."

"You *are* serious, then."

"I am indeed."

"But really, Brooke," said Wilkes. "You can't do that. You've got to go back and try again."

"Do I? Why?"

"Because," Wilkes stammered, "Well, old man, it must be obvious to you. You can't let this beast win by default . . ."

"Wrong. I can, and I will. Your damned rag of a newspaper has made this into a kind of sporting event. You know, Superman versus Superbeast. All that nonsense. The fact is, I've lost. I'm just too old and too tired, I can't cut the mustard anymore. Shaitan's just too much for me. He's taken the heart out of me; he's outwitted me and exhausted me. On your terms, writing this as though it were some kind of boxing match, I was the challenger. Well, sir, I lost. And I give you the winner, and still champion of the world—Shaitan."

"Dennis," said Sir John. "You'd be wise to reconsider. Think it over, think of the consequences."

"What consequences?"

"First, to your reputation."

"Bugger that. I don't care about it any more."

"Second, consider what the Indians are going to think . . ."

"It doesn't make any difference any more, Sir John. Whether I kill that leopard or somebody from Mars or Jupiter, doesn't really make that much difference. The point is, the tide's rushing against us, and it's too big to hold back any more. My little duel with Shaitan is now tremendously unimportant, only a little sideshow to the main event, a kind of diversion—it signifies nothing. The only regret I have is that I couldn't help your people up in Chakrata and the other villagers. I love those people, as you know; I've lived with them, and slept with them, and at times, *felt* like one of them, rather than who I really am. And there's where my guilt lies, gentlemen, and it lies deep. The fact that I couldn't help *them*."

Both his listeners were silent. Their faces were expressionless. They seemed unimpressed by what he had just said.

"Then you've made up your mind?" said Evans. "You *are* going home?"

"Yes."

"I see. Well, you're your own man, Brooke." The deputy commissioner spoke evenly, but there was a chill in his voice and in his eyes. "Nobody can make you do what you don't want to do. You seem determined to pack it in, and that's the end of it." He paused. "What are your plans?"

"I'm going to Lahore from here. Report personally to the colonel of the Regiment, explain what happened to Tony. He's certainly entitled to that."

"I agree. It seems the proper thing to do. And after that?"

"Delhi for a few days. Then, the first ship sailing out of Bombay."

The deputy commissioner nodded. His blue eyes studied Brooke as though he had met him for the first time. Wilkes was busy taking notes.

"How long will you be staying in Dehra Dun?"

"Just overnight."

"Very well," said Sir John. "I'll have my secretary book you a room at the King's Arms." He rose, glanced at Wilkes, then said: "Well, I suppose that's all. Good luck."

He did not offer to shake hands. Brooke turned, left the office, and walked out into the blazing sun. Now he had had his first taste of it. On the many occasions he had come through Dehra Dun, Sir John Evans had never failed to offer him the hospitality of his own home, a drink, dinner and a bed.

Now it was different.

The deputy commissioner had deliberately made the needle sharper, the potion a little more bitter, by booking him into the King's Arms. This was a small hotel, and rather on the shabby side. And it was patronized almost exclusively by box *wallahs*, the name given by the Indians to the British small businessmen or door-to-door salesmen. In terms of caste, this was the lowest order in the hierarchy of the Raj. The box *wallah* was held in contempt both by the covenanted Brahmins of the ICS and the officer ranks in the Indian army. The Indians understood that this class of Englishman, among his own people, could be compared to the low-caste Vaisyas, and almost to that of the Sudras, the outcasts.

That night Dennis Brooke dined alone. He thought of Lahore, and knew how difficult his visit to the regiment would be. At a nearby table were four salesmen who sold Doulton's pump filters, Twilfit corsetry, Beecham's pills, and Gaylord's portable toilets. They stole curious glances at him, knowing who he was, but they did not acknowledge his presence by so much as a "good evening," sensing that he wanted to be alone. They, too, had apparently heard the news.

The army cantonment housing the Royal Guards at Lahore had been built in the nineteenth century. At first sight, the dusty parade ground and the polo field, the high roofed BOR barracks with their thick walls and huge verandas, the officers' club, the administration building and the armory filled Dennis Brooke with great nostalgia.

It reminded him of younger and better days, when he reveled in action on the Northwest Frontier, or drank with his fellow officers and enjoyed the keen sense of loyalty, and the sense of belonging to one big family— *bhai bund*, it was called. He remembered the polo matches, the pig-sticking contests, and the hill stations during the hot season, when he and his fellow officers were given leave to go to Simla or Naini Tal or Ooty or some other place, and drink, carouse, flirt with the ladies and sleep with some of them. He remembered how exhilarating it was to stand at attention while the regimental band played, and then to march at the head of some fifteen hundred men for fifteen miles or more, with not one man dropping out, in a show of pride. He thought of small things, of the colonel and the other Old Boys, boring their captive audience at mess dinner with tales of their experiences in the Third Afghan War, back in '18 and '19, when the regiment was fighting the Afridis and Mohmands, traditional enemies of the British. He remembered even the small things, the beer *wallahs*, the crows swooping down to rob the food from the plates of the soldiers as they ran across the open area from their own field mess to shelter. He even thought of the three or four bearers he had had when he was with the Guards, remembering each by name. And he even remembered the name of the regimental *nappi*, or barber, who came in and shaved the officers while they slept so that they would be rid of the chore in the morning. And he even remembered the name of the regimental *banya*, or Hindu moneylender, who would come around by the back door of your quarters in the dead of the night by appointment, and lend you a thousand rupees, for which you signed a chit, a promise to pay. And of course, as an officer and a gentleman, you would never demean yourself by asking for the rate of interest.

The guilt hit deep within Brooke, and he thought: "The least I could have done was to make Tony's death worthwhile, to have it *mean* something, by killing that spotted bastard while I had the chance.

It was late afternoon when he arrived. He had sent word ahead that he would be coming to Lahore, and when he appeared at the outer office of the colonel, there was a stirring of excitement among the young subalterns and the clerks, the regimental staff.

"Welcome back, major!" The colonel's ADC saluted smartly. "Good to see you again, sir."

"Thank you, Dillon. Is the colonel in?"

"In and waiting, sir. Orders were to show you right in the moment you arrived."

Brooke was aware of the eyes watching him, the excited whispers, the complete and sudden stoppage of work on his appearance. Among all personnel, officer and British Other Ranks, it was Dennis Brooke who had made the regiment famous throughout the empire and world. There were the great regiments of India, Probyn's Horse, the most pukka of them all, sometimes called the "Hindu Blues" because of their aristocratic lineage; the outstanding Guides Cavalry and Infantry, the Third and Fifth Gurkha Rifles, John Cotton's Light Infantry Regiment, the Green Howards, the Bengal Lancers, and of course, the King's own Royal Regiment. But although they were all widely known and respected throughout India, it was the Royal Guards that was known worldwide. And all because of Brooke's exploits, and the wide newspaper publicity.

Colonel Sir Gilbert Cashmore, KBE, CIE, was a tall, handsome man, graying at the temples, with ice-blue eyes, and a large walrus mustache. Everything about him said army; his father had been a member of the Guards, and his father before him. It was said that Colonel Cashmore had the sharpest tongue and the most rigid back of any officer in the army. But now, as he rose from his desk, Brooke snapped to attention and saluted, forgetting for the moment that he was no longer in the army, and hadn't been for years. He flushed, embarrassed.

"Sorry, sir. Stupid of me. I didn't mean . . ."

The colonel extended his hand, and clasped Brooke's in a hearty handshake. He smiled:

"That's all right, my boy. Once you're in the army, you're always part of the family. Doesn't really matter whether you're in uniform or mufti." He sat down and studied Brooke. "Well, you've had quite a time of it, I understand, with this man-eater, Shaitan."

"Yes, sir. I wouldn't call it exactly—ripping."

"I know. We've all heard. Crafty beggar, I must say, if you haven't been able to bag him. But of course, sooner or later, you will."

"No, colonel. It may be someone else—but not I."

"I don't believe that."

"It's true."

"Look, my boy, you're done in. You're tired. And losing Lassiter before your eyes, having to take him out of his misery that way you did—well, that would shake any man. What you need is a rest, Brooke. Get your mind off what happened. The leopard will wait, everything will wait, until you're up to going back."

"I don't believe you quite understand, sir. I can't go back. I've reached the end of my rope, physically and otherwise. I simply don't have the skill for it any more—nor the stomach, nor the spirit. A man has his limits and I—well, I've exceeded mine. I feel badly that it was Tony Lassiter instead of me. Believe me, sir, I wish it had been the other way around. But there it is. I have some business in Delhi. After that, I'll be sailing for England."

"And that's final?"

"Yes, sir. It's final. I came here because I knew you'd want to hear from me personally what actually happened, how Tony—."

The smile on the colonel's face had gone. His blue eyes seemed covered by a cold film. He looked away from Brooke and studied the papers on his desk.

"Save it until dinner, major. Rather busy right now, got this damned paper jungle to penetrate. Might as well tell it to the whole staff at dinner. Save me the trouble of repeating it." He did not look up, and concentrated instead on the papers on his desk. "Dillon will arrange quarters for you. Dinner at the mess at seven, as usual."

Brooke hadn't wanted to stay for dinner. He had no desire to face the whole staff and retell his story. He had hoped to give his report to the colonel alone, and then quietly leave.

But the colonel, in his own way, was twisting the knife into Brooke, punishing him. He knew that it would be embarrassing for Brooke. He knew how the officers of the staff would react when they found out he was quitting cold. In addition, he would have to tell them how Tony Lassiter had died. And that would be the hardest of all.

The officer's mess of the Royal Guards was the center of life in the regiment, a sanctum sanctorum, especially for those officers who were bachelors. They spent much of their leisure time there, and dined together every night. The mess looked the same as that of any other British regiment in India. It was built of bricks and stone by the troops themselves, and it was completely functional, with no architectural merit whatsoever. Much of the furniture was barely post-Victorian, and some of it was made in a haphazard way, by local Indian chairmakers. When Brooke entered the foyer, he saw that nothing had changed. There were the same stuffy motheaten heads of tigers and leopards and antelope on walls. On the left of the foyer was the billiard room, with the walls similarly covered with stuffed and dusty heads. The dining room, as well as some of the walls in the foyer, were hung with pictures of those officers who had previously commanded the regiment. They were framed in gilt, and the frowning faces all looked more or less the same, with hard eyes, thin mouths, and great mustaches and beards.

Brooke felt conspicuous in his mufti. The colonel and the officers of the staff were already there, dressed in the full regimentals of long tradition—stiff shirts, skin-tight trousers, tight jackets and shining boots. Brooke was offered the traditional glass of sherry which always preceded dinner, and he instantly sensed the mood in the room. Apparently the colonel had alerted the others beforehand. These were old friends of his, old companions at play, at work and on the battlefield. Normally, they would have greeted him warmly, even though he had been out of the regiment for years. But now they were coolly polite, almost frigid. They shook his hand and murmured the phrases they might have offered to some stranger: "Nice to see you back, old man" or "Good of you to drop in."

The hostility was veiled, but it was there. He hated the idea of being here, he knew that the ordeal was yet to come and cursed himself for not giving the colonel some excuse for not attending mess. But now it was too late. He withdrew within himself. He told himself he no longer was going to worry about their opinion, or anyone else's. He was all through with that, he had gone to the well too often on everyone else's behalf, and he intended to live his own life. And if they didn't like it, and that included his once-fellow officers in the Guard, why, to hell with them as well.

If they preferred to have their backs up, then he

would have his up as well.

The mess sergeant appeared, saluted the colonel, and announced that dinner was served. The officers trooped in according to ritual, in order of rank. Normally a guest, and in particular a guest of the stature of Dennis Brooke, would enter the dining room with the colonel first, and sometimes arm-in-arm. But the colonel made no effort to extend this courtesy. The cut was, of course, deliberate, and observed by all.

As soon as the officers were seated, the colonel at the head of the table, and the others in order of rank, the *khitmagars* stepped forward and served what was called the first toast. Actually, it was the first course, which was almost always a slice of toast topped by a sardine or half of a hard-boiled egg. Dennis Brooke would not have hesitated to place a wager with a bookmaker on what would come next—some kind of tinned fish, then a joint, then a pudding and a savoury, which was called the second toast.

It was Colonel Cashmore who initiated the opening topic of conversation. Brooke thought, the army never changed. The talk was informal, but everyone observed the unwritten law that the colonel, being the senior officer, was the most intelligent of all, the majors were more intelligent than the captains, and the captains were superior to the lieutenants. There were other points well understood. You never mentioned a lady's name at dinner. And you never disagreed with the general opinion after the cue had been taken from the senior officer.

Traditionally, the colonel would have begun the dinner by choosing rather innocuous subjects, the up-coming polo match with the Sixth Lancers, or how many whiskeys he had seen Brigadier So-and-so, of Skinner's Horse, down without batting an eyelash at the officers' club in Rawalpindi, or the great black buck he had shot at the European *durbar* in Mysore.

Brooke expected that the colonel would immediately ask for Brooke's account as to what actually happened at the swing bridge at the time of the tragedy. This was clearly the story in which the staff was most vitally interested. After all, they had lost one of their own—Tony Lassiter. But the colonel deliberately held off. Brooke realized that he was being subtly malicious. He knew the wait would make Brooke uncomfortable. The colonel knew his guest wanted to get it over with, and he wanted to see Brooke squirm a little beforehand.

Brooke sensed this, and so did the others in the room. They talked of other things, but they kept eyeing Brooke. None of them addressed him directly. He was irritated by this, then angered. Damn them all, he thought, they're really laying it on. If they get onto me, I'll give them as good as I get.

The regiment had been preoccupied with its orders to proceed soon to the Northwest, and had been looking forward to its chance for action. It was scheduled to join the "Piffers," the famous regiments of the Punjab Frontier Force, not just to pacify the tribes, but to police those radical followers of Gandhi who were raising the cry of independence. The chief object of the regiment's hatred, and especially that of Colonel Cashmore, was Mahatma Gandhi, and now the senior officer set the key:

"Gentlemen," he began. "This rabble rouser simply baffles me. He's just refused to meet the Simon Commission sent out by Parliament. The damned impertinence of the man, ordering his people to meet the commission with black flags and then declare a general boycott. I must say, I cannot see why this emaciated fanatic has been able to achieve such power. It is not merely alarming, gentlemen, it is nauseating. I mean, to witness this half-naked fakir, as Mr. Churchill calls him, walking up the steps of the Viceregal Palace as pretty as you please, to parlay with Lord Irwin on equal terms.'' Colonel Cashmore's voice rose. ''On equal terms, mind you. Imagine him allowed to sit down with the viceroy, when everybody knows he was still organizing this campaign of civil disobedience—what the devil do they call it . . . ?''

''The *Satyagraha* movement,'' volunteered a major.

''Right. Thank you, Pierce. Been in India forever, and still can't remember these damned Hindu names. Anyway, to my thinking, we should put the bugger into jail again and let him rot there.''

''Hear, hear,'' came the murmur from the table.

''That would be a bad mistake, sir,'' Brooke heard himself say.

There was a sudden silence in the room. Every head turned to look at Brooke. The colonel glared at him incredulously. Brooke hadn't meant to open his mouth. He had been simmering at his cavalier treatment, and the words had just popped out. But now that they had, he thought, to hell with it. I'm in for it now. He stared back at them, defiantly. Finally the colonel said:

''You have just ventured an opinion, Major Brooke.''

''Yes, sir.''

''Would you care to tell us *why* this fakir should not be put down, once and for all? Why we should let him run footloose to arouse his unleashed mobs, create riots and challenge the Raj?''

''Because, Colonel, putting him in prison now would create a great deal of havoc and bloodletting. There would not be riots in just a few places, as we've had in the Punjab, in Benares, in Allahabad, Calcutta and elsewhere. What we would have is a mass rebellion all over India. What we would inherit would be a hundred massacres like Amritsar, back in '19. It would be positively hellish. And with all due respect to you, sir, and the Indian army in general, there simply would not be enough men or firepower to put something like this down." Brooke paused a moment. "There are, I believe, something like ten provinces of British India and over five hundred native states. That would spread us pretty thin."

"Us?" The colonel raised an eyebrow.

"I'm sorry, sir. Perhaps I've misused the word. But I still feel part of the regiment and the army, although I'm out of it." He paused again: "With your permission, sir, I'd like to make another point."

"Go on."

"The mass of Indians believe in Gandhi. They believe he's right, that they've been exploited by us, humiliated by us. They believe we've been stiff, arrogant, unyielding, deaf to their dreams and desires. That's why they're more determined than ever to achieve *purna swaraj*."

The colonel frowned. "*Purna* what?"

"Complete independence, sir."

"And do *you* believe we have been abusing our subjects, Major Brooke?"

Brooke was silent for a moment. He did not really want to get into a brouhaha with his former friends at this point. All he wanted to do was deliver his report of what had happened and get out. But he was clearly aware of their hostility and he knew they were trying to bait him. Perhaps, he thought, it was useless to even argue with these officers. They treated the common soldiers, the British Other Ranks like dirt. They were India's version of a samurai class. They were insular, ingrown, and although they lived in the country for years, they refused to learn the language, they did not even know the common words. Colonel Cashmore's asking what *purna swaraj* meant was not unusual. Their whole world was the regiment and the army, and its men and officers had very little contact with or knowledge of the millions of people who lived around them outside the walls of their cantonments.

You wore the regimental uniform and its insignia, you carried its particular mess kit in the field, you wore its special symbols on your topee, and sported its unique badges on your shoulders. The regiment was everything, the biggest and proudest entity in your life. It was your family. If you knew any Indians at all, it was a special breed—the Hindus, Muslims, and Sikhs who served in the two India regiments comprising each brigade. Otherwise, the only contact you had with the natives, or ever wanted to have, was with your servants or the various *wallahs* who tried to sell you everything from beer to fresh fruit, or for that matter, in the case of the British Other Ranks, their sisters.

"I repeat the question, major," said the colonel. "Do you believe we haven't behaved properly toward our subjects?"

"That's what the Indians believe," answered Brooke, carefully.

"I didn't ask you what they believe. I asked you how *you* feel about the matter."

Brooke thought, to hell with it, I'm really in for it, might as well go all the way.

"Well, colonel, since you put me to it, I will answer. Yes, I believe we British have made some mistakes. We haven't made real contact with these people. We haven't really listened to them. We've kept ourselves an elite for almost two centuries. We saw ourselves as rulers, ushering in a golden age and bringing to an uncivilized nation what we called Western enlightenment. We've never really trusted them. We've ostracized ourselves from them socially, economically, and politically. The point is, sir, we don't really *know* these people, we just rule

them." Brooke leaned back. "Sorry, sir. I didn't mean
to make a speech."

"But you just did, Brooke."

"Again, sir, I'm sorry."

"Since you seem to sympathize with these natives,
perhaps you can tell us how we misguided fools can start
reforming ourselves."

The colonel spoke sarcastically, baiting Brooke again,
and the others smiled their appreciation.

"I'd rather close the subject, colonel."

"No, no, Brooke. I find this fascinating. So do the
rest of us. How could we make some kind of start to
pacify these people?"

"Colonel, I'd really rather not get into this."

"But I insist that you do, major."

"I'm sorry, sir. But I insist on closing the subject. I
don't have the answers to your question. And at this
point, it may be too late for *any* answers."

Then one of the officers, Major Rupert Symington,
caught the colonel's eye:

"Permission to address Major Brooke, sir."

"Permission granted."

Symington fixed an eye on Brooke. He was a big
man, with beetling eyebrows, red face, and a great
walrus mustache. Brooke had soldiered with Symington, had found him brave enough in battle and efficient
in handling his troops in the cantonment. But he knew
that Symington resented him for something that had
happened a year before Brooke had left the service.
Symington's great passion was the sport of pig-sticking,
and his reputation throughout the regiments of India
was high in this regard. But at a great *durbar* in honor
of the Maharajah of Bikaner, Brooke, in the opinion of
the judges, had beaten Symington soundly, both in his
technique and as attested to by his larger bag of porkers.
Symington had resented this, and had not even spoken

to Brooke during the *burra khana*, or great dinner following the outdoor events, although they sat directly across from each other at the table. After that, Symington had been polite but frosty during Brooke's last year with the regiment. And being human, Brooke had reacted in kind.

"I can't believe what I've just heard."

"Sorry."

"I must say, Brooke, some of your statements seem downright—well, almost disloyal."

"I'm sorry. But I stand by everything I've said. I was only stating the facts—as I saw them. If you see them as blasphemy, or unpatriotic—a remark by you I consider insulting—then that's *your* interpretation."

"What makes you so sure of your ground, Brooke? Why should you present yourself as an expert on the Indian mentality?"

"Is that your idea of sarcasm?"

"Make whatever you want of it."

"What I make of it is this, Symington. You don't seem to have the foggiest notion of what is going on outside this cantonment. But I think I do. I've been on many hunting expeditions, as you know. I've met a lot of the simple people, the villagers who really make up this country. I've lived in their houses, eaten with them, slept with them, talked by the hour with them. They still respect the Raj, but they're hard put to keep doing so unless we begin to respect them. Very well, let us say admittance to our clubs, even of selected Indians, is a little farfetched, or a long time away. The point is that sooner or later we're going to have to break some of the hidebound traditions, reach out to these people, make some decent concessions. Or we'll lose them. In fact, we *are* losing them."

"Really, Brooke," said Symington. "Perhaps you ought to get a black flag and march in the streets along with . . ."

"All right, major," said Colonel Cashmore. "I think
we've all said enough on the subject—exhausted it, so to
speak."

"Yes, sir. As you say, colonel."

The rest of the meal proceeded in a chill. The officers
of the Guards went back to their mundane conversation, conspicuously excluding Brooke. But he knew
they were very restless to hear Brooke's account at what
had happened, and were waiting for a cue from their
senior officer. But the colonel was taking his time, and
Brooke became more and more tense. Why doesn't the
bastard give the signal? he thought. Then we can all get
it over with.

But Colonel Cashmore remained unhurried. After the
last course was finished, the mess sergeant appeared and
with a flourish placed three decanters before the
colonel. The first was port, the second madeira, and the
third, marsala. Since this happened to be Saturday
night, which normally was guest night, it was customary
to drink to the health of the King-Emperor. Then the
regimental bagpipe band appeared and paraded around
the table. Brooke had been away a long time, and now
he found the noise deafening. When the band finally
marched out, Brooke began to hope wildly that the
colonel had changed his mind and decided not to have
Brooke tell his story to the staff after all, in view of the
strained feeling between himself and the other officers,
especially Symington. But Colonel Cashmore did not
rise and thus signify that it was time to leave the table.
Instead, he leaned back and lit a cigar. This was a signal
to the others that they could smoke, and soon the mess
dining room was filled with curling blue smoke, from
cigar, cigarette and cheroot, swirling and eddying in the
currents of air created by the ceiling pull-*punkah*s.

"Gentlemen," said the colonel. "Major Brooke has

done us the courtesy of coming back here to his old regiment to give us a personal account as to his experiences in hunting this man-eater, and the regrettable loss of one of our own, Captain Anthony Lassiter. Let him know that we appreciate his thoughtfulness, and we await what he has to say."

The men around the table all nodded to Brooke, almost reluctantly. Each face was set in a hard mold. Brooke noted this. He began his story and told it stiffly, without emotion or change in his expression, and making it as brief as he possibly could. When it was over, there was a long silence.

"Thank you, major. Now are there any gentlemen here who have any questions?"

"Yes, sir," said Major Symington. "I do." He turned to Brooke. His hard blue eyes glinted.

"Brooke, you were the best shot with a hunting rifle in the regiment. Everybody here will acknowledge that. Yet you missed this man-eater at close range? Why?"

"I don't know. Why does *anybody* miss a shot? Shaitan surprised me by his sudden appearance." He had a sudden urge to tell them about the smile; it was the smile that had rattled him, shaken him up. But he suppressed the notion. "He was pushing Tony onto the bridge before I could get to my gun."

"I see. You know, Brooke, we're going to miss Tony Lassiter here. We were all pretty fond of him."

"So was I," said Brooke, evenly. "I was closer to him than any of you." He paused, staring at his questioner. "But I don't quite see why that remark was necessary, Symington."

"Because Tony is dead, and that animal is still alive. And while he's alive, I should think you would find it very hard to live with yourself until you go back and bag him. Yet you're packing it all in and going home."

"I told you why."

"Yes. We know. You told us why. But to my mind—and I'm sure I'm speaking for several of us here—it seems to me you'd want to hang on and avenge Tony Lassiter's death. That this would be the proper and honorable thing to do. After all, you owe your life to him. You walked away once, five years ago, perhaps for good reason. But this time—this is different."

Brooke saw the ring of faces watching him, and he knew they were all thinking of the same thing. Behra. He had tried to repress his anger at what he saw as an inquisition, but now it was getting to him.

"I don't need a lecture from you, Symington. And what I do or don't do is really my own business."

"No, old man," said Symington. "I don't believe it is. Your intention to quit is everybody's business. You came out here to kill that animal, and you funked out. The fact is, and I'll be blunt about it, you've let down the side. You've hurt the prestige of our people here, and among other things you've let the regiment down. And why? Whether you like it or not, I'm going to speak my mind."

"Your privilege."

"The truth is, you never got over Behra. You lost your nerve when you missed this man-eater, Shaitan. And in quitting now, you're showing the feather."

There was a heavy silence. Brooke saw the ring of faces, expectant now, curious as to how he would respond. Then Brooke said:

"I'm going to give you a chance to retract that, Symington. I want an apology, and I want it now."

"I stand by what I said."

"You understand you have publicly insulted me, and called me a coward."

"That was what I intended."

"And of course, I am going to demand satisfaction."

"At your service, major." Symington smiled.

"I'd like to settle this right now," said Brooke. "Tonight."

Symington smiled again and turned to the colonel. "With your permission, sir?"

"Permission granted," said Colonel Cashmore.

Somewhere in the book of military rules and regulations, there is a law which says that no officer of rank is allowed to physically strike any other officer of rank. But this was ignored, or observed very loosely in the British army in India. Each regiment, despite its close family esprit, occasionally had what might be called family disputes. And each regiment settled them in its own official way. In the Bengal Lancers, for example, the standard of excellence was horsemanship. It was rumored that disputes were settled by the two aggrieved men in an old-fashioned joust, where each man tried to knock the other off his horse. Another regiment settled grievances by wrestling, still another by a kind of human cockfight, where two officers sat on the floor trying to throw one another over.

In the Royal Guards, the two officers fought it out with boxing gloves.

The match was held in a corner of the parade ground, and only the officers of the regiment were privileged to witness it. It was temporarily off-limits to the enlisted men, and all BORs were ordered to remain in barracks until it was over. The rules were simple, and had nothing to do with the Marquis of Queensbury. The two contestants stripped to the waist and entered a ring marked off by lines drawn in the ground. There were no rounds, no rest in between. The two men would fight until one quit, was clearly knocked senseless or was knocked down three times.

It was a hot night, terribly humid, and Brooke felt the sweat rolling off him as he stripped to the waist. He

watched Symington take off his tunic, blouse and
undershirt, smiling and chatting to some of the other
officers. He seemed cocky and confident. He out-
weighed Brooke by some fifteen pounds. And beside his
reputation as a pig-sticker, he was known in the
regiment as a rough and ready boxer, and a heavy
puncher.

There was no referee. The colonel merely reminded
them of the simple rules and stepped back outside
the ring. He could see, by the happy smile on Symington's face, that his opponent relished the situation. He
had deliberately goaded Brooke into demanding satisfaction, and now was looking forward to taking his own.

Brooke was seething with anger. He saw Symington
advance on him, the sweaty, hairy chest glistening with
perspiration, the muscular arms raised. They closed and
hit at each other. Symington swung heavily, hit Brooke
in the face with his left, crossed with his right and
knocked Brooke down.

Brooke sat there for a moment, stunned, tasting the
blood from a cut lip. He looked up at his grinning
opponent. Suddenly, he translated the face and the
smile into something else. The face was furry and bewhiskered, the eyes opaque yellow, the mouth half
open, revealing the great jaws and rows of sharp teeth.
The smile was tantalizing; it was maddening in its
superiority and contempt. Brooke rose slowly.

He was aware of heavy blows thudding around his
head, but somehow he was numb to their sting. He hit at
the face again and again, trying to wipe off that smile.
He kept hitting at it, again and again and again, until
the face fell downward and disappeared from view.

Brooke stood there, swaying. Again, through a red
haze, the furry face appeared before him. But now it
was not smiling. It glared at him, the teeth were bared
and he heard deep growling come from its mouth.
Again, he was aware of the thud of blows to his head.

He tasted his own blood. He hit at the face again and again, pumping blow after blow into it maniacally; he wanted to smash it into pulp, to close the yellow eyes forever. He continued to feel the heavy blows to his face and to his stomach, but they seemed to come from some distant source; he was numb to them, totally numb, and this time he did not go down, because there was this face before him, this jeering face, and he hit it again and again as hard as he could, and finally it dropped out of sight.

Then, a moment or two later, it came into view again, and this time he saw something else, another face, the cruel and obscene face of a great black snake with glittering eyes, and he hit this new face again and again, and he felt no more blows on his own face and body, and wondered where they had gone. But the face he was hitting was a mask of blood, and he felt a wild sense of exultation, and suddenly it dropped out of sight, as had the other.

He was suddenly tired, very tired, and the blood was filling his mouth, and the face appeared again, but this time it was a different face, and he tried to strike out at it, but now he could hardly lift his arms, and finally he felt himself caught from behind by a pair of arms. The face in front of him said:

"Easy does it, old man. It's over."

The face was that of Colonel Cashmore. It was then that Brooke dropped his arms, and everything went black; he started to fall, and dimly he was aware that other arms had caught him, he was lying prone in the sand of the parade ground and someone was applying a cold compress to his face.

He lay there, staring upward at the ring of faces looking down at him, and he was so tired that he wanted to lie there forever, but he felt good, good, because he had made that smile go away, perhaps for all time.

23

WORD HAD COME through from Lahore that Brooke
would be on the train arriving at 3:30 that afternoon in
Delhi. And even as the train slowed within the station, a
group of reporters spotted him through his compartment window. They began running along the platform,
fighting through the usual manswarm, trying to esti-
mate exactly where he would get off.

When he came down the steps, followed by his bearer
carrying his luggage, they were there to meet him. Many
of the Hindus in the station crowd, recognizing him on
sight, stopped what they were doing to stare at him. His
arrival had been heralded, but now he noted, ruefully,
there were no one from the Viceregal Palace to meet
him, no Rolls Royce and chauffeur to take him
wherever he wanted to go.

Flashlight powder exploded in his face, the barrage of
questions assaulted his ears. The reporters wanted to
know whether it was true that he was *really* abandoning
the hunt and going back to England, and could he tell
them more in detail about Major Lassiter and how he
died, and asked him where he was staying, and on what
ship did he plan to sail, and was it possible that he might
change his mind at the last moment, and had he heard
personally from the viceroy, or from anyone at the
Viceregal Palace, and did he plan to visit the widow of
his best friend, Sir Hugh Clymer. They wanted to know
about Shaitan, and what he looked like, and how
Brooke felt after missing that shot, and a hundred other
things. He fought his way through his questioners,

saying only that he had no comment, he had nothing whatever to say except that he had done his best, and his best hadn't been good enough.

He took an ancient taxi to the Royal Princess Hotel and went to the desk. The desk clerk, who wore a stiff collar, tie and jacket despite the stifling heat, stiffened a little when Brooke approached.

"Good afternoon."

"Good afternoon, Sir Dennis."

"You have my reservation?"

"Yes, sir. We do." The clerk hesitated a moment. "Welcome to the Royal Princess, sir."

"Thank you."

"Will you be staying with us long?"

"A week. Perhaps a little longer."

"We all feel badly that—well, sir, you know—"

"Yes," said Brooke, curtly. "I know." Then: "I'd like some newspapers sent up to my room. Whatever you have available. And a little later, I'll need a *chaprassi*."

"Right, sir. You have only to ring us when you're ready."

The clerk averted his eyes as Brooke signed the register. He seemed somewhat uncomfortable in Brooke's presence; he seemed to squirm a little. The pariah, thought Brooke sardonically, gives off a certain odor. He noted there were several people in the lobby, all British, some reading newspapers, some engaged in conversation, others having tea at the small tables just off the lounge. They had all stopped whatever they were doing and were watching him blankly. The lobby suddenly became quiet, except for the swish-swish of the ceing *punkah*s.

It's this face of mine, thought Brooke. I'm really stuck with it now. No matter where I go, there's no getting away from it. They're going to know who I am, and they're going to sit in judgment. Maybe I'll have to change it surgically, or else wear a mask.

He realized that he was still a celebrity, but of a different kind.

In his room he undressed and examined his face in the mirror. It was still a little puffy from his fight with Major Symington. His upper lip was slightly swollen, and when he touched his cheeks they felt tender. But otherwise he seemed all right, and he reflected that it could have been worse, much worse. He shaved, bathed and then phoned down for the *chaprassi*. Almost instantly, it seemed to him, the messenger was knocking on his door.

He wrote a short note to Nora, telling her where he was staying and asked when he could see her. He put the note in an envelope, wrote Nora's address on it, and gave it to the boy.

"*Juldi!*" he said. "*Chelo*. Right away. And wait for an answer. You understand?"

"Yes, Sahib. Understand."

Brooke tipped the messenger generously, lay back on the bed and picked up the two newspapers which had been delivered moments after he had checked into his room.

One was a copy of the *Times of India*, the other, the *Delhi Statesman*. Both carried his photo on the front page, and the story that he had withdrawn from the hunt for Shaitan.

And each, in a black-bordered box, also carried the item that since Brooke had left Chakrata, Shaitan had made a meal of two more victims, one a pilgrim of Champur, and the other, the boy from Chakrata, the son of the village sweeper.

The messenger returned an hour later with a note

from Nora. It was brief. She simply asked him to come to dinner at seven.

When he arrived at the bungalow on the lane leading off Prithviraj Road, he was immediately ushered into the parlor. He had expected Nora to be alone. And he was surprised to find her with two visitors.

He saw the look in Nora's eyes that said, *I'm sorry, but this just couldn't be helped*. She said, formally:

"Oh. So good of you to come, Dennis." She nodded toward her guests. "Sir Arthur Wickham, Lady Diana Wickham. Sir Dennis Brooke. Sir Arthur is an ADC to the viceroy, Dennis. He worked very closely with Hugh."

They said their how do you do's. Wickham did not offer his hand. Both he and his wife looked frostily at Dennis. Sir Arthur said:

"We know of Sir Dennis, of course. And Hugh always spoke highly of you, sir. We've all suffered a great loss."

"Yes." Brooke turned to Nora. "I can't tell you how shocked I was when I got the news. I'm sorry, Nora."

There was a long and awkward silence. Then Sir Arthur glanced at his wife.

"Well, Nora, we must be off. Come, Diana." They rose and each brushed Nora with a kiss. "Head up, Nora. Chin up." Lady Diana said, "If there is anything we can do, dear, *anything*, please call us. We were so fond of Hugh, so fond, and of course, yourself. Delhi simply won't be the same without him."

They nodded to Dennis. Again Sir Arthur did not offer his hand, nor did he recite the ritualistic "So glad to meet you." They were almost ostentatious in the way they cut him. They simply turned their backs and walked out.

The moment they were gone, Nora was in his arms.

"Oh, darling, darling," she said. "You're back, you *did* come back!"

He kissed her hard, and again, and then she pulled away and started to babble.

"No, Dennis. Not now. Not here. We must be careful. I'm too recently a widow. I'm still getting condolence calls, as you've just seen. Sir Arthur and his wife overstayed. They simply would *not* get up and go home. I didn't want anybody here when you arrived, *anybody*." Her eyes suddenly filled with tears. "Thank God, you're here, you've survived . . ."

"Nora, I'm sorry about Hugh. I'm terribly sorry . . ."

She put her finger to his lips. "Dennis, don't say any more. Please. About Hugh. In a way, it was a mercy that he went so quickly. He was dying by inches, he had another stroke, you know, one I didn't tell you about. But he's gone, darling. He's dead, and we're alive, and that's the way it is. I suppose I should feel guilty—you know, about you. But I don't. I did what I could for Hugh. I loved him when I married him, and then I grew to love him in another way when it happened—the stroke, I mean. And when he began to waste away, it broke my heart. I knew he wanted to die, he said so many times. And I knew he felt badly about me, about my taking care of him the way I did, and I knew he wanted me to *live*. You know, darling, I think he knew about us—he *must* have known about us—and I like to think that he—well, maybe he even approved. I remember when he insisted on my going to Ooty, where he knew you would be—he was throwing us together, don't you see, he wanted me to have some kind of fun, get something out of life, some satisfaction . . ."

She was running on and on, almost hysterically now, and Brooke put his hand over her mouth and his arm around her, and finally she rested her head on his shoulder and cried a little. At last she drew away and wiped her eyes.

"I know, I know. I've been running on and on,

darling. It isn't just Hugh, it's you as well. Every morning when I've got up and looked in the newspapers, I expected to hear that you were dead, that he'd caught you—Shaitan, I mean. When Tony Lassiter died, I thought, my God, oh my God, you would be next, he, I mean this awful man-eater, would catch you like all the others, and then I'd be alone, really alone. Selfish of me, darling, I know, to think of myself this way, but I don't think I could have stood it, I think I would have gone mad, I love you so." She tried to laugh. "Oh, I'm sorry, I'm sorry. There I go, running off again. And what's worse, I've forgotten my manners. I haven't even offered you a drink."

She picked up a bell and tinkled it, and summoned the *khitmagar*. She ordered whiskey for him, and a gin and soda for herself.

After that, they went in to dinner.

He told her everything that had happened, and then, over coffee and dessert, he said, abruptly:

"Nora, has anything changed . . . I mean, between us?"

She stared at him. "What do you mean?"

"I'm not the man you knew when I came here. At least, not in the opinion of the rest of the world. I've failed this mission, Nora. To everybody we know and everybody else, I've let the side down, as they say." He paused. "I've been treated like a pariah ever since I came back. Everywhere I go, they've been cutting me. They think . . ."

"Damn them, Dennis," said Nora, her eyes flashing. "I don't care what they think. I care about *you*."

"Nora, I'm bringing this up because you must realize that a future with me—well, it isn't going to be much fun. I mean, you'll be the wife of an outcast, we'll both be ostracized. At least, in the circles in which we move.

Here, or in London, or anywhere else in the world, they'll remember . . .''

"Darling, you didn't quit. You simply showed some good sense. You tried as hard as you could. But you simply had too much on your plate. More than any other man could stand. They insisted that you go, they *forced* you to go against your will. They ordered you about, treated you like some chattel. You went out and risked your life for them. You owe them nothing, *we* owe them nothing. As far as I'm concerned, you should have come back from Chakrata weeks ago."

"Nora, you're sure you still—well, feel that way?"

"Darling, you know what I'm going to do?"

"What?"

"I'm going to prove it to you—later."

Her voice was low and husky, her sensuous mouth was parted a little, her eyes shone in a special way. He thought of the long, lonely months he had spent without her, and the daydreams he had had, of a darkened room and a soft bed, and his body melded against hers, the excitement of her touch, the smell of her flesh and perfume, the soft brush of her hair in his face. He even heard, in these daydreams, her small cries and moans of pleasure as she tossed from side to side and dug her nails into his back when he penetrated her. And now, seeing the promise in the violet eyes and the hunger as well, he shivered a little in his anticipation.

He could not stay overnight at her bungalow for obvious reasons. Hugh Clymer had died only recently, and his ghost was still in the house. Moreover, it was just too blatant, the whole idea of a man's very recent widow and his best friend copulating in the dead man's own bed. They themselves would feel guilty and inhibited, and the servants would certainly spread the news, a new sahib coming in very soon after the old one had gone, and topping the memsahib. And so they arranged a rendezvous at his hotel. He would go back to his room and wait for her, and she would come to him some hours later.

"What about your night watchman?" he asked.

"My *chowkidar?* What about him?"

"He'll be opening the gate for you late at night. And he'll see you come back in the morning. He'll certainly put two and two together."

"If he does—let him."

"You don't care?"

"No, darling. I really don't. I'm tired of being a proper English lady at this point. I've been inhibited all these years by the rituals that started back in the days of Queen Victoria. What you are seeing now is a totally repressed memsahib spreading her wings a bit. I am going to bed with my lover—my future husband—and I really don't care if everybody at the Viceregal Palace knows about it, right up to Lord Irwin himself. We'll be out of this damned country in a week or two, Dennis, and since you expect to be separated from the herd, and I with you, a whiff of scandal isn't going to make a bit of difference. I can't wait till we leave India. I've grown to hate the country, and the idea of getting out of here just when the hot season is really coming into full swing, simply makes me drool. I don't think I could stand another few months of this hellish furnace they call Delhi. Which reminds me, Dennis."

"Yes?"

"There's a ship leaving for England in about ten days. It's the good old P and O Line, and I think it's called the S.S. *Devonshire*. The people at the hotel can book passage for it."

"Are you sure you can leave that soon?"

"I'll arrange everything. This bungalow is on lease from the Viceregal Lodge, and the ADC who's going to replace Hugh will certainly want it." She brightened. "I just thought of something marvelous."

"Yes?"

"We'll get married aboard. Have the captain do it."

"It's an interesting idea," he said. "But you're supposed to be in mourning. People may think it's a little too soon."

"I don't care what people think, darling," she said. "I'm growing old and I want to sleep in the same stateroom with you, and I just don't have time to wait."

"The passengers will know who I am, Nora." He grinned. "And they may snub us. What will you do if nobody comes to the wedding?"

"Why then," she said brightly, "we'll have all that champagne for ourselves."

He grinned and kissed her.

"Oh, one more thing, Dennis. About tonight."

"Yes?"

"Don't forget to leave me your room number. It'd be easier for me to go straight up. You've just heard my declaration of independence, but I don't want to shout it aloud. At least, not yet."

That night something happened to Dennis Brooke that he found entirely unbelievable.

Holding Nora's naked body against his, he began to make love to her. But to his surprise and consternation, he was unable to get an erection. He had never had a problem like this, never in his whole life. Sexually he had always been a vital and virile man. When they had been together in Ooty, he would become excited simply by Nora's closeness when she stood and kissed him, fully clothed. And in bed with her, it had been three or four times a night. He had always been ready, erect. Now, he remained limp, no matter what he did, no matter what Nora did to try and stimulate him.

He was shaken; he felt the deep cut of humiliation, the kind almost any man finds under the same circumstances. He turned away from Nora and stared up at the ceiling.

"I'm sorry, Nora."

"About what?"

"I just can't . . ."

"Perform, you mean?"

"Yes."

"Darling, you're a fool. Like all men. Nobody's asking you to perform. I hate that word, anyway. You're not some trained monkey at a carnival. You're a man, and I love you. Just lying in bed with you like this, with your arms around me, just being as sweet and gentle as you are, is enough for me right now."

He didn't seem to hear her. "This has never happened to me before. I just don't understand it."

"It could be for any other reasons. You could just be tired, darling. Or upset emotionally. About Tony, other things. You've been through a lot lately. It'll come back, of course. Give it a little time." She turned her head on the pillow and kissed him gently on the mouth. "It's not important now, don't you see? What's important is just to be with you, to be together."

"The thing I don't understand is *why?* Why *now?*"

Nora suddenly sounded disgusted. "You men. You're all so stupid. You and your ridiculous male egos. You all have this one symbol of your sexuality and you all have to prove your manhood by that thing between your legs. If it doesn't come up, if it doesn't harden, if you can't push it inside a woman on every occasion and every situation, no matter who the woman is, you think you've lost your manhood. But darling, that's ridiculous. There's more to a man than just that. Ask any woman. Ask me." She paused for a moment. "You know that Hugh was paralyzed from the waist down and he couldn't well—do anything."

"Yes," he said. "Of course I knew. And I often

wondered how you—."

"Lived with it?" She was silent for awhile, and he felt
that she was trying hard to organize her thoughts, to be
clear about what she was going to say. "I'll be honest
with you. Sometimes it was difficult. Sometimes, I felt
so frustrated that I—well, anyway, there's no point in
going into detail. I'm a healthy, passionate woman, as
you know, darling; I love sex, and I love the right man
beside me and inside of me, and I love to have that
marvelous feeling of orgasm." She laughed. "Good
Lord, if the long-nosed and very proper Englishwomen
here heard me speak like this, they would have the
vapours, as they used to say, and faint dead away. They
would think me some kind of Jezebel, a tart. Sometimes
I've wondered whether they all dress in the dark before
going to bed with their husbands, or call them by their
first names even in bed. The ghost of Her Majesty
Queen Victoria still haunts this country, darling, believe
it or not. But new ideas are breaking loose all over the
world, although they're very slow in reaching India. I've
been reading some of the newspapers sent from home,
and there's a movement going on where women are
beginning to take the bull by the horns, and telling
males that females are human too, and that it's perfectly
natural to *want* sex instead of just submitting to it. And
then there's this doctor from Vienna, Freud, who's
broken down a lot of doors with his id, and ego and all
those new ideas about sex, and there's this man in
America, Judge Lindsay who's come out with the idea
of companionate marriage and—well, I'm getting off
the track, I'm afraid. What *were* we talking about?"

"Hugh."

"Oh. Yes. Well, of course, I missed the physical part
of it. But in every way, I felt—almost compensated. He
was so gentle, so kind, so considerate. So much a man.
And I knew how badly he felt, how much pain he felt

because he couldn't consummate our marriage in the strictly sexual sense. Darling, you feel it's some kind of blow to your manhood, because for this one night you're limp. But think of Hugh, how terrible it was for him, knowing that it was permanent. Anyway, darling, you're a very potent and powerful male who's just had a temporary setback, and when you get back to normal you're going to frighten me with the length and hardness of that huge weapon you carry around with you. Now, why don't you just accept the fact that tonight's not the night, and put your arms around me, I'll turn my back and you can hold me close, and we'll sleep away the night that way."

"Damn it," he said. "I still don't believe it. I wanted to take you all the way . . ."

"Darling," she said. "My foolish Dennis. If you insist, then let me tell you. There are other ways to please a woman. Maybe you know them, and maybe you don't, but I'm going to show you, anyway . . ."

They spent four nights together. And still he could not perform.

He was angry at himself, frustrated, humiliated. And he continued to ask why, *why?* He was totally baffled by the mystique of the male. The mystique that had haunted so many other men over the centuries when it came to what they regarded as the crucial test of their manhood: the ability to penetrate a woman. He knew there was nothing wrong with him physically. He was as healthy a specimen as the next man of his age. He knew it was a matter of the mind. It was something he could never understand. The brain told you to wiggle a toe, and your toe wiggled. The brain told you to raise an arm, or bend over, or told your fingers to pick up some object, and every limb, every part of your body responded instantly to the brain's command.

Except one.

You could beg it to rise, you could plead with it, shout at it, swear at it, but it was as though it were something foreign and separate in your body; it did not or would not listen to your brain, it seemed to have a mind of its own. And it could stubbornly go down and stay down, until something inside of you was unlocked, until somewhere in your mind you pressed a magic button that would release you.

On the fourth night, after his latest failure, he said to Nora:

"Look, it's no use."

"Darling, don't be impatient. Give it time."

"I can give it all the time in the world. And I don't think anything will help. I've been driving myself around the bend trying to think of why, why this has happened. And as far as I can see, Nora, there's only one answer."

"Yes?"

"Shaitan."

She stared at him. "Shaitan?"

"It's the man-eater, Nora. I'm sure of it. If you look at it, it's simple enough. Before I went on this hunt, I had no problem. No problem whatever. Now that I've faied—and he's still running around loose—something has happened to me. Something deep in—what do these mind doctors call it?"

"The unconscious."

"Right. That's the word. The truth is, Nora, the damned leopard has made a eunuch out of me. Somewhere, deep in my mind, or deep beneath it, he's shamed me, beaten me, castrated me. Maybe he didn't kill me physically, but he's destroyed my manhood mentally. And there's only one way to get it back."

She turned towards him, she knew what he was thinking, and she was afraid.

"No, Dennis. No. You can't."

"I've got to."

"If you go back," she said, urgently, "he'll kill you."

"That's a chance I'll have to take."

"Damn you," she said, suddenly angry. "*Damn* you, Dennis. Here I just get you back, and you go running off after that monstrous animal again. What about me? I'll ask you that again, darling. What about me? I've just lost one man. Now I'm going to lose another. It's going to be the same old thing again. Hardly sleeping every night, then getting up in the morning and reading the newspaper, looking for your photo and the announcement that this horrible beast has finally caught you and made a meal out of you. What about me?"

"I'm sorry."

"Fine. *You're* sorry."

"It's something I have to do. Otherwise I don't see how I can go on living with myself, or with you. I'm sure Shaitan is the reason, Nora. I *know* it. It's a matter of exorcising this particular devil. If I can kill him, then maybe I can be myself again, a whole man."

Once again he was tempted to tell her about his belief that Shaitan had a human brain. But he drew back. No matter how close Nora was to him, she would not believe him. No one would believe him. Except the Hindus, of course.

"How do you *know* the reason is Shaitan?"

"I don't know for sure. But it's a pretty good guess. Anyway, I've got to try. I don't want to go on like this."

She was silent for a time, and then she said, bitterly:

"I know you're going to go ahead and do what you think you have to do. And nothing in the world I can do or say is going to make you change your mind. I hate the whole idea, but to be honest, I think I have some vague idea what this means to you. If I were a man, I'd probably do the same. I'm trying to think of it in terms of myself, as a woman. If I couldn't function as a woman, if I were under some threat of someone trying to cut off my breasts, or pull out my ovaries, or whatever it is that makes me a complete woman, then I suppose I'd do everything I could to stop it." Suddenly she laughed, a little hysterically.

"What's so amusing?" he wanted to know.

"Don't you see it, darling? This has to be the world's most bizarre *ménage à trois* in the world. You, myself, and a man-eating leopard—all caught up in each other!"

24

THE NEXT DAY Brooke called a press conference and informed the reporters of his intention to' go back and resume the hunt. He gave no reason for his change of heart, and they did not ask for any. The fact that he was returning once more to match himself against Shaitan was news enough.

When he arrived in Dehra Dun, he checked in briefly at the office of Sir John Evans. The deputy commissioner greeted him enthusiastically. Peter Wilkes, who was scheduled to leave that day for Bombay and then sail back to England, had now been instructed through the Delhi bureau to stay on.

"Damned glad you decided to come back, old man," said Evans. "Knew you would. All you needed was a little rest, and of course Tony Lassiter's death had to be a nasty shock. Now, is there anything I can do for you?"

"I'll need to reopen the bungalow at Chakrata, of course. And I'll need the usual servants . . ."

"Right. I'll arrange everything. Meanwhile, you'll stay at my place as my guest, of course."

"Sorry, Sir John. Thank you, but I've made other plans."

"Yes?"

"I've already booked a room at the King's Arms. I think I'll be more comfortable there."

Sir John Evans blinked. "I see." Then, a little sourly: "Well, that's up to you, of course."

All through this, Wilkes had been silent. But clearly

he was amused at this exchange.

"Sir Dennis, I wonder if you'd grant me a favor?"

"Yes?"

"I'd like to go up to Chakrata with you. Be an interesting experience for me. And for our readers. A first-hand report, directly from the scene, so to speak."

Brooke studied Wilkes. He was about to refuse, and then he thought sardonically, why not? Wilkes would not follow him into the field and thus get in his way. And it might be enlightening for the bastard to see what real fear meant among helpless people, and to witness what a human corpse looked like when Shaitan had finished chewing it to shreds. It would give Wilkes a sharp and nauseous dose of reality, to counter his view of the hunt as a game, complete with numbers and the scores of official kills.

"You won't find it very comfortable up in Chakrata, Wilkes. It's rather primitive."

"Oh, I've roughed it before."

"Very well, Wilkes. Come along. I hope you really have something to report."

"I have a feeling I will, sir. And soon."

"My death, for instance?"

"I hope not."

"But that's what you really expect, isn't it? Based on what has happened so far, the odds are all in Shaitan's favor. That one day he'll make a dinner out of me."

Wilkes smiled. "Remember, *you* said that, Sir Dennis. Not I."

"But either way, it's a story."

"Right. That's what I'm here for."

He knew that Wilkes, the *Times* and the public itself still saw this as a game. It was still Superman versus Superbeast. One of the participants had been badly beaten so far, had almost given up. But not quite. He had come back to make his challenge. So far, the battle had been long drawn and there was no decision. But sooner or later there would be one. And based on the performance of the two gladiators so far, it was Shaitan who would raise a bloody paw in victory.

This time his reception at Chakrata was quiet, yet joyful.

"We prayed in our temples and at our shrines for you to return," said Bahalji Singh. They were drinking tea in the headman's house and, as always, they spoke Hindi. "It must be, Sahib, that the great god Vishnu heard our prayers and sent you back to us."

"Perhaps you are right, Bahalji Singh. But I have my own reasons for returning. And they are private and personal."

"It does not matter. You are here, and therefore we can hope again."

Walking back to the bungalow, Brooke reflected on what he alone knew. That this was not simply a hunt for a killer animal. This was truly a *manhunt*. Think whatever you wanted, believe it or not, this leopard had a human brain. To Dennis Brooke, this manhunt had become intensely personal and obsessive.

He was no longer the professional, hunting an impersonal man-eater as he had done so many times in the past. This was different. He had a personal and deep hatred of Shaitan now. Not just because of what had happened, or not happened, with Nora. He realized with a certain horror that Shaitan had dulled the sharp edge of his professionalism. He had outwitted Brooke time and time again, made him look like a fool, an insecure amateur. He admitted to himself that not only did he respect the leopard, he was now *afraid* of him. He had never been really afraid before, not once, except for the incident at Behra.

Brooke realized that he was emotionally involved

now, his confidence had been eroded, and he had to be careful. Very, very careful. He was aware that he might become overeager to get Shaitan, make some wrong move, forget his customary caution, and this could be dangerous. Shaitan knew who he was. The man-eater had singled him out, had toyed with him and had extended the game. But Brooke knew that Shaitan would not go on in this way indefinitely. He would tire of the game one day, and precipitate a conclusion.

He thought of the shot he had fired at Shaitan back at the swing bridge. Normally, he would have made it ninety-nine out of a hundred times. Yet, incredibly, he had missed. He was beginning to feel superstitious. Missing that easy shot was some kind of omen. He had had his chance, and he had lost it. More and more he was seeing the leopard as someone human, thinking of him as Ram Gwar rather than Shaitan.

He remembered Behra again, the gaping jaws and mouth and teeth of that leopard only a foot in front of his face, and for a moment he pictured himself in Shaitan's great mouth, the huge jaws snapping shut, and he fancied he could hear the snap of his own neck before darkness came . . .

Then he pulled himself together and told himself, steady, *steady* . . .

All he wanted, prayed for, was for this dreadful thing to end soon. One way or the other.

He had no way of knowing that he would get his wish. And very soon.

Two days later Shaitan struck again.

The place was a path leading from Chakrata to the nearby village of Ramnagas. The man-eater had used this particular path often, and the villagers had been warned to avoid it, to go around the forest to Chandpur and from there proceed to Ramnagas. A circuitous route, seven or eight miles longer than going by the direct path, but more open and populated. The victim, Hari Ram, had an appointment to drive a herd of bullocks from Ramnagas to Bijnor, and he had been late for his appointment. Since it was broad daylight, he had decided to chance the direct route. His son, a young man named Punwa, had gone along with him.

Halfway along the path, the leopard had leaped out of hiding from beneath a grove of tall bamboo and seized Hari Ram before the horrified eyes of his son. With one twist of his jaws, he had broken the father's neck. The son, Punwa, had been carrying a walking stave at the time, and instead of turning and running, he had shown great courage, and smashed the man-eater across the head with the stave while his father was still in the leopard's jaws. Shaitan had then released the body of the father, dropping him on the path, and fixed his yellow eyes on Punwa.

After that, the son babbled, he had simply stood there, paralyzed with fear, waiting for Shaitan to kill him too. The blow with the stave had hardly affected him. The leopard had studied Punwa for a moment and suddenly . . . he couldn't believe it . . . the young man saw him *smile*. He swore this was a human smile, the kind one would find on the face of a man. The older villagers, to his amazement, accepted this without reservation.

On a curious whim of his own, Shaitan had allowed Punwa to live. He had trotted off with the body of Punwa's father clamped in his jaws.

The remains of the bullock driver had been found just off the path some two miles from the killing ground, in the direction of Ramnagas. The overhanging mango and cinchona trees had hidden the remains from the vultures. But when it was found, a flock of Himalayan magpies were perched on the body, picking away at the scraps of flesh.

Punwa had become hysterical and had gone half-mad on seeing the remains of his father. He began to froth at the mouth, buried his face in the dirt and beat the ground with his fists.

This time Peter Wilkes went along with Brooke to view the remains. When he saw what was left of the bullock driver, he turned deathly pale. Then he turned away and retched. Brooke noted sardonically that he didn't bring out his reporter's notebook.

Brooke wanted to track the man-eater. As the pugmarks indicated, Shaitan had left the path almost immediately after he had finished his feeding, and had entered the bush beneath a grove of trees. The remains had been discovered in the late afternoon. There was only an hour or so left before dusk, and Bahalji Singh pleaded with Brooke to discontinue his tracking and get back to Chakrata in a hurry.

Brooke knew this was very good advice. To be caught on this particular path after dark was asking for it. Asking for a ticket to the hereafter.

Later that evening Brooke was sitting on the veranda with Wilkes, drinking gin and soda. Miraculously, a cool breeze had come up, bringing some relief from the steady, unrelenting heat. Wilkes was still shaky from the sight of the grisly remains of Hari Ram, and was unable to eat dinner. Grimly, Brooke derived some satisfaction from this. Wilkes said:

"I must say, there's something I don't understand."

"Yes?"

"Why on earth would Shaitan let that young man go?"

"Hard to say. My guess is that Shaitan already had his dinner in his mouth—the boy's father, I mean—and at the moment he was not interested in more food.

Normally, the man-eating leopard often will kill wantonly, just for the pleasure of it. This time, he decided against it."

"But Punwa hit him with that stave."

"True. But apparently he didn't hurt him. And the leopard saw no threat in the son. It's all conjecture, of course. But he may have figured—well, what's the point? Why bother killing the son? What's to be gained?"

"I say, Brooke. You've got this animal thinking almost like a human being. I mean, you're giving him the power to reason."

"I suppose I am."

"But that's nonsense."

"To you, perhaps. And to me. But not to the Hindus."

"You're talking about this Ram Gwar legend."

"Yes."

"My dear fellow, that's pure rubbish. But it doesn't seem to appear that way—to you. Next thing you'll be telling me you believe in this whole balderdash of reincarnation."

Brooke studied the correspondent. "Wilkes, I'd like to tell you how I really think. But I'm afraid you'll print it in that damned newspaper of yours."

"I promise you this conversation will be off the record, if you so wish."

"You'll guarantee that?"

"I give you my word as a gentleman."

"Very well. On this subject of reincarnation. There are millions upon millions of people in this part of the world who believe it, to whom it is virtually a religion. In our world, the Christian world, we don't. Who's to say, really, if we're right, or they are."

"But nobody's ever proved it. Reincarnation, I mean. Nobody's ever come back in recognizable form, to document it."

All right. We, and the Church of England, believe in a deity we call God. Is that correct?''

"Yes."

"But no one's ever proved the existence of God, either. There are people these days who are coming out and saying we simply *invented* Him to fill deep needs of our own. No one has actually seen Him, or touched Him, or heard Him. The point is we *believe* in him. And if you believe in anything hard enough—it's true. The Hindus believe in reincarnation, heart and soul. Therefore, to them it's true. Actually, if you're going to believe in any kind of hereafter at all, I like the Hindu idea better. It would seem to me much easier to die if you know you're going to get another chance, another swing with the cricket bat, so to speak.''

Wilkes drained his glass, then put it down.

"I suppose you believed that boy, Punwa, when he made that ridiculous statement."

"What ridiculous statement?"

"That he saw that man-eater smile. "Wilkes smiled. "Imagine that. He saw the leopard *smile*."

"Maybe he did."

Wilkes stared at Brooke, unbelieving. "What?"

"I said maybe he did."

"My dear fellow, you must be joking. The leopard is an animal. And an animal cannot smile. The son simply *thought* Shaitan smiled. Of course, it's sheer fantasy. The lad was hysterical, he was in shock, he could imagine anything . . .''

Again, Brooke was tempted to tell Wilkes what he already knew. But that would be stupid. The correspondent would think he had gone off his head. So would anybody else. Brooke hadn't even told Nora. He could see where it would be impossible for anybody to believe him. He knew this was a secret he must keep all his life. The bullock driver's son had seen the same smile on Shaitan's face that Brooke had. But Punwa was a Hindu, and he, Brooke, was a Christian, and of course there was all the difference in the world . . .

"Amusing, all this," said Wilkes. "Reminds me of something that happened a few years ago. There was a chap who lived in Suffolk somewhere. One of your dyed-in-the-wool dog lovers. Wrote a letter to the *Times*. It seems that he had this Irish terrier who worshipped him. When this chap left the house for a time, away for the day, or just went down to the neighborhood pub for an ale, the dog was always at the door to greet him. Claimed the dog actually welcomed him with a smile when he came in. That set up a storm of other letter writers who wrote the *Times* and said that the man was daft, he was seeing things, animals could not smile. One of our chaps ran an interview with the keeper of the London Zoo. The man declared unequivocally that no animal he knew of was capable of smiling. Then we got this letter from an old lady who lived alone in Pimlico. She lived with three cats. Cats, mind you. And she said whenever she got them their food, after they were through eating it, they all jumped up on her lap and looked at her with an affecionate smile. Well, that set off a rash of other letters. Finally, the editors decided the whole thing was silly, and dropped the matter by refusing to print any more letters on the subject. Happened a long time ago, but I still remember . . ."

Wilkes cut off as both Brooke and he saw some of the villagers come around the bend to the bungalow path. They were carrying torches, and were headed by Bahalji Singh.

When they came up to the bungalow, Brooke saw that the bereaved son, Punwa, was leading the procession, side by side with the headman. Bahalji Singh said:

"Sahib, we have just burned the remains of this

young man's father, Hari Ram, and brought his ashes into the river, which is our custom. Six months ago, Punwa's mother, Padma, was killed by Shaitan, and we did the same. Now, Punwa here is alone; he has no more family, for he was the only child born to these two. He is heavy with grief; now that his people are gone, he no longer wishes to live."

Brooke and Wilkes looked compassionately at the young man. Brooke said:

"Bahalji, I understand Punwa's sorrow. But why do you bring him to me?"

"He wishes to speak to you—about Shaitan. He has a plan to help you kill Shaitan. Perhaps as soon as tomorrow night."

"Yes?"

"Sahib," said Punwa. He was a tall young man, muscular, and now his eyes glittered as he watched Brooke's face. It seemed to Brooke there was a touch of madness in them. "Sahib, hear what I have to say. This demon Shaitan has robbed me of everything I have in life, my mother and my father. I cannot suffer to know he is alive any longer. You, Sahib, have done your best. But it is not enough. Wherever you go, Shaitan eludes you. He is like some invisible spirit, a ghost. You may continue to hunt him for many months without success. Meanwhile, he will kill and eat many more of us during this time. There is only one way he can be killed." Punwa paused. "He must be made to come to you."

"How can this be done, Punwa?"

"We all know Shaitan is no ordinary man-eater. To tie a bullock or a goat to a tree and then wait in a *machan* for Shaitan to appear is useless. There is only one kind of food he craves. Human flesh. Therefore, I offer myself, Sahib, as the bait to lure Shaitan into the range of your gun."

Brooke and Wilkes looked at each other, startled.

Then Punwa continued: "There is a stream along the forest trail leading to Ramnagas. We know that Shaitan often goes to this stream to drink at night. I will place myself there, alone, by the stream, while you are watching from a *machan* nearby. I will be in a place so that you can easily kill him with your rifle if he appears. I will seem to be easy prey for him. Surely, he will come to get me. On the first night, or the second, or the third."

Brooke looked at Punwa a long time. Then he turned to the headman:

"What do *you* think of all this?"

Bahalji Singh met Brooke's steady gaze. "I have talked to others in the village, Sahib. They all agree that this could be done. If you cannot find Shaitan, then in this manner he will find you."

"But you're talking about setting up a human being as bait, Bahalji. As you did with the *samadh swami*. But the *swami* was very near death already, and Punwa is healthy and alive. You must know he could be killed. The leopard is very fast. And very clever. Punwa here would never know what hit him. He would be dead before I could get a shot at Shaitan."

"But you *would* get a shot at him. Is that not true, Sahib?"

"Yes. Nobody could know for sure. But I suppose it's possible."

"I am willing to take the risk, Sahib," said Punwa. "If it means the killing of Shaitan."

"I will have my men build the *machan* by the stream tomorrow," said Bahalji. "In a tree that gives you a close and clear view of the river bank, when the game goes to drink. Then . . ."

"No, Bahalji," said Brooke. I won't do it."

"But Sahib . . ."

"It is out of the question."

"My life is only one," said Punwa. "By its sacrifice, I may save many others. After Shaitan took my mother, I thought I should become a disciple of yoga, and became a *sadhu*. Shaitan is an Evil One, destroyer of life, enemy of good. I have been to the temple and prayed to Ganesh, who you know is our Hindu god of luck, or good fortune. I have placed flowers at his feet, burned incense before him, prayed that he may spare me from the jaws of Shaitan, that you kill the Evil One before he kills me. But if he does, then my *karma* will be good, and I will be rewarded in my next life . . ."

The young man looked up at Brooke, his black eyes pleading. Brooke was reminded again of the incident where they had set up the *samadh swami*. The same passion to sacrifice a human life for the common good. Brooke was tempted for a moment. It *could* work. If Shaitan did indeed strike, it would take him a moment to secure and kill his prey. It might take another moment or two to pick the body up in his jaws and carry it away. Under these circumstances, if the light was right, he could easily get off a shot at the man-eater. This time, though, he would have to be sharp. He couldn't afford to duplicate his performance at the swing bridge. This time his eye would have to be keen, his hands steady. If it came off, the whole thing would be over. Chakrata and its surrounding villages would be free at last. And he could get back to Nora . . .

Suddenly, he hated himself for even toying with the idea. He knew Wilkes was watching him closely, and he pulled back.

"Sorry, Punwa. But I·can't be a party to this."

"I beg you, Sahib . . ."

"Sorry."

Punwa turned and walked away without another word. Bahalji looked at Brooke, disappointed, then he stood, turned and walked away. The others followed, and it was clear that they were depressed at his refusal.

Brooke turned to his companion.

"Wilkes, I need a drink."

"So do I." Then: "I could see you were sorely tempted, for a moment."

"I'm ashamed to say I was."

"Can't blame you. Had a chance to pack it all in at one stroke." Wilkes paused. "I wonder what I'd have done, if I were you."

"Well? What *would* you have done?"

"I don't know, Brooke. Damn it, I just don't know."

Later that night Punwa committed suicide.

He was staying at the house of Bahalji. The headman owned an ancient rifle of prewar vintage, the kind of weapon allowed to some of the responsible members of the Hindu community. It was of small caliber and used for hunting small game.

While the headman and his family were asleep, Punwa had taken the gun from its pegs on the wall, and apparently had gone out to hunt Shaitan. He was half-mad with grief over the death of his father, disappointed and angered by Brooke's rejection of his plan, and his hatred of Shaitan was hysterical. He was so wrought up, in fact, that he had forgotten the taboo on any Hindu killing Shaitan and thus releasing the demon of Ram Gwar himself on the villages and towns of the district. Not that this could happen. Not with a gun of that caliber, which might kill a partridge or a pheasant, but would have very little effect on Shaitan. It was an exercise in futility.

Late the next morning they found Punwa's remains lying on the path, not far from where his father had died.

When they brought the young man's body back to the village to be burned, Brooke and Wilkes were there.

Suddenly, the villagers turned sullen. They avoided
Brooke, turned their backs on him, made it a point not
to speak to him. Brooke was upset. He cornered Bahalji
Singh:

"Bahalji, what is the matter with them?"

"They are angry at you, Sahib. They blame you for
what happened to Panwa."

"They blame *me?*"

"They say he died for nothing. That if you had
watched over him in a *machan*, he might still have died.
But Shaitan would have been killed, as well. And it
would be all over. They say that perhaps sacred Ganesh
would have let him live and saved him from the teeth
and claws of Shaitan. Then with Shaitan gone, Punwa
would have married in good time, and raised a family of
his own, and so would not be abanoned and lonely."

"Bahalji, I just couldn't do it . . ."

"I know, Sahib. You have spoken of this before. It is
a matter of your religion. A human life is sacred. But
the people here do not understand. All they understand
is that Punwa was willing to die, was not afraid to die,
in order to bring about the end of an Evil One. They
knew that he would be amply rewarded in his next life
for doing this brave and courageous thing." He paused,
then: "Sahib, perhaps all this has come to an end for
you. We have loved you, and we know you love us, and
we remember the man-eaters you have killed on our
behalf, and the peace you have given us. We are grateful
for all this, Sahib. But we believe now that Shaitan is a
demon of great magnitude. Of a kind that no human
being can ever destroy. That only Vishnu or other gods
have the power to do this when they tire of his evil
deeds. There is talk of moving out of our villages,
leaving our houses and our fields forever, and going to
some other part of India. Many have so done already,
and soon Chakrata and Ramnages, Jhirmoli and Kotd-

wara, Khurja and Bisalpur will be ghost villages, once inhabited by men . . . It is no use, Sahib. I do not mean to demean you, but Shaitan has proved your master. One day, if you continue, he will certainly kill you. I love you like a brother, and I do not wish to see this happen. Leave the hunt then, Sahib. Go home and pursue your own life. It is better for all.''

Brooke went back to the bungalow and thought about this for a long time.

He thought of all the miles he had walked, the blazing sun and torrential rains he had endured, the endless hours of sitting in *machans*, persecuted by swarms of insects, all for nothing. He thought of the weeks and months he had wasted here in total futility, of the frustration he had suffered and the humiliation. He thought of all the great expectations, and the fact that he had never even come close to fulfilling them. They had dubbed him Superman, and the nickname was now a cruel joke. He thought of his nemesis, his bête noire, Shaitan, and remembered the smile on the animal's face, a smile he began to see in his sleep, a smile that tormented him, and laughed at him, and held him in contempt. He thought of Nora, holding her close in his arms, the woman he wanted and needed and loved, and with whom he could no longer function as a man. Not as long as Shaitan lived. He thought of the grief of Bahalji's people as they lost father, mother, sons and daughters. And he thought of Punwa, foolish Punwa, who was willing to give his life, put himself up for bait to draw in Shaitan.

Put himself up for bait.

It was an idea that was slowly growing on him. What was the saying? If the mountain wouldn't come to Mahomet, then Mahomet would go to the mountain. He wasn't sure whether this was relevant. But he knew

now, in his heart, that he was incapable of tracking
Shaitan down into a position where he could get a shot
at him. He had used every skill, every tactic, every
strategy he knew, without success. In the time he had
spent hunting Shaitan, he might have killed ten man-
eaters. The Dharkot Leopard, for example, had taken
him only two weeks to track down and kill; the Bangthal
tiger, three weeks; and the Sindarwandi Tiger had
eluded him for five weeks. But he had spent months on
the trail of Shaitan, and this could stretch out forever.
An ordinary tiger or leopard with an animal brain,
relying only on the instinct and tools of his species, was
one thing.

But this man-eater, Shaitan, was something else.

Put himself up for bait.

That was the only way Brooke could think of to
surely close the issue. Forget about being a professional.
Throw away all caution and finesse. Deliberately walk
into Shaitan's trap on the leopard's terrain with every
advantage on its side, and hope for the best. It was more
than dangerous. It was suicide. But it has come down to
him or me now, thought Brooke. There is nobody else in
this arena. It's something between the two of us.
Shaitan knows it, and I know it. Perhaps he is tired of
the game and wants to end it, too. Perhaps he, too, has
decided that enough is enough.

He realized he was indulging in fantasy. Obviously,
he could not know what was in Shaitan's brain. His
chances for survival, if he offered himself as bait, were
very small. He might not live out the week. He might
end up as a crushed mass of chewed flesh and broken
bone in the upper branches of some mango tree, or in
some open field as a grisly meal for the vultures.

It would be a horrible death. But he would feel
nothing. It would be no worse than the living death he
would face if he simply turned his back and went home.

The point was, the issue would be settled—one way or another.

He made his decision, and was surprised at his calm. He felt totally at peace with himself. And, he decided, the sooner the better. He would begin to tempt Shaitan out of hiding that night.

Later, as he checked his weapons, he told Wilkes what he proposed to do.

His strategy, he explained, would be very simple. Shaitan was known at present to be lurking along the path from Chakrata to Ramnagas. His pugmarks at the drinking hole had been very fresh. He might move out of the territory suddenly, as he had on other occasions. But it was Brooke's feeling that having been so successful in acquiring prey in the region, he would stay for a while.

It was Brooke's idea to walk the path to Ramnagas. At night. And alone. And thus set himself up as bait, invite a showdown. He knew that Shaitan would be aware of his presence, would be watching him.

When Brooke finished, Wilkes was staring at him, horrified.

"My dear fellow, surely you're not serious."

"Oh, but I am."

"Damn it, man, you're asking for it. Suicide, I mean. The man-eater could be hiding in the shadows, or among the leaves of a low branch. He'll be able to come out of the darkness and at you, he could be upon you before you even knew it."

"I'm aware of that."

"Don't you see, Brooke? I know you haven't liked some of my dispatches to the *Times*. Perhaps they've been a little critical. But that was when I was back in Dehra Dun, and I didn't know you. I know you now, and I realize what you've been up against here, and the press has been damned unfair about all the time you had to take, and so on." Wilkes fell silent, watching Brooke, as though not quite knowing what to say next. "I must confess, I've grown to like and respect you, Brooke. I've always thought of you as some kind of blown-up celebrity image, and that rather turned me off on you. I'm sorry for that; I apologize for it."

Brooke smiled sardonically. "At least you'll get what you came up here for—a story. A particular kind of story."

"I didn't expect you to set yourself up as a sitting duck, Brooke. And I don't want to write your obituary on this one. Give it up, man. For the love of Christ, give it up."

"Give it up and go back? To what?"

The correspondent avoided his eyes. Brooke went through his guns, and now he made a decision. He decided against the .450; it was powerful, but too heavy to swing around quickly. It was a choice between the .275 and the Mannlicher. Finally, he chose the Mannlicher, because it had a hair trigger. And even the fraction of a second it took to get off a shot with an ordinary trigger could make the difference.

It was almost dusk when Brooke walked to Chakrata. Everybody in the village already knew of his intention. News travels fast in rural India. The *khitmagar* or one of the other servants had no doubt overheard his conversation with Wilkes, and had run to notify the villagers.

Bahalji Singh said to Brooke:

"This is a brave and noble thing you are doing, Sahib. But it is useless. The demon of Ram Gwar will kill you."

"I must settle with him, Bahalji, one way or the other."

"I know. I see it in your face, Sahib. Shaitan has made you sick to your soul, he has soured your life and made it bitter."

"He has made it not worth living."

"We will go to our temples and pray to the gods. Only they can save you. Only they can destroy such demons as Shaitan. Perhaps, tonight, the great Vishnu himself will be tired of Shaitan's evil. We will pray that this is so."

There were tears in the headman's eyes.

"Thank you, Bahalji. And for the prayers of your people as well." Then, quickly: "Bahalji, if—if Shaitan finds and kills me he will leave certain remains of my mortal body—a few bones, a few scraps of flesh. If you find them in some tree, or field, please burn them—in the Hindu way. I am a Christian, and had always expected to be buried in the Christian way. But I do not want the ugliness of my body to be seen by those beyond Chakrata. You understand?"

"Yes, Sahib. I understand. And if this dreadful thing comes to pass—we shall do as you say."

Brooke nodded, and started to walk across the rice fields toward the path leading through the jungle. Wilkes ran after him and caught him by the arm:

"Brooke, for God's sake, don't do it. Don't go out there and offer yourself as dinner to that damned monster . . ."

He smiled. "Too bad you can't come along. This could be the eyewitness story of the year."

"Damn it, man, if you think that's a joke, I simply don't appreciate it."

"Goodbye, Wilkes. The least you could do is wish me luck."

He thought he saw tears in Wilke's eyes.

"Good luck, you fool. Oh, you damned idiot, good luck!"

25

HE LEFT THE rice field and entered the forest, carrying his Mannlicher. He decided to leave his electric night-shooting light, a German model called a petromax, at home. Normally, the amount he entered the forest on any night, he would turn on the lamp. The Hindus themselves carried oil-burning lanterns in the event that they were caught outside at night in maneater country. It was said that the tiger or the leopard might hesitate at seeing this bright blob of light bobbing through the forest.

Brooke knew that Shaitan would take his victim without hesitation, light or no light. Brooke had used the petromax with Tony Lassiter, when they thought they had a man-eater spotted. Lassiter would turn on the blinding light in the quarry's eyes. The quarry would blink for a moment, paralyzed, and this would give Brooke time to get in a shot. They had used this method successfully, when perched on *machan*s, on other hunts.

At the last moment he had brought along two hand grenades, which were now hooked to the belt of his bush jacket. There was a chance, just a chance, that they might be useful. He smiled a little grimly, when he remembered that during the war, when out on night patrol to try and capture a Boche or two, he had carried the same equipment. But that had been a manhunt.

The trees, pines and mangoes at this point towered over him in a dark canopy. A light *dadu* wind, which always blew south during the day, now blew north, rustling the leaves. The moon was riding through the clouds, dappling the path in alternate light and darkness, and Brooke knew that if Shaitan attacked, he would do so when a cloud blanked out the moon. When the moon was blacked out, Brooke caught an occasional view of the *bhoota* star. This was the packman's guiding star, so to speak. They waited until it reached a certain ascension, about four o'clock in the morning, before they resumed the story. The *bhoota* was their heavenly talisman, and brought them good luck and fortune.

For a while Brooke followed a solid bed of twigs and scattered pine needles. Then the terrain turned rocky, and after that became a series of damp buffalo wallows.

He saw tracks of other animals—ghooral, pig and serow—but nothing that suggested the man-eater's pugmarks. Another one of Shaitan's little tricks, Brooke thought wryly. He veered off the pathway, knowing a hunter would obviously expect him to follow that route straight to Chakrata. Brooke calculated that Shaitan usually made his approach to the village through the brush, probably circumventing the rice fields, and moved up on the town from the opposite direction.

Brooke had lived in silence for too many hours of his life to be imaginative or easily shaken. He had spent too many days sitting in tree platforms, waiting and watching to see whether his quarry would come in and take the bait, usually a tethered goat or a bullock calf. He had spent night after night watching bridges, rivers, paths, and crossroads without reward, and once, in the case of the Duwa Man-eater, he had sat in a tree for thirty straight days before the leopard walked into the sights of his .275, or .450.

The forest seemed extraordinarily quiet. Even the sounds of the night insects seemed muted, and the crawling sounds made by small and slithering animals were gone. It was as though they were all waiting and expecting some spectacle, some dramatic event to come.

When well along the path, Brooke knew that he was being watched.

He had no visible proof. It was just a *feeling*. Shaitan was still in the area. The path was his domain at night, and he would be aware of a person passing along it. The hair on Brooke's neck bristled. He felt the adrenalin begin to flow. He knew that the man-eater could be lurking behind any bush or tree now, watching him, prepared to spring. This time, he knew, Shaitan was no longer interested in extending the game. This time, the man-eater was serious. Shaitan had not eaten any human flesh for a week. He would be ravenous.

Brooke had known fear on many an occasion. He had known it in the trenches in the Somme and in the skirmishes with the Pathans on the Northwest Frontier. He had never really felt it when hunting the big man-eating cats, until his near-death at Behra. But he had never known fear like this. And he felt helpless. Shaitan could see him, but he could not see Shaitan. You did not virtually invite an animal to eat you alive.

The moon rode in and out of clouds. When it was out, Brooke kept walking, holding his gun ready, safety catch off. With the light of the moon, he at least had a chance. When the moon went under, he immediately stopped, stood silent with his back against a tree and waited. In this way, at least, he could not be attacked from the rear.

He saw no yellow eyes watching him from the bush. No twig cracked to indicate the weight of a heavy paw. There was no telltale silky rustle of a large animal's body through the bush.

There was only silence.

He left the main path, and took a sidepath to the waterhole where many of the forest animals came to drink at night. It was his forlorn hope that Shaitan might possibly appear. His old pugmarks indicated that he had been here before. Brooke climbed the lower branches of a nearby tree, and waited.

In about an hour, he saw a deer, a hind, come down to the water's edge. It began to drink.

Suddenly, the hind lifted its head and looked fixedly into the nearby forest. Then, in a flash, the deer left the waterhole and vanished into the forest.

Brooke knew that the deer had detected Shaitan, either visually, or by scent. Otherwise, she would not have dashed off in such a hurry. So Shaitan, as well as Brooke, had been watching the deer. Did Shaitan now know where his quarry was—perched on the lower limb of the tree? If he knew, all he had to do was to wait for Brooke to climb down. Descending a tree was an awkward maneuver for any hunter being stalked by an adversary, and it would be easy for Shaitan to spring, leap up, and claw Brooke down.

So Brooke, not knowing for sure whether Shaitan had him located, decided to sit there and wait. Wait till daylight, if necessary. All he wanted now was to close the issue. But he wanted some kind of fighting chance when it happened. He did not want to play the total fool for the man-eater. One of them was going to die, Brooke knew, but he did not want this to be a mere execution, to offer his neck for the blade. He wanted some chance, however slim, to execute the executioner.

He was well-hidden by a bower of leaves. He knew that leopards had a poor sense of smell, and did not rely on this as a tool of the hunt. Temporarily, then, and for the first time that night, he felt safe. He waited two hours, hoping against hope that it would all turn out to be unexpectedly and ridiculously easy. He hoped that Shaitan might appear, stride to the edge of the waterhole and drink. He caressed the muzzle of his Mannlicher. It would be an easy shot, so easy.

And this time, he would not miss.

But this hope vanished when he saw four samburs

come down to drink. He knew that this was a wary
species, highly sensitive to the presence of any tiger or
leopard in the vicinity.

Since they showed no signs of alarm, Brooke descended from the tree and walked up to the main path.
No sooner did he reach it when he heard the alarm bark
of a kakar deer a few hundred yards up the path. The
bark started again, then was abruptly cut off. After
that, nothing but silence.

Shaitan.

He knew the particular bark of the kakar, and knew
that it meant that a leopard or tiger was very close by.
Brooke moved up on the path, alert, the Mannlicher
ready. His eyes darted to the left and right, his ear
strained for the sound of a twig cracking. The moon
came out, flooding the path with light.

Finally, Brooke reached the kakar. It was lying dead
in the middle of the path, its throat slashed. Clearly,
Shaitan had killed the kakar so that it could give Brooke
no further warning. And then Brooke saw something
else.

This particular portion of the path was damp. Brooke
saw the traces of his own footsteps, impressions he had
left when he had walked into the forest path from
Badrinath.

And just behind his footsteps, and somewhat fresher,
were the pugmarks of Shaitan. With a shiver, Brooke
now realized that the leopard had been following *him*,
at least for some distance, and then, still not ready to
attack, still waiting for the sure opportunity, had veered
off into the brush or forest.

He recalled that Shaitan had pulled the same trick on
himself and Tony Lassiter some time ago, after they had
tried to blow up the man-eater by planting the grenade
in the neck of the bullock calf.

Suddenly, Brooke heard a twig crack under the

impact of a heavy foot. It came from less than twenty yards away. He fancied he saw the slight movement of a big animal as it lay in the brush. He raised his rifle, quickly, but in an instant his target was gone.

Still, he did not hear the sound of a body moving through the brush. As graceful and sleek as a leopard was, he could not move through low-lying brush without making some sound. And Brooke knew he was somewhere in that clump of bushes. It was pointless to fire; he had no clear-cut target. But there was another way, one he had prepared beforehand, for exactly this kind of situation.

He unhooked a grenade from his belt, pulled the pin, and hurled it into the bushes. It exploded with a shattering roar. If Shaitan was still in that small area, the impact would kill him, or certainly wound him.

After the explosion, pandemonium broke out in the forest. The tree monkeys awoke and started to scream and chatter. Birds whooshed up from the branches, screeching, and headed for the night sky. Brooke stood still, waiting, his gun ready.

There was no sign of life from the bush.

Gingerly, he approached the area where he had thrown the grenade. He knew he was taking a calculated risk. Shaitan could have moved a few yards away, just out of the grenade's explosive range. He could be waiting for Brooke to get just close enough.

But there were no remnants of the leopard to be found.

Instead, Brooke found a huge boar, his body blown into chunks of meat, the head still intact.

Halfway along this woodland path was an abandoned forest hut built of sturdy stone and used as a protective shelter by those who, through some mishap or miscalculation, had been caught in the path at night.

At dawn Brooke arrived at the shelter and found it locked. Clearly, there were inhabitants inside, and when he shouted to be allowed to enter, he received no answer. Irritated, he threatened to blow the lock of the door open with his gun. A frightened voice called to him to wait a moment, and the door opened. Brooke entered, and the door was slammed behind him and rebolted.

A few months after Shaitan had appeared and begun to take his terrible toll, the hut had been abandoned for any official purposes. It had been strengthened by the forestry service and made sturdy, the small windows heavily barred and a new door installed, heavy enough even to withstand an angry charge by the man-eater. The main room was small, and there were two other smaller rooms, a kitchen and a supply room. The whole place, although kept quite clean by the refugees from the man-eater, stank of mold and human perspiration, and in the fierce heat slanting down through the roof and blasting in through the windows, it was difficult to even breathe.

The place was filled with men. There were two or three villagers Brooke recognized from Chakrata, but the rest were holy men in flowing saffron robes, wearing caste marks of sandalwood paste on their foreheads. Brooke was offered a hookah to smoke, but he refused, saying he was a *bhakti*, or abstainer. The group of *sadhus* looked common enough, but their equipment he found most uncommon.

On the floor was a stuffed effigy of a huge leopard. And in one corner was a pile of gongs and trumpets. While Brooke was staring at all this, the man who had admitted him, apparently a leader of the *sadhus*, said:

"I am Bhajrang Bahadur. I am sorry we did not allow you to come in sooner, Sahib. We thought perhaps you might have been Shaitan himself."

"But how could that be? You heard my voice."

"True. But Shaitan is a demon, and we believe that he can speak as a human, with the voice of Ram Gwar, when he finds it of advantage. We believe that he can also turn himself into a human, if necessary, to accomplish some evil deed. It was only when our friends assured us—" he pointed to the villagers— "that this was indeed your voice we heard, that we gave you entry. Accept our most profound apologies, Sahib."

Brooke returned the *sadhu*'s bow, and then asked, in Hindi:

"Where are you from, Bhajrang Bahadur?"

The leader of the *sadhu*s waved his arm vaguely, in a westerly direction. Brooke knew he should have not asked the question. Many of the holy men of India often had no place they called home. The entire country was their home. They moved incessantly, traveling from shrine to shrine, temple to temple, living on alms thrown in their beggars' bowls. As the Hindus themselves maintained, no one could tell where a *sadhu* had come from, nor did they have the right to ask him where he was going.

But it was the effigy that fascinated Brooke. The leader explained:

"This is a leopard we have built. We will take it to Chakrata, and there have a *tamasha*, with gongs and trumpets. By our prayers we shall make the evil spirit in Shaitan restless. He may wish for a new home. Finally, if he listens to our prayers, it is our hope that he will leave the body of Shaitan and enter that of this leopard here, which we have fashioned. Once this spirit, this demon of Ram Gwar, is imprisoned in this new coat, we shall burn this leopard so that the demon will be destroyed for good."

They offered Brooke a meager breakfast of porridge and tea. He decided not to go back to Chakrata but to stay in the shelter for the day and start the hunt again

that night. The villagers from Chakrata who were
present left him what food they were carrying. He
thanked them and instructed them to tell Bahalji Singh
that he was safe, but not to come out to the shelter, nor
send anyone else out.

The shelter was steaming hot, almost unbearable. But
Brooke was exhausted and tired of walking. Moreover,
he had not slept the entire night.

He threw off his clothes, and just before he dropped
off to sleep, he thought, tonight's another night, and
maybe we can finish it then.

26

THE BEWHISKERED FACE was close to his, the cruel, fixed yellow eyes looking straight into his, and then he saw the great jaws of the monster open, the red tongue and the rows of sharp teeth, the obscene saliva drooling from the lips, and the mouth was just about to suck in his head and bite it off, or twist it from his neck like the head of a sawdust doll, and he could not cry out, he was unable to utter a sound, he was paralyzed. He heard the growl and smelled the stink of the monster's breath, and simply waited for the end. But the end did not come.

Surprisingly, another face came into view, the face of his friend, Tony Lassiter, but actually there were two faces, for Tony's was covered with an evil black head with two small glittering eyes, the head of a serpent, his teeth fixed in Tony's neck, and Tony's eyes were crying "Kill me! kill me!" and suddenly, there was the head and face of another snake, very different from the first one, only a few feet away. And Dennis Brooke awoke from his nightmare, and to his horror he realized that this reptilian face was not any part of his nightmare, but was *real*.

He lay on his mat, his naked body drenched in sweat, and stared, paralyzed, at the horror before him. The head of the huge snake was raised two or three feet above the ground; its eyes glittered, looking directly into his. The hood encasing the head was the size of a dinner plate, the throat of the reptile was crimson, shading down to a yellow and gold color on that portion of his body which reached the ground. The back of the snake

was dark green, lined with ivory colored stripes, and the
area near his tail was glistening black, striped with
white. From head to tail, it measured some fourteen
feet.

Brooke recognized it as a hamadryad, a species
known to be very aggressive when disturbed, and able to
travel at great speed. It must have crawled through some
hole in the hut's foundation, seeking relief from the
blazing heat of the sun, and now it was directly in front
of him, almost within actual striking distance. Brooke
realized that the odor of his naked body must have
attracted the snake, and he was aware that at this
moment the hamadryad was studying him, undecided
whether to attack.

He stared at the glittering eyes, and the vibrating
forked tongue flickering out of the cruel mouth. His
Mannlicher was at his side, and he thanked God that he
had left the safety catch off. He knew he could not
make an ostentatious move without alarming the snake,
who would instantly react and attack. Fortunately, the
gun was not on his open or right side, facing the snake,
but nestled between his body and the wall. Far enough
away so that he could not roll over onto the gun in his
sleep, and accidentally set it off.

His left hand, which was hidden, moved imperceptibly toward the gun. Finally he was able to touch it, and
his sweaty palm closed around the stock. Then, with one
quick movement, he snatched up the gun, swung it
around, and fired straight at the middle of the hood,
praying that he would beat the snake's reaction. Luck
was with him. He heard the roar of the Mannlicher, and
saw the head of the snake mush into a bloody pulp,
spraying drops of blood onto Brooke's face and his
body. The hamadryad, though headless, was still
apparently alive. Its coils moved, the body slithered
toward Brooke. Brooke leaped up and put another shot

into the snake's neck. This time, there was no further movement.

Brooke sat there for a few moments, trembling. That had been close, very close. There had always been a chance that the snake would close his hood, lower his head, and slither away. It depended on how hungry it was. But Brooke, his body dripping perspiration, was sure that it would have decided, in the end, to attack.

He started to laugh. First lightly, then hysterically. The suffocating heat of the forest hut was frying his brain. Otherwise, why would he feel so light-headed, so dizzy? He had a certain appointment tonight, a rendez-vous with the Devil. He had sought it out himself and now he looked forward to it, and he was sure the Devil looked forward to it, as well. It was a very important appointment, very, it had been brewing for a long time, and certainly it was long overdue. To have missed it now would be intolerable.

He had expected it to take place the night before, but it hadn't. But this was another night, fast approaching, and he was sure, he knew it, he felt it in his bones, that tonight would be the night, and everything would be finally resolved, one way or the other.

He was suddenly aware of the stink of the dead snake, and the nauseating stench of its still wet blood all over his face and body, mixed with the sweat of his own.

He knew there was a small stream, only two hundred yards from the forester's hut, where Hindu travelers on this path made their ritual morning ablutions, according to *darshar*, or custom. He did not bother to dress. He walked out into the sunlight, stark naked. The brassy sun slammed at the retinas of his eyes, burned into his back and spine, seemed to hit like a hammer into his face. He walked down to the stream, threw himself into it, and floated on his back. The water was tepid, but he still enjoyed its silky caress, and he washed off the snake's blood from his face and body. Then he floated a little, inert, dreaming, staring up at the leaves of the shade trees overlooking the stream. Then he looked toward shore, and saw the rifle he had taken with him, leaning against a tree. It had been impossible for him to carry it into the water with him, and still take a thorough bath. He had taken a calculated risk and he knew it, but he wanted that bath badly, very badly. Shaitan could be anywhere in that clump of bushes, that patch of thick reeds, watching him. The moment he stepped ashore, he would be a sitting duck for the leopard's charge.

Strangely, he was not afraid. He found the situation somewhat amusing, in a black and light-headed way. This was even more ridiculous than simply being caught with your trousers down. His position was totally absurd, and although Dennis Brooke at this moment could very possibly be a helpless victim, he could not help but laugh. Then he began to laugh and laugh hysterically, he could not stop. He saw it as some kind of cartoon that *Punch* would run. There would be this naked bather in the water. He would be paunchy, of course, with one of those huge military mustaches. His pith topee and his clothes would be hanging from the limbs of a tree, and his rifle would be leaning against the tree. On the shore, there would be an enormous tiger looking at him. The face of the tiger would be wreathed in a great, drooling smile of anticipation, his tongue sticking out, the teeth showing. The rotund bather's face would be red with indignation as he spoke to the tiger. And the caption would read: "Really, old chap, have you no modesty? This is a damned impertinence, I must say. I demand that we meet in more modest circumstances." It would be something like that; of course, very British in its humor.

He went back to the shelter, dressed, and with a heavy

forked stick managed to drag what was left of the hamadryad out of the shelter. The stench of the huge snake lingered on, ripened by the intense heat of the hut, but there was nothing he could do about that. Finally, when dusk began to fall, Brooke ate a few hard biscuits, reloaded his Mannlicher, and made his way toward the forest path again.

Two hours before dawn, it happened.

On this night the moon had favored Brooke. It was almost at its full. Its soft yellow light exposed him fully; he felt naked in its luminescent bath. Yet, in an insane sense, that was precisely what he wanted. He wanted to be exposed, conspicuous. At the same time, if Shaitan charged, he would have a little light to shoot by—if he ever had a chance to raise his gun. Again, to Brooke's advantage, he could detect a shadow if anything moved. And Shaitan would cast a big shadow. He would have to stay totally concealed before he made his move.

Brooke walked slowly along the path, the Mannlicher held ready in his sweating hands, his body tense. He was sure Shaitan was watching him, he *knew* it. The man-eater was somewhere behind that big rock, he was curled on the lower branch of that mango, hidden by leaves, waiting for a strike as Brooke walked underneath him; he was lying flat on his stomach in that patch of brush, creeping along slowly, body low, tail moving up and down slowly, stalking him, and now the powerful muscles were tightening in his hind shoulders and legs, where he would generate the terrible power to leap like a released spring before Brooke had a chance to even turn . . .

As the hours of the night passed, Brooke's nerves began to jangle. A chill ran up and down his spine, his skin prickled. What was that damned leopard up to? Why didn't he make his move? Was he deliberately pro-

longing the moment of attack simply to increase the
tension of his quarry? Was he holding off, suspicious
that Brooke had some new and dangerous trick up his
sleeve? Otherwise, Shaitan might think—yes,
think—why would Brooke deliberately expose himself
in what was clearly a suicidal position? Brooke would
not put this beyond the reasoning capacity of the man-
eater; he was now convinced that Shaitan possessed a
human brain. The leopard had been pursued by many
hunters, had outwitted and devoured many of them, but
none had foolishly walked a jungle path like this, alone
at night, and without a lantern. Perhaps, thought
Brooke, Shaitan *did* expect some new trick, and would
not attack at all.

The possibility of this shook Brooke. If Shaitan did
not attack now, it meant more weary weeks, perhaps
months of futility, trying to hunt the man-eater down.
The thought unnerved Brooke. He started to shake.
Suddenly, he heard himself shouting obscenities at the
invisible leopard. "*Damn you, Shaitan, here I am.
Here's your dinner, you bastard. Come out and get it.
Why don't you come out and finish it?*"

The forest was silent. It listened, but answered only
with a slight echo of his own voice. No night bird
squawked, no langurs awoke and replied with surprised
chatter. It seemed that all life had left this section of the
forest. Or, if it were present, it preferred to wait silently,
for what was to happen.

Brooke sat down at the base of a mango. He tried to
pull himself together to quiet his screaming nerves. He
realized he had gone over the edge, that shrieking his
challenge into the forest like this was an act of insanity.
He knew he was on the verge of a breakdown. If
nothing happened on this night, then he knew he simply
could not take another. He was now sure that Shaitan
had somehow smelled some kind of trickery, and had

decided not to take the bait.

He rose and began to walk, stiff-legged, continuing on the path to Chakrata. This time he did not bother to look to the left or the right. He was convinced that his strategy of seeking a final confrontation had failed, and he just didn't give a damn any more.

Suddenly, Brooke thought he saw a shadow move along a rock. In an instant, it vanished. A moment later, he heard a twig crack. Then silence. He saw no movement of grass or reed. But he knew the leopard had the remarkable facility of moving through low grass or bush, twisting and turning its low graceful body so that it made the least disturbance possible.

Brooke felt his mouth go dry. His hands broke out into a sweat. He hoped they would not slip when he had to use the gun—if he had a chance to use it. Now, he stood still and waited. He did not stir for a minute. Two minutes. He studied the immediate terrain. At this point, the moonlight was dappled by an overhanging bower of tree branches and leaves. Light and dark were serried in weird patterns, so that the visibility was tricky.

There was no sound from the forest. No sound, no movement. No shadow crossed the rock again. But Brooke knew Shaitan was somewhere in there, very close, watching and waiting, tail twitching up and down slowly. He could *feel* the yellow eyes upon him.

Still, he did not attack. The man-eater, he decided, knew that Brooke had seen his shadow, perhaps heard the breaking twig. Shaitan could tell that by the fact that his quarry was standing stock-still in the middle of the path, ready for the attack. Perhaps the man-eater had decided to wait a little longer, catch him somewhere else, off-guard.

Then it occurred to Brooke that he had seen the shadow cross the rock in front of him and to one side. If

Shaitan wanted to attack, the last thing he would do would be to rush his quarry from the front. If Brooke's reflexes were fast enough, he might have time and good vision for one direct shot right into one of the leopard's vital spots.

Brooke decided that Shaitan, wherever he was hiding now, was somewhere to the front of him, and did not like his position. And Brooke thought grimly, *if this is true, then let's make it easy for you, you bastard.*

He started to walk forward again, slowly. He moved up the path, legs tense, body sweating, hands gripping the Mannlicher tightly. Now, he calculated, if there was an attack at all, he would come from behind, where Brooke would have to turn to fire.

He knew it had to come now. From somewhere.

And it did. Not from the back, as he had expected, but from his right side. Brooke had heard the slight cough, the faint hiss. He whirled, and luckily he turned to the right instead of the left. He saw the great hulk of the man-eater coming at him in two big springs of his powerful legs, then leaping into the air, jaws open claws extended.

Brooke fired blindly, having no time to aim. He fired straight into the hurtling body as it hung over him in midair, feeling the Mannlicher's kick in his shoulder. He had no time for another shot. Shaitan hit him heavily and bore him down by his sheer weight. The gun flew from Brooke's hand. Yet, Shaitan's teeth did not find Brooke's neck. Instead, the leopard rolled off Brooke, spun over once on his back, screaming, regained his footing and then darted into the forest.

Brooke lay there for a moment, half-stunned, the breath knocked out of him by the impact of Shaitan's body. He lay there, wondering how it happened that he was still alive. Then he saw it. There was blood on the trail. Brooke's face felt wet. He put his hand to his face.

It came away with blood—Shaitan's blood. The front of Brooke's bush jacket was soaked in it.

He knew that he had made a good hit somewhere, that Shaitan was bleeding heavily. But that did not mean the man-eater was finished. Brooke had seen many a tiger and leopard survive hits that were thought to be fatal. They wre tough and durable beasts. Brooke had no idea whether he had caught Shaitan in a vital spot or not. It might merely be a superficial flesh wound.

All he knew was that he was very, very tired. He saw the forest around him through a red blur. He found a tree and sat down beneath it, leaning his back against its trunk. He was in a state of shock; the confrontation had drained him emotionally. He started to laugh exultantly, and thought *at last, at last, I got a shot at the bugger, I put one into him*.

Then he sobered. He realized that Shaitan was still out there, somewhere in the forest. There was a blood trail to follow, and Brooke would have to wait till morning. Shaitan might be dead, but Brooke doubted it. Wasn't it true that this particular man-eater had magical powers that other leopards did not possess? Was it possible, since he was a demon, that he would recover from his wound and later go out and resume his kills again?

Was he, in some mystical way, actually indestructible?

In the morning, Brooke would find the answer. He tried to sleep, but he could not. His brain whirled with scenarios of what would happen when he began to track Shaitan's blood trail the following morning.

There was still unfinished business to conclude, a final accounting.

Half an hour later, Brooke saw the procession of torches and lanterns moving toward him from the direction of Chakrata.

27

SHAITAN KNEW THE Man had hurt him badly, the Man who had been after him so long.

He had been hit just forward of his left shoulder; the bullet had smashed some bone within him, then glanced off, torn through some muscles, and, having finished it journey, was lying somewhere deep in his belly.

He realized now that he could have stayed a moment or two longer, even with the blood gushing from him, and killed the Man who had hurt him in this way. But his instinct had won over. He knew that he was badly hurt, he needed cover above all, and he had streaked into the forest to find it. He did not believe the Man would come after him now. Not in the dark, not at night. But he knew it would be different in the morning. He knew the Man would not wait. Not this time. The Man would come and seek him out. If so, he, Shaitan, would find the right place to wait. And finish what he had set out to do.

That is, if he had the strength to so do.

A few hundred yards into the forest, Shaitan felt the great pains throbbing through him, saw the blood staining his coat. He stopped and lay down to rest. He was very tired. He found it hard to breathe now. He rolled over on his back, waving his paws into the air, trying to fill his lungs. He tried to lick the blood oozing from the ragged hole in his shoulder. It was difficult for him, since he had to turn his head in an awkward position to do so.

Suddenly, he felt the blood welling up in his throat,

and he started to gag and choke, and he coughed hard to spit it out. He felt his wound throbbing, and the blood welled out in intervals as he moved.

Even at night, the jungle was alive with small sounds, creeping, slithering creatures, the squawking and chattering of birds. But now it was eerily silent. They were all apparently waiting for him to die.

He was tempted to simply lie here and rest, and close his eyes and bleed to death. But the instinct to survive was still strong within him, and painfully he rose to his feet and began to move slowly, wearily dragging his body so low that it scraped along the ground, uncaring whether anything or anybody heard the sound or not. Dimly now, Shaitan recalled a possible place of refuge, a cave in a stone formation some distance away, one cave among many, where an animal of his size could rest and hide, and it would be very difficult for the Man to find him once he reached this haven. Shaitan knew that he was leaving a blood trail, and this the Man could easily follow, but if the bleeding finally stopped and caked, there would be no more droppings to follow.

The forest was still silent. There was nothing but the small whine of the wind, rippling through the trees. Shaitan coughed again and again as the blood gagged up in his throat. His mouth was dry. He needed to drink. He needed to drink desperately. And he had not eaten in some time. He needed food. Perhaps, if he could find food, any kind, surprise a small deer perhaps, the meat would replace the blood he had lost and his strength might come back. But he was too weak now to hunt. His muscles and legs had very little spring left.

But above all he needed to drink. He knew this territory well, since it was his own, and he knew there was a small stream some distance ahead. He could even hear its flow, but he did not know whether he could make it or not. He lay down again, under the rotting branch of a mango tree, wincing at the savage pain in his shoulder and belly.

He was suddenly aware that he had company, and he made out the shapes of two jackals warily circling him. They had smelled the blood, and now they sat patiently, watching Shaitan carefully, waiting for him to die. Finally, one of them rose almost impatiently, and delicately moved closer to Shaitan to better study the extent of his injuries and calculate how long it would be before they could appease their hunger without danger. Suddenly, Shaitan shot out a clawed paw, slashed at the muzzle of the jackal, turning it into a cruel gash of blood. The predators ran off, one of them screaming in its pain.

Then Shaitan rose and moved ahead again slowly, dragging his body against the ground, head lowered in weariness, his tail limp.

Finally, he came to the stream.

It was a pleasant spot, shaded by overhanging trees, and he had often rolled in the cool green moss lining its bank in order to clean his coat of any parasites or insects that might have lingered there. Now he walked into the water and cleansed his coat of the caked blood, watching it redden the stream. He walked back to the bank and for a while lay on the bed of soft moss, resting. He was feeling a little better now. The water had refreshed him. And for a time the bleeding seemed to have stopped.

But he still felt the shooting pains within him like streaks of hot fire. And when he rose and walked only a few yards the weakness came upon him again, and he saw that the motion of his muscles had caused the blood to come oozing out again.

It seemed incredible to him now, dragging along in this manner, foot by foot, that this could be. He remembered the power he had had in his sleek muscles,

the speed with which he could run and leap, the ease in
which he could overpower and and eat the two-legged
animals he favored. He remembered how weak they
were, how they would cry out and try to run, how they
would scream when he broke their necks, the feel of
their soft limp bodies in his jaws as he carried them
away, and the delicious taste of their flesh.

Now the sun rose, and soon its merciless heat took its
toll of him. His head dropped lower, the pain within
him came in agonizing waves, the blood seeped up into
his throat again and he choked and fought for air as it
clogged his windpipe. He coughed hard and spat out the
blood on the sand so that he would not strangle. The
blood made black blotches on the sand.

He crawled into the shade of a tree and lay there
awhile, panting. His eyes seemed blurred now; he did
not seem to see so well. He wanted to die here under this
shade. But not yet. Not quite yet.

He wanted to wait for the Man who had hunted him
for so long, the Man he had expected to kill like all the
others, but who instead had hurt him so badly. He
wanted to conserve his strength for that meeting.

He knew that here, under the tree, was not the place.
There was too much open space; he could not conceal
himself. He did not have the strength to make a charge
at the Man, and the Man would have plenty of time to
put the fire into him that caused him such an agony of
pain.

No, this was not the place.

But a short distance away, he saw a clump of wild
arum lilies. They were high enough to conceal him, yet
give him a small amount of shade.

He crawled into the clump, lay down and waited. The
pain never stopped; it was as though a forked stick was
turning in his vitals. Blood still oozed from his wound.
He felt weak, desperately weak. He looked up into the

sky, his yellow eyes blinking into the sun. And now he saw them appear and start to circle.

The vultures.

He had seen them often, circling over a feast he had just finished, waiting for them to go away. Now, he would be the feast.

He put his head down, breathing hard, now and then coughing up blood.

And waited for the Man to come.

The group that had come from Chakrata, alerted by the distant sound of his shot, gathered around him.

"You're not going in there after him," said Wilkes.

"I have to."

"Sahib," said Bahalji Singh. "No man, even a great *shikari* like yourself, follows a wounded leopard into the brush. No man, Sahib."

"He may already be dead," said Brooke.

"Ah, yes, Sahib. This may be so. But he may also be alive, and waiting for you."

"I don't know how badly I hurt him, Bahalji. It may just be a superficial wound. It may be that he will recover in time, and come back to kill again. We do not know for sure. But we must find out."

"You're not going in there, old man," said Wilkes. "Damn it, I forbid it. Absolutely. For God's sake, Brooke, don't be a bloody fool."

"It's my decision, isn't it?"

"If you go in there, you're simply asking for it."

"Precisely. I have to know whether I did him in, or not." He looked at the group of villagers who had come out along with Bahalji Singh and Wilkes. "We all have to know. Otherwise, we'll never be sure."

"Sahib, wait. Later in the morning, I will gather my people. We will follow you and beat the bushes. If Shaitan is alive, he must show himself or run . . ."

"No, Bahalji. By that time, if his wound is only superficial, he may be a long ways off, hiding somewhere. He will be leaving a blood trail, and if we wait, we may lose it. Besides, I would prefer to find him—alone."

"Alone?" Wilkes stared at Brooke. "But why?"

"Because I'm the great white hunter," said Brooke, sardonically, staring back at Wilkes. "Remember the way your newspaper put it? Superman versus Superbeast. We must give the public a climax, a high ending to the whole show. Right? That's what they expect, that's what they're entitled to, and that's what they're going to get."

Wilkes frowned. "I don't find that very amusing."

"It isn't supposed to be."

Yet, thought Brooke, as he left the group and started on Shaitan's trail, the press and the public were actually going to get what they expected. Again, and as he knew it would, it had all come down to this, Shaitan and himself. He thought of it as a personal matter. He hated this man-eater, he hated him with every fiber of his soul. What he wanted was revenge. It was Shaitan who had brought him here and humiliated him, and kept him away from Nora, and, temporarily at least, had robbed him of his manhood. If there ever was a time to settle the issue, it was now.

He had no illusions about the danger of tracking a wounded leopard into the brush, especially one as formidable as Shaitan. He knew only a fool would take the chance. If it had been any other big cat, he would have taken Bahalji Singh's suggestion, and waited for the beaters.

But this was not any other animal.

He followed the blood trail slowly and very carefully.

It was easy tracking, an invitation to go forward. When Brooke came down to the stream, he saw

Shaitan's pugmarks in the soft ground near the edge.
Studying their contours, Brooke noted that the man-
eater was favoring his left front leg. That particular
pugmark was lighter than the others, and it indicated
that he had probably caught Shaitan somewhere in the
area of the left shoulder. He noted, too, that the other
three pug marks bit deeply into the damp ground,
indicating that the leopard was moving heavily, and
without his usual lightness and grace. There were also
scrape marks of his belly dragging along the ground.

Brooke knew by these signs, and by certain stops the
maneater had made to spit up blood, that he had hurt
Shaitan badly. But how badly? He had wounded more
than one big cat who had left a blood trail even heavier
than this, and the tiger or leopard had survived. It all
depended whether they had been hit in a vital spot.
Otherwise, if they found some kind of shelter where
they could lick their wounds and rest, they could re-
appear months later and start killing all over again.
Brooke, more than anyone else, agreed with the Hindu
saying that it was never safe to say a leopard is dead
until it was skinned.

Brooke knew that the man-eater would not proceed
very far now. The bleeding was too heavy. He would
not vitiate whatever strength he had left, trying to put
distance between himself and his pursuer. If he was still
alive, he would be hiding somewhere now, watching
Brooke from some concealment, waiting for him to
come close, close enough so that he could reach his
tormentor by a single spring. The advantage would be
heavily in his favor. He could see Brooke from wherever
he was concealed. But Brooke could not see him.

Brooke felt the sweat break on his brow; gooseflesh
popped out all over his body. The blazing sun seemed to
penetrate straight down through his pith topee, and
made him light-headed. The nearby trees and brush

seemed to waver a little. The telltale drops of blood had suddenly stopped. That meant that Shaitan was close.

Brooke stood stock-still. His hands were damp with sweat as he gripped the Mannlicher. It was possible that Shaitan was lying dead in some patch of brush, very close. But it was also possible that he was waiting, waiting for Brooke to make some move, a move in a direction that could be fatal.

Brooke looked up into the sky. Now he knew that Shaitan was not dead, but still very much alive. The vultures were circling high over the area, gliding, leisurely dipping their wings. They had seen their prey below, but since they were still circling, still waiting, it was clear that Shaitan was still alive, wherever he was hiding. How did the vultures know that Shaitan was wounded or dying? Could they smell the blood? Did they have an instinct for future carrion? He did not know.

Suddenly, Brooke got a fix on Shaitan's hiding place. He could not place it accurately. But he knew the general area in which the leopard was hiding.

Now, from the large field of wild arum lilies, he saw a pair of golden-winged doves suddenly shoot upward and skim along the top of the lilies. An instant or two later, only a few yards away from where the doves had emerged, there was the faint whoosh of wings as five or six upland pippets sprang up, flew over the tree tops, settled on the branch of a tree for a moment then flew off again. Brooke knew that although these species had no alarm calls, as did the others, they were always disturbed by the presence of a big cat.

Brooke noted the location from which they had emerged, and saw that it was almost in the center of the field. That meant that Shaitan was somewhere near that location, and completely hidden. He might have been twenty feet away from the alarmed birds, or fifty feet, or even fifty yards. It was hard to know exactly.

The only way for Brooke to make contact with Shaitan was simply to wade through the lilies until he came upon him. If Brooke did this, Shaitan could watch his every move, yet stay concealed. And since the leopard was clearly still alive, he was very dangerous. His advantage was heavy, and it was a clear one. He was in a position to get the first jump on Brooke.

Brooke hesitated. For five minute he stood staring at the field of lilies. He had certain options. He could sit and wait, as the vultures were doing. He could fire his gun, and bring Bahalji Singh and his beaters in to finish the job. But by that time, Shaitan could move to another location. Brooke said to himself, to hell with what the bloody vultures expected. Shaitan was alive, and waiting for him.

He began to walk slowly through the lily field, step by cautious step. He had the Mannlicher ready, his finger close to the trigger. He stopped for a time, standing and listening, hoping to detect a hiss or a grunt or a cough somewhere up ahead. But he heard nothing. He was coming close now to the area where he had seen the alarmed birds rise, he had marked the point distinctly where they had emerged. Again he stopped and listened for a telltale grunt or cough.

And again he heard nothing.

The silence was overwhelming, oppressing. A sudden slight breeze arose, but it was hot rather than cool, and it bent the heads of the lilies as it passed. He looked up. The vultures were still circling, but now they were much lower. They had seen him now, as well as Shaitan. And now they expected, more than ever, to fill their voracious bellies.

He felt faint, light-headed. He could not stand here, knee-deep in these damned lilies, and wait all day. For a moment he was tempted to retreat, call for Bahalji

Singh, and take a chance that the leopard was still
around. It would take time for Bahalji to organize a
beat from the village. He would find many who would
refuse to participate; they would be afraid, they
wouldn't come within a mile of Shaitan, let alone stir
him up in the bush. The beaters who worked for the
maharajahs *had* to stir up the big cats; when their
masters hunted for amusement, they had no option. But
they were always afraid, and many of them had been
mangled by an angry tiger or leopard hiding in the bush.
By the time Bahalji had managed to find enough beaters
to tackle the job, it could be nightfall. And after that,
they could possibly lose the quarry.

Brooke took a few tentative steps toward the area in
which he knew Shaitan was hiding, and then he suddenly stopped and remembered something.

The grenade in his belt.

He had left Chakrata with two of them, and had used
one on the wild boar. Now, he thought wildly, and with
shuddering relief, I have a card to play.

He unclipped it from his belt, held it in his hand for a
moment, and thought out the situation. If he threw the
grenade in the general direction of where he thought
Shaitan might be hiding, there was a chance that he
could score a near hit, and kill the man-eater. The odds,
however, were against this. What *could* happen, what
he hoped would happen, was this. The grenade, even if
it exploded some yards from the man-eater, would
startle the leopard. He would jump away, or up out of
the lilies, and thus reveal his position. And at that
moment, Brooke would have his gun pointed.

He pulled the pin, held the grenade for a moment,
then stiff-armed it, sent it flying toward the place where
he had seen the alarm birds rise.

There was a tremendous explosion.

Dirt and plants flew skyward. And then suddenly

Brooke saw him coming. Straight at him. Shaitan. But
Brooke saw that he did not have his usual speed. Instead
he was coming at Brooke slowly, almost wearily.
Brooke trained the sights of the Mannlicher straight
onto the leopard's head. He had plenty of time, he
wanted this shot to be good. Then, just as he was about
to flick the trigger, he saw Shaitan stop, fall and roll
over on his back, his paws waving in the air.

Brooke stood, amazed at what he saw. He heard
Shaitan crying and whining. He saw the leopard painfully try to get up. Shaitan at last rose to his feet, and
stood for a moment, his body trembling with the effort.
He ignored Brooke completely. Then he toppled over
again, and lay still.

Brooke knew he should simply put a bullet into
Shaitan. Put him out of his misery and make sure he
was dead. But his curiosity got the better of him. He
wanted to see this animal who had been his bête noire
close up. He could see that Shaitan was still alive. He no
longer waved his paws at the sky, and his belly was
heaving wildly as the leopard fought for air.

Brooke moved toward the man-eater, gun ready. He
saw the now-gaping wound just above the left shoulder
and the blood gushing from it. Already the flies were at
the blood, swarming around Shaitan's eyes and face.
The shadows of the vultures, now flying very low,
crossed over himself and Shaitan, waiting.

He looked down at the face of the man-eater. The
mouth was open, the whiskers flecked with blood where
Shaitan had tried to lick his wound. A swarm of flies
settled around his mouth.

The yellow eyes of the dying animal looked directly
up into Brooke's. Brooke could have sworn they were
not cat's eyes. He could have sworn they were human.
They seemed to have a soft expression now, almost sad.
They said to him, or it *seemed* that they said to him, *It is*

*over, and you have won. Put me out of my misery. Kill
me now.*

The yellow eyes turned up and stared into the sky,
following the course of the sailing vultures. Then
Brooke pointed the Mannlicher and shot Shaitan
through the head, near the left ear. Shaitan's eyes
turned toward him again, for an instant, in what seemed
to Brooke to be a flicker of thanks. Then they glazed,
became dull, and finally hardened into cat's eyes again.

After that, Brooke sat down next to Shaitan, trying to
come to grips with the fact that Shaitan was dead, he
was really dead, and it was truly over. And somehow,
sitting there, staring at the dead leopard, his hatred for
the animal disappeared. He felt a vague sense of regret
that he could not explain to himself.

The vultures had come down close now, waiting for
him to go away. He raised the Mannlicher and shot one
of them. The others, realizing they were to be deprived
of their meal after all, flew away angrily and settled on a
dead branch in a tree in the nearby forest.

In the distance, Brooke saw the group he had met on
the path running toward him. He felt an immense sense
of weariness. He wanted to lie down here, beside
Shaitan, here in these lilies, and sleep. He wanted to
sleep for a long, long time.

They came by bullock cart, by *tonga*, and on foot, up
the pilgrim road and along the many forest paths. They
came by the hundred to Chakrata, from neighboring
and distant towns, to witness the burning.

Bahalji Singh, as headman and master of ceremonies,
had decided to delay the death of the demon for three
days, so that all who were able to come would be in time
to witness the end of Ram Gwar, the Evil One, encased
in its furry body. This was the real Shaitan, not the
effigy they had burned a few days ago.

In Chakrata and the other villages, there had been
nothing like this celebration before. Hundreds of people
now choked the freshly-swept main street of the village.
The women wore their best silk saris, glittering with
lace; the men wore clean *dhoti*s wrapped with red silk
upper cloth around their shoulders. Their joyous faces
were smeared with sacred ash, sandalwood paste vermillion. Bahalji Singh wore a white *khaddar* cap, a long
mull jibba, a *dhoti* topped by a lace upper cloth over his
shoulders.

The temple was illuminated day and night. The path
to it was swept clean and watered every five minutes and
strewn with flowers. Hundreds came to thank Krishna
and Vishnu and Radha for their deliverance, and to
place offerings at the feet of their images. The bazaar
was jammed with customers buying sweetmeats, and
one delicacy in particular was very popular, balls of rice
cooked with jaggery, made from palm sap and spiced
with cardamom and coconut. Another, and especially
favored by the children, was a sweet Bengal candy called
mishti. Women, dressed in their best jewelry, sat by the
side of the road and wove garland after garland of
flowers.

The music was incessant. Men played sitars, harmon-
iums, flutes, tablas and *dholak* drums. The sound was
one great discord, the musicians were unable to play
together or in harmony, but nobody seemed to care.
Children were underfoot and everywhere. They played
all manner of games, and one of their favorites was
chasing each other by running under the legs of the
adults. No one reproached them at this time for their
high spirits, for this was indeed a very special *tamasha*,
a celebration to be remembered and spoken about for
years to come.

There were special dances performed in Brooke's
honor. Along with Wilkes and Bahalji Singh, he sat on

an elevated platform and watched the performance. First, a group of young women, dressed in silk saris of many colors with bright shawls and garlands of flowers, danced the two classical Indian dances, the fast and vigorous *kathakali*, and the graceful and flowing *manipuri*. But the main event was the stick dance. Wilkes, who had never seen one, was enchanted by the performance. There were about thirty performers, the girls now being joined by young men dressed in white, with orange turbans and waistbands.

Each dancer carried two sticks. As the music began, they held them high. Then with each beat, they hit the sticks together with a loud clap, sometimes one dancer's stick hitting another's, sometimes the dancer clapping together his own sticks. The start of the dance was slow, but it built slowly, and in the end it was executed with speed, precision and enthusiasm.

Finally, on the third night, it came time for the burning.

Shaitan lay trussed on a bamboo bier, shaded against the sun, above a great pile of firewood. It was so constructed that when the fire was ready, men could pull ropes attached to the bamboo bier and drop the leopard into the flames.

This was a solemn moment. The crowd, pressing shoulder to shoulder far back up the street, fell silent as Bahalji Singh addressed them.

"First, we give thanks to the great Krishna and Vishnu for hearing our prayers, and in their mercy, deciding that the Evil Demon, Ram Gwar in his leopard's coat, must finally be put to rest. Next, we give our profound thanks to the Sahib, to Sahib Brooke, who went through so much and risked his life to kill Shaitan so that we could open our houses again, and our children could laugh, and we could grow our crops and walk our paths without fear. The Sahib did not want to

come, but he did. He came a long way from his home-
land to do this thing because he loved us, and because he
knew we loved him. He knew we could not kill Shaitan,
for in so doing we would release his demon who would
harm our villages in another way, perhaps by plague or
sickness, or drought. The Sahib was our only hope, for
only his skill was enough to kill the demon of Ram
Gwar, and perhaps we will build a shrine to him as a
way to thank him. And so he is going home, and we will
miss him, and always remember him, and his name will
be a legend to our children and their children's children,
and theirs after that for years to come. And that is all I
have to say.''

Bahalji Singh turned to Brooke, and there were tears
in his eyes. Suddenly, he reached out his arms and
embraced Brooke, who was deeply touched, and the
crowd raised their fists and shouted his name: ''Sahib,
Sahib'' over and over again, and surged forward, trying
to touch his garments and to touch his feet.

Then, at last, Bahalji called order, and it was time for
the burning. Some in the front row picked up pebbles
and tossed them at the body of Shaitan, not yet convinced, even now, that their nemesis was dead. Brooke
looked at the man-eater, legs spread-eagled and tied. It
was Shaitan's once magnificent coat that seemed to
have suffered the most. The gloss was gone, the coat
looked drab, the hair was beginning to fall from the
pelt. In the hot season, it was a must that any leopard or
tiger killed must be skinned on the spot, otherwise the
sun would ruin the pelt. Shaitan had been lying on his
bier for three days, shaded only by a cloth overhang,
and the stench of his rotting flesh was almost overwhelming. For some reason, this bothered Brooke. It
seemed to him that it was undignified for this
magnificent animal to be seen in such shoddy circumstances, even if he had been a cruel and vicious killer.

Now, watching Shaitan lying there, he felt empty. He did not know why; he had hated the bastard while he had hunted him. But now—well, there was no longer anything to hate.

"I say, this is a damned shame," said Wilkes.

"This burning, you mean?"

"Yes."

"Why?"

"I saw that pelt after you shot him, Brooke. It was magnificent. It was yours by right, and you should have had him skinned on the spot, and kept it. Do you realize how valuable it was? Even historic. I have no doubt that it would have hung in the British Museum if you offered it. What a trophy it would have been. A bloody sensation." Wilkes frowned. "Why the devil did you let them do it, Dennis? I mean, let the pelt go to pot, let them burn it?"

"They have to burn it, Wilkes. The whole animal. And especially his coat."

"Otherwise the demon will get away. Is that it?"

"That's it."

Wilkes snickered at Brooke.

"My God, Brooke, I almost get the impression you still believe this bloody legend. I mean, this Ram Gwar nonsense."

Brooke was silent, and Wilkes pressed him: "It *is* rot, of course. Superstitious rot."

Brooke was silent for a moment.

"Of course, Wilkes. As you say, superstitious rot."

There's no point in my contradicting him, thought Brooke. I have a life to live with Nora. I can't go around having people think I'm crazy. They'd never believe me anyway. So it's my own private affair. But I know what I know what I know. Or—I *believe* I know.

At a signal from Bahalji Singh, two men applied torches to the pile of firewood beneath the bamboo bier.

The fire crackled and then blazed. At another signal from the headman, the ropes were pulled, and the body of Shaitan was tipped over and dropped into the roaring flames. The great carcass of Shaitan hissed and sizzled in the flames, sending up the stink of burning flesh, and the crowd was silent as the body of the leopard became a faint outline in the fire and disappeared completely.

Then the crowd laughed and cheered and cried, and seized hands and danced in their joy. For a few minutes Brooke watched this triumphant outburst. Then, feeling sad, empty, he turned abruptly and took the path to the bungalow.

He had packing to do, and Nora was waiting in Delhi.